THE
BONE
JAR

THE BONE JAR

SW KANE

THOMAS & MERCER

Published by Thomas & Mercer, Seattle

www.apub.com

Amazon, the Amazon logo, and Thomas & Mercer are trademarks of Amazon.com, Inc., or its affiliates.

ISBN-13: 9781542018876
ISBN-10: 1542018870

Cover design by Dominic Forbes

Printed in the United States of America

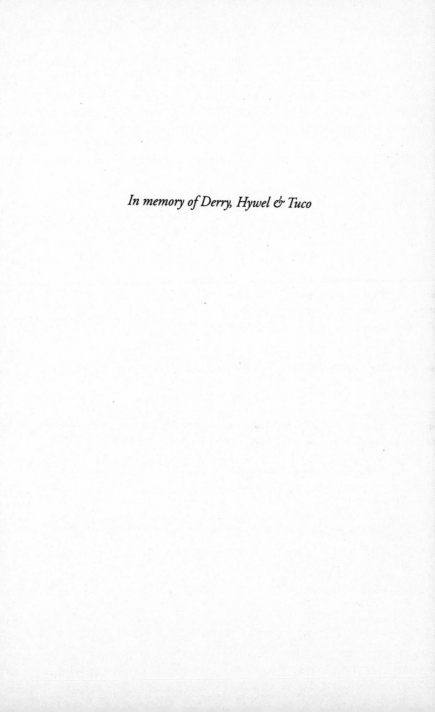

In memory of Derry, Hywel & Tuco

There they stand, isolated, majestic, imperious, brooded over by the gigantic water-tower and chimney combined, rising unmistakable and daunting out of the countryside — the asylums which our forefathers built with such immense solidity to express the notions of their day. Do not for a moment underestimate their powers of resistance to our assault.

Enoch Powell, 1961

PROLOGUE

He made his way up the staircase, palms sweating, nerves kicking in. He shouldn't be here; in fact, he'd specifically been told not to go upstairs, yet he couldn't help himself. It was a beautiful summer's day, and he'd taken himself off to the lake, but even there he couldn't shake the feeling of impending doom; so he'd returned. He hadn't encountered anyone on his way back and had felt like he was in one of those sci-fi films where everyone disappears, and you're the only person left. When he'd finally got back, there was no one there either: the building still and quiet, the only noise the gentle ticking of the hall clock. As far as he knew there were no visitors coming that afternoon, and the doctor wouldn't arrive until much later. The whole place appeared deserted.

As he reached the top of the stairs he paused, surveying the landing for any signs of life. All the doors off it were shut except one: right at the end, which was ever so slightly ajar. After a few minutes, when he felt as sure as he could be that he was alone, he slowly began moving towards it. He'd only taken one or two steps when he heard something – a slight whimper – and felt the hairs on the back of his neck stand up. Despite his sweating palms, which he wiped on his trousers, his throat was bone dry, and he longed for a drink of water.

Then he heard it again – the whimper – only louder this time. He stopped halfway across the landing, heart pounding in his chest, and looked back at the staircase, wondering whether he should go and get help, but he found himself unable to move. The landing suddenly appeared vast, but retreat seemed out of the question and the compulsion to go on non-negotiable. He crept forward, passing through a shaft of sunlight catching dust in the air, and as he got nearer to the door he heard another sound: someone breathing – heavily, but with control. Then came another whimper, only fainter and slightly muffled. By now, his heart was racing faster than he deemed possible, and he briefly thought of his mother, a pang of sadness rippling through his body. After another few steps the door was within reach, and as gently as he could he pushed it open. He knew it wouldn't creak; the door's hinges had been specially oiled.

Inside the room the curtains were drawn, as they often were, but he could still make out the bed on the left and a familiar shape beneath its covers. A small lamp cast a pool of light on a nightstand, intensifying the dark shadows in the rest of the room. As his eyes adjusted to the dim light, he realised that there was someone else in the room, the source of the breathing. They were leaning over the bed; he watched, transfixed, unsure of what he was witnessing, but instinct telling him it was something intensely private. He saw the bedclothes twitch, then lie still, and sensed the figure hunched over the bed relax. Suddenly aware that he'd been holding his breath, he let it out gently as the figure slowly straightened up; a long sigh, almost a sob, coming from somewhere deep inside. In that moment, he knew that no breath would ever leave the woman on the bed again, and was about to back away when he saw the figure bend forward and brush something from the prone body.

What little light there was in the room caught the feather as it floated to the floor and danced across the worn boards towards him. He shrunk back from the door, as the feather, caught on a summer breeze, drifted out of the room and settled on the landing by his feet. He bent down to pick it up, and when he stood up there she was, standing in the doorway, watching.

'It's over,' she said. 'She's finally asleep.'

CHAPTER 1

DI Lew Kirby hated hospitals – it was the smell, although today that wasn't going to be a problem. Shoving his hands deep into the pockets of his down jacket, he turned away from the dead woman lying on the bed and looked out across the snow-covered landscape of South London, an icy-cold wind making his eyes smart as it sliced through a crack in the window. The capital was in the grip of one of its coldest winters on record, and the ornamental lake that stood on the hospital grounds was iced over. Everything in London was frozen: the ponds on Hampstead Heath; the Serpentine; even the river between the houseboats where his own boat was moored had chunks of ice floating on it. After the previous night, it was all dusted in fresh snow and rather scenic. Dragging his eyes away, Kirby turned back to the room and the less-than-scenic picture there.

He had taken the call just as he was leaving home that morning. He'd spent the night at Isabel's, neither of them getting much sleep – the joys of the new relationship had yet to wear off – and had only popped back to his own boat for an hour or so, to shower and grab some coffee. He'd just started his second espresso and was seriously contemplating going to wake Isabel when Vicky, the dispatch caller, had rung and told him to skip the office and head to what everyone referred to simply as 'Blackwater'.

Blackwater Asylum, later renamed Blackwater Psychiatric Hospital, sat on the banks of the Thames at Battersea and had been closed for over two decades, its buildings left to rot on what was one of London's most valuable pieces of real estate. The journey from his mooring at Nine Elms should only have taken him twenty minutes tops, but because of the weather it had taken almost twice that. Snowploughs and gritters were out on the main roads; the side streets were all but impassable. When he'd eventually pulled up at the gates of the derelict hospital in his police-issue Corsa, which he loathed with a passion, a young red-nosed PC had directed him to the admin block, where he'd parked and been shown the way to Keats Ward, in which he now stood.

The ward was located towards the river end of the asylum's grounds – equidistant from Daylesford Road on one side of the site and a private property on the other, and well out of view from either. The room he was in was on the first floor and contained nothing apart from six old hospital beds: five of which were empty. On the sixth bed, the one that held his attention, was the body of an elderly woman. She lay on an old mattress, stained by decades of use and neglect. Kirby guessed the woman to be in her late seventies or eighties, although it was hard to tell under the circumstances. Her face had been badly beaten; her jaw was dislocated, judging by its unnatural angle. Her features had taken on the hue of the decaying surroundings, smudged blues and pinks, darker patches where the blood had smeared. The hospital-issue bed was a steel frame, a faded number 19 stencilled at its foot. The entire scene made him feel queasy.

A police arc light stood over the bed, its beam now switched off, and Scenes of Crime Officers moved carefully around the space, walking on tread plates, which always made Kirby think of a bizarre game of Twister. He watched as the police photographer recorded the body, the digital camera shutter snapping like teeth, the woman's injuries garish under the harsh light of the flash.

'Not exactly Sleeping Beauty,' said a voice Kirby recognised as belonging to his partner, Pete Anderson.

Anderson appeared in the doorway, practically filling it, and walked over to the bed, where Kirby heard him mutter *'Jesus Christ'* under his breath. Ten years his senior, Anderson was a great hulk of a man – not overweight, just large; his fingers like sausages. In his spare time he practised taxidermy, although how those big fingers managed such delicate work, Kirby had never figured out; perhaps that was why some of Anderson's creations were less than perfect, like the fox with three legs Kirby had back at the boat.

'Who said that line in *Withnail and I*, about no true beauty without decay?' said Anderson.

'Fuck knows – you're the one who stuffs dead animals.'

'Uncle Monty,' mumbled the photographer without looking up.

'That's it, Uncle Monty,' said Anderson, snapping his fingers. 'Mind you, it's more like bloody *Psycho* than *Withnail*. I keep expecting to bump into Norman Bates. This place gives me the creeps.'

'You and me both.' The two detectives fell silent while the photographer finished his work.

'What kind of lowlife does this to an elderly woman?' said Anderson, when he'd gone. 'She wouldn't have stood a chance.'

Kirby shook his head. 'No, she wouldn't.' Whoever had done it had hit the victim more than once, the bruising visible on both sides of her face and jaw. Kirby walked around the bed, hands still firmly in his pockets – nitrile gloves were no protection against the cold – and studied the woman's clothing. The first thing that struck him was that, although she was fully clothed, she wasn't wearing any kind of coat, which in this weather was peculiar. Her dress was in good condition, but dusty, and her shoes – flat and sensible, like

7

he'd seen advertised in the back of the *Telegraph Magazine* – were also dusty. He bent down for a closer look at her hands, which were gently resting on her stomach. The knuckles and a few of the finger joints looked swollen – probably arthritis. No sign of a wedding ring, and the nails were dirty but not broken.

'How in God's name did she get here?' said Kirby. 'It's not as though you can simply stroll into a place like this.'

'And why *here*?' asked Anderson, looking around. 'What's an elderly woman doing in a derelict mental hospital?'

It was a good question. Although there were no visible signs of decomposition, it was so cold that she could have been there for days.

'The security guard who found her says there was a site visit about a week ago and that she wasn't here then,' said Anderson, as though reading his thoughts.

A week, Kirby thought grimly. Surely she'd have been missed if she'd been here that long? 'Have you spoken to the guard?'

Anderson shook his head. 'Only briefly. He's waiting for us in his Portakabin.'

'What about the phone that he found, you got it?'

Anderson pulled an evidence bag from his pocket and held it up. 'Samsung. Several missed calls on the home screen. Security guard found it over there,' he said, pointing towards a marker near the door. 'I'll get it over to Newlands and checked ASAP.' Newlands was where the communications investigation unit was based.

Kirby looked around the bleak room. It was relatively spacious and probably would have held at least six more beds when it was a functioning ward. Four large arched windows ran along the outer wall, one of which had been blocked up. The floor was littered with broken glass, plaster, and decades of dust and bird droppings; a used condom by the skirting. Looking up, he saw a dead pigeon hanging from a light fitting, its wings spread as though crucified.

A road map of frozen damp was spreading across the ceiling, and the walls, which had once been pale pink, now peeled like burnt flesh, revealing layers of decades-old paint beneath. It was hard to imagine it as a place where you were meant to recover.

'Who the hell comes to a place like this?' said Anderson, eyeing up the dead bird.

'Let's talk to the security guard,' said Kirby, with a sudden urge to be out of there. He skimmed the room a final time. The dead pigeon was now gently swaying in an unidentifiable breeze and he hoped that it wasn't the last thing she saw.

CHAPTER 2

The security guard's name was Leroy Simmons, and he was reading a copy of *Carpworld* when Kirby and Anderson arrived at the Portakabin.

'This fuckin' weather,' Simmons moaned, as they brought in a waft of cold air with them. 'It ain't no good for man nor beast.' He waved his magazine as if to demonstrate the plight of carp.

The cabin was small and basic: a compact kitchen at one end, with a sink and microwave, and a small table and chairs at the other. Two dirty glasses rested on the draining board. Simmons sat at the table; piles of paper and magazines had been pushed to one side, a deck of cards hastily stacked on top. He was a large man, and even through his uniform Kirby could tell that he worked out. He'd have no problem carrying an elderly woman through the hospital grounds and up a flight of stairs.

'I'd sooner be on my rounds than sat on my butt in here,' said the security guard.

'You won't be doing any rounds today. Once we've spoken to you, you'll need to make a formal statement at the station. Then you'll be free to go,' said Kirby, taking a seat opposite. Anderson stood by the door and rattled a box of Tic Tacs before flipping the tab and popping one into his mouth.

'But I haven't finished my shift. Will I get paid?' asked Simmons.

'You'll have to take that up with your employers,' said Kirby. 'But first we need to ask you a few questions.' He took out his notebook, a battered Moleskine, and opened it on a fresh page. 'How long have you worked for Emeris Security?'

'Six months, give or take a day or two.'

'What time did you arrive here today?' asked Kirby.

'Six a.m. That's when we change shifts.'

'So the snow didn't hold you up at all – getting here, I mean?'

'Uh-uh, I walk. Live over there,' he said, gesturing. 'On the estate.'

'Okay. So who did you take over from this morning?'

'Guy goes by the name of Chips. Dunno his real name, but you best speak to him about what went on in the darkness.' His hands gripped the *Carpworld*, which he'd rolled into a tube.

The darkness? He made it sound like some sort of religious state, and Kirby saw Anderson shift his weight and lean on the door frame, arms folded.

'And where were you last night?'

'In my bed, sleeping. Tries to get a good night before I gets here.'

'Can anyone verify that?'

'Uh-uh. I lives alone now the wife is gone, God rest her soul.' He crossed himself.

'Okay, walk us through what happened. Before and after you made your discovery.'

Simmons rubbed his eyes; he looked tired, the opposite of a man who'd had a good night's sleep. 'I got here, made my coffee, waited for the sun to come up and then went out on my first round. That was about seven-thirty. I went to the main part of the fence on Battersea Fields Drive, then I cuts down through the airing courts

11

and checks the chapel, and then down to the water tower and back. I don't go down to the lake very often.'

'But today you did. Why was that?'

'I heard a noise. Couldn't fathom what it was. Then, when I got nearer, I realised it was a phone.'

'You heard the ringing from outside?' asked Anderson, speaking for the first time since entering the cabin.

Simmons nodded. 'Sounds crazy I know, but what with the snow, it was so quiet. Reckon I'd have heard an ant shit.'

Anderson smiled. 'Right.'

'And then what did you do?' asked Kirby, wondering what an ant shitting would sound like.

Simmons paused. 'I was scared. Don't get me wrong, I'm no coward, but this place gives me the creeps. I stood there for a moment, rooted to the spot. Then I thought, *Pull yourself together, Leroy, ain't nothing but a phone.* So I goes in. Wish to God I hadn't.'

'What made you go upstairs – is that where the ringing was coming from?'

'Uh-uh. It stopped when I got inside,' he said. 'Then I heard a buzz, like when someone leaves you a voicemail. I dunno, maybe whoever it belonged to is deaf and needs the volume up high.' He stopped, crossing himself again. 'And then I seen her, lying there.'

'Did you recognise the woman?' asked Kirby.

Simmons looked genuinely shocked at this. 'Course not. Why would I?'

'Did you touch anything?'

'You gotta be joking. I legged it, called you lot.'

'Have you seen anyone hanging around the perimeter recently, near the front gate, perhaps, when you arrive and leave?'

'No. No one.' He squeezed *Carpworld* into an even tighter roll.

'How about young kids, or vandals – any trouble with them trying to get in?'

Simmons shook his head again.

'So you've never seen anyone on the site who shouldn't be there?'

'No, I ain't. No one came or went last night. I checked the cameras while I was waiting for you lot to show up. We've only got the two, one at the main gate and one on Daylesford Road.'

'The Daylesford Road entrance is still used?' Kirby remembered it as a small, gated affair, rusted and overgrown the last time he'd passed it.

'Uh, yes. It's the one Mr Sweet uses.'

Kirby looked up from his Moleskine. 'Who's Mr Sweet?'

'You mean you don't know? He lives here, down near the river.' He jerked his thumb back over his shoulder. 'In the Old Lodge. Been there ever since the place shut.'

Kirby glanced at Anderson, who had now straightened himself up, phone at the ready.

'That was over twenty years ago,' said Kirby. 'Surely there can't be any staff left after all this time?'

'Oh, he ain't staff,' said Simmons, looking from one detective to the other. 'He was a patient.'

CHAPTER 3

It was the snow, its muffled silence creeping into his dreams, that had caused Raymond to wake with a start. He lay in bed, his heart pounding, trying to figure out what was different. Then he realised there were no sirens, no birds, no exhausts backfiring; even the aircraft making their early flyovers were a dim rumble. The light seeping into the room also had a different quality to it, so propping himself up on his elbow he peered out of the window and could hardly believe his eyes. He'd seen a few flakes fall last night, but never in a million years did he think it would snow this heavily. A feeling of relief swept over him – the timing couldn't be better – and he sank back on to his pillow, a smile on his face.

Raymond had lived in the grounds of Blackwater Asylum for nearly twenty-three years, and before that had lived in the hospital itself as a patient. He'd been admitted shortly after his mother died in a house fire when he was seventeen, and when Blackwater closed some twenty-seven years later, Raymond had never left. Officially he had, like everyone else, except he kept coming back: again and again. He'd found it impossible to stay away and had eventually set up home in the old caretaker's lodge, on a small corner of the site, down by the river. No one knew he was there to begin with; or if they did, they didn't care. He never bothered anyone and kept himself to himself, generally avoiding any kind of confrontation. And then *they* had come, a whole succession of them. 'They' were developers, and he hated every single one. Naturally, they all wanted shot of him, but it wasn't that easy. The truth was that Blackwater wasn't just his home, it was his entire world; to leave Blackwater would be tantamount to destroying himself. He'd lost count of the various schemes he'd seen fall through over the years. The pattern had repeated itself so many times that he had genuinely come to believe that Blackwater had a life of its own. It had a way of sucking you in and, if it didn't like you, spitting you out. It would take more than a sharp-suited property developer with pound signs in his eyes to destroy it. Or, that's what he'd thought until Patrick Calder had come along.

At first he'd seemed like the rest of them, and Raymond didn't pay him too much attention, but after a few months it became clear that Patrick Calder was different. When the realisation hit him that Calder wasn't going to make the same mistakes as those who'd gone before him, Raymond became convinced – for the first time in more than two decades – that it really might be the end. On the brink of giving up hope, he took the advice of his friend, Mrs Muir, at the Lavender B&B, where he was supposed to have lived when Blackwater closed, and sought legal help. To his amazement it turned out that he had squatter's rights – he'd lived there for over twenty years, after all – and, as a result, the small pocket of land on which the Old Lodge stood was now legally his. He still found it hard to believe that he'd won, that he'd actually beaten a man like Patrick Calder. Calder had been furious, making it very clear that should Raymond be found wandering the grounds outside his designated boundary, the consequences would be severe. It was a small price to pay, and the reality was that Raymond did what he liked; he just had to be careful he didn't get caught.

After a few minutes, he heaved himself out of bed and began looking for a match to light the gas stove so that he could make some tea, and pondered his situation. His home was safe, that was guaranteed; but other elements of his existence at Blackwater were now under threat. Not only were the contractors due to start work that very day, which presented certain logistical problems, but also in recent months someone else had been poking around Blackwater – someone he'd dubbed the Creeper. The snow would scupper the contractors for a few days, he was sure, but not the Creeper. The Creeper was a law unto itself.

He grabbed a mug off the draining board and reached up for the tea caddy, his fingers brushing the urn that was nestled between it and the sugar jar, and smiled. He popped a teabag into the mug and returned the caddy to the shelf. 'I wish you were here,' he murmured.

Climbing back into bed, he pulled the duvet up to his chin – it was ruddy freezing – and waited for the kettle to boil. Over the years, Raymond had developed a strong sixth sense: trespassers, unwanted visitors, urban explorers, vandals, whatever you wanted to call them – he always knew when they were here. Over the past few months, however, someone else had been visiting regularly, and he'd seen them again last night. After the first couple of sightings he'd assumed that it was just another trespasser or vandal, or even one of the explorers, but as the months had gone by, doubt began to set in. Those visitors rarely, if ever, came alone, and for the most part they didn't know their way around; they also didn't come on a weekly basis. Whoever this was, they did all those things; or rather *whatever* this was, because Raymond had recently come to the conclusion that the Creeper was a ghost. It was the only logical conclusion, and once he'd embraced the idea he felt vaguely comforted by it.

The kettle started to boil – he could see it from his bed misting up the windows of the small front room – and he got up and poured hot water into his mug. He watched the teabag float in the water, bleeding out into the rapidly darkening liquid, until the tea was almost black. Then he fished out the bag and dropped it into the sink with a moist thud, where it lay steaming like fresh cat prey. He managed to extract a few dribbles of milk from a frozen carton and then reached up for the sugar, his fingers again brushing the urn next to the jar. He added two teaspoons of sugar and hurriedly took a slurp, instantly burning his mouth.

He lit the paraffin heater and quickly got dressed while his tea cooled to a more manageable temperature. He needed some new shoes – the ones he had had developed a leak – and he wondered whether there might be a bring-and-buy at the church. Perhaps he could prevail upon Mrs Muir at the B&B for a bath afterwards, and, if he played his cards right, maybe even some supper; that's if she hadn't started on the sherry. Once he was dressed, he opened the front door and stood on the porch, sniffing the cold, deliciously fresh air, and he was about to take a sip of tea when the sudden feeling he wasn't alone ran through him. He paused, straining his ears for the slightest sound, and scanned the woodland around the lodge. There was nothing but silence – or Blackwater Silence, as he called it. It couldn't be the Creeper at this hour, surely?

As he turned to go back inside, a noise made him stop in his tracks: a voice, somewhere in the distance. He'd been right, there was someone out there; the contractors must have arrived early, despite the snow. He downed the tea, leaving the mug in the sink, quickly made the bed, and turned off the paraffin heater. He put on his coat, wound his scarf around his head turban-style and locked up. As he made his way to a pathway through the trees, he felt a blister forming on the roof of his mouth where he'd scalded it. His mother had always told him off for drinking his tea too fast. *You'll burn your tongue, Ray, love.* He smiled at the memory, as banal as it was. God he missed her.

CHAPTER 4

'Why the fuck didn't anyone mention this Sweet character earlier?'
Anderson growled, as they made their way towards the Old Lodge.

Kirby wondered the same, but fumed quietly.

The lodge was concealed in a small clearing, completely surrounded by trees and tangled undergrowth. A path had been beaten
through, but to the untrained eye it was all but invisible. What he'd
been expecting, he wasn't quite sure, but the small house in front
of him came as a surprise. All the buildings he'd seen so far reeked
of neglect and decay, but the Old Lodge was the converse. It was
a raised one-storey building, with a small flight of steps leading up
to a wooden porch and gabled entrance. The paintwork was well
maintained, albeit in a variety of colours, and the fabric of the
building looked to be in good nick. Window boxes, empty at the
moment, hung from the two front windows. A lean-to had been
erected on the left-hand side of the property, made up of sheet
metal and what looked like the side of an old shed. Even that had a
rustic charm about it. If nothing else, Sweet was house-proud, and
Kirby wondered how much the land was worth if Simmons's claim
that he had squatter's rights was correct.

Anderson was peering through one of the lodge windows in
an attempt to see if Raymond Sweet was at home. No one had
answered the door when he'd knocked, and the place was locked

up. Fresh footprints in the snow led from the porch off into the trees, and Kirby was willing to bet that they led to the entrance on Daylesford Road.

'He's not here,' said Anderson, unhelpfully, as he moved around the property.

Kirby followed the fresh prints in the snow, being careful not to disturb them. They disappeared beneath the trees, but a clear path trailed through, and sure enough the footprints began again at the other end, where Kirby tracked them to the side entrance that opened on to Daylesford Road. The entrance consisted of large wrought-iron double gates and a smaller gate to one side. The large gates had been blocked off with sheet metal and had security spikes along the top. The smaller side gate was also spiked, but unlike the larger gate it hadn't been blocked off, so he could see through to the road outside. A new closed shackle padlock gleamed against the rust-flecked metal chain that secured it. The footprints led to the small side gate, and the snow had been pushed to one side in a quarter-circle where the gate had recently been opened and closed. Kirby headed back to the lodge, his mood darkening.

'Anything?' asked Anderson, when Kirby arrived back at the small clearing.

He shook his head. 'He's gone.' He pulled out his phone and punched in the number for the office, where Mark Drayton picked up.

'Lew, what's up?'

'Run a check on a Raymond Sweet for me, will you? Apparently he's an ex-patient of Blackwater Asylum and lives on the site. I want to know everything about him.' Kirby's eyes roamed over the lodge, and the Heath Robinson-esque lean-to, as he hung up.

Anderson's phone pinged. 'The ME's arrived,' he said, reading the message. 'You coming?'

'I'll follow you in a minute,' said Kirby. He wanted a few moments to himself to get a sense of the place – and of Sweet. As Anderson's muffled footsteps receded into the distance, silence engulfed the small clearing. Kirby would never have guessed how near he was to an inner-city road, let alone flats and houses where people had left for work that morning or were now cosy in their beds after the night shift. Life went on all around, but the clearing felt like a world apart. Snow clung to the tree branches like thick icing – a good few inches had fallen overnight – and the ground was smooth with unspoilt snow. He wondered what it was like to live here all alone – and not only that, but in the grounds of the very institution that had once removed you from society.

He moved around the lodge and peered in through the windows, images of the dead woman flashing through his mind. It was hard to see much inside, as the interior was dark and his eyes had to adjust from the brightness of the snow. The main areas looked tidy enough – the draining board and small kitchen table were clear, even the bed was made – but every other available space was crammed with objects. He went back round to the window nearest the bed and looked in again. On the bedside table were an alarm clock and a framed photo. He was about to move away when something caught his eye, half hidden in the shadows. He cupped his hands around his eyes in a bid to see better and at first thought it was Sweet, watching from inside. As his eyes accustomed themselves to the dark interior he soon realised that it wasn't Sweet at all, but some kind of dummy. What was it, a dressmaking model? He moved along the window, his breath steaming up the glass, and peered in again, holding his breath. Although he could see more clearly, it was still too dark to make out much detail. One thing was clear though, the dummy was wearing a coat; and, as far as Kirby could discern, it was a woman's coat.

CHAPTER 5

'Ed, it's me. Where are you? Call me. Let me know you're okay.' Connie ended the call and slipped the phone back into her pocket and pulled out her keys. Where the hell was he? She pushed open the heavy wooden door and manoeuvred herself and a large roll of drawings into the building, letting the door slam shut behind her. Her friend Ed worked in a local school, which was shut today due to the weather, so there really wasn't any good reason for him not to have called – especially after last night.

Propping the roll of drawings against the wall, Connie went over to the small cupboard where the alarm was kept, and was about to open the door when she realised it wasn't bleeping. She'd been so preoccupied coming in that she hadn't noticed. The alarm pad looked normal, and the error light wasn't flashing; perhaps her boss, Richard Bonaro, had forgotten to switch it on last night when he'd left. It hadn't been her, she knew that much. She'd been on her way back from Oxford with the blasted drawings she'd just lugged in through the snow, on a train that had crawled along. She could feel the frustration returning just thinking about it: no buffet, no heating and no information. Fucking nightmare. It wouldn't have mattered so much if she hadn't been meeting Ed.

Heaving the roll of drawings under her arm, she began making her way up the stairs to the main reading room.

Connie's official job at RADE, the Repository for Architectural Drawings and Ephemera, was archivist, but in reality she did a bit of everything – she'd even given the odd tour of the place, not that many people knew it existed. Somehow, RADE had ended up as a 'hidden gem' on a trendy culture website, and every now and then some intrepid Japanese students would ask for a guided tour. This had actually given her an idea, which so far she hadn't confided to anyone, not even Ed and their good friend Mole.

Reaching the top of the stairs, Connie paused. The door to the offices was ajar. Perhaps that's why the alarm hadn't been set properly; all the main internal doors had to be closed properly before it would engage. Bonaro must have had one of his wealthy buddies over, pumping them for cash, and forgotten to close up properly – not realising the alarm hadn't kicked in. Nudging the door open, she stepped into the small reception room. Off this was the main reading room, where she unceremoniously dumped the roll of drawings. She went over to her desk and shrugged off her coat before rolling up the blinds, revealing large French windows that overlooked the small square outside. Today, the square looked picture-postcard pretty, the trees covered in snow and hardly a soul in sight. With natural light restored, Connie began to make her way through to the small kitchen at the back of the building – she was gasping for a coffee, as her usual pit stop had been closed due to the snow. As she passed Bonaro's office, to her right, she paused; she could have sworn that she'd heard a noise. The wooden floor in his office had a characteristic creak that Connie would recognise anywhere. Except Bonaro wasn't due in that day. Who else could it be, though?

She stopped by the door and hesitated, before knocking gently. 'Hello, Richard?' Another creak. Someone was moving around inside. It had to be Bonaro, surely? No one else had the access code to the alarm apart from the trustees of the collection, and none of them would be here; they lived in a massive pile in Wimbledon and rarely set foot in the place, much to her and Bonaro's relief.

Now she couldn't hear anything and realised that she was holding her breath. This was ridiculous; no one could get in without disabling the alarm, and who would want to break into a place like RADE anyhow? She was just about to reach out for the doorknob when she heard another, louder creak. Whoever was in there was now standing right beside the door.

She knocked again, this time more forcefully, and grabbed the doorknob, giving it a good twist, only to find it was locked. She let go quickly and backed away, unsure what was going on. Why would Bonaro lock himself in his own office? Then she heard the key being turned in the lock and saw the doorknob moving. The door opened a few inches towards her, and she took another step back, wondering whether to make a run for it. Before she could decide what to do, the door was pushed open entirely and Bonaro's startled face appeared.

'Connie? What are you doing here?' he asked.

'Dropping off the drawings that I collected from Oxford yesterday. Jesus effing Christ, you gave me a scare. Didn't you hear me knocking?'

Bonaro shook his head. 'Sorry, no . . .'

'I didn't think you were coming in today, I thought you were a burglar.'

Bonaro looked slightly confused. 'I was on the phone – I didn't hear you.'

'Why was the door locked?' she asked.

'Oh, that. I've had a duplicate key made and was trying it out.'

'Oh, right,' said Connie, wondering why he needed a duplicate. 'I see.'

'I left my damned wallet here last night,' he said, patting his jacket pocket. 'Good job, actually, because the phone rang as soon

I came in. That call I was on just now, it was the executor of Helen Linehan's estate.'

Connie frowned; the name was familiar and yet she couldn't place it. 'Remind me?'

'Her family owned Marsh House – you know, the place by the river in Battersea? She died at the end of last year.'

Connie knew exactly where Marsh House was; it was the house next to Blackwater, where she would have been meeting Ed had she not been stuck on that frigging train. 'What did they want?' She tried to keep her voice even.

'Mrs Linehan has left us some drawings of the house and garden.'

'Really? That's great news. Do we know how many?' Her mind was racing as she spoke. 'Or whether there's anything else?'

Bonaro shook his head. 'Only that it's all in one portfolio, apart from a couple of journals. As to its exact contents' – he shrugged – 'they're anyone's guess. I doubt the executors have even looked.'

'So there *could* be plans for Blackwater mixed in . . .'

Bonaro smiled. 'Don't get ahead of yourself, but yes, I suppose there could be. Regardless, they'll be a significant addition to the plans we already hold of James Neville's other hospital buildings. I've arranged for you to collect them next Monday at noon. There's a family member there clearing the house. The name and contact number are here.' He handed her a piece of paper torn from his notepad, then looked at his watch. 'Damn, I'd better get going. I'm late. Dentist.'

'I'm surprised it's open,' said Connie, thinking of all the closed businesses she'd passed on the way in.

He grimaced. 'Typical, isn't it?'

'Urghh. Well, good luck.'

'Oh, and there's something I need to talk to you about tomorrow. First thing, over coffee?' he said, pulling his office door closed. 'Assuming I can still speak.'

Connie smiled. 'Okay. Can you give me a clue?'

'You'll have to wait. It's nothing to worry about though,' he said, hurrying past, leaving a waft of Floris aftershave in his wake. 'Bye.'

'Bye.' She listened as the metal Blakeys on his shoes clipped the stone stairs, followed by the echo of the front door slamming shut in the hallway. When she was sure he'd gone, Connie opened the door to his office and peered in. A box of James Neville drawings sat on the table, and she went over and lifted the lid: Neville's drawings of mental asylums from the nineteenth century, the ones she'd painstakingly catalogued a year ago. RADE held all of Neville's asylum designs, except the ones for Blackwater, which had never been found. She wondered who Bonaro had been showing them to, and let the lid fall back into place. Leaving the room, her thoughts returned to Ed – he really should have called by now, he knew how anxious she'd be – and a sickening feeling began to grow in the pit of her stomach. *Please don't let it happen again*, she thought, as she headed to the kitchen.

CHAPTER 6

Revulsion bubbled away in Kirby's gut as he descended the creaking wooden staircase to the ground floor. Decades of grit, plaster and pigeon guano crunched under each step. The medical examiner had estimated the time of death somewhere between 10 p.m. and midnight – probable cause, the combination of a blow to the head and hypothermia. The blow to the head hadn't been the one to break the elderly woman's jaw: that had been meted out separately. The ME couldn't say much more until he'd examined the body in detail at the mortuary.

What kind of person would commit such a brutal act on someone so vulnerable? The pressure would be on to solve this as soon as possible, and he sincerely hoped that they did. The location wouldn't do them any favours; the media loved Blackwater despite professing to hate it.

Which all brought him back to the location: why *Blackwater*? The hospital was deeply embedded in the fabric of the entire local area, even after all these years. It was a place about which everyone had a tale to tell, from seeing ghosts to knowing someone who'd worked there. It had also been the location of various criminal acts since its closure in 1993 – arson and drug dealing to name but two – and one poor soul had chosen it as the backdrop to their suicide. It was the stuff of urban legends, and the press lapped it up. That the victim had been left there was no accident, he felt sure. And then there was the ward itself: Keats. What was the significance of that? It was deep in the grounds of the asylum, a fair walk from either of the two entrances. The killer would have passed plenty of other hiding places en route – not to mention locations where the body may not have been found for weeks. It could have been a random choice, but Kirby didn't think so.

Kirby stepped outside, glad to be out of the decaying ward block, which he found profoundly depressing. A path had been marked out, for police coming and going, in an attempt to preserve any evidence outside, but the truth was that whoever had done this had come before the snowfall ended. When the first police had arrived, there were no other tracks leading into the building, or anywhere in the immediate area, apart from those belonging to Leroy Simmons.

He spotted Anderson talking to one of the SOCOs, and he waved Kirby over.

'There's a breach in the fence by Daylesford Road,' said Anderson. 'Big enough to crawl through, but difficult to drag a body through, at least without snagging it or its clothing.'

'We're checking for fibres,' said the SOCO before wandering off.

'Sweet's got a woman's coat in his house,' said Kirby. 'It's on some sort of dummy.'

Anderson raised his eyebrows. 'Maybe he likes dressing up.'

'Or it could belong to our victim,' Kirby said, stamping his feet. He was frozen to the core. 'Look, I'm going to check out the house next door, the big posh place. You want to come?'

Anderson shook his head. 'Site manager's on his way.' He looked at his notes. 'Brian Kaplinsky. I'll wait for him, otherwise we'll be here all day.'

It was true; they were so short-staffed that if they did every-thing in pairs, cases would take twice as long to get solved. 'I'll call you when I'm done then,' said Kirby, and he began to make his way back towards the admin block.

He was keen to have a proper look around, but that would have to wait until the SOCOs had finished their search. When he reached the admin block, a handsome Queen Anne-style building, he skirted around the Corsa – preferring to walk, despite the cold – and set off down the asylum's main driveway. Away from the police activity, silence once again shrouded him, like it had at Raymond Sweet's house. It was like nothing he'd ever experienced before in London. He stopped for a moment and took in the beauty of the white landscape, the snow off the main driveway pristine and undisturbed. It reminded him of a film set, and he imagined Father Christmas hurtling into view with reindeer and sleigh any moment; although, in truth, Jack Torrance from *The Shining* was more like it.

When he reached the main gate, the same young PC who'd first admitted him – now a lovely shade of blue – let him out of the grounds, and he turned left to walk along Battersea Fields Drive towards Marsh House. The asylum perimeter along this part of the road was boarded up: difficult to climb over in any cir-cumstances, but with a body in tow? Impossible, thought Kirby. On the opposite side of the road to the asylum, their lower floors masked by trees, sat large, Victorian, red-brick mansion blocks. The flats at the top would afford perfect views of the asylum grounds and beyond, although the likelihood of anyone seeing something last night was slim. Officers were doing door-to-door, and Kirby hoped their efforts yielded something – the glimmer of torchlight in the dark, a strange vehicle – that might lead them to the elderly woman's killer.

After several minutes of brisk walking, the asylum's boarded-up perimeter came to an end, replaced by a brick wall over which he could just make out the bare branches of trees covered in thick snow. A few feet further on and he came to an open gate, flanked on either side by ivy-covered stone gateposts, the inscription *Marsh House* barely visible on the left-hand post. He turned off the main road and began walking up the drive. The house was easy to miss from the street, and although he had no idea of its history, he wondered if at some point it had been part of the asylum. Whatever its original purpose, it was now a highly desirable residence. Kirby rang the bell and waited.

The man who answered the door to Marsh House introduced himself as Charles Palmer and was a slender man in his fifties. Judging by his accent he was either Australian or Kiwi. After explaining the reason for his visit, Kirby was led into the kitchen, where Palmer offered him a coffee. 'I was just about to make myself an espresso,' he said, gesturing towards an expensive-looking Gaggia.

Kirby could almost feel himself salivating at the thought. 'That'd be great, thanks.'

'Milk?'

Kirby shook his head. 'As it comes.' He watched as Palmer made the coffee, neither man speaking – as though some kind of ritual was being observed.

When the dark liquid had finished filling two small espresso cups, Palmer handed one to Kirby. 'Let's go next door, it's more comfortable.'

Kirby followed him into a handsome living room, where they sat down. The room was a jumble of partially filled boxes and crates, but despite the chaos a fire roared in the grate. Kirby finally felt himself warming up.

'Are you moving in or out?' Kirby asked.

'I recently inherited the place, so I'm busy clearing things out at the moment. But I have been living here for the past month or so.'

'Where are you from? Australia?'

'Perth.'

'Do you intend to stay?' Kirby looked around, thinking how lovely it would be to have this much space. Mind you, he'd only fill it if he did.

'I'll probably sell. Go back to Perth.'

'Will the development next door affect the sale?'

Palmer shrugged. 'I hope not, although it's not ideal. The whole area seems to be being redeveloped, what with the American embassy down at Nine Elms and all those apartments going up.'

Kirby knew about that only too well; it was a stone's throw from the boats. Not to mention the development going up right next to the moorings. He drained his coffee. 'Thanks, that was good. Right, perhaps we could move on to last night. Were you here?' He took out his Moleskine.

Palmer hesitated. 'No, I was out last night. I got back late; the snow held me up. I'm not used to driving in it.'

'And what time was that, roughly?'

'I suppose I left here at about seven and didn't get back until gone midnight. It was snowing heavily by then – the roads were deserted.'

'I see,' said Kirby, noting down the times. 'Can anyone verify your whereabouts?'

Palmer looked taken aback. 'Why do you need to know?'

'I have to ask.'

Palmer paused as though weighing up the options before speaking. 'I was at the Vauxhall Tavern. The barman, Vihaan, will remember me.'

Kirby wrote down the barman's name. 'And you drove back, you said?'

'Despite what you might think, not everyone who frequents the Tavern is high or drunk. I don't drink, for the record. Or do drugs.'

Kirby ignored the dig and went on. 'When you drove back, did you see anyone outside the house or on the road – either on foot or in a car?'

Palmer shook his head. 'No one. It was a whiteout. Never seen anything like it in a city.'

He was right – Kirby had never seen snow like it in the capital. 'Have you seen or heard anything suspicious in the last twenty-four hours?'

'No. What's this about?'

'A body was found this morning in the grounds next door,' said Kirby.

'*What?*' Palmer looked genuinely shocked. 'A body? Jeez, that's terrible. Was it an accident?'

'It's unlikely.'

'D'you know who it is?'

'Not at this point, no. I don't suppose that you've seen anyone hanging around recently?'

Palmer shook his head. 'No, but then again, I don't go that way very often – past the main entrance, I mean. I usually turn left and head to the shops, or into town, that way.'

'I believe that there used to be access to the asylum from your grounds, is that correct?' Kirby went on.

'There's a door in the garden wall, but it's been blocked off for years.'

'Is there any other way into next door from here?'

'Are you saying that someone got in through the garden on this side?' Palmer looked shocked at the thought.

'We have to explore every possibility.' Kirby had noticed a path down the right-hand side of the house, which he assumed led to

31

a back entrance. 'Do you mind if I take a look in the garden?' He glanced through the window at the snowy scene outside; he felt warmer now than he had done in the past twenty-four hours, dammit.

'Be my guest, but I can tell you now that whoever got into the old asylum didn't get in through here.' Palmer got up and led Kirby through to a drawing room, which had French windows that opened straight on to the garden. He unlocked the doors with a key that he took from the top of the doorframe.

'Does this lead directly down to the river?' Kirby asked, stepping out on to the crisp, white snow.

'Yes, there's an old boathouse down there, beyond the maze.' Palmer pointed off to the left, his breath clear and white in the cold air. 'I wouldn't go in, though. I don't know if it's safe. Everything's a bit of a mess these days.'

Kirby walked away from the house, leaving Charles Palmer watching him from the warmth of the drawing room. He wasn't quite sure what to make of the man. He'd been helpful and certainly knew how to make coffee, but Kirby wondered whether his hesitation over his whereabouts the previous night concealed anything more sinister than reticence. And the inheritance. *I'll probably sell.* Kirby thought back to when his grandmother had died and his mother had sold the house. It was fraught with emotion. He'd got none of that from Palmer, and wondered if he had siblings or a family of his own. Just because he hung out at one of the best-known gay bars in London didn't preclude a wife and kids tucked away in Perth.

After a few yards, Kirby stopped for a moment, the same feeling that he'd had outside Raymond Sweet's house returning. London felt miles away, although in reality Chelsea Bridge and its traffic were only a few hundred yards to his right. A siren wailed in the distance, but the snow muffled even that, as though it were in another world running parallel to his.

As he carried on towards the boathouse through the thick, undisturbed snow, he could tell that the garden had once been beautiful. The lawn he was crossing led to a parterre on the right – its layout just visible under the snow – and a wooded area to his left. Directly ahead, he could see a statue, and beyond that a small frozen pond and a line of trees. Although the Thames was shielded, he could feel its presence beyond the treeline. He veered off to the left and found himself in a small maze, and *The Shining* sprung to mind for the second time that morning. Unlike the maze in the film, however, these hedges were no more than four feet high and would once have been neatly trimmed; now, they sprouted unwieldy shoots, which hung heavy with snow.

Out of the maze, he found himself on what must have been the path that Palmer had mentioned. He could feel the frozen gravel through the snow as he crunched his way forward. He could sense the river ahead of him strongly now, and smelt its familiar tang. To his left there was a high wall overgrown with ivy and topped with razor wire, and he spotted the bricked-up doorway. He went over for a closer look, but it was clear that no one had been through it in years. He gazed up at the wall, trying to imagine the elderly victim scaling it in the middle of the night; there was simply no way, unless she changed into Catwoman in the early hours. He turned and looked back at the garden. It really was magnificent; there was even what he took to be a small folly – a short, stumpy structure covered in ivy.

Heading towards the river, he made his way over to the boathouse, which was on raised stilts, and looked out over the water. In contrast to the snow, the Thames looked brown and sluggish, and yet despite this it was still a magnificent sight. A flight of steep steps led straight into the river; the tide was out and the steps were exposed right the way down to the foreshore. He moved around to the boathouse door, which he saw was fitted with a new lock. It was heavy-duty – more than you'd need to secure a lawnmower or a rowing boat. What few windows there were in the boathouse had been blacked out, and he couldn't see anything inside. He was about to head back to the house when his mobile rang; it was Anderson.

'What's up?' Kirby asked.

'Raymond Sweet's back. He's waiting for us at the Lodge and doesn't look too pleased.'

CHAPTER 7

Raymond had been waiting at the Old Lodge for over half an hour – a policeman standing guard outside – and his stress levels were escalating by the minute. He only took the odd thing from the asylum, things that no one else could possibly want. It was the more delicate acquisitions, as he liked to think of them, that he was worried about: things that should never have been left behind in the first place. Was *that* what this was about? Or maybe it was his drawings? He often drew little faces on the walls to help him navigate – smiley faces, sad faces, sometimes faces making a noise, depending on how the mood took him – as parts of Blackwater were so overgrown that sometimes even he had difficulty finding his way around. He spoke to them sometimes, too – little helpers, he called them. They did no harm to anyone, so it couldn't be that, surely? Suddenly, there was a knock on the door. He got up and, despite the situation, felt a surge of pride opening the door to *his house* – the house that if Patrick Calder had his way would be demolished with the rest of Blackwater.

'Mr Sweet? I'm DI Kirby,' said the man outside. 'And this is DI Anderson.'

Raymond pulled himself together and managed to say 'hello'.

'May we come in?' asked the detective. 'We have a few questions for you.'

'Oh, erm, yes.' Raymond stood aside as the two men entered the small room, then pushed the front door closed.

The three of them stood awkwardly in the centre of the room. Raymond had never had guests before – well, not like this – and he wasn't sure how to conduct himself. He tried to think what Mrs Muir would do, but realised that he didn't have any sherry, let alone those funny little glasses she used.

'We'd like to speak to you about last night,' said the one called Kirby. 'Why don't we sit down?'

'Oh, erm, yes,' said Raymond. He must stop saying 'erm', but before he knew it another one had popped out. 'Erm, yes, sit down. There.' He pointed at his old sofa. 'I'll perch.' He'd heard Mrs Muir say that on several occasions. *I'll perch, dear.* Somehow it didn't sound the same when he said it.

'Last night,' the policeman began.

Last night. His mind began to race.

'Could you tell us where you were?' The second one, whose name he'd already forgotten, interrupted his thoughts.

'Oh, I was at home,' he replied, relieved at being asked such a simple question.

'You mean here, in this building?'

'Well . . . no . . .' He looked nervously from one man to the other. The first one was looking around the room. His eyes were darting over everything, including some boxes in the corner, like a fly looking for something to land on. They lingered on the bedroom door, which thankfully he'd remembered to close, then eventually came to rest on Raymond.

'Well . . . I, erm . . .' He paused. Perhaps it was best to come clean. 'I was playing cards with Leroy.'

The two detectives looked at each other and then back at him.

'You played cards last night with Leroy Simmons, the security guard?'

36

He nodded, wondering why this was so interesting.

'What time was this?'

'I – I suppose it must have been about eight o'clock?' Unlike his own clock, the one in the cabin ran on a battery and kept good time.

'And what time did you leave?' The man was making notes now in a shabby-looking black book, which Raymond quite liked the look of.

'Quarter to eleven.'

'And what time did you get back here?' shabby-notebook man asked.

Raymond couldn't be bothered to explain about his own clock, about how he kept forgetting to wind it, so made a guess. 'Quarter to twelve?'

'You were with Mr Simmons from 8 p.m. until 10.45 p.m., then walked back here arriving at 11.45 p.m.?'

'Yes.' He nodded, vigorously.

'Can you explain how it took you an hour to get back? It can't be much more than twenty min—'

'Twenty-two minutes if I walk fast,' he interrupted. 'But I get chips on a Tuesday night from the Rock Bottom Fishcoteque. Sometimes they save me a piece of cod, or if I'm very lucky, a Peter's Pie. Last night it was chicken.'

The two policemen were now staring at him intently, and he didn't like it.

'Have . . . have I said something wrong?' Raymond asked.

'So you left Mr Simmons at 10.45 p.m. and went to get chips? Which exit did you use?' asked shabby-notebook man.

'The main one on Battersea Fields Drive. It's the only time I use it. Leroy lets me out.'

The second policeman, the one without the notebook, got up and pulled out his phone. 'Excuse me,' he said, and went outside.

'And then what did you do,' the first policeman went on, 'after you got the chips?'

'Peter's Pie,' corrected Raymond. 'They'd run out of chips.'

'Okay, so after you got the pie. What did you do then?'

'I came home along Daylesford Road. And went to bed,' he added, before being asked.

'And you were alone?'

'Well, yes . . .' It was sort of true.

'Did you see anything unusual, either on your way to the cabin or on your way back, last night?' The policeman stood up and began wandering around the room. He stopped by the sink and looked up at Raymond's kitchen shelf, where the tea and sugar were – and the urn.

'No,' he managed, his heart beating a little faster.

The policeman turned. 'You didn't see or hear anyone?'

Raymond shook his head again. He'd taken a small detour and strolled down to the lake – to walk off his pie – and seen the Creeper, but he didn't think the police would want to know about ghosts. Plus, he wasn't supposed to go down there and didn't want Calder getting wind of the fact.

'How long have you lived here, Mr Sweet?' The policeman was now leaning on the sink, his arms folded, watching him from across the room.

'A long time,' replied Raymond, slightly confused by the change in subject. 'I do have permission.'

'So I understand. You can't be pleased about the redevelopment.'

Raymond didn't know what to say. Was this a trick? He couldn't even tell if it was a question. 'Has something happened?' he asked tentatively. He still didn't know why the policemen were here.

'A body was found earlier; Leroy Simmons discovered it on his morning rounds. Do you know anything about it?'

'Who – I mean, no . . .' He was stunned. 'Where?' he managed to ask.

'Keats Ward. By the lake.'

Something registered in Raymond's subconscious, shadow-like, and then it was gone. His throat was suddenly dry and he wished the detective would move away from the sink so he could fetch some water.

'Do you have any idea how a body might have got there?'

'I . . . No, I don't,' he said, shaking his head. An uncomfortable feeling had come over him, and he felt his heart beating even faster.

'Or why someone would leave a body there?'

He shook his head.

'Have you been in Keats Ward recently yourself?'

'No.' He never went to that place. Ever.

'Do you own a woman's coat?' the policeman asked suddenly.

'Pardon?' said Raymond, taken aback.

'A woman's coat. Only I thought I saw one through your bedroom window.' The policeman was now staring at him with such intensity that Raymond felt his cheeks burning.

'Oh, erm, yes, I suppose I do.' What on earth did they want with his mother's coat?

'Would you mind showing it to me?'

It wasn't a question, and Raymond eased himself off the armrest of the chair, relieved to get off his 'perch'. Goodness knows how Mrs Muir managed it; she must wear padded underwear.

'It's in here,' he said, leading the policeman into the bedroom. 'There.' He pointed. 'It was my mother's.' The coat hung on an old anatomical model that he'd found in one of the basement storage areas. It made a very good clothes stand.

The policeman went over and studied it carefully. 'It looks burnt,' he said, lifting a sleeve.

'There was a fire . . .' Raymond began, trailing off. The policeman was now looking at the exposed heart and lungs of the torso that lay beneath.

'What is this?' the policeman asked.

'It's not real,' Raymond answered quickly. 'I found it. It lights up, look.' He reached behind the door and flicked a switch, and his mother's coat lit up; the holes where the fire had caught it glowed pink from the illuminated organs underneath.

'That's quite something, Mr Sweet,' said the policeman, smiling. 'And collectable, I imagine.'

Raymond shrugged. He had no idea.

'That's made my day,' said the policeman. 'Fascinating.'

Raymond followed the detective out of the bedroom and back into the living room.

'Tell me, do you know of any other ways into Blackwater, apart from the two entrances?'

Raymond shook his head.

'Are you sure?' the policeman pushed.

'The river?' ventured Raymond, feeling he should contribute something useful. He wasn't sure how the Creeper came and went, but then again, the Creeper could probably walk through walls.

The detective nodded. 'Okay, thank you. And there's no other way in that you know of?'

Raymond shook his head for the millionth time, wondering why it was so important. After reiterating that he mustn't go wandering about the grounds and should stay on his own part of the property, the detective finally left. When he'd gone, Raymond stood by the window and surveyed his small patch of land, trying to decide what to do. In truth, he'd been putting off the inevitable for months, the task too daunting, but the reality of the situation was now very clear; somehow, without being seen, he was going to have to move his collection.

CHAPTER 8

Kirby was sitting in the dreaded Corsa, which even his mother took the piss out of, calling it a 'student car'. He was outside MIT29's headquarters, known to everyone as Mount Pleasant. MIT29 was one of the Met Police's twenty-four Murder Investigation Teams in London and was located in an old abattoir in Southwark. Why it was MIT*29* was a mystery to everyone, as was the name; Mount Pleasant was neither pleasant nor on a mount.

Kirby's boss, DCI Idris Hamer, had called an 8 p.m. briefing to go through what information they'd been able to glean throughout the day, and Kirby was taking a few minutes to himself before going in. In his mind he ran over what they had so far: an as-yet-unidentified elderly woman, brutally beaten and left on a hospital bed in a derelict asylum; a mobile phone; and an ex-patient with access to the grounds. And then there was the bloody weather, erasing any trace of the murderer and confusing the sniffer dogs. Which brought him to the question foremost in his mind: how the murderer and victim had got into the asylum. Neither of the cameras over the two entrances to the asylum had shown anyone entering or leaving with an elderly woman – dead or alive. Had someone tampered with the camera and let them in – Raymond Sweet, Leroy Simmons? There was now an added problem: Leroy Simmons was missing. After Kirby had spoken to him in the Portakabin, he'd been escorted to the station where he'd made a statement. By the time Kirby and Anderson had spoken to Raymond Sweet several hours later, and discovered the discrepancy in their statements, Simmons had been released and was now AWOL.

A knock on the car window brought Kirby back to the present. It was Hamer. 'You ready for the briefing, Lew?' he asked through the glass.

'Yeah, sure. Coming.' Kirby grabbed his phone and notebook from the passenger seat and climbed out of the car.

Hamer was about the same age as Anderson, mid to late forties, and had been head of MIT29 for just shy of two years. Kirby thought he did an efficient job of managing several murder teams and was talented at the stuff Kirby knew he'd hate if he were ever to rise up the ranks – namely, being good on camera and kowtowing to the upper echelons of the Met Police. Not that Kirby was particularly anti-authority; he just couldn't be arsed with it beyond a certain level. He had, however, detected a change in his boss over the past six months or so. He'd first noticed it at a colleague's leaving do, when Hamer had seemed awkward and on edge, almost as though he were on his guard. Perhaps his marriage was in trouble – there were no kids that Kirby knew of – or perhaps it was simply the pressure of work.

'Anyone been able to get hold of the security guard yet?' Hamer asked as they walked into MIT29's headquarters.

'Not yet. We've been to his house but he's not there. We're trying to trace any friends or family.'

Hamer grunted. 'We need to find him ASAP. The last thing we need is a missing suspect.'

'Tell me about it.'

Hamer glanced at Kirby as they waited for the lift. 'There's something about this case that worries me already.'

Kirby felt the same. 'Anything in particular?'

'The location, the victim, the lack of witnesses.' Hamer reeled them off one by one, using his fingers. 'Something tells me this isn't going to be straightforward. The press will have a field day.'

He was right, they would. Anything to do with Blackwater and the press were all over it like a rash.

'Even my wife says Blackwater's cursed,' Hamer went on. 'And she's about as sceptical as you can get.'

Kirby had heard the rumours: from ghosts of past patients and strange glowing lights at night, to the land being cursed. That every major redevelopment plan had fallen through – for one reason or another – had only added fuel to the fire. Not to mention the few unfortunate souls who'd perished there in the intervening years: an urban explorer, two drug addicts and a suicide had all made the headlines when they'd died at Blackwater.

'Ten minutes, everyone,' called Hamer as he strode through the main office to his own, slamming the door shut behind him.

Kirby went over to his desk and sat down, absent-mindedly flicking through a pile of messages, most of which he could now bin. However, the one on the top in Anderson's handwriting was a surprise – *Jon Kirby called 19.40*. His father. He checked his mobile and saw the missed call. Kirby wondered what he wanted; they didn't see each other as often as they would have liked – his father lived in Cornwall and they both led busy lives. It was strange that he'd called the office and left a message.

'You spoke to my father,' he said, looking up at Anderson, whose desk was opposite.

'Yup. Called just before you walked in.'

'Did he say anything?'

Anderson shook his head. 'Just that he was trying to get hold of you. Everything okay?'

'Hope so.'

'Probably wants to meet this new girlfriend of yours. Talking of which, how's it going? You know . . .' He raised his eyebrows.

'Fine. Thanks,' said Kirby, cutting him off.

'Good. The stuffed fox didn't put her off then,' Anderson chuckled.

'No, although she was concerned about the missing leg.' Kirby looked at his watch – if he was quick he could call his father now. He'd just picked up his mobile when he heard his name.

'Lew.' A young sergeant named Steve Kobrak was approaching his desk.

'What is it?' he asked, putting the phone down.

'Initial report from Newlands, about the phone found at Blackwater.' Kobrak handed Kirby a piece of paper.

He skimmed the contents. 'Good work. Have you run him through the system?'

Kobrak nodded. 'He's clean. Two uniform are on their way to his flat now.'

'Okay, thanks.' Kirby got up and went over to Hamer's office and knocked, going in without waiting.

'We've got the mobile owner's name,' he said. 'Teaching assistant at Royal Oak School by the name of Edward Blake. Uniform are on it now.'

'Good,' said Hamer, looking at his watch. 'Okay, let's get this started.'

Kirby followed the DCI out of his office.

'Listen up, everyone.' Hamer clapped his hands and the room quietened.

Kirby went and stood by the water dispenser, pouring himself a cup. The room was stiflingly warm, despite the Arctic temperature outside.

'This is what we know so far,' Hamer began. 'At around 7.30 this morning an Emeris security guard called Leroy Simmons heard a phone ringing inside Blackwater Asylum and went to investigate. He discovered the body of an elderly female in one of the derelict wards. Injuries to her face show that she was badly beaten, probably somewhere else, and, although the ME has yet to confirm the cause of death, he thinks a blow to the head and hypothermia are likely causes. Estimated time of death is somewhere between 10 p.m. and midnight. It began snowing heavily in central London at approximately 11 p.m. and didn't stop until 4 a.m., which gave our killer plenty of time to dump the body and make his escape without leaving any trace.'

People around the room exchanged glances. The death of a child was always the worst-case scenario, but the suspicious death of someone elderly and vulnerable was equally shocking in its own way. Photographs of the victim had been pinned to a board, as well as shots of the building where she was found and the surrounding area.

'The victim was carrying no ID,' Hamer went on, 'and was not wearing a coat or any protection against the cold, which could indicate that she was taken from home. Since being questioned this morning, Simmons, the security guard, has disappeared.' A general murmur went around the room.

'Raymond Sweet, sixty-seven,' Hamer went on, tapping a photo of a much younger-looking Raymond than Kirby had met earlier, 'an ex-patient at Blackwater, who lives in the Old Lodge within the grounds of the asylum, claims to have played cards with Simmons last night between 8 p.m. and 10.45 p.m. Simmons then let him out of the main entrance on Battersea Fields Drive, and he walked to the Rock Bottom chip shop. The owner's son, Nick Katsaros, confirms this. They give Raymond whatever's left at half-price on a Tuesday night.'

'Last night it was a Peter's Pie,' said Kirby, remembering his gruelling conversation with Sweet.

'What filling?' asked Mark Drayton, provoking a ripple of sniggers around the room.

'Chicken. Allegedly.'

'Okay. So we know what Raymond Sweet ate as he walked home. Moving on . . .' said Hamer. 'The camera at the Daylesford Road entrance shows him entering the asylum grounds at 11.36 p.m. What he did once inside, we have no way of knowing. But he was alone when he left and alone when he returned.'

'We need to find Simmons,' said Kirby. 'And find out why he lied.'

'According to Emeris, 6 a.m. was his allotted shift and Danny "Chips" Monahan should have been on shift last night. When Mr Monahan was questioned, he told us that Simmons had asked if he could do a double shift as he was hard up, and Monahan agreed,' said Hamer, reading from the statement he had in his hand.

'Does Simmons have a record?' asked Anderson.

'He's clean,' replied Hamer. 'As Lew said, we need to find him and establish why he lied – and we know that he did lie; the security camera on the main gate clearly shows him arriving at 6.30 p.m. on Tuesday night.'

'Idiot,' muttered someone.

'He might not be the brightest spark, but it does suggest that he wasn't expecting the footage to be checked,' said Kirby. 'Ergo, that he'd have to be a *real* idiot to commit a crime the same night.'

'Going back to this Sweet character, what's his story then?' asked someone else. 'He was in the loony bin for years, wasn't he?'

'Correct. He was a patient at Blackwater for over twenty years after losing his mother in a house fire in 1966,' said Kirby. 'The exact reason for his admittance is vague. According to social services, the records covering the period when he was admitted no longer survive.'

'How come?' asked Anderson.

'The doctor in charge, a Dr Alistair Brayne, took them all when he retired in the mid-seventies and he's long gone. Anyhow, when the hospital closed in 1993, Sweet was sent to live in a B&B, only he kept returning to Blackwater and eventually began squatting – dropping off social services' radar in the process. He won squatter's rights and now legally lives in the Old Lodge in the grounds. He has no criminal record and no history of violence.' He could see people exchanging glances. 'Initial contact with him suggests that he's lucid, albeit eccentric. How reliable he is remains to be seen.'

'He has free access to the grounds,' someone piped up.

'So does Simmons,' said Kirby. 'And any number of people employed by the developers.'

'The site manager, Brian Kaplinsky, is compiling a list of everyone who had access to the site,' said Anderson. 'There actually aren't that many. Not with direct access.'

'Maybe they were in it together, Sweet and Simmons,' said Kobrak.

'It's possible,' said Kirby, glancing at Hamer. 'What we don't know is how our victim and killer – if it's not Simmons or Sweet – gained access to the site. None of the security cameras show either man entering the asylum with anyone, let alone an elderly woman.'

'And none of the CCTV footage from the surrounding streets shows our victim in the area – not yet, at least. There's still a fair bit to go through,' added Anderson.

'So, apart from finding Simmons, our first priority has got to be identifying the victim,' said Hamer. 'Someone must be missing her and she didn't get there by herself. Once we know who she is we might be able to establish some kind of motive, and then hopefully things will be a bit clearer.'

'There's also the mobile phone that was found at the scene,' said Kirby. 'It belongs to twenty-seven-year-old Edward Blake, of 3 Worcester Gardens, SW18. A teaching assistant at Royal Oak

School. There might be a perfectly innocent explanation as to why his phone was there – it might have been stolen, although it wasn't reported – but we need to find him and eliminate him from the enquiry. Uniform are on their way to his flat now.'

The room fell silent for a moment, then Anka, one of the recorders on the case, spoke up. 'A robbery or mugging I could understand; but killing an old lady and leaving her somewhere like that just doesn't make sense.'

'Agreed. The location may well be significant, but we won't know that until we know who she is. Let's hope that by the morning someone has missed this woman and raised the alarm,' said Hamer.

'SOCOs have finished searching the site for today but have so far found no other means of entering other than the main gates on Battersea Fields Drive, the Daylesford Road entrance and a small hole in the fence just past it, near the river. It's big enough to crawl through.'

'Awkward to pull a body through, don't you think? Unless the victim crawled in willingly and was beaten in the grounds,' said Anderson. 'In which case, what was she doing there?'

'It could that be our victim was taken in during the day by someone working on the site and kept there,' said Kirby. 'The place is massive. There must be plenty of places to hide a body or keep someone prisoner for a few days without anyone ever knowing.'

It was a grim thought that the elderly woman might have been held against her will at the old asylum before being killed. Kirby wasn't discounting it, but she'd looked generally well fed and clean; whereas if she'd been held captive for a few days there would have been signs on the body and clothing. He hadn't noticed anything himself, but until the forensics report came back they couldn't be sure.

'I talked to the owner of Marsh House, the property adjacent to the asylum, name of Charles Palmer, and he neither saw nor heard anything suspicious. I checked the grounds and there's no way in from the house – there used to be an entrance in the dividing wall, but it's long since been bricked up.'

'What's Palmer like?' asked Hamer.

'Fifties, Aussie. Recently inherited the house. In the process of clearing it at the moment. He was out last night, at the Vauxhall Tavern. I swung by there on the way back here,' said Kirby.

'Oh yeah?' said Anderson, cracking a smile. 'And there I was thinking you had a new *girl*friend.'

Fuck's sake, thought Kirby; now everyone knew he had a new girlfriend on the go. As a rule, he liked to keep his work and his social life separate. 'I spoke to the barman, Vihaan James, and he remembered Palmer. Said he left just before closing, which is midnight. That matches up with what Palmer told me – that he got in at gone midnight. We can check traffic cameras to verify this, but it looks like he's in the clear.'

'What about the developer, Patricey Developments?' asked Anderson. 'They must have plans and access.'

Kirby was about to say something when Hamer jumped in. 'Patricey Developments is headed by Patrick Calder, who is currently in Scotland,' he began. 'He flew up there yesterday on business, gets back the day after tomorrow. As I'm sure you know, this is a huge redevelopment, worth billions. It's important both financially and politically, so he's not going to take the news of a murder on his land very well, I imagine. I should also add that Patrick Calder is a highly influential man.' He scanned the room as he said it, as if to emphasise his point.

'What do we know about him?' asked Kirby, wondering how Hamer knew the developer's whereabouts so quickly.

'Late fifties, self-made billionaire, has several offices around the world. Bought Blackwater Asylum from Tamanaka Holdings two years ago. And before you ask, he has no record,' said Hamer, directing his last comment at Kirby, who shrugged. What the hell was that supposed to mean? Wealthy and influential or not, Calder was still a suspect until his alibi checked out.

'Could be a rival wanting to discredit him,' said Kobrak.

'It's possible, I suppose,' said Hamer. 'Lew, go and see him first thing on Friday.'

Kirby looked up, surprised. 'Don't you want to handle him, given how influential he is?'

'No. I think it's better if you do. He won't be pleased at having his project held up, so be nice. And take it from me, he's not someone we want to upset.'

Yeah, right, thought Kirby, smiling to himself. 'I'll be on my best behaviour. *Sir.*'

'Good. That's it then, folks. Tomorrow's a new day. Onwards!' Hamer headed back to his office, where he shut the door.

Kirby crumpled up his water cup and chucked it in the bin. Patrick bloody Calder. He hated property developers about as much as he hated hospitals. Why couldn't Hamer slip on the kid gloves himself for once?

CHAPTER 9

When Kirby got back to the mooring later that night, instead of doing the sensible thing and going straight to his own boat, he headed to the end of the jetty and jumped down on to a red Dutch barge. In summer the boat overflowed with flowers and herbs, but now the snow-covered terracotta pots on deck glowed in the moon-light, distorted silhouettes gently bobbing with the boat's sway. He knocked gently on the door, and as he waited he wondered where Edward Blake, the missing teacher, was. He wasn't at his flat and none of his neighbours had seen him since the day before.

After a minute or two, the door of the barge opened, and a waft of rose and geranium floated out.

'Lew, come in.' Isabel was dressed in an old pair of faded, ripped jeans and a T-shirt. She looked like she'd just come out of the shower, and she shivered at the cold air.

'I'm sorry it's late,' he said, stepping inside and closing the door behind him.

'Don't worry, it's fine. Come on in and get warm. Drink?'

'Thanks.' Kirby took off his coat and hung it by the door, kicking off his shoes at the same time. He followed Isabel into her small galley kitchen, where there was barely enough room for two people to pass each other. She was at the sink rinsing a wine glass, and he stood behind her and slid his hands around her waist.

'I didn't hear you leave this morning,' she said, turning off the tap. 'You should have said goodbye.'

'I almost came back, but . . .' He kissed her neck and closed his eyes. He saw the elderly woman from Blackwater on the hospital bed, surrounded by decay and forgotten memories, and quickly opened them again.

She wriggled around so that she was facing him. 'But what?'

'A new case. I'll tell you later.' He kissed her, moving his hands up her back, and felt that she wasn't wearing a bra.

'You're insatiable, you know that?'

'And you're not?' He slid his hands round the front, pushing her T-shirt up, and felt her leg curl around his as he pushed her against the sink.

'You're also incorrigible,' she whispered, as he carried her into the bedroom.

Afterwards, they sat on the sofa, Isabel in an old kimono, Kirby stretched out next to her in a pair of tracksuit bottoms she'd found – presumably from some long-gone lover.

'Cheers.' They clinked glasses and fell into a comfortable silence. Kirby's mind wandered back to the body at the asylum. How did someone like that get into a place like Blackwater? It really was bugging him.

'I had a call from the developers today,' said Isabel, after a while.

'What did they want?' The moorings were in dispute with the developer of one of the new riverside apartments, and Isabel was the driving force behind the residents' fight against them. Now he thought about it, wasn't it the same bunch who'd just bought Blackwater? He must remember to look into it tomorrow.

'Same old bullshit. They want a meeting. I said no, not unless they have something new to offer us.'

Kirby was deeply sympathetic towards the boat owners, some of whom had lived here for fifteen years or so. He was a relative newcomer, and hadn't yet attended residents' meetings.

'If they give you notice, then it'll have to be a good period,' he said.

'You mean *us* notice. You live here too.'

'I know. I just don't feel part of the crowd.' He propped himself up and took a sip of wine.

'That's because you're hardly ever here,' said Isabel. She said it with no hint of reproach, merely as fact.

'I'm here enough,' he said. The truth was that he wished he were here more. He loved the boat, would love to take it elsewhere – move around, stay in other places. It just never happened. 'Where would you go, if you – we, sorry – lose?' He lay down again.

'I don't know.' She paused. 'I might leave altogether.'

He didn't say anything.

'Would you care if I went?'

'Of course I would.' He sat up. 'I . . . we . . . It's good,' he said, smiling. They hadn't been seeing each other for very long, a few months at most, but he liked her a lot and hoped it was reciprocated. He looked at his watch. 'D'you mind if we watch the news?'

She shrugged. 'Sure.'

He got up and switched on Isabel's small television. The national ten o'clock news was just coming to an end, the local news about to start. Only the basic details about the Blackwater murder had been released to the press so far, and he watched as the news reporter stood outside the main gates of the asylum relaying what little she knew. Remarkably, Raymond Sweet's name didn't come up, and once the short piece was over he switched off the television.

'Is that the new case you mentioned?' asked Isabel.

Kirby nodded. 'You might not see much of me for a while. In fact, I should be going. Sorry.'

53

'It's the same developer who wants to move us out,' said Isabel.

So he'd been right. 'Who have you been dealing with – not Patrick Calder?'

'I wish. If I could deal with him we might get somewhere, but I can't get past his PA. It seems more than her life's worth to grant me a meeting with him.'

'It is what she's paid for,' said Kirby.

'I've heard his staff are all terrified of him.'

He made a mental note to look into Patrick Calder's past himself; the developer might not have a record but that didn't mean he was clean.

Kirby suddenly remembered his father and the message he'd left earlier. 'Bollocks. I meant to call my dad.'

'Why not call him now? Is he okay?'

'Yeah, I'm sure he's fine.' Kirby finished his glass of wine. 'I really do need to get back to the boat, so I'll call him from there.' He went and got dressed, wishing it were warmer and he could just sprint back to his boat in the hope no one would see him. As it was, he'd freeze his balls off if he tried that tonight.

'I wish you could stay,' said Isabel, as he stepped on to the deck. She held the kimono tight around her, the thin cotton no protection against the cold night air.

'Me too. Go back inside before you get frostbite.' He kissed her forehead and then climbed on to the walkway that linked the boats and headed back to his own berth. As soon as he was inside, he dialled his father's number. After a few rings his stepmother Meredith picked up.

'Oh hi, Lew. How are you?'

'I'm good, thanks. Is everything okay with you both? Only, Dad phoned earlier . . .'

'Yes, we're fine. It's . . . well, actually it's Liv we're worried about.' Livia was Kirby's mother, but most people called her Liv.

'Why, what's wrong?'

'She called a few days ago and sounded confused,' said Meredith. 'Didn't seem to know what day it was or when your father's birthday was—'

'Lew?' His father's voice interrupted on the extension. 'I'll take over now, Meredith, thank you.'

'But Jon—'

'I said I'll talk to Lew. You go and make some tea.'

'Bye, Lew,' said Meredith. 'Hope we see you soon.'

'Bye.' Kirby waited for her to put the phone down before he spoke. It was unusual to hear his father speak to her like that, and he wondered what was going on. 'Dad?'

'Sorry, Lew. This is just, well, *you know*,' said his father.

'No, I don't know. What's the matter?'

After a pause his father spoke quietly and seriously. 'You need to go and see your mother. There's something she needs to tell you.'

'What do you mean, there's something she needs to tell me? Why doesn't she just call?'

'Because—' He stopped himself. 'You know what she's like. Just go and see her.'

'Okay . . .' said Kirby. 'Can't you tell me what it's about though? Come on, Dad, we don't keep secrets.'

His father was silent on the other end of the phone, and for a moment Kirby thought the line had gone dead. 'I'm sorry, Lew,' he said eventually. 'You need to speak to her about this.'

'About what?'

'I need to go, we're in the middle of a film,' his father said quickly. 'That tea'll be ready now too. Meredith will never forgive me.'

'But Dad—'

'You must come and visit soon. Bring Isabel if you like. Speak soon.'

He'd only told his father about Isabel in the last couple of weeks and wasn't sure he wanted things to get that cosy just yet. 'Night,' said Kirby, but his father had already hung up; it was as though he couldn't get off the phone fast enough.

Kirby sat for a few moments trying to figure out exactly what had just happened. Had his father been drinking? He hadn't sounded drunk, far from it. *There's something she needs to tell you.* What the fuck was that supposed to mean? Was she ill? Christ, did she have cancer? *Dear God, not that.* Kirby now felt irritated by the conversation – angry with his father for not explaining, annoyed that within minutes his father had cast worry into his mind. He almost called him back but then decided against it.

Instead, he called Livia's home number and waited impatiently as it rang. His parents had separated when he was twenty – for reasons he was never entirely clear about – but had remained on good terms. That said, they didn't make a habit of calling each other for long chats, so what could have led to this conversation was beyond him. He cast his mind back to the last time he'd visited his mother and searched his memory for anything unusual. She had seemed a little distracted and, now he thought about it, forgetful. At the time he'd put this down to being tired – she'd said she was having difficulty sleeping, and who didn't get like that after a few sleepless nights? Several times during his visit she'd forgotten what they were talking about and struggled for names. They'd joked about it, Kirby saying he'd wear a badge with his name on if she ever forgot who he was. Suddenly, it didn't seem so funny.

The phone rang and rang, and eventually he hung up. She was either in bed or out with friends; God knows her social life was busy enough, so he tried her mobile. It went straight to voicemail, so he left a message asking her to call him back, and hung up.

That night, Kirby went to bed and dreamt he was at Blackwater, walking through what seemed to be an eternal ward – bed after bed of patients, some strapped down, others sedated and staring into space; the elderly woman from this morning was there, lying on her back, grinning up at the ceiling. Eventually he came the last bed – the end of the ward was bricked up with no way out – only to see that the last patient was his mother.

He woke up in a cold sweat during the early hours, his father's words churning about in his mind. *There's something she needs to tell you.* He'd call Livia again later today and get to the bottom of it. Perhaps she was thinking of moving back to Italy, where she was born and raised, and was worried what he'd say. He'd miss her, obviously, but on the other hand it would be lovely to have an excuse to visit Italy on a regular basis.

Kirby drifted back to sleep with thoughts of long Italian lunches and the sparkling sea; however, like a dark shadow, the dead woman from Blackwater was never far behind.

CHAPTER 10

As soon as Kirby walked into the office at MIT29 the following morning, he knew something had happened. He was late; the bastard Corsa didn't like the cold and had to be coaxed awake. And then, when he'd finally got the car going, an accident at Vauxhall had brought the already crawling traffic to a standstill.

Anderson was eating a bacon sandwich, while listening to someone on the phone, and trying to put his coat on at the same time. He was doing a remarkably good job and motioned with his eyes towards Hamer's office. Kirby didn't have time to reach the door before his boss came out.

'We've got an ID for our Blackwater victim,' said Hamer. 'Ena Massey, 79 Chartwell Road. This is next of kin.' He handed Kirby a piece of paper. 'Go and break the news.'

Kirby read the name – Karen McBride, née Massey – and an address on Downchurch Road: the victim's daughter. He hated these visits – they all did. 'How was she identified?' he asked.

'Through a neighbour. Apparently our victim volunteered at a hospice, only she didn't turn up for a home visit yesterday afternoon. The neighbour was known to the hospice – she has a relative there – so they called her and asked if she could check on Ena, to make sure she was all right. When the neighbour got no answer yesterday she didn't worry too much, but when it happened again this morning she called it in.'

'And it's definitely her?'

Hamer nodded. 'Hospice website. There's a page about volunteering and she's on it.'

'Bloody hell, she must be the same age as the patients,' said Kirby, wondering if there was any age limit on volunteering.

'Older, in some cases – she was eighty-four. The hospice is sending us a list of people Ena Massey dealt with directly. It could be that she fell out with a relative. You do hear about elderly people who change their will without telling anyone, so perhaps Ena became a beneficiary and pissed off the family.' Hamer didn't sound convinced, but he was right; Ena could easily have been left something valuable, and a family member with a grievance might have decided to take matters into their own hands. It wouldn't be the first time, although it didn't explain what she was doing at Blackwater on the coldest night of the year.

'And,' Hamer went on, 'Edward Blake didn't go back to his flat last night, and his grandfather, who he's very close to, was expecting a visit. Blake never showed up.'

'Shit,' said Kirby. 'You think he could be our man and has done a runner?'

'It's certainly possible. Or he could be a witness.'

'When was he last seen?' asked Kirby.

'Tuesday afternoon. He went back to his flat around 4 p.m., which is usual, then his upstairs neighbour saw him go out at about 7 p.m.'

'Okay. We'll need to check CCTV, see if we can trace his movements. Are his phone records back yet?'

Hamer nodded. 'There's a name that keeps cropping up: Connie Darke. Looks like Blake was going to meet her on Tuesday night. She's called and texted him several times, and she's also the

59

last person he called from that phone. Go and talk to her once you've seen Ena Massey's daughter. Pete's going to speak to the school – finding Blake is a priority. So far, he's all we've got.'

'What about the hospice?'

'Send Kobrak after he's been to see Blake's grandfather,' said Hamer, checking his watch. 'The post-mortem's in an hour, and I need to see the pathologist about another case, so I'll cover that. I'll let you know when we have something.' Then he turned and disappeared into his office.

Kirby went and sat at his desk and logged on to his computer; he wanted to look through Blake's phone records before leaving. He scrolled through the information that Newlands had sent. Blake's phone usage followed a regular pattern: on weekdays he rarely used his phone between roughly 8.15 a.m. and 3.30 p.m., presumably when he was at work, and at the weekend he made and received calls sporadically throughout the day and night. The calls were to a variety of numbers, including Connie Darke's, and he called his grandfather, Harry Joyce, regularly – almost every other day.

Kirby looked through some of the texts, noting that a lot of them were late at night and appeared to be places to meet, although where those places were was a mystery, as Blake and his friends seemed to have a language all of their own. Blake was up to something, but what? He'd contacted Connie Darke frequently over the past month and, as Hamer had said, it appeared that they had arranged to meet on the night of the murder, but something had stopped them. He typed Connie Darke's name into the system. Like Blake, she was clean, not even a parking ticket between them. However, there was something of interest there.

Anderson finished the call he'd been on and came over. 'I swear to God that woman knows when I'm eating a bacon sandwich and need to leave the building.'

'Not Mrs Star Witness again?' said Kirby.

Anderson nodded. 'Apparently, her neighbour was murdered – *again* – last night at 3.45 a.m., and the perpetrator legged it through her back garden, leaving footprints. Footprints she'd like *me* to come and take a look at with a view to having casts made. For fuck's sake.' Mrs Star Witness was a seventy-year-old woman who repeatedly reported serious crimes that had never been committed.

'You've got to stop giving your number out to older women, Pete.'

'Fuck you.' Anderson smiled, then glanced at Kirby's computer screen. 'Are those Blake's phone records?'

'Yup. There's not much to go on, except someone called Connie Darke. Says her address is the Four Sails – why do I know that name?'

'It used to be a pub; the screws from Wandsworth nick used to drink there. Been empty for years. Strange place to live – maybe she's a squatter. Look, I'm heading over to the school and then to the victim's house. Meet you there later?'

'Yeah, sure,' Kirby mumbled, busy looking up the Four Sails on Google images. Anderson was right; the place had been empty for five years. The pub was a small, weather-boarded building, and its old sign showed a windmill. It must have had a connection to the old windmill at Wandsworth Common, and was indeed a strange place to live. Kirby stood up and put his coat on, a fleeting sense of dread in his stomach at the thought of having to deliver bad news to Karen McBride. As he took the elevator down to the ground floor, he tried not to dwell on it and instead thought about Ed Blake and Connie Darke. Although neither had a police record, they were both in the police database for another reason: five years ago, they had both been questioned in relation to another suspicious death. The death had eventually been ruled as misadventure, but what had caught Kirby's eye was the location: Blackwater Asylum.

CHAPTER 11

'Well I'll be buggered,' said Ena Massey's daughter.

Kirby was sitting on an overstuffed sofa at 14 Downchurch Road feeling extremely uncomfortable. On arrival, he'd been ushered into the front room, where every surface was cluttered with objects: mainly pink, and more often than not in the shape of a dog. The place reeked of air freshener, and he could hear whimpering noises off to the left, which he assumed were coming from the kitchen. Karen McBride sat opposite him and was wearing a tight, pink onesie. The years hadn't been kind to her, and the onesie suited her about as much as it would have suited Kirby. He felt like he'd wandered on to the set of some crazy, late-night chat show, and to add to his misery the heating was on full tilt – not just to a nice, cosy temperature to ward off the freezing temperature outside, but a full-on furnace of Mount Etna proportions. He could feel his face smarting and sweat starting to trickle down his back.

'You have my condolences, Mrs McBride,' said Kirby. 'Can I get you something – a glass of water, some tea, perhaps?'

'Tea?' She looked at him aghast and reached for a packet of Silk Cut. '*Water?*' She pulled out a cigarette and lit it with a poodle-shaped lighter, the flame shooting out of its mouth as she clicked on its ears with a nail-bitten thumb. 'No, ta, but you can get me one of them blue things from behind there.' She jerked her thumb towards an authentic 1950s cocktail bar.

Kirby was glad to get off the sofa, which itself seemed to emit heat – it had to be flammable. The cocktail bar was shaped like the hull of a boat with a red Formica top. Two portholes were cut in the sides, one of which was embellished with a gilt chain anchor, and despite himself Kirby could envisage it sitting very nicely on his houseboat next to Pete's stuffed fox. Bottles of WKD Blue were neatly lined up on the shelves behind the bar, and he opened one with a bottle opener shaped like a bulldog's head, then looked around for a glass and some ice.

'I'll have it as it comes,' said Karen, taking a deep drag on her cigarette. 'Have one yourself, if you like.'

Kirby would rather poke his own eyes out than drink a warm, blue alcopop – let alone at this hour of the day – and politely declined. He passed her the drink and sat down again. Karen raised the bottle and nodded upwards. 'To Mum,' she said, and took a long swig.

'I'm afraid I do need to ask you some questions. Are you up to it?'

'You can ask me what you like, but I doubt I can help you much,' she replied, stifling a burp. 'What happened to her anyhow?'

'Your mother was found in the grounds of an old hospital in Battersea.'

'What, that body what was on the news? That was my mum?'

Kirby nodded. 'Yes, I'm sorry.' *Shit*, he thought, as he remembered that he still hadn't phoned his mother – he'd been on the go since abandoning trying to sleep at some ungodly hour, and hadn't had a moment.

'Ain't your fault. What the effing hell was she playing at, at her age, poncing about an old hospital?'

'That's what I need to find out, Mrs McBride. When did you last see your mother?'

'1978,' she said without hesitating. 'Same year Rod Stewart brought out "Do Ya Think I'm Sexy?"'

Bloody hell, that was before Kirby had even been born. He did the maths: according to the register of births, marriages and deaths, Karen had been born in 1962, which meant that she'd been sixteen in 1978. 'And you never saw her again?'

'No. And bloody glad I was too. Got out as soon as I could. We spoke on the phone over the years, but I never saw her again.' She paused to take another swig of WKD. 'To say we didn't get on would be an understatement. She didn't like Rod Stewart, for starters.'

Kirby smiled politely and half expected Mike Leigh to pop up and shout, 'Cut!'

'I need to build up a picture of what she was like, Mrs McBride, so anything that you can tell me about her would be useful. Do you know any of her friends? Where did she work? That type of thing.' He paused. 'Can you think of anyone who might have wanted to harm your mother?'

Karen snorted at his last question. 'Like I said, I hadn't seen her for almost forty years. She was a nurse up at that loony bin, Blackwater. Bleedin' horrible place.'

Kirby's ears pricked up at the mention of Blackwater – finally, something useful. 'When did she work there?'

'She was there when I was born and worked there until it shut.'

Which, thought Kirby, meant they needed to talk to Raymond Sweet again; he had to have known her.

'No idea what she did after that,' Karen continued. 'Probably went on torturing poor sods somewhere else, knowing her.'

'What do you mean, *torturing*?' he asked.

'Mr Kirby,' she began, as though explaining something to a small child. 'My mum weren't very nice. Christ knows how she became a nurse, but she did. It was different back then, not so many checks and that. And if you had a bit of nous' – she tapped the side of her head with a finger – 'you could get away with murder. Fuck knows, she did.'

'You mean, she wasn't qualified?'

Karen shrugged. 'Well, I never saw her studying, put it like that.'

'Okay . . . Before you left home, where did you live?'

'We lived in the hospital grounds. There was accommodation for the nurses, and them what had kids could go on a list for one of the chalets. Chalets, my arse; more like a frigging bunker. I wanted us to move, but *oh no*, we had to stay. All she cared about was herself and that sodding place.'

'What was her role there?'

Karen shrugged. 'Dunno, matron or something. She never talked about it, but I remember she worked weird hours. We didn't see much of each other.'

'And where did she go when it closed in 1993?'

'Fuck knows. You're the detective, you'll have to crack that one.'

Karen drained the last of the WKD Blue and began looking for the lighter, which had slid down the back of the chair. Kirby could have sworn the zip on the onesie was now lower than it had been when he arrived, and he caught a glimpse of her bra strap as she wrestled the poodle lighter from the cushion behind her. He looked away quickly and concentrated on his notes. 'What about your father?'

'Gotcha, yer little blighter,' she said, recapturing the lighter. 'My dad? Never knew him.' She lit another cigarette and leant forward to rest it in the ashtray. 'I'm not being very helpful, am I?'

'This must be difficult for you – I appreciate that – but you never knew who your father was?'

Karen shook her head. 'Some doctor at the loony bin would be my bet. They were at it like bleedin' rabbits up there.'

'I have to ask this, Karen, but where were you on Tuesday night?'

'What, you think I did it? Give me a break! Frankly, I wouldn't waste my time.' She studied Kirby for a few seconds before continuing. 'As it happens, I was down at the Welcome. My mate runs the place and was short-staffed. I was pulling pints all night. Ask anyone who was there – I'm quite popular,' she said, winking.

Kirby couldn't help but like Karen, despite her apparent indifference to her mother's death, and wondered what kind of child she had been. Had Ena really been that awful, or was she simply not suited to motherhood? Even when Kirby had been at his worst growing up – and he shuddered now at some of the things he'd done as a teenager – his mother had always forgiven him.

'Can you tell me anything about your mother's recent life – the volunteering at the hospice for example?'

'You what?'

Karen's expression was comedy gold, and Kirby had to remind himself why he was there. 'She never mentioned that she volunteered at a hospice?'

'No, she never bloody did. Probably knew what I'd say if she had. Bleedin' hell, you've come with a right load of eye-openers, haven't you?'

That was one way of putting it, thought Kirby, suppressing a smile. 'You said that you talked to her on the phone. When was the last time you spoke?'

'Christmas . . . No, hang on, she *did* call at Christmas – bloody miracle, nearly choked on my prawn cocktail – but she also called a couple of weeks ago. Timing wasn't her strong point – always phoned up when I was in the middle of something.'

'What did she want?' he asked.

'Nothing. I'd had a few drinks, like you do. Couldn't wait to get rid of the old cow.' She leant forward and retrieved the burning cigarette. 'Is it hot in here, or is it just me?' Karen lowered her zip another inch and sucked on the cigarette so hard that it glowed like a red-hot poker.

Kirby stood up before he'd even realised what he was doing, and headed to the window. 'I'll open this for you, get some air in.'

Opening the window was easier said than done; the window-sill was covered in a herd of ceramic dogs, amongst which sat a pink Cadillac-shaped telephone, and it took all his powers of coordination not to knock them over. The last thing he needed was a tsunami of porcelain dogs in the mix. He couldn't remember an interview like this in his entire career, and prayed that he wouldn't get run over as he left the house, making it the last thing he ever did.

'You want one of these blue things yet?' he heard Karen say from the cocktail bar. 'Only I can get you a glass if you like?'

'No, I'm fine, Mrs McBride, thanks all the same.' He stayed by the window, glad of the cool air that went some way to dissipating the stench of Silk Cut and air freshener, which on top of the heat was making him feel nauseous.

'So, what did Ena say when she called? It might be important,' he asked, trying to steer the conversation back into safer waters.

Karen was now doing a very good impression of a Blackpool B&B hostess by leaning on the cocktail bar, toying with the bottle opener in a way that made Kirby relieved there was a bar between them.

After giving it some thought, Karen replied. 'Seemed to me that she'd rung to boast.'

'About what?'

'Ah, well, that's the thing.' Karen came out from behind the cocktail bar and sat down again. 'I might have had a few bevvies, but I do remember her saying that she was coming into some money. Who in their right mind would leave that old cow anything, I don't know.'

'Did she say where this money was coming from, and how much?' Money would certainly provide motive, and Kirby wondered if he was finally getting somewhere.

'Nah, some old acquaintance or something. And before you ask, no, she didn't say who. I just wanted her off the blower to be honest. Get back to my socialising.'

Kirby felt disappointed. 'Did she say anything else?'

Karen shook her head. 'Like I said, I'd had a few. Hey, you don't think she made a will, do you?' She took a long swig of the blue liquid, which was beginning to stain her lips, excitement in her eyes.

'If she did and you're mentioned, I'm sure you'll be notified. Do you know if she had any more children after you left home?' Kirby knew that she hadn't, but wanted to know if Karen knew.

'Now you really are pulling my leg with that question.' She laughed. 'I was bad enough. She wasn't going to go through that again.' She looked him over as though she were eyeing up a new ornament. 'You ain't bad for a copper, you know that?' She downed the rest of the second bottle of WKD in one, a burp the final flourish.

Kirby decided it was time to leave before she hit bottle number three, and made a move towards the door. 'You have a son, don't you?' he asked.

'Douglas,' Karen said from her armchair. 'Good-for-nothing little sod, if you ask me. Still, I am his mum, and I love him.'

Kirby felt a pang of sadness for Karen, whose mother had clearly never loved her. 'Do you know where I can find him?'

'Probably in the boozer, the Welcome, with that nasty shit Lloyd who he hangs out with.' She hauled herself out of the armchair, giving Kirby an eye-watering view of her cleavage. 'Let me show you out.'

'Did Douglas and his grandmother have a relationship of any kind?' he asked.

'They never met, let alone had a bloody relationship,' said Karen, squeezing past him into the hall before he had time to get out of the way. He could have sworn he felt an electric current from the pink onesie as they touched. 'If my Douglas done this, it'll be the first bloody useful thing he's ever done in his life,' she said, holding the front door open for him.

Kirby thanked her for her time and beat a hasty exit into the fresh air. Despite the cold, he opened the window when he got into the car, to try to rid himself of the aftermath of Silk Cut, and sat for a few minutes thinking over what Karen had told him. Two things struck him: the first was Ena's connection to Blackwater; and the second was that she'd told Karen she was coming into some money. The latter, if true, would certainly provide motive, but it was the connection to Blackwater that really intrigued him. It couldn't be a coincidence, could it?

As he started the engine and pulled out on to Downchurch Road, strains of Rod Stewart drifted from the open window of the house, and he pictured Karen swaying to the music behind the hull-shaped bar, drunk and alone, the zip on her onesie fighting a losing battle.

CHAPTER 12

The meeting that Bonaro had scheduled over coffee that morning took much longer than Connie had expected, and when she came out it was almost lunchtime. What she'd anticipated would be some sort of housekeeping meeting, or perhaps about the James Neville drawings she'd catalogued, turned out to be something quite different: Bonaro was going away on a research scholarship and had offered her the temporary curatorship of RADE while he was gone. He'd mentioned the scholarship vaguely a few months ago, but she'd never expected it to happen so suddenly and found herself accepting without a thought. Despite the incredible opportunity just given to her and with so much to discuss, she'd been distracted throughout the rest of the meeting, one eye on the clock, and was relieved when it ended.

It had now been over thirty-six hours, and Ed still hadn't called. Last night she'd spoken to their closest friend, Mole, who was away exploring in Poland, and he hadn't heard from him either; in fact, no one had. She'd called every mutual friend that she could think of and checked every social media outlet Ed used, but there was no sign of him anywhere. Then, just as she was getting ready for work that morning, listening to the radio, came the bombshell: a body had been found at Blackwater. The news had sent her into a spiral of anxiety. It couldn't be happening again, could it?

Relieved to be out of Bonaro's office, Connie went straight to her desk in the reading room and checked her phone. Her stomach groaned, reminding her that she hadn't eaten – not that she had any appetite. Her phone yielded nothing – no missed calls, no email, no nothing. She checked the BBC News app in case the Blackwater victim had been named yet, but they hadn't. *Damn, damn, damn.* There was now only one thing for it; she'd have to call the police. It wasn't a call that she wanted to make from RADE when Bonaro was around – so, grabbing her coat and bag, she headed for the stairs and was halfway down when the doorbell rang.

They didn't get many unscheduled callers at RADE – it was mostly appointment only – but there were a few ageing academics who popped in regularly, so she assumed it would be one of them. When she pulled open the heavy front door and came face to face with a striking-looking man in his thirties, she was slightly taken aback. 'Can I help?' she asked.

'I'm looking for Connie Darke,' said the man. 'Detective Inspector Kirby, Met Police.' He held up some ID, which she barely registered as a feeling of nausea passed through her. 'May I come in?' he asked.

She nodded, letting him in to the reception area. The door swung closed with a deafening slam. 'I'm Connie Darke. What's this about?' she managed to say, trying to keep her voice even.

'I need to ask you some questions about a friend of yours, Edward Blake,' he said. 'Is there somewhere we can sit?'

She felt her legs wobble. 'Is he okay?'

'I hope so. Can we sit?'

The relief was instant; it wasn't Ed's body that had been found at Blackwater. *Thank God.* 'Oh, yes, of course. This way.' She led him up the gently curving stone staircase and into the main reading room, where she closed the door, hoping that Bonaro wouldn't come in. 'So, what's this about?' she asked, offering him a chair.

'Mr Blake's phone was found at a crime scene yesterday morning, and we need to speak to him quite urgently,' said DI Kirby, sitting down. 'I was hoping that you might be able to help. According to his phone records you've been trying to contact him. You were also the last person he called.'

'A crime scene? I don't understand.' Her mind was racing – was this to do with Sarah?

'You may have heard that a body was found at Blackwater Asylum, the derelict psychiatric hospital in Battersea, yesterday. Mr Blake's phone was found nearby, and we need to trace him as soon as possible. Do you know where he is?'

'No, I don't.' She wasn't sure how much to say, so decided to leave it there.

'Can you think of any reason why he might have been at Blackwater?'

He was watching her carefully – he must know about Sarah, he had to. She noticed that he was wearing a silver ring on his middle finger; it looked too chunky for any policeman she'd ever seen, more like something Mole might wear.

'Miss Darke?'

'Um, actually, yes, I do.' She looked down at her own small hands, the silver ring on her thumb. She twisted it off and held it out. 'This belonged to my sister, Sarah.'

He took the silver band and turned it round in his hands. 'I read about her accident. I'm sorry.'

'There's an inscription,' she said. 'On the inside.' She watched as he read the words on the band.

'Ed Blake was your sister's boyfriend?' he asked, looking up.

She nodded. 'Yes. You obviously know that she died at Blackwater, but what you might not know is that Tuesday was the fifth anniversary of her death.'

'No, I didn't know that,' he said, handing back the ring. 'What did you plan to do?'

She pushed the ring back on. 'Go to Blackwater and – well, I don't know really. Mark the occasion somehow. It felt like the right thing to do.'

'So the two of you had arranged to meet at Blackwater on Tuesday night, and then what?' The detective's stare was quite unnerving. 'Break in?'

'It's not breaking in, it's different. It's . . .' How could she explain to a policeman?

'Am I right in guessing that you and Mr Blake are urban explorers like your sister was?'

There didn't seem much point in denying it, and she nodded. 'Yes, we planned to "break in", as you put it, and head to the water tower where the accident happened. Except we didn't – or rather, I didn't.' She relayed the events of Tuesday night: how she'd got stuck on the train due to the weather; how Ed had said he'd go to Blackwater alone. 'It was a stupid idea, but he was determined. He loved her and always felt guilty that he hadn't been with her on the day of the accident.'

'Have you spoken to Mr Blake at all since then?'

'No, and it's not like him not to be in touch. I'm worried, I have to admit.'

'So you have no *real* idea of whether he actually made it inside the grounds or not, then?'

Connie shook her head. 'No, I suppose I don't.'

'How did you plan to get in?' he asked.

'There's a hole in the fence on Daylesford Road. It's been there since last summer.'

'Just to be clear, you've had no contact whatsoever with Mr Blake – no text, no email?'

DI Kirby's eyes were the darkest green that she'd ever seen, and something about them unsettled her. 'No, nothing.'

'Can you think of anywhere he might go – family, a girlfriend?'

'There's his grandfather, Harry. They're very close. Ed's mum – well, she wasn't around very much. Harry pretty much brought him up.'

'Does he have a girlfriend?'

She shook her head and fiddled with the ring on her thumb. 'Not since Sarah.'

'What about other urban explorers?'

'What about them?' she asked, looking up. 'Look, Ed knew loads of urbexes – sorry, urban explorers – but that doesn't mean he'd go off-radar with any of them.'

DI Kirby looked thoughtful. 'How many of them have been into Blackwater?'

'Loads. Half the urbex community in London have been in. Not to mention people who've travelled to London especially.'

'Right.' He smiled. 'A cast of thousands. Tell me, do you know of any other ways in apart from the broken fence?'

She shook her head. 'Not unless you can bribe the secco.' She didn't know of any other way in, but even if she had, she wasn't about to tell the police – not even the striking DI Kirby.

'The secco?' he asked.

'Security guard. There's been the odd one over the years who'd turn a blind eye, but they never lasted long. Why?'

'We're exploring the possibility that the victim and perpetrator entered the site from somewhere other than the main entrances or the hole in the fence.'

She was suddenly intrigued. 'You mean you don't know how they got in?'

'Not yet, no. If you have any ideas, I'd be grateful if you could let me know.' He paused, as if mulling something over. 'Tell me, how did you get into all this, the urban exploring? Was it through your sister? Just being nosey.'

'I didn't know anything about it until Sarah died. I'd never heard of people exploring derelict buildings for a laugh – I didn't even know she was involved, to be honest. Her accident came as such a shock, then to find out she had this secret life.' She shrugged. 'I wanted to find out more.'

'Is that how you met Mr Blake?'

'Sort of. I'd met him once or twice, very briefly, with Sarah. He seemed nice. Initially, I just wanted to get into Blackwater to see where the accident happened, but then I wanted to understand more about why she explored in the first place. I couldn't do it alone and, well, he was the only urbex I knew.'

'And did you – understand, I mean?'

'Totally. It's exhilarating. I got bitten by the bug. The adrenalin alone is worth it—' She stopped. 'It's not just that though. I don't expect you to get it, but I feel close to her when I'm at Blackwater. It's hard to explain. Ed's been great, he's one of the loveliest people I know. Best drainer I've met too.'

DI Kirby looked bemused. 'Drainer?'

'Drainers specialise in exploring sewers and storm drains, that kind of thing. Ed loves them; in fact, he's known as RatRun to some of the urbexes after—'

'Tunnel rats.'

'Yes, how did—'

'Educated guess. Sorry, I interrupted you.'

'Oh, yeah – well, anyhow, he and another explorer friend really helped me. I don't know what I would have done without them.' She was talking too much. 'Are we done?'

'Who's this other friend?' he asked, standing up.

Bollocks. She'd walked into that one. 'I don't know his real name – everyone calls him Mole. He's been in Poland since the weekend and isn't back until tomorrow or the day after, I'm not sure which.'

'I see. Okay, thanks. You've been very helpful. And satisfied my curiosity.'

'Good. I say "good" as long as you don't arrest me.' She smiled.

'Not today, no.'

'I'll show you out,' she said, suddenly feeling embarrassed. Was she flirting with him? Christ, Mole would never forgive her. Fraternising with the enemy is what he'd call it, never mind that DI Kirby was good-looking.

'Are you allowed to tell me whose body it was that you found?' she asked, as they descended the stairs.

'The name will be released to the press this afternoon, so all I can tell you now is that it was an elderly female.'

She didn't know what she'd expected to hear, but an elderly woman hadn't even entered her head. 'That's awful. What on earth was she doing there?'

'We don't know yet.'

They reached the entrance, and when she opened the door an icy gust hit them both.

'Damn, that's cold,' muttered DI Kirby, stepping on to the pavement and zipping up his jacket. 'Thanks for your time, Miss Darke. If you hear from Mr Blake, or anyone who knows where he might be, let me know immediately.' He handed her a card. 'Call me any time. I can see this must be difficult for you, after losing your sister.'

'Thanks.' She took the card and slid it into her pocket. 'You know they never found out who my sister was with when she fell. It's haunted Ed ever since.'

'You too, I imagine.'

'I just hope he's all right. If something's happened to him, I . . .' She trailed off. She didn't want to think about it.

'I'm sure we'll find him, so try not to worry. Remember, call if you hear anything or have any concerns.'

Connie watched him cross the street and turn right along the square, until he disappeared round the corner. She stood for a second, absent-mindedly twisting the ring on her thumb, with a nagging feeling – not entirely unpleasant – that she hadn't seen the last of him.

CHAPTER 13

Seventy-nine Chartwell Road was on a small, neat little street of bungalows; not bad for a nurse's pension, thought Kirby as he pulled up in the Corsa. A Scenes of Crime van was parked outside, as well as Anderson's Astra. Kirby would give anything to be able to drive his own car for work – he owned a 1974 Citroën SM – but it was strictly forbidden. The Corsa affronted him on every level, but Pete's Astra was just as bad, if not worse.

He was aware of being watched as he got out of the car. Chartwell Road looked like one of those streets where nothing much happened and yet everyone knew what everyone else was doing. Kirby hoped the neighbours were talkative, as well as curtain-twitchers.

A SOCO, who had been sitting in the van talking on his phone, climbed out and said hello, handing Kirby protective overalls and bootees to slip over his shoes.

'There's another entrance around the back,' said the officer, pointing towards the side of the house, where Kirby could see a path. Once he'd pulled the overalls on over his clothes, the SOCO handed him some nitrile gloves.

'Thanks,' said Kirby, and headed towards the house.

There were two access paths to the house – one leading to the front and one towards the rear – and both had been clearly labelled by SOCOs so as not to disturb any footprints. A wooden gate separated the front garden from the street, and several sets of prints led up the garden path to the front door, most likely belonging to the postman and the neighbour who'd reported Ena missing. The curtains were drawn, and Kirby sensed an empty house; before the circus had arrived, that was. He followed the other designated path down the side of the property, which led to a gate and a small patio area, and stopped for a moment, every now and then catching Anderson's measured tones from within the house. He was on the phone, Kirby could tell.

Ena clearly hadn't been a gardener, and even under a blanket of snow he could tell that most of it was concrete. There was no sign of human activity, only a few animal tracks criss-crossing the small area and the narrow path the SOCOs had marked out. The garden was boxed in on three sides by adjoining gardens, which limited access for any intruder. A back door, the top half of which was glass, led into a small kitchen. Kirby pulled on the nitrile gloves and went in. Anderson was indeed on his mobile, now talking in more hushed tones, and he nodded as Kirby walked in.

Grey roller blinds were down in the small kitchen, diffusing the light, and it took Kirby's eyes a few seconds to adjust after the brightness of the snow outside. Washing-up was draining next to the sink – a plate and a small saucepan. He wandered over to the fridge and opened the door: a half-litre of milk still well within its use-by date; eggs – again, fresh; cheese; tomatoes; and an unopened packet of sliced ham. He checked the cupboards – a few tins of soup, sardines and pineapple chunks in one. Another held sugar, tea and a half-full jar of instant coffee; and a biscuit barrel stood on the work surface near a kettle.

He moved into the hallway, where he met a SOCO called Asia Barsetti coming out of a room to the left, which looked like the living room.

'Hey, Lew, how are you?' She smiled, her breath fanning out before her. The house was freezing.

'I'm good, thanks. Found anything yet?'

'No. Nothing looks out of place. It's as if she simply walked out and never came back,' said Asia.

A lone envelope lay by the front door, along with a couple of takeaway pizza menus. It didn't look like the accumulation of someone who'd been gone for more than one or two days. He picked up the envelope, a bill of some kind, and put it on the table, along with the pizza menus. He examined the front door; it was locked from the outside, and the chain was off.

'Have you found a key for this?' he asked Asia.

'Not yet. We all came in through the back.'

Kirby went into the room Asia had just come from, the sitting room, and went over to the window. He drew back the curtain and noticed movement in the window opposite. Mrs Valance, who had called the police to report Ena missing, was out until six, he knew, but whoever it was had a prime view of the front of Ena's house; he hoped that they had a good memory too.

Letting the curtain fall back into place, he turned to survey the room. Floral wallpaper covered one wall, while the rest of it was painted a dusky pink. The carpet looked new, as did the furniture. In fact, the place looked fairly recently decorated. A large television filled one corner of the room – a Sony, not cheap. The remote sat on a shelf below, along with several TV guides. The rest of the wall was filled with shelves; not shelves for books but the kind of useless shelves that Kirby hated – the kind of shelves that accumulated dust and 'things'. Ena's collection of things was sparse: three elephants in varying sizes, some Russian dolls, and a snow globe with the Virgin Mary inside. Kirby picked up the snow globe and shook it. The Virgin stared at him through the plastic dome, her

80

arms outstretched, palms turned upwards, as though inviting him in. He put it down and moved towards the bedroom.

He stood in the doorway for a moment, and Asia came and stood next to him.

'We haven't searched in there yet. You want to have a look first?' she asked.

'Give me a few minutes and then it's all yours,' Kirby replied, and stepped into the room.

Secrets: invariably, the bedroom was where people kept them. Why, Kirby wasn't sure. Was it the darkness at night, the feeling of being close to something private? It was also a room that visitors rarely entered, a room of privacy and seclusion. *What secrets did Ena have?* he wondered. Her death had not been random; of that, he was fairly certain. Ena had been chosen – for whatever reason – and her body placed somewhere very specific.

On first impression, Ena Massey's bedroom looked more like a hospital room than a private room in someone's house, and was quite unlike the living room. The walls were off-white and bare, save for a crucifix over the bed. The bed itself looked like standard hospital-issue – metal-framed and narrow – and not unlike the one she'd been found on in Keats Ward. A medical chart wouldn't have looked out of place at its end. The bed was neatly made, with starched white linen folded over at the top to reveal a flat, white pillow; a green eiderdown was the only concession to winter. A bedside cabinet in wood veneer sat to the left, on which stood an alarm clock and bedside light. Kirby walked over to the small cabinet and opened the drawer: an open packet of paracetamol, some Vicks VapoRub and a bible. He picked up the bible; the brown cloth cover was worn at the edges, the front held on by a thread. He opened it carefully, noticing that the first page was printed in red and black ink and resembled a bookplate. 'Presented to ____ by

_____' was typeset in Gothic script, and the blank spaces had been filled in with an ink pen: *Presented to Ena by Father.*

He smelt the bible's pages and was reminded of the second-hand bookshops he used to love trawling as a child. He never seemed to have the time these days, and a pang of nostalgia hit him so forcefully that he was transported back to a summer's day in Hay-on-Wye. His parents had let him roam the Cinema Bookshop alone; its labyrinthine interior, lined with books, felt as big as an aerodrome to the young Kirby. It was the smell, however, that had stayed with him the most – of old paper worn by a million human touches. Thinking of his parents reminded him that Livia hadn't returned his call; usually she was chomping at the bit to speak to him.

He flicked through Ena's bible, a book he hadn't read since being at school, and it fell open about halfway through. A passage from the Proverbs had been marked with a black pen: *When thou liest down, thou shalt not be afraid: yea, thou shalt lie down, and thy sleep shall be sweet.*

'Found something?' said Anderson's voice, from behind him.

'Not really. Just a bible given to her by her father.' Kirby closed the book and returned it to the drawer.

Anderson waved his mobile. 'Neighbour across the road saw Ena leave here at around three yesterday afternoon. She was wearing a fur coat and talking to someone on her mobile. He didn't see her return.'

'So we need to find her phone,' said Kirby. 'And she wasn't wearing the coat when we found her either.'

'Kobrak's going to get on to the phone when he gets back from the hospice, although my bet is it's at the bottom of the river.'

Kirby sat on the bed and looked around the austere room. 'Nothing happened here, did it? It's as she left it.'

'That's certainly how it looks. This room wouldn't be out of place at Blackwater, if you ask me. How did it go with the daughter?'

Kirby recounted his visit with Karen, while looking through the other drawers in the bedside table.

'Bloody hell,' said Anderson when he'd finished. 'Sounds like you barely got out alive.'

'Yeah, the way she fondled that bottle opener will stay with me forever. Anyhow, if Ena worked at Blackwater, then Raymond Sweet must have known her. They were both there for decades.'

'We'd better bring him in. What about this money Ena mentioned to Karen? If it's true, and she did come into some cash, then we should find the paperwork here somewhere. Not that Sweet strikes me as someone who'd kill for money . . . Does he to you?'

'No, he doesn't, but he might have had some other reason.' Kirby went over to the wardrobe and opened the doors. It was full of the usual clothes and shoes that you might expect from a woman in her eighties: sensible shoes, plain dresses, skirts – no trousers – and a few coats. There was nothing hidden – no suitcase full of stolen money, no stash of drugs; nothing worth killing for. He sighed and closed the door. Anderson was going through a chest of drawers, which sat in front of the window. He'd just opened the second drawer when his phone rang.

'It's Hamer,' he said, glancing at the screen. 'Initial post-mortem results must be in. You want to carry on?' he asked, stepping aside to concentrate on the call.

Kirby went over and continued searching the drawer. It contained nothing but cardigans and scarves. The third drawer contained the same, only there were a few other items, such as belts and gloves. He found what he was looking for in the fourth drawer, the bottom one. Amongst some cardigans and a few scarves sat an old shoebox with *Saxone* printed on it. He took it over to the bed and carefully took off the lid. It contained jewellery and correspondence, and he took out an envelope at random.

The envelope was addressed to Ruth Abbott, Blackwater Asylum, Battersea. The postmark was smudged, but he could just about make out the date: 1964. Inside was a handwritten letter, which began, *Dear Ruthie*. Kirby skimmed the letter and took out another – and then another. He glanced at Anderson, who was listening intently to what Hamer was telling him on the phone, then back at the letters.

There were fifteen in total, and all appeared to be letters written from relatives and friends to patients at Blackwater Asylum. There was nothing revealing in the letters themselves, but one stood out. It was addressed to Catherine Edwards, and yet the letter inside began, *My Dearest Sarah*. It must have been put back in the wrong envelope by mistake, although the handwriting was the same on both. Kirby replaced the letters and began going through the jewellery. There wasn't much: a few brooches, an old school badge, a locket containing two sepia photographs and some rings. He was looking at each in turn when Anderson finished the call with Hamer.

'Looks like Ena died of a fractured skull, although she wouldn't have lasted long in an unconscious state in these temperatures. Toxicology report to follow.'

'Christ,' muttered Kirby. 'What on earth could she have done to provoke that?'

'It's hard to imagine.'

'Look at this.' Kirby handed him one of the letters.

'What about it?' asked Anderson, skimming over the contents and then looking at the envelope. 'It's probably an old letter to one of Ena's patients – what's the big deal?' He handed it back to Kirby.

'There are fifteen of them, six different patients in all.' Kirby put the letters back in the box and stood up. 'Don't you think that's strange?'

'Not necessarily. Could be she just cleared out an old desk before the hospital closed.'

On their way out, Kirby stopped Asia. 'There's a shoebox on the bed in the bedroom. I need a list of its contents and copies of the letters and envelopes.'

'No problem,' replied Asia. 'Anything else?'

'See if you can find any correspondence relating to the victim being left some money. Solicitor's letter, anything like that.'

It was dark when they left the house and headed back to the van parked at the front. They began stripping off their protective clothing.

'Ena Massey wasn't married, was she?' said Kirby, pulling off a plastic bootee.

'There aren't any records of her marrying. Why d'you ask?'

'Because she had at least seven wedding rings in that shoebox, threaded on to a piece of string,' said Kirby. 'So if she wasn't married, whose were they?'

'Heirloom?'

'If I hadn't seen the letters, then I wouldn't have given it much thought. A couple of letters, yes, but fifteen?'

'What are you trying to say? That she was killed because of the letters and the rings? I don't see how.'

'It's not that,' said Kirby, as they crossed the street. 'It's more what they say about Ena's character. If she deliberately withheld the letters, or stole them – and the same with the rings – then she was clearly abusing her position.'

'Well, it's certainly possible,' said Anderson.

Kirby halted on the pavement, outside the house opposite. 'And if she was, then that makes me wonder what else she might have been capable of.'

CHAPTER 14

'Is Livia there? It's her son, Lew,' said Kirby. Alarm bells were ringing in his mind because the voice that had answered his mother's phone wasn't hers. He'd taken the opportunity to call while he waited for Ena's neighbour, Julia Valance, to get home.

'Lew, it's Kate from next door.'

He recognised the voice now. 'Is something wrong?'

'Hang on . . .' She lowered her voice and he heard her close a door. 'I've been wanting to call you, only Livia insisted that I didn't.'

Kirby didn't like the sound of this at all. 'Go on.'

'She hasn't been herself these past few weeks – you know, forgetful, a bit confused. She's lost weight too. Then, when I came round for coffee this morning, she was much worse.'

'In what way?' His mother was rarely forgetful – let alone confused – apart from the last time they'd met up, and he now wondered whether he'd been in denial. It hadn't been that bad, had it?

'She kept going on about the snow. Almost – this sounds daft, I know – like she was afraid of it. Anyhow, we had a coffee, chatted, the usual, but when I came to leave she wouldn't come near the door – it was the snow thing again. It was so odd that I thought I'd come and check on her before supper. She's in the bathroom at the moment, she asked me to answer the phone.'

Kirby wasn't quite sure what to say. He couldn't imagine his mother behaving like that and wondered what was going on; at least she hadn't fallen off a ladder and broken anything. 'How does she seem now?' he asked.

Kate was silent for a moment. 'She didn't remember that I was here earlier.'

Fuck, thought Kirby. Was it the onset of dementia? The thought made him feel sick.

'Oh, here she is, I'll pass you over. Nice talking to you, Lew.' He heard her pass the phone to his mother and say goodbye.

'Mum, how are you? I tried calling yesterday, but you weren't around. I thought you were out gallivanting.' He tried to sound as though nothing were wrong.

'I'd hardly call playing Briscola gallivanting. I must have left the phone in the kitchen or upstairs.' Kirby's mother had taught some of her friends how to play the game, and they had regular card-playing sessions, although Kirby suspected it was just an excuse to get together and drink too much wine.

'Kate said you weren't very pleased about the snow. Has some-one cleared your driveway?' He didn't quite know how to bring up what his father had mentioned the previous night, let alone what Kate had just told him.

There was a pause before his mother replied, her voice a whis-per. 'I can't go out in it, Lew. It's everywhere, and I mean every-where – roofs, cars, parks, even the pavements. I don't want to be anywhere near it.'

'But, Mum, you love the snow. You can't ski without snow.'

She carried on as though he hadn't spoken. 'I can't sleep prop-erly either, knowing it's all over the house.'

'Mum, it's just snow. It won't hurt you.' He waited a few beats before going on. 'I spoke to Dad last night—'

'Kate's husband cleared the drive for me, and offered to do some shopping, so that was kind,' Livia cut in, oblivious.

'I spoke to Dad,' Kirby repeated with more force than he'd intended. 'He said you needed to talk to me.'

'Really? I always want to talk to you, Lew. You're my son.'

'Yes, but—' He stopped. 'Look, I'll come over this weekend, okay? I've got a new case, so I can't say when exactly, but I'll call and let you know.'

'That would be lovely. I'll look forward to it. Take care, *ciao ciao*.'

'Bye, Mum.'

Kirby sat for a few moments. Since when had his mother disliked snow? She was Italian, from Trentino, and practically came out of the womb on skis. Admittedly, London snow wasn't exactly the Dolomites, but he'd never heard her moan about it before. At sixty-two, she'd easily pass for a youthful fifty. On one occasion, about ten years ago, she'd even been mistaken for his wife – something they'd both giggled about like teenagers at the time.

Several people – no, most people he knew had difficult relationships with their parents. Some didn't speak at all, so he'd always considered himself lucky with his mum and dad, who were more like friends than parents. Something was definitely wrong. He'd have to see her this weekend no matter what was happening with the Blackwater case, even if it was only for an hour, although God only knew when he'd find the time.

A woman was walking up Chartwell Road with two children in tow, and disappeared into the house opposite Ena's; it must be Julia Valance. Kirby gave her ten minutes to get the kids' coats off and sort herself out, then got out of the car and walked up to the house.

Two minutes later he was sitting in the Valances' kitchen with Julia. Her two children – Poppy, aged five, and Mikey, aged four – were in the front room watching television. Julia was busy preparing the children's supper – she would be eating with her husband, John, when he got home later. It felt so different to Kirby's existence on the boat.

'I can't believe it,' she was saying. 'I mean, who'd want to kill someone like Ena?' Julia Valance was a yoga teacher in her mid-thirties; tall and slender, she was wearing a figure-hugging black tracksuit, and her streaked hair was scraped back into a ponytail. Two discreet silver-orb earrings adorned her small earlobes, and Kirby recognised them as Vivienne Westwood. He wondered how much an hour's yoga session with her would set him back.

'I gather that Miss Massey was a volunteer at a hospice where a family member of yours is living?' he asked, as he watched her prepare the food. He'd hardly eaten and was suddenly starving.

'Yes, St Elizabeth's Hospice on Valentine Road. John's mother is there. They do a wonderful job. We simply don't have the time, or the room, to look after her here.'

'How well did you know Miss Massey? Did she look after your mother-in-law?'

'Actually, we don't – I mean, didn't – know her very well at all. Ena wasn't involved with the care of John's mother, as she's a resident at St Elizabeth's. We gave Ena a lift up there once or twice, when the weather was bad, but I think Ena mainly did home visits. The hospice had nothing but praise for her. She was an incredible woman.'

'You mean because of her volunteering?'

'Yes, of course. To have given your working life to a profession and yet still be prepared to devote your retirement to it is quite something, don't you think? She must have really loved her job.'

Yes, thought Kirby, *she must.* 'So you knew that she used to be a nurse?'

'That's why the hospice was so grateful for her time.'

'Did she ever mention any family to you – children, that sort of thing?'

Julia Valance shook her head. 'No. As far as I was aware, she had no family, or at least wasn't in touch with them if she did. I never saw anyone visit her.'

'Didn't you find that a bit odd?'

'Now you mention it, I suppose it was a bit. She seemed such a nice lady that I can't believe she didn't have any friends. Maybe they all met up elsewhere.'

They chatted some more about Ena – how she and Julia would pass the time of the day on the street, and how, if there was an emergency of any kind, she always offered to help. Julia hadn't seen anyone suspicious hanging around, nor seen any visitors – ever.

As he got up to leave, Poppy ran into the kitchen clutching a stuffed-toy rabbit.

'Is tea ready yet, Mummy? I'm hungry.'

'Yes, darling, nearly ready. I'm just showing this nice man out.'

'Are you a pleeceman?' Poppy asked, looking at Kirby eagerly.

'Yes, I am. Your mummy has been helping me.'

'Is it about Miss Massey?'

Julia Valance looked at Kirby and then at Poppy. 'Have you been listening to us, you monkey?'

Poppy stuck out her lower lip and shook her head. 'No, Mummy, but there's vans outside her house and men in romper suits.'

'That's right,' said Kirby. 'They're my special team.'

'Have they come to take Miss Massey away?' asked the little girl.

'Poppy! What kind of question is that!' said Julia. 'Of course they haven't. They're just making sure her house is okay.'

'I don't like her,' said Poppy, suddenly.

'Poppy! I'm so sorry, Detective Kirby.' Julia Valance looked at her daughter, unsure what to say.

'Well, we can't like everyone, can we, Poppy?' Kirby smiled. 'I'll let you into a secret,' he went on, lowering his voice. 'There are some people I don't like either.'

Poppy giggled. 'I don't like her 'cos she don't like me.'

'What do you mean?' said Julia, kneeling down beside her daughter. 'You must tell us if she said something nasty to you.'

Poppy seemed to sense a shift in the room. 'Mummy . . .'

Julia smoothed her daughter's hair. 'Did Miss Massey tell you off for playing outside? Was that it? Were you making too much noise one day?'

Poppy shook her head. Julia looked up at Kirby for some kind of guidance.

'It's okay, Poppy. You don't have to tell us now, if you don't want to. But if you do, it can be our secret. Just the three of us,' said Kirby gently.

'I only don't like her 'cos she don't like any of me.'

'*Any* of you?' asked Julia.

'Yes, Mummy. That's what she told me one day. She said, "I don't like any of you." She didn't even like Mikey, and he's cute.'

Julia stood up, frowning.

'Am I in trouble, Mummy?' asked Poppy.

'Of course not,' said Kirby, smiling. 'I won't tell anyone, promise.' He put his finger to his lips.

'Now, go and wash your hands and tell your brother to do the same. Tea in five minutes,' said Julia.

The two adults watched Poppy run back to the living room and then looked at each other.

'I have no idea where that came from . . .' began Julia.

'It's fine, don't worry about it. I'm sure it's nothing.'

The yoga teacher led Kirby to the front door and held it open for him. 'If there's anything else we can do, please let us know.' She looked across the road to the small bungalow. 'What will happen to the house?'

'I honestly don't know,' replied Kirby. 'Good night, Mrs Valance.'

CHAPTER 15

After parting company with Kirby, Connie had grabbed a sandwich and gone back to work. Bonaro continued to bombard her with information on her soon-to-be new role, most of which went in one ear and out the other. The relief that the body found at Blackwater wasn't Ed's had been short-lived. She'd gone through every conceivable scenario to explain his absence – from having the mother of all hangovers to eloping with a secret lover. The most likely one she could come up with was that he had injured himself and was stuck somewhere – there were a shitload of ways to injure yourself exploring derelict buildings, especially at night, not to mention if you were alone. But if that were the case, wouldn't the police have found him? Regardless of any of that, the fact was that he was missing and a woman had been murdered. None of it was good.

When Connie eventually left RADE at 5 p.m. the snow-covered pavements were glowing eerily under the new street lamps, which cast a cold, harsh light, and although the roads had been gritted, there was still very little traffic. Most places had closed early, and it already felt like a ghost town. The one place that was still open was the nail bar, where a forlorn-looking girl sat behind the counter chewing her hair. There were no trains or buses, but if you wanted a new set of nails, no problem.

She began the trudge back to the Four Sails and thought about what Kirby had said about the Blackwater victim: an old woman. What the hell had she been doing at Blackwater, let alone at night in the middle of winter? Like Ed's phone, it didn't make sense. And then there was the mystery of how the elderly woman had got in – every urbex enjoyed the challenge of infiltrating a new building, and Connie was genuinely curious. A sudden urge to do something swept over her; the question was, what?

She reached the intersection with Queenstown Road and stood waiting for the lights to change, mindlessly pushing the button at the crossing, when out of the jumble of thoughts something popped into her head: a pub. Ed had mentioned it – it was where some of the Blackwater Asylum staff had gone to drink when the staff facilities at the hospital had closed. He said it was a right old dive, but that his granddad, Harry, still loved going there. Connie looked at her watch; it was only just gone half five. Mole was still away, and she felt like she needed someone to talk to. It couldn't hurt, could it? That's if she could find the damn place.

The pub was somewhere near the station, she remembered that much, because Ed had joked about the bottles rattling when a train went past. Problem was, he hadn't said which station: Battersea Park Road or Queenstown Road? He'd also commented on its name, which she couldn't remember, but she could hear him laughing and saying, *How fucking ironic is that?* She seriously doubted that an elderly man would be out on a night like this, but she had nothing better to do.

The lights eventually changed, and she set off in the direction of both stations. As it turned out, there were no pubs directly next to Queenstown Road station, so it had to be Battersea. There were a few pubs on Battersea Park Road, but given what she could remember of Ed's description, she dismissed them and turned on to a small side street. None of the snow had been cleared from here, and she felt it creeping over the tops of her boots. After a few minutes, she came to the only turning off the small street, and there, at the end of a small boarded-up terrace, stood the Welcome Inn. The irony of the name hit her immediately because it looked like a shithole. But, shithole or not, her feet were now so cold she would have gone into the mouth of Hades just to warm up.

From the outside, the Welcome Inn looked like a rundown corporation pub from the seventies, most likely built to accommodate the surrounding estate. A 'Value for Money' sign was badly painted on a board outside. She took a deep breath and went in, stamping the ice and snow from her boots on a threadbare doormat just inside the door.

'JD and coke,' she said to the barmaid, after walking across the sticky carpet to the bar. 'A double.'

The Welcome Inn was anything but. Shabby didn't cover it; it was a total dump. A sign on the wall read *Top Radio DJs* and *Caribbean Food Friday*. Connie was the only customer.

'Anything else?' the barmaid asked, looking her over.

'Um, no thanks.'

'That'll be five quid.'

At least it was cheap. The barmaid snatched the ten-pound note she held out.

'Actually, there is something else. I'm looking for someone who drinks here.' Connie looked around and found it hard to imagine anyone coming here regularly out of choice.

'Who's that then?' said the barmaid, peering into the till. 'Got no change, luv, 'cos of the snow, see.' She waggled the tenner between her nicotine-stained fingers.

'Oh, right.' Connie dug about in her wallet and managed to find enough change to pay for the drink. 'Here you go,' she said, pushing a pile of coins towards the barmaid. 'The person I'm looking for is called Harry. He's a regular.'

'Joyce or Merrill?'

Connie had no idea. 'He's an older bloke, granddad of a friend of mine.'

'Joyce then,' said the barmaid, looking around the empty room. 'He's not here.'

'Any idea when he might come in?'

'No.' The barmaid pushed the till shut. End of conversation.

Connie went and sat down at a small corner table so that she could see anyone who came in, although she wasn't holding her breath. She took a large slug of the drink; the Coke had come from a hose and tasted watered down, but the JD did its usual trick and she instantly felt herself beginning to warm up.

After another sip of the sweet drink, she took a more careful look around the room. It really was a dive; nothing short of a wrecking ball could make the place attractive. The sticky carpet was worn down, reflecting the flow of clientele to the bar and the toilets. A badly painted sign featuring a pointing four-fingered hand grandly informed her that there was also a 'rear-garden'. What the fuck that was like was anyone's guess.

There was a conspicuous rectangular patch of carpet where something had obviously stood until recently, the garish colours of the swirly pattern at odds with the rest of the faded, monotone decor. The place didn't look as though it had been painted, or cleaned, since the smoking ban had come into effect over ten years ago. It was intensely depressing, and Connie now wished she'd just gone back to the Four Sails.

She pulled out her phone and checked it for the umpteenth time, just in case, but there was still nothing from Ed. She logged into her email account to see if he'd contacted her that way, but he hadn't. Christ, where *was* he? Maybe he did have a girlfriend, someone tucked away he didn't want to mention, and just hadn't realised his phone was missing. It was a ridiculous thought – not the girlfriend part, perhaps, but that he'd fail to notice his phone was gone. He could easily have borrowed someone else's to check in with her – or, God forbid, used a public payphone.

Two men wandered in from the back, Connie guessed after having a smoke in the 'rear-garden', and leant on the bar. They appeared to be on good terms with the barmaid and ordered two pints of Carlsberg. One of the men was tall and skinny, arrogance etched on his face. His companion was the physical opposite: chubby and meek-looking. They looked like Laurel and Hardy minus the laughs, and Connie now had an even greater urge to leave.

She looked down at her phone in the hope they wouldn't notice her, although given there was no one else in the pub, she may as well have had a neon sign over her head. She took a sip of her drink and tapped on the BBC News app icon on her phone. She was about to click on the Blackwater story when she became aware of someone standing next to her table. It was the skinny one; the other, larger man was still at the bar, watching. This was the last thing she needed.

'Mind if we join you?' The man pulled out a stool from under the table.

'I was just going. Sorry.'

'You haven't finished your drink,' he said. 'You'll enjoy it more with some company.'

'That's doubtful.' Connie stood up to leave.

'Never seen you in here before,' said Skinny, his tongue licking his lips. 'I think we'd've remembered.'

She looked over towards the bar, seeking some reassurance from the barmaid that they were harmless, but she was nowhere to be seen. She glanced outside at the deserted street and the boarded-up terrace, and suddenly realised how isolated she was.

The larger of the two men had now sauntered over, and she was trapped behind the small, round table. To get out she'd have to move past one of them, and neither was an attractive proposition.

'I think the lady wants to leave, Lloyd,' said the fat one, casting a quick glance at his friend.

'No, she doesn't. Do you?' He flashed a bad-toothed smile. 'We were just getting to know each other.'

'Excuse me.' Connie edged round the table, brushing past the fat one, who she'd decided wasn't quite as scary as the skinny one. She felt his body lean back a fraction to let her pass and was grateful even for that.

'What are you doing in here, anyway?' asked the skinny one.

Now she was free of the table, with the door on to the street a short sprint away, she felt more confident. 'I *was* having a quiet drink. Not that it's any of your business.'

'Disturbed you, have we?' said Skinny. 'Only I was hoping we could spice up your evening.'

The barmaid reappeared from wherever it was she'd disappeared to but totally ignored them and began pouring a large gin.

Connie headed to the door and had just grabbed the handle to pull it open when a booted foot stopped it, and she felt someone's breath on the back of her neck.

'Lloyd, let the lady out.' The barmaid had a voice that could shatter glass.

The breathing on the back of Connie's neck stopped suddenly, and when he exhaled it was all she could do to stop herself gagging.

'Sure. I was just opening the door for her.' She recognised Skinny's voice. He moved his foot. 'Showing her some manners, that's all.' He then whispered in her ear, 'Show you a lot more if I had my way.'

Connie yanked open the door and stumbled out on to the pavement, nearly knocking an elderly man flying. 'Sorry,' she mumbled, rushing past. Her skin was crawling and her heart pounding as she walked away, her short breaths leaving white puffs in her wake. When she reached the corner of Battersea Park Road, she risked a look behind to make sure the bastards weren't following; but instead of Laurel and Hardy, she was surprised to see the old man she'd nearly knocked over gingerly making his way along the badly lit pavement towards her. He was waving his stick. 'Wait!' he called, breathlessly.

'Did I forget something?' She checked her bag – her phone and wallet were still there.

'No, it's not that,' the man said. 'It's . . .' He caught his breath, leaning heavily on his stick.

'Yes?' She wanted to get away from there as soon as possible – before Laurel and Hardy decided it *was* a good idea to follow her.

'The barmaid said you were asking for me in the pub.' He held out his hand. 'I'm Harry Joyce.'

CHAPTER 16

After the stress of the previous day when the police had found the body, followed by the news only an hour or so ago that the police wanted to interview him again – this time at the station – Raymond had been very pleased when Mrs Muir invited him round to supper at the B&B. She was preparing his favourite meal – beef stew with dumplings – so as far as he was concerned it was a no-brainer. Mrs Muir had her faults, but when it came to dumplings, no one could touch her. Not only that, she had also promised to let him play his memory video. It wasn't exactly a video, it was now a DVD – as her son had had it put on a disc for him – but Raymond was old-school, and in his mind it would forever be a VHS.

The radio was on in the steamy kitchen – an old Roberts with a swivel base, sticky from several decades of close proximity to food. The headlines for London sounded muffled in the warmth and smell of Mrs Muir's cooking. Raymond had had twenty-four hours to go through things in his head – speed wasn't his style – and had finally come up with a plan to move his collection. He was deep in thought about the finer details and trying not to worry about his police interview the next day, when a news item caught his attention.

'Police have identified the body of an elderly woman found in the grounds of Blackwater Asylum yesterday morning,' said the newsreader.

Raymond's ears pricked up immediately – as, unfortunately, did Mrs Muir's.

''Ere, Raymond, you get that? Your home's on the news again.'

He nodded. Of course he had heard it. He was trying to listen, if only Mrs Muir would shut up.

'Sorry,' she mouthed, miming pulling a zip across her lips.

' . . . named as Ena Massey, a former nurse at the asylum, which is about to be redeveloped into luxury flats,' the newsreader went on. 'It's still unclear what the former nurse was doing in the abandoned hospital, and police are asking any members of the public who might have seen her in the hours leading up to her death to contact them.'

Raymond sat stunned, the newsreader's voice coming in and out of focus as he took in what he'd just heard. The voice washed over him, because all he could concentrate on was the name of the dead woman: Ena Massey.

'Raymond, love, you all right?' Mrs Muir's voice penetrated his thoughts. She was looking at him, all plump and concerned. 'It's not the dumplings, is it?'

'What? Err, no. The dumplings are delicious.'

Her hand patted her heart. 'Thank goodness for that – you were giving me palpitations. For one moment I thought I'd messed up. Now wouldn't that be a thing!'

But Raymond wasn't listening; Ena Massey was dead. In his head he saw a little smiley face, winking at him. He popped a dumpling in his mouth – they *were* delicious – and wondered why it had taken so long for someone to finally kill her. He wasn't sorry at all – not that he'd be telling anyone else that, of course. As he continued with his meal he realised that a weight had been lifted from his shoulders, a weight that he'd never truly acknowledged – or perhaps hadn't even known was there until it was gone. Moving his collection suddenly didn't seem as daunting as it had when he woke up. Crumbling it might well be, but once again Blackwater had done the right thing and spat out the bad apple.

'What a business though,' Mrs Muir was saying. 'Fancy going to a derelict hospital at her age. Do you think she was dealing, Raymond, like one of those matriarchs you see in films?'

Raymond had no idea what a matriarch was, but wouldn't put anything past Ena. 'I don't know,' he replied, through a mouthful of dumpling.

''Ere, you didn't know her, did you?' Mrs Muir's eyes gleamed with excitement. 'Wouldn't that be a thing, you knowing a murder victim!'

'It was a long time ago,' he said, adding, 'Poor woman,' for good measure. He didn't want to discuss Ena.

'Yes, of course, poor woman,' echoed Mrs Muir, with about as much conviction as Raymond.

'The stew and the dumplings were lovely, thank you.' He pushed his empty plate to one side.

'My pleasure, love. Shall we go and watch your little film then – wait for that lot to go down before we have some afters?'

'That would be very nice,' he said.

The video had been given to Raymond by the staff at Blackwater as a leaving gift. Most of the long-stay patients had received one to remind them of the happy times they'd had at the hospital; and it was one of his most prized possessions. There was even a short black-and-white clip of his old pal Gregory Boothe playing cards, which always made him smile.

Once Mrs Muir was ensconced on the sofa with a small sherry – Raymond usually took the recliner – she put on the television. 'Go on then, Raymond. Do the honours, will you?'

He pulled the DVD out of his jacket pocket and took out the disc. As he slipped it into the machine, Mrs Muir flicked through the TV channels.

'I do miss Parkinson, you know,' she was saying. 'And here's the thing – he only had two O levels.'

One of the channels she flicked through had the news on. It was the Blackwater story, and a man's face came up on the screen. It was the man the police were trying to trace, the one whose name Mrs Muir had talked over in the kitchen and which Raymond now caught: Edward Blake. He didn't recognise the name, but the face was vaguely familiar. Hadn't he spoken to him once, at Blackwater? Then came an image of Ena, so he quickly pressed 'Close' on the DVD machine, and the disc slid in.

He lowered himself into the recliner and gave Mrs Muir the nod, and she pressed 'Play'. Her technique with the remote was akin to someone being knighted.

As the video began, Raymond felt himself drifting off to a different place, the footage of Blackwater flooding his head with memories – not to mention the drowsy effect a stomach full of dumplings had on him. He had no idea how much time had passed when Mrs Muir suddenly screeched, 'Oh my giddy aunt! Look!'

She had paused the video, the remote held aloft.

Raymond looked up; he'd been totally lost in thought, his eyes adrift in the swirls of Mrs Muir's wallpaper, but now he refocused on the television, where Ena Massey's face stared out at him from the screen. The shock was instant. It wasn't just seeing her face again; it was seeing her in that room. He'd deliberately pushed Keats Ward to the back of his mind after the detective had mentioned it yesterday. But now it came charging back, knocking all other thoughts out of the way and dragging something with it. Something nasty and frightening.

CHAPTER 17

After he'd introduced himself, Connie walked Harry Joyce back to his house, two streets away. He was quite unsteady on his feet, and she marvelled at how he'd got to the pub without coming a cropper in the first place. As they walked, she explained to him who she was and how she and Ed had met.

'We were in daily contact almost every day – until now. I'm so worried,' Harry was saying.

They were sitting in his front room, a cosy space with a small gas fire, complete with fake logs, burning in a cracked, 1930s tiled fireplace. Connie sat on the sofa, an old worn-out thing that was surprisingly comfortable, and tried to imagine Ed sitting in her place. It was a far cry from the man she knew, who spent his spare time diving into sewers and forgotten corners of the city. It felt weird.

'Me too,' she said. 'I hope the police don't think he had something to do with that poor woman's death.'

'My Ed would never get mixed up in anything like that.'

'*We* know that, but until he comes forward and explains himself it doesn't look good to the police.'

'I can't think what's stopping him,' said Harry, with a troubled look.

'The police thought he might be with someone. A girlfriend, maybe.'

'Don't be daft, love. After what happened to your sister, well . . .' He shook his head. 'Knocked him for six. Pleased as punch I was when he landed that teaching job. A good solid job like that, we'd've killed for one of those in my day. I don't know what he sees in this buggering about in old buildings.'

'He's pretty obsessed with Blackwater, isn't he?' said Connie.

'Probably my fault, telling him stories as a kiddie.' Harry chuckled. 'We lived in BelleVue Tower when he was growing up, eighteenth floor, looked down right over the whole asylum. Been pulled down now, of course, but he'd spend ages with my old pair of binoculars studying the place.' Harry sighed at the memory. 'He's even started an oral history of Blackwater. Now *that* I can see the value in.'

'He brought the idea up a few times, but I didn't know he'd actually made a start.'

'Oh yes. I gave him a few names – people I know who used to work there. And he interviewed me, of course. I was groundsman. Not a bad job, but not as good as being a teacher.' He smiled, proudly. 'Places like Blackwater get under your skin. He was off to talk to someone last Sunday afternoon, some new lead he'd got. He's such a live wire, is Ed. Keeps some of his stuff here – no room for it at his studio flat.'

'What kind of stuff?' asked Connie.

Harry shook his head. 'I leave him to it. Have a look if you like – it's upstairs.'

'I don't think I should. It's his personal stuff. It just doesn't seem right.' It had only been forty-eight hours, after all. Or was that a long time for someone to be missing? Christ, she had no idea.

'None of this seems right. Maybe there's something up there that might tell us where he is.'

'I'm not sure.' Connie hesitated. 'He might walk through that door any moment. Like, it's only been two days.'

'Right,' mumbled Harry. 'Only two days.'

'Okay, I'll take a very quick look, but I won't disturb anything. Promise.'

'First room on the right.' He pointed upwards with his thumb.

'And I'll make you a cup of tea when I come down, then I really must shoot.'

Mike Mower's theme tune to *Bargain Hunt* came on in the living room as Connie climbed the stairs. The merry saxophone riffs sent a wave of depression through her, which was only heightened when she stepped into the small room where Ed kept his stuff. A writing desk stood in one corner with a chair tucked under it, and a single bed was pushed against the opposite wall, over which hung a vintage mirror, its glass mottled with age. Connie stared at her reflection, imagining Ed's face looking back at her. On the wall behind she could see a framed photograph; it was Blackwater, the ornamental lake and water tower unmistakeable. It looked like a staff photograph with nurses in uniform, although some patients were also present, their body language making them stand out from the straight-backed, formal-looking staff. She recognised a young-looking Harry in the back row, and immediately saw the resemblance between grandfather and grandson.

Apart from the desk, chair and bed, the rest of the space was taken up with box folders, books, and bits of what most people would call junk. She recognised a 'HAZARD' sign that Ed had taken from an old factory they'd visited in Surrey. The urban explorer's motto, 'Take only photographs and leave only footprints', was in general adhered to, but even Ed hadn't been able to resist the odd trophy. The memory of that day felt like a stab to the heart. *Where the hell is he?*

Connie went over to the desk, which was covered in files and folders. A Post-it note caught her eye, a name – Tom Ellis – and address scrawled on it as though written in haste. She didn't recognise either; but below – underlined twice – was one word that made her catch her breath. *Sarah*. She racked her brains, but the address meant nothing. Her immediate thought was of her sister, but in truth it could be any Sarah.

She opened a box file, but it was empty apart from a USB stick. She closed the lid and randomly chose a folder, leafing through the pockets inside. It mainly contained copies of newspaper articles about Blackwater. She pulled one out from the *Wandsworth Guardian* dated 14 April 1993 and headlined BLACKWATER ASYLUM CLOSES ITS DOORS FOR THE LAST TIME. An aerial photograph showed the sprawling mass of buildings – many of which had been closed years before – that made up the asylum. The article went on to talk about the last two patients, who had only left the week before, and about how mental health needs had changed and most people wanted to be cared for in the community.

She put it back in the plastic slipcase and pulled out a few more. One from 2008, BLACKWATER DEVELOPMENT AXED; another, STAFF CLEARED OF MISCONDUCT, showed two women leaving Blackwater's entrance with their heads down. Another article, BLACKWATER NURSE FOUND DEAD, told how a female nurse was discovered after taking an overdose at the hospital in 1966. A grainy photograph showed a family leaving the funeral. She flicked through the rest of the folder and was about to close it when a cutting from 2015 fluttered out. It was another from the *Wandsworth Guardian* and was titled LIFE IS SWEET.

Squatter Raymond Sweet was today handed the title deeds to a small area of land within the infamous Blackwater Estate. The land, which is home to a former psychiatric hospital, has lain derelict for twenty-two years but has recently been bought by Patricey Developments. Sweet, who has squatted on the land since 1994, made a claim for adverse possession when the developer moved to evict him. Patricey Developments will now have to move forward with their plans to turn the former mental asylum into luxury flats with Mr Sweet still firmly in residence in the north-west corner of the site.

She closed the folder and sat still for a moment. Raymond Sweet. She'd almost forgotten about him – a dishevelled figure, well known locally and harmless enough. He always looked like a man who was doing something he shouldn't. Ed had tried befriending him once in the hope that he might let him in the grounds, but as far as she knew Raymond had proved a tough cookie, quiet and reclusive.

She suddenly became aware of the TV channel being changed downstairs and Harry's voice calling her name.

'What is it?' she asked from the top of the stairs.

'You need to come and see the news.'

As she headed downstairs, she wondered if Raymond Sweet had seen anything on Tuesday night.

'Here we go,' said Harry, turning up the volume when she walked into the living room. It was now ear-splitting, but Harry didn't appear to notice. She sat down.

The main story on the weather was just coming to an end, and the studio newsreader began talking about Blackwater. 'Police are appealing for witnesses after a body was found at the derelict Blackwater Asylum site early yesterday morning. The victim, who has been named as eighty-four-year-old Ena Massey, is thought to be a retired nurse from the hospital, which closed in 1993.'

Connie stared at the image on the screen and felt a shiver run down her spine.

The newsreader went on. 'Police are particularly keen to trace a man seen in the vicinity of the old asylum on Tuesday night and have released CCTV footage of the man they want to speak to.'

She gasped as a fuzzy image of Ed walking past the main entrance to the asylum came up on screen.

'The man is believed to be twenty-seven-year-old Edward Blake, a teaching assistant from Royal Oak School. Police are also trying to trace Leroy Simmons, a security guard from the old hospital who went missing shortly after reporting the body. If anyone has any information on the whereabouts of either man, they should contact the police on this number – 0845 1221221.'

When the story ended, Connie grabbed the remote and turned the volume down. She could barely hear herself think.

'She worked at Blackwater,' said Harry, pointing at the now-blank screen. 'Ena Massey did. They called her Nurse Ratched behind her back.' He shook his head at the memory.

Connie frowned. 'Why?'

'*One Flew Over the Cuckoo's Nest.* I remember going to see it when it came out. They may as well have modelled her on Ena. Nasty piece of work, if ever I've met one.'

She'd seen the film and remembered the Nurse Ratched character vividly.

'I'm hardly surprised some bugger's killed her,' said Harry, glancing at Connie. 'Sorry.'

'What did she do?'

'It's all in the past now,' he said, batting the comment away. 'She won't be missed, let's leave it at that.'

She wasn't quite sure what to say. 'Did Ed know her?'

Harry shook his head. 'I doubt it. I'd never have put him in touch with the likes of her, not that I even knew she was still knocking about.'

They fell silent for a few moments, then Connie realised that she needed to get going. 'How about that cup of tea then, before I leave?'

'That'd be grand. You'll find everything you need.' Harry waved vaguely towards the kitchen.

She felt bad at the thought of leaving him alone, but she couldn't stay. Terror, her cat, needed feeding, and she had to be up for work the next day.

In the small kitchen, she put the kettle on and rootled around in the cupboards for the tea-making stuff.

Connie carried the mugs of tea – and a lonely Penguin she'd found in the biscuit barrel – into the front room, and as she set them down on the table she asked if it was okay to use the bathroom.

She took the stairs two at a time and ignored the bathroom, instead slipping straight into Ed's room, where she picked up the folder of newspaper clippings and began searching for the one she'd seen earlier. She found it soon enough, STAFF CLEARED OF MISCONDUCT, and stared at the photograph, then at the caption below. Although the photograph showed two nurses with their heads down, the caption left no room for doubt. One of them was Ena Massey. Nurse Ratched.

CHAPTER 18

An arsehole in Armani was Kirby's first thought on entering Patrick Calder's office. The second was that Anderson would concur – and the *third* was that if Hamer ever got wind of the description he'd bollock them both to Blackpool and back. He was feeling tired and irritable that morning, having only slept a few hours the night before. He needed to keep his prejudices in check.

After leaving Chartwell Road the day before, he'd gone back to the office to write up his report and to read through the door-to door statements and CCTV reports. No one had seen anything, which was hardly surprising given the weather and the fact it had been night-time. Ed Blake had been caught on CCTV on Battersea Fields Drive and outside the main entrance, and the only other sighting of him was at the junction with Daylesford Road. There was no sign anywhere of Ena Massey, or anyone even vaguely resembling her. It was bugging Kirby more and more how she'd got into Blackwater and how the killer – or killers – had got out. After several hours of learning very little, he'd gone back to the boat tired and frustrated.

'Detective Inspector, please sit down.' Patrick Calder indicated a leather chair opposite the desk at which he sat. 'Sorry I wasn't available when this tragedy unfolded. I was away with some of our investors.'

Kirby detected a subtle Welsh accent, which lent a richness to Calder's voice, and immediately envisaged him being able to talk his way into – or out of – anything. A useful skill to have for a property developer. Kirby sat down, taking in the minimalist decor and looking around for evidence of what he'd call work: files, reports, a printer – a fucking pen, even. Hamer's words sprung to mind – *be nice* – so he mustered a smile.

'It's a great view, don't you think?' said Calder, swivelling slightly in his chair to face the expanse of glass behind him. It was a clear, bright, savagely cold morning.

'Magnificent.' Kirby couldn't help but agree. They were directly opposite Blackwater, on the Chelsea side of the Thames, and Calder's office had a clear view of the asylum and its grounds. It was, without doubt, a sprawling mess by comparison to what surrounded it, although not without interest. If Kirby had an office with a view like this, he'd never get any work done. As it was, his desk was nowhere near a window, and even if it had been, all he'd probably see would be the car park and the fucking Corsa.

'Slightly spoilt by the old asylum, but that shouldn't be there for too much longer.' Calder paused. 'I don't suppose you have a high opinion of developers, do you?'

Kirby was startled by the question. 'That depends.' Across the river he could just make out the outline of the boathouse at Marsh House, through the willow trees. Further along sat Tidal Wharf, where his boat was moored, and the massive redevelopment at Nine Elms next to it.

'Indeed it does,' said Calder, turning back to face Kirby. 'There are sharks in our profession, I agree, but I like to think we do things differently here.' He smiled. He'd had his teeth whitened, which enhanced his tan and the whiteness of his shirt collar. 'It's dreadful what's happened. I hope that we'll be able to move forward with the work on-site soon, but until then I'm here to help.'

'As you know, we're investigating a murder. Does the name Ena Massey mean anything to you?' asked Kirby.

Calder sat with his legs crossed, one arm casually thrown over the arm of his expensive chair – Eames, Kirby realised with a pang of jealousy. He'd kill for an original and had little doubt he was looking at one now.

Calder had a habit of rubbing his thumb over the tip of his wedding finger, as if rolling some piece of imaginary fluff between them. 'No, I'm afraid not. Is that the name of the victim?'

'Yes.' Kirby pulled out a photograph of Ena and laid it on the desk. 'Ena Massey. She was eighty-four. Do you recognise her?'

Calder leant forward and glanced at the photograph. 'No, sorry. Who'd want to kill a sweet old lady like that?'

'That's what we're trying to find out. You've been in Scotland, I gather?'

'Correct. I flew up on Tuesday morning and back early this morning. You can check with the airline.'

Kirby already had. 'Can you think of any reason why Miss Massey might have been on the Blackwater site? She worked at the hospital before it closed – perhaps she wanted to see it before it was knocked down?'

'Absolutely none. And we certainly don't allow sightseers on to the site. As I said, I didn't know her.' Calder sat back and resumed his casual position, flicking an imaginary speck off his immaculate trousers. Kirby couldn't imagine him on a building site for a second.

'What about the name Edward Blake, do you recognise that?'

Calder stared at him blankly. 'No. Should I?'

'His phone was found at the scene and he's now missing.'

'I don't know what to say. I've never heard of either of them.'

'What about urban explorers, ever had any problems with them?'

'Ah, an arty-farty name for trespassers,' said Calder. 'There have been problems in the past, but nothing recently that I'm aware of.'

'I see. What about your neighbours at Marsh House – are they in favour of the redevelopment?' Kirby asked, changing the subject.

Calder pursed his lips slightly before smiling. 'They've made no objections, if that's what you mean. In fact, I'd say they've been very helpful.'

His voice was really quite magnetic. Kirby knew a high court judge with a similar timbre to his speech, who every time he summed up had the court eating out of the palm of his hand. 'The security firm that you use, Emeris, have you been happy with them?'

'They were suitable for a derelict property and kept costs down, but not for a development of this scale. We have a new firm taking over next week.'

'Okay, but you've had no trouble with people breaking in recently?'

Calder shook his head. 'None, to my knowledge.'

'And you would know – I mean, if someone had tried to break in, you'd be informed?'

'Of course I would. You can't seriously be suggesting that some-one working for me has done this?'

'I'm not suggesting anything, Mr Calder. Tell me, are there any other access points to the site, apart from obvious ones?'

'What do you mean?' Calder looked surprised.

'Just that. Do you know of any other means of entering the site, apart from the two main entrances – perhaps via an old service tunnel, or something like that?' Kirby watched the man's face care-fully, looking for any kind of recognition, but saw nothing.

'I don't.' Calder started rubbing his fingers again.

'What about Raymond Sweet? He must have caused you a few problems.'

Calder flashed the smile again. 'We made him an excellent offer that he chose to decline, which is his prerogative, of course. He's making a huge mistake in my opinion.'

'Your investors can't be very pleased.'

'The situation will resolve itself. They always do. I'm just not sure how easy Mr Sweet will find living on a building site for the next few years. Still, we'll do our best to accommodate him. Once the project is completed, you must come to our launch, Detective Inspector. You never know, you might fancy moving in yourself.' He chuckled.

'On my wages, doubtful.' Calder was a smooth operator; Kirby had to hand it to him. 'I'll let you know when we've finished down there,' he said, standing up, his eyes drawn to the view again. 'And then you can give your people the go-ahead.'

'Excellent,' replied Calder, and he swivelled in his chair to face the river again, his back now to Kirby. 'Give my best wishes to Idris. My secretary will see you out.' He emphasised the name Idris, the Welsh accent now unmistakeable.

Kirby stopped by the door. 'Pardon me?'

'I said, my secretary will see you out,' he said, over his shoulder. 'And to give my best wishes to DCI Hamer.'

Against his better judgement, Kirby had almost warmed to the developer, thinking that his initial impression had been wrong. But now he left with a nasty taste in his mouth; using Hamer's first name had been deliberate, so perhaps he was an arsehole in Armani after all. On his way out of Patricey's offices, he stopped to look at a scale model of the proposed new development for Blackwater. The water tower and chapel were the only two buildings left from the original asylum, the rest of it demolished and replaced by fancy apartments and landscaped gardens. The model also showed what was planned for the lower ground levels, which included a gym, cinema, casino, car park and sports facility. One area lay blank, as though earmarked for something, but with no indication of what. It was where the lake currently lay.

'Excuse me,' Kirby said to the man at reception. 'Can you tell me what's going to be built there?' He pointed to the void in the model.

The man shook his head. 'That'll be phase two of the project. It hasn't been announced yet.'

Kirby left the building wondering what plans Calder had for the lake. It seemed a shame to fill it in, if that was the intention.

His phone started ringing as he stepped on to the pavement. It was Anderson.

'We've found Simmons. And guess what?'

'What?' asked Kirby, watching a boat chug past on the Thames.

'His name crops up in one of the hospice's visitor books. The same hospice where Ena worked.'

CHAPTER 19

When Kirby got back to Mount Pleasant, Anderson was in the process of interviewing Raymond Sweet, so he had the pleasure of talking to the security guard all to himself. He still couldn't get over Calder's words: *give my best wishes to Idris*. He'd amended them when Kirby had asked him to repeat himself, but nonetheless the implication had been there. *I know your boss.*

Leroy Simmons looked worn-out and nervous. There was no rolled-up *Carpworld* magazine for him to fiddle with this time; his large hands lay flat on the table in front of him, idle. A man of his size would have no problem carrying someone like Ena, thought Kirby, as he started the interview.

'Mr Simmons, you lied to us about when you arrived for your shift. I think you'd better start from the beginning.'

The security guard sighed and rubbed his face. 'I ain't supposed to do no double shifts, but Chips is a friend an' I said I'd help him out. If Emeris found out they'd have my hide. So would Mr Calder.'

'So you're saying that Mr Monahan asked if you would do his shift on Tuesday night, as well as your own shift, which was due to begin on Wednesday morning – correct?'

'Correct.'

'And Mr Monahan is a friend?' asked Kirby.

Simmons nodded.

'Not much of a friend, I'd suggest. Because according to him, the double shift was your idea, not his. He said you were desperate for the money, and he agreed to swap shifts as a favour. What do you say to that?'

'It ain't true! I swear, as God's my witness. It was him asked me.'

Kirby noticed that Simmons wore a silver cross around his neck; he could see it, as his shirt was undone. When they'd spoken on Wednesday he'd been in uniform with a shirt and tie. 'Why would Monahan lie?'

'Look, it ain't none of my business what he gets up to in his own time, but he wanted the night off for something. I didn't ask what, and, yes, I was glad of the money.'

'Why did you disappear then? You knew that we'd talk to Raymond Sweet. Surely the sensible thing would have been to just tell us what happened?'

'I need this job. I didn't want my boss to find out, see?'

'Tell us about Ena Massey,' said Kirby, leaning back in his chair and folding his arms. 'I think that's something else that you've been lying about.'

'What you on about?' Simmons looked nervous. 'I don't know her, I told you.'

'Are you sure about that?' Kirby asked.

'Course I'm sure. Seeing her lying there with her face all beat up, I'd have still recognised her if I'd known her. But I don't. You gotta believe me.'

'The thing is, Mr Simmons, Miss Massey volunteered at a hospice – St Elizabeth's Hospice in Streatham. The same hospice that your father went to six years ago.'

Kirby watched the information register and thought of his own parents. He dreaded the day when one of them might have to be admitted to somewhere like that.

'I never seen her there, honest to God,' Simmons was saying.

117

'Really? According to the hospice, Miss Massey visited your father on several occasions before he moved into the hospice permanently. Are you saying that you didn't know?'

'No.' Simmons's hand went up to the cross round his neck. 'I swear to you, I don't know her. Truth is' – he looked down, guilt etched into his face – 'I didn't always see eye to eye with my dad, God rest his soul.'

'What are you saying?' asked Kirby.

Simmons looked up. 'I never visited him. I ain't proud of it, and I pray for his soul every day, but I never visited him when he was sick. Knew the hospice would take good care, and they did. I don't know who visited him.'

'How come your name is in the visitors' book then?'

'What?' Simmons looked genuinely surprised. 'It can't be.'

Kirby opened the file in front of him, took out the photocopied sheet and slid it over to Simmons. 'Your signature is right there.'

Simmons peered at the list and shook his head. His large hands were now clasped, fingers flexing. 'My son. That's my son's writing. Leroy Junior.' He sighed. 'I didn't think he'd go. He never told me.'

'Your son is also Leroy Simmons?'

Simmons nodded. 'He's Jason Leroy. We don't talk much. You ask me, he's signed as Leroy as a dig at me.'

Karen McBride had barely seen her mother in thirty years and had despised her, and now here was Leroy Simmons, who'd left his father to die in a hospice without ever visiting him. Kirby wondered what it was they'd fallen out over that had led to such a grievance.

'So you never once visited your father at St Elizabeth's Hospice, or came into contact with Ena Massey?'

'No. I wish I had. I'd have thanked her if I'd met her. Thanked her for doing what I should've done. God rest that poor woman's soul.' He crossed himself, the gesture oozing shame. 'Who'd want to kill a fine person like that?'

It was a very good question: who would want to kill an elderly woman who by all accounts was a saint? A sudden thought popped into Kirby's mind. 'Did your father leave a will, Mr Simmons?'

'A will? Not that I know of – why? I doubt he had anything to leave: lost most of it on the horses.'

So that was it, the sin of gambling. Not easy watching a loved one betting their livelihood away – or their pension. 'Is that what you fell out over, gambling?'

'It's a sin.' Simmons began to shake his head slowly. 'A love of money is the root of many evils. Same as drugs or drink, it pierces your soul and eats you up. He was deaf to all that, stubborn fool.'

'We'll need to contact your son to corroborate what you've just told us.'

He nodded.

'Tell me a bit more about Raymond Sweet,' said Kirby. 'Do you see much of him?'

Simmons shrugged. 'Not much. He comes to visit me once in a while. We play cards, chit chat, you know. Truth is, I appreciate the company sometimes.'

'Did you play cards with him on Tuesday night?'

Simmons nodded. 'Will you have to tell Emeris?'

Kirby ignored him. 'What time were you and Mr Sweet together?'

'Dunno, I suppose about eight 'til eleven, or thereabouts.'

'Can anyone corroborate that? You and Sweet could have killed Ena together – you both have access to the asylum. Why should we believe you?'

'I ain't done nothing!' cried Simmons. 'Please, you got to believe me. I never seen that lady before I found her laying there, honest to God.'

'When you're not playing cards, what do you and Mr Sweet talk about?' Kirby was intrigued what the two men had in common, apart from loneliness.

'This and that. I fear for him once they start knocking that place down. It's his home – his only home. He ain't got no other place to go. Tells me I'm the custodian of something very special, that I have a great responsibility to look after it. I goes along with it, makes him happy.'

'Has Mr Sweet ever mentioned Ena Massey? Perhaps he knew her when the hospital was still functioning?'

'Uh-uh. I never heard her name until I heard it on the news. And that's the truth.'

Kirby questioned him for another twenty minutes, then stepped into the corridor just as Anderson was coming out of the interview room where he was questioning Sweet.

'Anything?'

Anderson let out a long sigh. 'He says there's a ghost.'

'Oh Christ.' Ghost stories about Blackwater were ten a penny. 'What kind of ghost?'

'He's only seen it from a distance – a "dark shape", calls it "the Creeper". But get this, he says he saw it on the night of the murder, down by the lake.'

'What time was this? He didn't mention it yesterday when we spoke to him.'

'It was when he returned from the fish and chip shop. He went to the lake before going back to the lodge. He only saw it for a second and didn't think anything of it.'

'What makes him think it's a ghost and not a real person?' asked Kirby.

'He says it knows its way about, plus it's always alone. Trespassers are never alone, according to him, and for the most part they're not familiar with the grounds.'

'You think there's anything to it?'

'Honestly? Fuck knows. I believe he thinks he saw something, but whether it actually exists is open to conjecture. You've met him, he lives in his own world.'

'What did he say about Ena? Did they know each other?'

'Now this is more tangible. Yes, they did know each other. In fact, she treated him for a number of years – along with Dr Brayne, who ran the place – but he hasn't seen her since the place closed down. He gave the distinct impression that he didn't like her.'

'Why?'

Anderson shrugged. 'Said she kept putting him to sleep. When I asked him to elaborate, he said he couldn't remember and clammed up.'

'Did he know anything about the letters and rings?'

'Nope.'

He told Anderson about his conversation with Simmons.

'Bollocks. I suppose they could both be lying.'

'There's nothing from Forensics yet to connect either man to Ena, or to Keats Ward. And why would Simmons call it in if he was the perpetrator? If he'd wanted to hide a body, there are plenty of places he could have done so quite easily, where she wouldn't have been found for months. Same with Sweet.'

'We need to speak with Monahan again and find out why he wanted the night off. He could have come back.'

'I don't see how,' said Kirby, feeling frustration growing. 'I know he had the keys and the passcode to the main gate, but we'd have seen him in one of the surrounding streets by now. We know he didn't come in through the main entrance or Daylesford Road.' He paused. 'There's got to be another way in. Something we've overlooked.'

'Every inch of that perimeter's been searched,' said Anderson. 'There's no way in other than the breach on Daylesford Road, and we're pretty certain that she didn't get in there. Her clothes would have snagged if she'd been dragged through, plus there would be drag marks of some kind. There's nothing.'

He was right. Kirby had even been in touch with the Port of London Authority to see if there had been any reports of unregistered vessels on the river that night – there hadn't. The fact remained, however, that Ena Massey had been taken to Blackwater by someone, and that someone had also managed to leave. The question was, how?

'Let's go back to Marsh House,' said Kirby suddenly.

'You think Palmer is hiding something?'

He shrugged. 'I don't know, but I can't think where else to look.'

CHAPTER 20

Anderson swung the Astra into the driveway of Marsh House and pulled up by the front door. A rabbit's paw hung from the ignition keyring – not his own work – and it swung gently as the car came to a halt. It was the only thing about Anderson's Astra that Kirby liked.

'Well, Palmer's car's here at least,' said Kirby.

'Luck of the paw,' said Anderson, grabbing his keys and climbing out of the car. The rabbit's paw had an almost mythical status at MIT29; God forbid it should ever go missing – the place would go into lockdown.

While Anderson rang the bell, Kirby wandered around to the side of the house, where a gate led to a path that ran the length of the house. At the end, he could see another gate, which he presumed must lead into the garden. He tried the first gate and found it locked. There were paw prints, probably a cat's, but no sign of human activity. The murderer could have come this way before the snow on Tuesday night – that's if they had a key.

Kirby turned and looked back towards the road. The secluded driveway had one large electronic gate, which, like today, had been open the last time he was here too. He wondered if Palmer closed it at night or whether it was permanently open. The house was fitted with several security lights, but without those on, anyone on the drive would be difficult to spot from the road.

It took Palmer several minutes to answer, and he looked surprised to see them.

'This is DI Anderson,' said Kirby. 'May we come in for a bit?'

'Please . . .' He held the door open and they went in. Palmer led them into the kitchen. 'Coffee?' he asked.

Kirby recalled the coffee from his last visit as his eyes rested on the Gaggia in the corner. 'Thanks.'

Anderson shook his head. 'Gives me acid.'

'How's the investigation going?' asked Palmer, as he put coffee in the machine. 'Do you have any leads?'

'A few,' said Kirby non-committally. 'We're trying to trace a young man who we believe was in Blackwater on the night of the murder – you might have heard his name on the news, Edward Blake.'

'Yes, I did hear something. Is he a suspect?'

'He's certainly someone we'd like to talk to. I don't suppose you know him, do you?'

Palmer shook his head. 'No, sorry.'

Kirby watched as Palmer wiped an espresso cup with a tea towel and placed it on the tray of the Gaggia. 'We identified the victim as a woman called Ena Massey – she used to work at Blackwater. Does that name ring any bells?'

'None.' Palmer had his back to them and pressed a button on the machine, which sprung to life with a shudder. 'Who was she?'

'A nurse. She worked there for thirty-odd years,' said Anderson.

'Is there a connection?' Palmer set a saucer down on the kitchen top and switched off the machine, still with his back to them both, busying himself with the coffee.

'That's what we're trying to find out,' said Anderson.

Kirby wandered over to a door to his right. A circular glass window was set into the wall next to it. It was purely decorative, and he could see the wall outside through the mottled glass. 'This door must lead to the passage that runs down the length of the house, down to the garden, mustn't it?' he asked.

'I can show you if you like,' said Palmer. 'There's a gate into the garden. It's always locked, if that's what you're thinking. And I double-checked the locks after your last visit.' He handed Kirby the coffee.

It was every bit as good as it had been the last time, and he downed it in one, handing the cup back to Palmer. 'Thanks. You certainly know how to make good coffee.'

Palmer smiled. 'Pleasure.' He retrieved a bunch of keys from one of the kitchen drawers and unlocked the side entrance. 'I rarely use this door. If I want to go into the garden I use the French windows in the drawing room – the ones we used the last time.' He stepped outside and led the two detectives down the narrow path, to a gate at the end and the garden beyond.

'Is the key to both gates on that keyring?' Anderson asked, as they followed Palmer down the narrow pathway.

'Yes.'

'Do you know if anyone else has copies?'

'I actually have no idea. There might have been a gardener at some stage, but whether they had a key, who knows? Why are you so interested?' he asked, as they approached the heavy-looking ironwork.

'We're still having difficulty in working out how whoever did this – the murder next door, I mean – got into the site. We just need to be sure we've looked at every possibility,' said Kirby.

'I see.' Palmer began unlocking the gate. It was set into a tall brick wall, which had security spikes running along the top. The image of Ena Massey trying to negotiate that was almost comical.

The gate itself was locked with one large padlock, and Palmer swung it open for them to go through.

'Do you have the keys to the boathouse on there?'

'I guess so. I'm not sure, to be honest. As I said, the boathouse isn't very safe, or at least that's what I've been told.'

'Do you mind if we take a look?'

Palmer hesitated for a second, glancing from one detective to the other.

'It won't take us long and then we'll leave you in peace. We don't want to discover a speedboat and a length of climbing rope in there in six months' time. It would be embarrassing, to say the least.'

'Point taken,' said Palmer. 'This way then.' He began walking across the snow-covered lawn towards the maze.

'There was something I wanted to ask you,' Kirby said, as he and Anderson caught up with him. 'Does the name Raymond Sweet mean anything to you?'

Palmer slowed down. 'No, I don't think so, why?'

'He was a patient at Blackwater and lives in the Old Lodge on the far side of the asylum's grounds. He won squatter's rights.'

'What, you mean he actually lives in the asylum's grounds?' Palmer looked surprised.

'That's right,' said Kirby. 'He's lived there on and off since the place closed. I'm surprised you haven't come across him. You could say that he's your neighbour.'

'I see,' said Palmer as they approached the boathouse, sorting through the keys looking for the right one.

Kirby's footprints from his previous visit were now invisible under a fresh layer of snow. It didn't look as though anyone had been there since then.

While Palmer began fiddling with the lock, trying various keys, Kirby and Anderson stared out over the Thames, through a gap in the trees, towards Chelsea. It was gone five, and the sun was setting in a clear, orange-streaked sky. It was going to be another cold night – the Met Office's promise of warmer weather unfulfilled. Calder's office was just out of view from where they were standing, but Kirby imagined him sitting in his soulless glass cube, looking out over Blackwater, eyeing up the next piece of land to snap up. A Marine Policing Unit Targa sped past heading downriver, leaving deep ripples in its wake, and Anderson waved.

'Beautiful, isn't it?' said Palmer. 'Even in winter.'

'Did you grow up here?' asked Anderson. Palmer had so far volunteered nothing about his private life, or the circumstances of his inheritance.

'Ah!' said Palmer, pushing the door to the boathouse open. He either hadn't heard the question or had chosen not to answer. 'Hang on, let's see if the light still works.' He stepped inside, and after a few seconds the small building lit up.

The interior of the boathouse was as Kirby had expected – rectangular, half-timbered, and with a dock that a boat could safely pull into from the river. The only difference was that the docking area had been completely covered over, so the building no longer functioned as a working boathouse, although there looked to be some kind of hatch in the floor towards the river end of the building. 'Does this open straight on to the water?' asked Anderson, pointing to the hatch.

'I don't know. I suppose it must,' said Palmer.

The river frontage itself was one large double door, which would have opened out on to the Thames but was now secured by heavy-duty bolts and padlocks. Garden tools and machinery were piled up around the walls, which themselves were covered in shelves and old canvases. An ancient-looking kayak hung from the ceiling. There was a smell that Kirby couldn't quite identify, sweet and slightly acrid. It was probably a mix of old fertiliser, varnish and paint, as he noticed several ancient-looking pots of Dulux and Ronseal dotted around the building. It certainly didn't look unsafe.

'It doesn't look as though anyone's been in here for years,' Kirby said to Palmer. 'But the lock is new – was that you?'

'No. It was here when I arrived.'

They took a last look around the small interior. It would be a great place to hide, but no one had stolen a boat from here and floated a few yards up the Thames, then climbed into Blackwater, that was for sure. The kayak didn't look seaworthy and had enough cobwebs on it to indicate that it hadn't been moved in some time.

They went back outside, Palmer turning the light off and locking up after them. 'You know, I've been thinking,' he said, as they began strolling back to the house. 'Surely the easiest way to get into next door would be to bribe the security guard. Or this man Sweet.'

Neither Kirby nor Anderson said anything.

Palmer went on. 'After all, people do get in, like drug dealers and vandals. Someone got in and set fire to one of the old ward blocks once, or at least that's what I've been told.'

Palmer was correct, and Kirby wondered who it was who'd told him. Over the years the place had been vandalised, and there had been several cases of arson, so people did find a way in. However, most weren't elderly ex-employees.

They were walking back up the garden when Kirby remembered the short, stumpy tower that he'd seen on his previous visit.

'Yes, it's a folly,' said Palmer, when Kirby mentioned it. 'We can go past it if you like.'

'You'd like to see the folly, wouldn't you?' Kirby asked Anderson.

As they walked, Anderson asked again if Palmer had grown up here.

'My upbringing was complicated, shall we say. But no, I didn't grow up here.'

'Perth, then?' Kirby ventured.

Palmer gave a curt nod. They'd now reached the folly and stopped in front of it. It was as Kirby remembered it from Wednesday – a squat tower, no more than eight feet high, octagonal in shape and topped off with a copper roof. An ornate iron gate was set into one of the walls. Wisteria had grown around the entire structure, the twisted stems now leafless, forming a basket-like cocoon for the strange building.

'Is it used for anything?' asked Anderson.

Palmer shrugged. 'It's empty apart from an old chair. Magical on a hot summer's day, I imagine.'

Kirby turned around and looked towards the river. It would be a very peaceful place to sit, with a view of the garden towards the Thames.

'Shall we go back?' said Palmer. 'Only I'm not really dressed for the outdoors.'

They walked back to the house, Palmer this time letting them in via the French doors.

'Thanks for your help,' said Kirby, once they were inside. 'And sorry you got so cold and wet.' He looked around as they made their way through to the hall and the front door, his eyes resting on a pile of post on a table by the door. 'I'm curious, but who lived here before you inherited?'

'My mother,' said Palmer. 'We weren't close,' he added quickly.

Close enough to leave you the house though, Kirby thought. He saw Anderson eyeballing the pile of post. 'One more thing,' said Kirby. 'The main gate, is it always kept open?'

'Yes. Or rather, it is at the moment.' Palmer opened the front door, suddenly appearing to want them out. 'It's operated by a remote, which I can't seem to find. It could be anywhere.'

'Do you remember when you lost the remote?' Kirby lingered on the threshold.

'I don't know, last week?' Palmer sounded irritated. 'I can't be specific.'

'I see. Well, thanks for your time,' said Kirby.

'And, our condolences,' added Anderson.

There was a second's hesitation before Palmer nodded an acknowledgement. 'Goodbye, detectives.' He turned and closed the door without giving either of them a chance to say anything else.

'He's hiding something,' said Anderson, once they were in the Astra.

'It was to do with his mother.'

'The post was addressed to a Mrs Helen Linehan. To be fair, he did say they weren't close.'

Anderson started the engine, and Kirby thought about Palmer, alone in the silent, beautiful house, packing up his mother's possessions. Who would clear Ena Massey's house – Karen? He couldn't picture that happening for a second. Though from what he'd seen, Ena's possessions, by comparison, were meagre. He felt a stab of sadness as he remembered his grandmother's house in Italy after she passed away. She'd died fairly young – sixty, or thereabouts – and the house had felt like an empty shell without her.

'What do you think?' asked Anderson, as he drove them back to Mount Pleasant.

'I can't believe we're three days in and still no nearer to finding out how the hell Ena's body got into Blackwater. I might need to pay Connie Darke another visit – someone has to know another way into that place.'

'An urban explorer's hardly going to give up trade secrets though, is she?'

'She might if – shit!' said Kirby. 'Stop the car.' A young man who looked like Ed Blake had just emerged from a bookie on the other side of the road and was lighting a cigarette outside.

'What is it?' Anderson veered into a bus lane and slammed on the brakes, prompting a cacophony of horns. A courier cycled past and banged on the bonnet, shouting 'You fucking cunt' as he went.

Kirby was already halfway out of the car. 'It's Blake, outside the bookie.' He ran around the car and impatiently waited for a lorry to pass before sprinting over the road. Blake had now been joined by another man and had his back to Kirby. The two men were huddled together, cigarette smoke mingling with breath as they talked. As he approached, he caught the other man's eye and saw him say something to Blake, who stubbed out his cigarette and headed back inside. The man he'd been talking to grabbed Kirby's arm as he walked past.

'Got the time, mate?' he asked.

Kirby shook him off and entered the bookmaker's. Three middle-aged men stood apart, mesmerised by a big screen mounted in the top, far corner. Fuck only knew what they were watching, but it certainly wasn't racing from anywhere in the UK.

Before he had time to say anything, a woman behind the counter with a perm worthy of an eighties porn star pointed a taloned finger towards the door to the fire exit and simply said, 'Khazi.'

Through the door, Kirby found himself in a dimly lit corridor. The fire exit was at the end, padlocked; the gents to his left. He pushed open the bathroom door and went in. 'Blake? Police. Just need a few words with you.' There were two urinals and one stall, its door shut. He tested it; it was locked from the inside. Crouching down, he looked under the gap and saw two trainer-clad feet, the heel of one bobbing up and down – nerves or drugs. He stood up. 'I'm not going anywhere until you come out.'

'Whaddya want?' shouted an unsteady voice.

'I want to talk to you about Tuesday night. I know that you went to Blackwater and I know that you lost your phone. I need to ask you a few questions. Please, come out now.' After a few moments he heard movement inside the stall and the bolt being drawn. He stepped back, blocking the exit in case Blake tried to make a run for it, but he needn't have bothered.

'Fuck,' said Kirby, as the man stepped out.

'Fuck,' said the man, grinning, off his face on something or other.

He heard Anderson outside in the corridor. 'In here!' he shouted, just as his phone started ringing in his pocket.

Anderson came in, filling what little space there was left in the room, and saw the man. 'Fuck.'

The man shrugged, looking from one to the other.

Kirby answered the phone, keeping his eyes on the man he'd mistaken for Blake. 'You're kidding,' he said, glancing at Anderson, mouthing Kobrak's name. 'Yeah, sure. Thanks.' He hung up and pocketed the phone. 'It's your lucky day,' he said to the man he'd mistaken for Blake. 'Now fuck off.'

Once they were alone Kirby recounted what Kobrak had told him. 'Cause of death was a fractured skull – no surprises there – but Ena Massey was also full of drugs.'

'So she'd been sedated first – with what, Rohypnol, something like that?'

'You're never going to guess this one: phenobarbital and methaqualone.'

'You mean Quaaludes?'

Kirby nodded. 'Yup. Disco biscuits.'

CHAPTER 21

Raymond's initial feeling of relief on hearing that Ena Massey was dead was now morphing into something else. Fragments of memory had been pushing their way forward since watching the video the night before, things Raymond would rather forget. And then this morning, at the station, the police had started asking questions about her. He didn't want to think about her, let alone talk about her. Even dead, Ena was proving a pain in the arse.

Raymond was down by the lake, its frozen surface covered in a smooth, white layer of snow. It looked so tempting, just to set foot on it, feel his feet sink into the soft, slightly squeaky flakes. He couldn't risk it, stepping on to the ice. It might crack, give way, and then he'd be sucked under. Sucked under the lake, down to . . . well, *down there*. No – there was a quicker, not to mention dryer, way to get *down there*.

The place he was aiming for was a bit like an old pillbox. The concrete structure had been covered in green moss for as long as he could remember and blended perfectly into its surroundings; over twenty years on, it was now completely obscured by ivy and bramble. It was located between the lake and Keats Ward, and as he went past the old ward block, he found himself pausing to look up at the window. Unlike the rest of the hospital, this was the one part that he'd happily see razed to the ground. He thought of it as an infected wound that wouldn't heal, yet despite that an invisible thread held him there, once in a while gently tugging, as if to say, *Come in, come upstairs.* A sudden image came into his head of Ena standing over a bed, a strange look on her face, and then it was gone as swiftly as it had arrived. Goosebumps broke out over his body, and he hurried on, startled by the intensity of the sensation.

The pillbox was located in a particularly overgrown patch that had once been a small vegetable garden. Japanese knotweed had long since taken over, and he had to carve a passage through to reach the entrance. Snow fell off the foliage like icing sugar, and he felt it cold on his neck. He hadn't been there in over a week; first Calder had been parading about with his site manager – Catapult, or whatever his name was – and then Ena's body had been found, and everything had been thrown into confusion. As he emerged from the tangle of branches in front of the pillbox, a helicopter flew overhead, momentarily disturbing the silence, and he remained still until it passed. Very little snow had penetrated this area, instead forming a canopy on the tangled vegetation, and what little light there was shone through like it was frosted glass.

He pulled out a small wind-up torch that he always carried with him and stepped inside. He played his torch over the small interior. Icicles hung from the ceiling, and one of Harry's – the old groundsman – pitchforks stood in the corner, caught in a web of ivy that held it like a skeleton clutching the bones of its decayed child. The familiar graffiti, *NYCHO*, sparkled in the torch beam, and beneath that the round face, its mouth forming an 'o' with *shhh!* coming out of it. Except something was wrong. He moved closer. Where had the *shhh!* gone? All that was left was a smear, which had taken half the mouth with it too. A fox, perhaps? Raymond patted his pockets, eventually finding a nub of chalk with which he quickly reinstated the missing part of the mouth and the all-important *shhh!* Satisfied that order was restored, he knelt down and flipped a two-inch block of wood from its niche in the floor, revealing a latch, into which he hooked his finger. Once he'd lifted the trapdoor a few inches, he was able to open it enough to swing his legs into the hatch and find the steps with his feet. With the torch between his teeth he lowered himself down, carefully closing the trapdoor behind him.

When he reached the bottom of the steps the familiar smell of damp tickled his nostrils, and he stifled a sneeze. He stood in the small tunnel and shone his torch towards an old, rusted metal door at the end, and made his way towards it. The only sound was the odd drip. He was a little worried about that – he'd yet to find the source – but he wasn't in any imminent danger, he was sure. When he reached the door he pushed it open it and shone his torch inside. It was pointless really; the darkness beyond was unlike anything he'd experienced until he'd come down here. The torch beam sliced through the dark for a few feet, then gave up, as if swallowed by the blackness. It was so dark that he could almost feel it caressing his hand, as he fumbled about to his left for the old Bakelite light switch.

The space ahead lit up, and he blinked a few times to adjust to the light, which illuminated the circular room in front of him – or, as he called it, the bone jar. Strings of small lights hung around the periphery, tacked on to shelves and hooks – anything he'd been able to find – and the effect reminded him of a galaxy. He had no idea where the electricity supply came from, or who paid the bills, but for some reason it had never been disconnected when the rest of Blackwater had.

He padded his way over to a cupboard that ran the entire circumference of the room, apart from where the two entrances interrupted it. The cupboard was divided into four segments, each quarter accessed by a series of sliding panels, and he carefully slid one open and looked inside.

His collection.

When he'd first found them, Raymond hadn't been sure what he was looking at – copper canisters of some kind, some over a century old, with names on them – and it was only after rootling about a bit more that he'd come across an old ledger and realised what they were: the unclaimed ashes of past Blackwater patients. That was how he'd come to call the room the bone jar. If he was going to be pedantic about it – another one of Mrs Muir's phrases – the canisters were the bone jars, but somehow the name had stuck for the hidden, subterranean, circular room. *I'm off to the bone jar*, he'd mumble, before leaving the Old Lodge.

Most of the ashes contained in the canisters went further back than Raymond could comprehend – anything before the year 1927, when Jaffa Cakes and the telly had been invented, was beyond his imagination. These were even older, going back to a number he didn't even recognise, which began with 18. There was one canister, however, which was more recent – 1968 – and which Raymond treasured above the others. It held the ashes of Gregory Boothe, perhaps the best friend he'd ever had at Blackwater, or maybe ever – not that he would admit that to Mrs Muir, who as far as she was concerned held pole position. He'd drawn his first smiley face on the day Gregory died, the scream inside his head so loud that he was afraid to open his mouth in case he broke a window. Not that that first little face he'd drawn on the inside of the toilet door – the only place Ena wouldn't find him – was smiling. It still haunted him that his friend's ashes had been left in the bone jar for thirty years before he'd come along and found them. It was then that he'd made his pledge; these unclaimed souls – fifty-two in total – were now his responsibility and would never be forgotten again.

Since the discovery of the canisters, his visits to the bone jar had become a regular part of his routine, and he enjoyed going there. He'd polish the canisters, dust the shelves and have a little natter with them. Along with Gregory, they now all felt like old friends, and he thought fondly of his mother back at the Lodge. He savoured his visits here, but with work on the redevelopment imminent he'd begun to worry. His forays to the bone jar to protect these forgotten people were going to become more difficult, if not downright impossible, so he'd decided to take action.

He began going through the canisters, trying to decide who would be the first evacuees – Gregory, obviously, getting first dibs. He'd arranged them in the cabinet in alphabetical order and thought that, for ease, he should probably begin removing them in the same order – then he'd know where he was. He picked up Roy Gallows, turning the canister round in his hands. He'd made up stories for some of the names – background, employment, what they ate for supper – and he'd resisted the urge to give Mr Gallows the job of hangman. Instead Raymond liked to think he'd been a clown, or a horse trainer – something a little more, well, sociable.

He put Gallows back and decided he'd better get cracking when he noticed that Gregory Boothe was next to Alardice. That was odd; he must have moved Barnes just now without realising.

Get a move on, Raymond, he could hear his mother's voice saying. 'Yes, Mother,' he mumbled as he slipped Alardice into one pocket and Barnes into the other. Picking up Gregory, he slid the cabinet door closed and stood up.

He switched off the galaxy lights and made his way back along the tunnel. As he emerged into the light and sat panting on the floor of the pillbox, he thought about the canisters. He must have imagined it, but like a few other things recently at the lodge, he could have sworn that they'd been moved.

CHAPTER 22

When Connie reached the Optic Bar at six-fifteen the place was heaving, and it took her a while to spot Mole slouched in a corner, nose buried in a book. He'd called to say he was back from Poland earlier that afternoon, and they'd arranged to meet that evening.

The small cellar bar was steamy and warm, filled with people finishing work for the weekend and the odd tourist who had wandered in. She pushed her way through the drinkers towards Mole, who looked up and smiled when he saw her coming.

Mole was tall and well-built and wore his dark hair shoulder-length, swept back off his face, his brown eyes radiating mischief. Tonight he was wearing a black long-sleeved T-shirt and faded black jeans, and an old sheepskin coat was slung over the back of his chair.

'You got a seat,' said Connie, when she reached the table. 'Well done.'

'Come here,' he said, standing up and giving her a big hug. 'You okay?' he asked, studying her at arm's length.

'Yeah, but boy am I glad to see you.' It suddenly felt as though the past few days had crept up on her. She'd had no one to talk to, apart from her evening with Harry, and seeing Mole she felt a bit overwhelmed.

'Come on, neck a couple of these, and you'll feel better,' said Mole. They sat down, and he poured two glasses of wine from a bottle on the table. 'You look tired.' He slid a glass towards her as she took off her coat.

'Thanks a bunch,' said Connie, taking a good long slug of wine. 'You're right though, I'm knackered.'

'You still look great, knackered or not.'

'Charmer.' They clinked glasses, and she began to feel slightly better, the wine hitting her system like a speeding train. 'So, how was Poland?' she asked.

'Oh, you know, just a bit awesome. Droog and Claus sorted some really amazing explores. Wish you'd been able to come, you'd have loved it.'

'Don't,' said Connie, thinking about her trip to Oxford and how dull it had been.

'Anyhow, Poland can wait – what's all this shit about Ed? It sounds serious.'

'It is.' Leaning forward so that their heads almost touched, Connie told Mole exactly what had happened, from her last conversation with Ed on Tuesday, to her visit from Kirby and her evening at Harry's when she'd found the clipping.

Mole sat staring at his glass for a few moments after she'd finished. 'I made a few calls before I came out,' he said. 'You're right, no one's seen or heard from him in three days, and I mean *no one*.'

'*Shit*,' said Connie under her breath.

'A couple of people have even had calls from the police.'

Kirby had obviously been doing his homework, and she guessed that before long she'd be getting another call.

'What about this dead woman, the nurse?' Mole went on. 'If what Harry told you is true, and Ed had started doing some oral history, he might have tracked her down. He had her name from the clipping you mentioned.'

She shook her head. 'No. At least that's what Harry said, and he seemed quite sure. Apparently they used to call her Nurse Ratched, like in *One Flew Over the Cuckoo's Nest*.'

'Fucking hell, really? We don't know Ed didn't meet her though – I'm sure he doesn't tell Harry everything. Great name though – wonder what she did to deserve that?' He chuckled.

'Even if Ed had interviewed her, what on earth could that have to do with her being killed? Whatever she did at Blackwater was, like, decades ago.'

'Yeah, true.' Mole went quiet, staring gloomily into his wine. 'Actually, there's something I need to tell you.'

'What?' asked Connie, who'd wandered off into her own little world.

'It was meant to be a surprise. I swore I wouldn't say anything but . . .' He took another slug of wine before continuing. 'Ed had found out who your sister was with when she had the accident. He had a name for you.'

'*What?* For a moment, she wondered if she'd heard him correctly, and almost asked him to repeat it. She'd long given up any hope of finding out who Sarah had been with that fateful day, because, despite the best efforts of the police – never mind Ed and Mole, who'd used all their urbex contacts to try to find out – it was like the person had never existed.

'It was going to be a surprise on Tuesday, being the anniversary and everything,' said Mole, quietly.

'Did he say who it was, how he found out?'

'No, he didn't tell me who, and I don't know how he found out. He called just as I was getting on the plane, and some dickhead was in my seat. I was zoning in and out of the chat.'

'You don't think it's connected to him disappearing, do you?'

Mole shook his head. 'I don't see how. Your sister's death was an accident. This is all to do with this old nurse.'

She suddenly remembered something Harry had said. 'Hang on, when did you go to Poland?'

'Sunday afternoon. Why?'

'There was a name and address at Harry's, on a Post-it. Ed had underlined the word *Sarah* beneath, and Harry said he went to see someone on Sunday afternoon. Maybe that was them.'

'Cons, don't get too excited. That could have been anyone. Really.'

'Hmm, maybe.'

Mole smiled. 'Sorry. I'm just trying to be realistic.'

'I know, and you're right.' She smiled back. 'How about we kill this bottle,' she said, topping up their wine. She didn't care what Mole had just said. The name and address had been clear, and whoever it was *was* connected to Sarah, she was now sure.

'Deal. Cheers,' he said, and they clinked glasses again. 'And Rats, wherever the fuck you are mate, give us a sign.'

They chatted about Poland and some new places that they planned to explore, but all she could think about was that Ed had found out who Sarah was with when she had the accident. After a while, fatigue kicked in.

'I'm done,' she said, draining the last of her wine. 'D'you mind if we go?'

'Lightweight,' said Mole, smiling. They put their coats on and began making their way out of the bar towards the stairs that led up to ground level. The crowd had thinned out now, but it was still a cramped space, with piles of bags and big winter coats to negotiate.

'That's better,' said Connie, once they were outside. The air was soberingly cold, and an icy wind was blowing. She pulled up her coat collar, her breath trailing out into the darkness.

'It was warmer in bloody Poland,' said Mole, as they walked to the Tube.

'Have you even been to Marsh House?' asked Connie, suddenly remembering her appointment on Monday.

'The place next to Blackwater? Went up the drive once for a nose.'

'The woman who lived there died and left us some plans. I'm going on Monday to collect them.'

'Apparently that outfit who've bought the asylum are desperate to get their hands on it,' said Mole.

'Who told you that?'

'Ed did, ages ago.'

'Jesus,' mumbled Connie.

'It's gotta be listed, but the land alone has to be worth a packet.'

'Maybe it'll get sold off now,' she said.

They'd reached the Tube station and stopped by the steps. Their breath mingled in the air between them.

'So, this is where we say goodnight then,' said Mole.

'I'll call you.' She pulled her coat tighter. 'And thanks for tonight. I'm glad you're back.'

'Me too.' He wrapped his arms around her and gave her a tight hug. 'Keep me posted. And if you need company, you know where I am.' Then he kissed her on the forehead and was gone.

She headed down the steps to the Tube, gusts of warm air enveloping her as she rode the escalator. As the train hurtled along, she stared out of the window trying to see past the reflections into the tunnel beyond. She remembered the thrill of her first foray into the Underground system as an explorer, of standing in a parallel tunnel as a train sped by, its passengers unaware that they were being watched. It was like seeing a snapshot of people's lives, and gone in a second.

As usual, it felt several degrees colder at the Four Sails than it had in central London. Terror wrapped himself around her ankles as she unlocked the door.

'What're you doing out here, big boy?' she asked, letting them both in. He was mewing as though he'd never been fed, and he followed her through the bar and into the kitchen. The Four Sails had been a small pub – quaint even – with a small front bar and an even smaller snug at the back.

She grabbed a tin of cat food and began opening it without taking off her coat, wondering why the heating hadn't kicked in – the place was like a fridge. While Terror tucked into his Whiskas Finest, she went over to the boiler and looked at the timer, frowning. She could have sworn she'd set the heating to come on for an hour tonight, but it was firmly in the 'Off' position. Just as she turned it on, hearing the familiar *whoomf* as the ignition kicked in, her phone started ringing.

'Yes?' she answered, going over to the cat flap as she spoke.

'It's DI Kirby. I'm sorry to call so late.'

'What is it? What's happened?' She stopped by the door, dreading bad news.

'Sorry, no news. That's not why I'm calling.'

'Oh . . .' Relief and disappointment flooded through her simultaneously. She nudged the cat flap with her toe.

'I was wondering if we could meet tomorrow. There are a few things I'd like to discuss with you.'

'Um, yes. Of course.' The cat flap didn't budge, and she bent down for a closer look. The damn thing was locked.

'Are you okay, Miss Darke?'

'Yes, sorry. Just fiddling with the cat flap. Carry on.'

'Perhaps we could meet at 11 a.m. at Blackwater? Main entrance?'

'Fine. Can I ask what it's about?'

'It'll keep until tomorrow. See you then.'

'But—' She was too late; he'd already hung up. Sighing, she turned her attention back to the cat flap. It was one that operated

143

with a magnetic collar that you could lock four ways, and somehow it had been locked so Terror couldn't get in – or out. She adjusted the lock so he could come and go freely, and stood up.

'Sorry, little man, dunno what happened there.'

Terror followed her around the pub as she checked all the windows as well as the front and back doors, something gnawing away in the back of her mind. Then she made sure the heating was set to come on again in the morning and climbed into bed, Terror shadowing her every move. Lying in the dark, the only sound Terror's gentle purring, her mind once again went back to what Mole had told her earlier. *He had a name for you.* She thought about the Post-it note on Ed's desk, with a name and address written on it and her sister's name beneath. It had to be the person who was with Sarah when she had the accident, didn't it?

She eventually drifted off to sleep, waking every now and then, feeling Terror's small body curled up next to her. It would only be when she woke early the next morning that she'd remember what had been bothering her the night before as she locked up. When she'd left for work yesterday, Terror had been indoors, she was positive. In which case, how had he got out if the cat flap was locked?

CHAPTER 23

Quaalude, the trade name for methaqualone, was known as Mandrax in the UK. By the mid-1980s, Quaaludes – or disco biscuits as they became known – had been listed as a Class B drug in the UK, making it illegal to manufacture or sell. Why the hell would Ena Massey, an eighty-four-year-old woman, be full of them?

Kirby put the pathology report down and rubbed his eyes. They felt as though someone had thrown a barrel-load of grit into them. He longed to be back on the boat, stretched out listening to some music. Instead he was at Mount Pleasant, where the heating was on overtime – pumping it out to a sub-tropical level – stripped down to his T-shirt and jeans. What he wouldn't give for an ice-cold beer right now. At least it was quiet, most people having called it a night – Kobrak was still floating about somewhere, and Anderson had gone off to meet a snitch about the Quaaludes.

Kirby gathered up the report, as well as the letters found at Ena Massey's, and started getting ready to leave. He was glad he'd been able to arrange to meet Connie the following morning. He wanted to pick her brains about Blackwater and anything she could tell him about the history of Keats Ward. Everyone Kobrak had managed to dig up only ever remembered the room Ena was found in as a television room – or rather, that's all they'd admit to remembering – and that had been short-lived, the ward block itself falling out of use in 1980.

He was about to put his coat on when Hamer stuck his head around the door.

'Lew,' he said. 'Step inside for a moment.'

He hadn't realised his boss was still there and he sighed, taking off a layer before going into Hamer's office and sitting down. A small desk fan whirred in the corner.

'Drink?' Hamer asked. He looked tired.

'Not unless you've got some cold beer and an iced glass.'

'I've called maintenance three times now about the bloody heating. Same every year,' said Hamer, pouring himself a generous measure of malt. 'Sure I can't tempt you?'

Kirby shook his head. If there was one thing he hated, it was malt whisky. He was convinced Hamer only offered it to him because he knew Kirby would say no. It was expensive stuff.

'The Blackwater case,' Hamer said, dropping into his chair. 'It doesn't feel like we're getting anywhere. I'm seeing the commissioner in the morning, and I'd like to have something to tell him.'

'You saw the pathologist's report, I take it? The victim was full of Quaaludes.' Kirby wondered what this was really about.

'They can't be easy to get hold of.'

'Pete's out asking around, but it's an odd choice, which I think could be important.'

'You mean the drug is significant, like leaving the body at Blackwater?' asked Hamer, taking a sip of whisky.

'Yes. I mean why not Rohypnol or GHB, something easily available? And why go to the trouble of leaving the body at Blackwater when it would have been easier to dump her somewhere else? Moreover, somewhere that she wouldn't be found.'

Hamer looked thoughtful for a while. 'What about this money the daughter mentioned? Any sign of it? At least that would give us motive, and God knows we need something.'

'Nothing. Her bank account looks normal and there was no paperwork at her home. Her daughter's alibi checks out, by the way. Jaycee Morgan, who runs the Welcome Inn, corroborated her story – Karen McBride was there until closing time and went straight home in a taxi to feed a litter of puppies. She ordered a takeaway and didn't go out again until the next day. She's got a security camera outside her house.'

Hamer frowned. 'Why?'

'Puppies. They're valuable cargo. Grand a pop.'

'What about her son?'

'Douglas? Worked the night shift at the twenty-four-hour Asda. Plenty of witnesses, not to mention store cameras.'

'Damn,' said Hamer, swirling the last of his whisky around the glass before knocking it back in one. 'This missing teacher worries me. I think we have to assume that his disappearance is somehow connected to all this. If he'd gone on a bender he'd have surfaced by now, surely?'

'Agreed. And from what we know about him, a bender of that magnitude *and* on a weekday would be very out of character.'

Hamer stood up and switched off the fan. 'We really don't want a second body, Lew. It wouldn't be good for anyone.'

Not least Ed Blake, thought Kirby. Or Patrick Calder. 'No,' he said, standing up. 'Oh, and we spoke to Mr Monahan again too, the security guard who Leroy Simmons said asked him to cover his shift on the Tuesday night. Seems Monahan has a poker problem, so no wonder he didn't tell Leroy why he wanted the night off. Simmons would never have agreed if he'd known.'

Kirby and Hamer left the small office and walked into the open-plan area where everyone else worked, and Kirby went over to his desk to get his coat. 'By the way, you know that I saw Patrick Calder this morning? He sends his best wishes.' He looked over to Hamer, who was standing by the door, his face suddenly tense.

'Really?' was all he managed.

'Yes,' said Kirby, gathering his stuff. 'I didn't know that you knew each other.'

'We barely do,' said Hamer, as they waited for the lift to clunk its way up from the ground floor. 'We met at some fundraiser, as you do. Patrick's the kind of man who crops up everywhere.'

When the lift arrived, they got in and headed towards the ground floor in silence, then said goodnight. Hamer left by the main exit, and Kirby stood for a moment wondering what had just happened. He had no reason to doubt that Hamer had only met Calder once or twice; it was just odd that he hadn't mentioned it until now. But first-name terms? It might have just been Calder's way of warning Kirby not to fuck with him, but judging by his boss's reaction just now, and his casual use of Calder's Christian name, Kirby felt there was more to it than that.

He took the back exit into the car park – fuck it was cold, especially after coming out of the sauna-like office – and drove back to the boat, lost in thought. He couldn't think of a reason why Calder would shit on his own doorstep, so to speak. Perhaps he felt he could oil the wheels of the investigation to turn that much faster if he name-dropped Hamer. As far as Kirby knew, Hamer was straight-up.

He passed the railway arch where he kept the Citroën SM. He might drive it over to his mother's in the morning. He'd go early – unannounced – and try to get to the bottom of whatever it was that was going on with her.

He pulled up at the mooring and resisted the temptation to leave the Corsa unlocked in the hope that someone might steal it. As he made his way to the boat, his eyes were drawn to Isabel's barge, and he pictured her inside, warm and beautiful. Reluctantly, and with some effort, he resisted the urge to sprint over, instead jumping down on to his own boat.

Inside, he cracked a beer and heated up some soup, thinking about Ena. What had she done to provoke this kind of attack, and why now? He wondered whether it could be a message or a warning – but if so, to whom? Her mobile phone was still missing, but her phone records did show that she had spoken to someone on the afternoon that she went missing. She'd been called on an unidentifiable pay-as-you-go phone and then presumably – for whatever reason – turned her own phone off, as there was no trace of her at all after that.

Kirby sat in the small kitchen area and ate the soup, copies of the letters found in Ena's flat spread out in front of him. Letters from anxious relatives to their loved ones in hospital – nothing unusual, just signs that life was going on as normal in the outside world to which the recipient would hopefully one day return.

We had Granddad and Grandma over yesterday. They were asking about your health and we told them you'd be home soon . . . Little Patty misses you and can't wait to have his mam home. Hang in there, we'll all be together soon . . . The tomatoes are doing well with all this sun. Hope they let you sit outside and enjoy this weather . . . The doctors and nurses tell us that you're doing well. Rex and Margie send their love . . .

Where were these people now? Kirby wondered; had their loved ones left Blackwater better than when they'd gone in? Had Ena treated them well? He hoped so, although Karen McBride's words echoed in his head: *Christ knows how she became a nurse, but she did.* It could just have been festering bitterness talking – after all,

Karen left home as soon as she could, with no love lost on either side by the sounds of things. And then there was Poppy Valance's comment, that Ena hadn't liked her, or her brother – in fact hadn't liked 'any of me'. What did she mean, 'any of me'? That Ena didn't like children? She certainly hadn't had much time for her own – that was clear. And then there were the rings. Kirby had been reliably informed that they were wedding rings, and in some cases, expensive ones. What was Ena doing with wedding rings?

He listened to the comforting sound of wood spitting in the burner, with a nagging feeling that there was much more to Ena Massey than what they had so far managed to find out. What if she'd never delivered the letters to her patients at Blackwater? What if she'd kept them – reading them herself? Why she would do such a thing he couldn't understand, but it was a possibility. And the rings – had they been left to her by grateful patients, and, if so, how did their relatives feel about it? The rings were almost impossible to trace, and none were engraved. It even crossed his mind that she might have stolen them.

The feeling in his gut was that this case was somehow rooted in the past. Women of Ena's age were regularly targeted victims of crime, but most often it was fraud, or cybercrime, and usually because of their age. Whoever had killed Ena had done so because of *who she was*. She may have been physically vulnerable, but that didn't mean she was all sweetness and light. They needed to dig into her past and find out what she was really like and what she'd done – and, more importantly, to whom.

CHAPTER 24

After falling asleep on the sofa and crawling into bed at 3 a.m., Kirby woke with a start at 6 a.m. He'd dreamt about Blackwater. He'd been on the frozen lake near Keats Ward, unable to move or speak, falling snow rapidly covering his body, landing on his eyeballs and being sucked into his nostrils. He would suffocate unless someone helped him, but he couldn't make any sound, and as he finally managed to roll on to his side the ice cracked beneath him. Suddenly, he was sliding in slow motion beneath the ice, the cold water of the lake caressing his body, numbing him into submission. As his head sunk beneath the ice a shape loomed above him, and then he'd woken, his heart pounding.

His mother was an early riser, so he thought he'd surprise her with breakfast. He had a shower and a quick coffee and then left the boat. The fresh snow was soft underfoot. He crossed the walkway, passing the Corsa – which was, unfortunately for Kirby, parked exactly where he'd left it – and headed towards the nearby railway arches where Malone's Motors had its premises. Mitch Malone Jr, known to everyone as Mad Mitch merely on account of his somewhat-unkempt appearance, restored classic cars and let Kirby keep the Citroën in his workshop. He'd been one of the first people Kirby had met when he moved on to the boat – after Mitch was lured out of the arches, unable to resist the sound of the Citroën's throaty roar. Kirby, in turn, had slowed down upon seeing the 'Classic Cars Restored' sign, and such was the grin on Mitch's face when he'd clocked the SM that Kirby had pulled over. The rest was history.

Mitch hadn't arrived yet – it was way too early for him on a Saturday morning – and so Kirby let himself in. It was one of life's small pleasures, feeling the Citroën's suspension gently rise, but this morning he barely noticed, his mind on other things. There was a bakery on the way to Ealing, where his mother lived, and he stopped off for baked cheesecake – Livia's favourite. The traffic was sparse despite it being Saturday, and he made good time. When he got to his mother's house, just before eight, the curtains were still drawn. Perhaps she was having a lie-in – if she was feeling below par it made sense – although he couldn't remember the last time his mother had slept in past 7 a.m. She had the constitution of an ox – even after a heavy night of wine and Briscola.

He grabbed the box of cheesecake and locked the car. The snow on the drive was fresh from the previous night, and he made a mental note to clear it before he left. At the front door, he rang the bell and waited. The plants in the front garden had been cut down; usually his mother left the seed heads, enjoying the way they caught the early-morning frost. He rang the bell again. Perhaps Livia was in the shower – she'd never hear the bell from there. After what seemed like an age, he heard a noise behind the door.

'Mum, it's me,' he said.

'Lew?'

'Yes. Come on, let me in, I'm freezing out here.'

He heard the chain being slid off and the mortise being unlocked. 'Hang on,' he heard his mother say, the door opening a crack. 'Count to five and then come in and shut the door.'

What the hell was this? It was too early for party games, but he did as instructed, waiting for five beats before going in and closing the door behind him. 'Mum, are you okay?'

Livia was standing in the kitchen doorway at the end of the hall in her dressing gown. 'I'm fine. I just didn't want to get cold.'

'I see,' said Kirby, who didn't see at all. 'I thought I'd surprise you. Got your favourite breakfast.' He held up the bakery bag. 'It's just that I've got a new case and I'm going to be really—' He stopped. 'Mum, are you sure you're okay?' He took a step forward.

'Stop!' she almost shouted. 'Take your shoes off!'

'Okay . . .' He did as she asked, and with his shoes off he headed towards his mother and kissed her on both cheeks. Kate was right, she had lost weight; her shoulders felt bony beneath her dressing gown.

'You're cold, Lew. Come in and get warm,' she said, leading the way into the kitchen before he'd had a chance to look at her properly.

The first thing he noticed was that the blinds were drawn; the second thing was that the kitchen was a mess. He put down the cheesecake and began lifting the blinds, but his mother screeched from behind him, 'No! Leave them shut!'

He turned and stared at her. 'What's wrong? What's going on?'

'Going on? Nothing's going on. It's just . . . just . . . I don't want to see outside.' She went over to the sink, bumping into the edge of the kitchen table. 'Ouch!'

'You okay?'

'Yes – clumsy, that's all.' She picked up the kettle and began filling it with water. 'Let me make some coffee, just how you like it. Did you bring cheesecake?'

'Of course. It's ages since we've had breakfast, and I haven't seen you in a few weeks.' He looked around the kitchen again. Maybe it wasn't as bad as he'd first thought. It looked a mess as a lot of stuff was on the counter, but from what he could see it was clean. 'Been having a clear-out?' he asked.

'What? Oh, that. Yes,' she said, switching the kettle on. 'I've been cleaning the cupboards out. I had mice, and they'd crapped everywhere.'

'You should put some traps down,' he said, opening a cupboard.

'I hate traps, you know that. Can't bear that snapping noise when they go off.'

He began putting some of the crockery on the counter back in the cupboard, watching his mother from the corner of his eye. She looked tired – worse, she looked old. Livia had never looked old, and he found the thought quite shocking. He was wondering how to broach the subject of what his father had said when she swore loudly in Italian.

'*Merda!*'

He turned around to see that she'd poured hot water over the work surface after missing the coffee pot.

'Now look what I've done,' she said.

'It's okay, Mum, let me do it.' He got a cloth and wiped up the water. 'Go and sit down – you look worn out.'

He finished making the coffee and put some milk on the hob to heat up, and stole glances at Livia whenever he thought she wasn't looking. He needn't have worried; she seemed distracted and didn't notice.

'How's this new girlfriend of yours – Isabella? I haven't spoken to you in ages,' she said, yawning.

'Isabel – she's fine, thanks. But we spoke a couple of days ago, don't you remember? Kate was here, she answered the phone.'

'Kate?' She looked momentarily confused. 'Oh, that Kate. Yes, she did pop in, but that was weeks ago. But stop changing the subject, when am I going to meet her, this Isabel? Maybe once all this snow has cleared up we can all go to, um, you know – *Porca miseria!* she swore, waving her hand in frustration.

'Alfredo's. We'll see. It's early days.' Alfredo's was a small, family-run Italian place and the food was quite exquisite, although Kirby wasn't sure he wanted his mother involved with Isabel just yet. He poured the coffee and put a slice of cheesecake on a plate for each of them, and sat down opposite her.

'I spoke to Dad,' he began, taking a mouthful of cheesecake. 'He said there was something you needed to tell me.' He looked at his mother as he spoke, but she was avoiding his eyes. 'Mum, what's going on?' He reached out and took her hand. It felt cold and small. She had dark rings under her eyes, and there was little doubt in his mind that she was unwell.

'We can always go somewhere else,' said Livia. 'If you don't want to go to Alfredo's.'

Kirby let his head sink down and stared at his coffee cup. 'Just tell me, Mum. Please.' He squeezed her hand. 'I can tell something's wrong. This stuff with the snow, you've lost weight, you're not sleeping. What is it?'

'I don't know what you're talking about.'

'Is it cancer?' he whispered.

'Whatever gave you that idea?' She pulled her hand free of his and began picking at the cheesecake.

'Dad knows, but he won't tell me. He was rude to Meredith on the phone the other night, so whatever it is, it's affecting him too.' He looked at his mother, who was now staring at him.

'It's not cancer,' she said. 'And it's none of your father's damned business. He shouldn't have said anything to you.'

'He only said it because he's worried.'

'Well, he needn't be. And it needn't worry you either.' She took a sip of coffee and smiled. 'You always did make the best coffee.'

'Okay, if you really want to change the subject, what's this thing with snow?' he asked. He wasn't letting her off the hook that easily.

'I don't know, I just don't like it anymore.' Her eyes darted to the window. 'I can't stand looking at it. I hate the way it gets trodden into the house. Everything about it seems deeply repellent.' She yawned again. 'I'm sure it'll pass. It's probably because I'm tired.'

'You can't stay indoors with all the curtains drawn. It's not healthy. How much sleep did you get last night?' he asked.

'I wish you'd stop asking me questions, Ludovico!' she snapped. 'All you've done is question me since you got here.'

He sat open-mouthed. There were only two times when she called him by his full name: one was when she was teasing – like she had a few weeks ago about the fucking Corsa – and the other was when she was angry. This was definitely the latter. He finished his cheesecake in silence and then got up and began clearing the table. 'Have you been to the doctor?'

'No,' came the curt reply.

'If you're worried about going out in the snow, I can take you,' he said, wondering where he'd find the time.

'You've got quite enough on your plate without ferrying me about. I'll be fine. They'll only put me on sleeping tablets, and I don't want to end up like Robert Downey Jr.'

'Mum, I think Robert Downey had a few other problems too. I'm sure there are different treatments you could try before things got that bad.' He tried to sound upbeat, as though her earlier outburst hadn't happened.

They chatted for a while, Kirby deliberately not asking any more questions, then he glanced at his watch – it was coming up to ten o'clock, and he had to meet Connie at eleven. He wondered whether he should take Livia to the emergency surgery, if such a thing existed on a Saturday morning, but envisaged her reaction if he suggested it. Now he thought about it, he didn't even know who her GP was, as she was never ill. 'I'm going to clear the drive for you, then I'm going to have to shoot. It's this new case.'

'Is that the Blackwater murder?' she asked. 'I heard about it on the news and wondered if you were involved.'

'That's the one.'

'Poor woman. Imagine ending up in a place like that.' She shivered and got up to wash the coffee cups.

'Well, thankfully it's something you don't have to worry about. That's my department.' He went over to the sink and gave her a hug. 'I'll come and say goodbye when I've cleared the drive.'

Outside, the sky was bruising for another fight. It seemed pointless to clear the driveway now, as it would be covered again in the next hour by the looks of things, but he did it anyhow, the act of shovelling the snow giving him time to think. Whatever it was his mother was hiding, she wasn't going to tell him without an argument – not today, at least. It could be anything, he reasoned: money, a new relationship, or perhaps she really was thinking of moving back to Italy. Any of those things might cause insomnia, but they didn't explain the memory loss. The drawn blinds and dim kitchen lights had helped hide some of the signs, but her eyes had dark rings around them, and her skin, which was usually flawless, looked tired and worn. He wondered if she was eating properly, as she'd barely touched the cheesecake.

He was putting the shovel back in the garage when the first few flakes of snow began to fall. He hurried inside and said goodbye to Livia, who was curled up on the sofa with a book.

'Why don't you go back to bed?' he suggested. 'And make an appointment to see the doctor.'

'If you insist.'

'I do,' he said, from the door. 'Promise me you'll do it?'

'If it'll stop you nagging at me, then yes. Now off you go. Catch that poor woman's killer. *Ciao ciao.*'

When he got into the Citroën he looked up at the house, its curtains firmly drawn. Snow was already settling on the driveway that he'd only just cleared. As he pulled away, thinking of his mother cocooned in her house, he was left with the lingering feeling that this was just the start. Of what, he wasn't sure.

CHAPTER 25

Connie arrived at Blackwater ten minutes early, so carried on walking along Battersea Fields Drive to keep warm. A fine snow was coming down, a strong wind driving it like needles into her face, and she pulled her parka hood further forward. She wondered what it was that Kirby wanted to talk to her about.

She'd spoken to Harry earlier and arranged to go over to his place once she'd finished at Blackwater. He'd sounded down on the phone, which was hardly surprising, so she thought she'd go and cheer him up. She also wanted to check the address on the Post-it note. In light of what Mole had told her, it had played on her mind all night, and she'd more or less made up her mind to go and confront this Tom Ellis person. That's if the address actually belonged to her sister's exploring companion – the truth was that he could be anyone.

She paused for a moment outside one of the mansion blocks that lined the road opposite Blackwater, and squinted through the snow up at the top flats. The views over the asylum – and beyond, to the river – must be awesome, and she wondered how the residents felt about the impending development. It would certainly turn this exclusive neighbourhood into a noisy and congested area for several years to come. Turning back to the road she suddenly realised how close she was to Marsh House, where she'd be going on

Monday. She thought about moseying over for a quick look – it was probably only a few more minutes' walk – but after checking the time she decided to leave it and began walking back to Blackwater's main entrance.

Just as she approached the gate a green car pulled up. It wasn't just any green car, but some sort of insane classic thing – even the shade of green was from another era. She watched, mesmerised, as it seemed to lower itself to the ground like some sort of crouching tiger. Who the hell drove a car like that? Connie didn't know much about cars but she did recognise the Citroën logo on the front, and she was actually thinking what a cool machine it was when the door opened and a blast of Savages poured out at full volume, followed by Kirby. This was a surprise.

He raised a hand in greeting. 'Thanks for coming.' He locked the car and walked over, zipping up a black North Face jacket.

'I didn't know the Met had such good taste. The car, I mean.'

'They don't. My work car is a Corsa. I shouldn't really be driving this on duty, but I'm just on my way back from somewhere.'

'What is it? It's – well, amazing.'

'It's a Citroën SM. Wildly inappropriate, no doubt destroying the planet as I speak, and older than I am. Shall we?' He gestured towards the main gate of the old hospital just as an Emeris security guard appeared. Kirby showed the guard his ID and they were let in.

It felt strange to be walking into Blackwater without looking over her shoulder. Two huge, brown arcs had been carved in the snow where the gates had opened and closed over the past few days, and the tyre tracks of multiple vehicles were now frozen in hard, uneven ruts, making walking difficult. The snow was undisturbed off the main driveway apart from the odd track, which Connie assumed must have been the Scenes of Crime people.

She and Kirby began walking up the driveway, their feet crunching on the frozen ice.

'Do you have any leads yet?' she asked, as they made their way towards the administration block.

'A few,' he replied.

'What did you want to see me about?' The wind and snow made conversation difficult. 'There's still no word from Ed.'

'There's something I think you can help me with,' said Kirby, turning his head towards her so that she could hear him. 'I was hoping you might be able to give me some historical background on the place. Recent history is relatively well documented but there's a big chunk that isn't.'

'I can try, but Ed's the one who knows this place inside out.' Moving to the side of the rutted driveway, they trudged on – which made the going easier, the snow squeaking beneath their boots.

'I can't help feeling like I'm missing something,' Kirby was saying. 'Something important. So much has gone on here.'

'Where exactly are we going?' she asked, wondering what she might know that could possibly help. 'The place is humongous.'

'Keats Ward,' he replied. 'Do you know it?'

'I think so; it's down towards the lake, away from the main ward blocks. It's a detached block?'

'Correct. It's where the body was found.'

It hadn't occurred to her that she'd be visiting a murder scene, and suddenly she felt slightly nervous. After a few minutes they reached the admin block, and she was glad that she'd worn her snow boots as the temperature seemed to be dropping by the minute – the cold was stinging her eyes and she could feel them watering.

The admin block was dominated by a central clock tower, and she squinted through the snow at the void where the clock face should have been. The space stared out like an empty eye socket. A weather vane atop the tower was bent, as though an unseen force had passed through it; an uneven top hat of snow was precariously balanced on the top, frozen solid. All the windows of the building had been boarded up, and Buddleja grew out of a first-floor balcony.

'This was used by security when the place first closed,' said Connie, who'd been in there two or three times in the past. 'It used to have lovely wooden panelling until the fire.' Large parts of it had been destroyed in an arson attack in 2004, but the front portion, which they were looking at, had remained fairly intact.

As they both stopped to look at the building, she stole a sideways glance at her companion. Kirby actually seemed interested in the place, as he had done at RADE. It could just be professional interest, but she sensed a curiosity that surprised her – like the car had. What sort of detective drove a Citroën SM and listened to Savages? She wondered what he did when he was off duty, and found herself blushing at the thought.

'We need to go this way,' he said, as though suddenly remembering why they were there, and pointed off to the left.

Glad to be moving again, Connie followed him as they skirted around what had once been the recreational hall, which had also been badly damaged by fire. All that was left were four walls and the remains of a decorative cast-iron railing, which now hung suspended in mid-air, and the rubble-strewn floor was covered in a layer of snow. The four walls gave a brief respite from the driving wind, which seemed to find every crevice it could in her clothing. She noticed a crude smiley face drawn on one of the walls, crumbling mortar giving it the appearance of having lost a tooth.

'I've never been here in snow before,' she said. 'Everything looks so different.'

'Don't you worry about getting caught?' Kirby asked. 'When you're exploring a place like this?'

'It's part of the buzz – not getting caught. Getting in, getting out. It's one of the things I learned to enjoy, but yeah, no one wants to get caught.'

'The old adrenalin rush, I get it,' said Kirby. 'I can understand your interest in the place because of your sister. Is it the same for Ed?'

'His grandfather used to work here – he was a groundsman – and they lived in a tower block that overlooked the place. He used to tell Ed stories when he was a kid. But apart from all that, it's an interesting place. It was also fairly easy to access at one point, and a lot of stuff was left behind – machinery, patient records, samples, that sort of thing.' Her lips were going numb, it was so cold.

'Patient records?' asked Kirby.

'Yeah, there's loads. And medical samples.'

'Isn't that illegal, or some kind of breach of privacy?'

'You're the policeman, not me,' said Connie. 'Anyhow, there's a lot to explore here. Plus, my job at the architecture library gives me a geeky interest in the design of the place.'

They had now reached the chapel, which was in good nick compared to most of the buildings and had been listed four years ago, along with the water tower. Beyond the chapel lay the kitchens and then the ward blocks. She'd give anything for a poke about while they were here, but it was hardly a sightseeing tour, so she said nothing.

They trudged on through the snow, passing wards Blake, Byron and Milton. Suddenly, the wind dropped and the place fell eerily silent, the snowflakes drifting dreamily to the ground. She tried to imagine what an elderly woman might have been doing here at night. Something had brought the woman back to Blackwater – or someone.

After ten more minutes they reached Keats Ward – all alone, facing the lake, the water tower to its right. It had stopped snowing by now, and the view was quite serene. *Keats* had been engraved into the stone lintel over the doorway and was just visible through the snow-covered ivy that clung to the brickwork.

'This is the building I was thinking of,' said Connie, as they ducked under the police tape that had been pinned across the door-less entrance.

Structurally, the building was in good condition, but the large day room on the ground floor had been used as a store space and was a chaotic jumble of old chairs, tables, bed frames and medical equipment – all of which was in poor condition, the metal rusted and the wood warped and mouldy. The air felt colder than it had outside, and even through the frozen air she could smell the decay. 'Fuck it's cold,' she said.

'I've had to dig out my skiwear this winter it's been so cold,' said Kirby, leading the way upstairs.

'You ski, then?'

'Used to. My mother taught me – she's Italian. Skied all her life.'

They made their way upstairs and Kirby led her along a corridor, cell doors opening off to their left. Connie had only been in here once – about two years ago – and had found it creepy then, but today it was even more so. At the end of the corridor was a door that bore a sign that read *Television Room*. It was where, instinctively, she knew Kirby was taking her.

'Is this where you found her?' Connie asked, as she and Kirby entered the room.

'Yes.' Kirby pointed to the far corner. 'On a bed, over there – with the number nineteen on it. Does that mean anything to you?'

She shook her head and pulled her jacket collar a little tighter. Her neck felt cold, and a sudden rash of goosebumps ran down her arms. There was something about the room that she didn't like; the atmosphere felt different to that in the corridor outside. 'You do

163

know that this used to be called the Narcosis Room or the Sleep Room?'

'No, why was that?'

'Basically, the patients were given a shitload of drugs, including barbiturates, to make them sleep for several days – in some cases weeks or months. They'd carry out ECT on them too.'

'Electroconvulsive Therapy?'

'Yeah. There's still a machine downstairs, or there was when I was last here. It gives me the creeps.'

'I'm not surprised. Did this deep-sleep stuff work?' Kirby asked.

'The opposite – quite a few people were permanently damaged, lost huge chunks of their memory.'

Kirby looked intrigued. 'Do many people know about it?'

'A lot of urbexes do, it became a bit of a thing – you know, the creepy room at Blackwater.'

'Can you tell me anything else about this ward, anything unusual?'

'Not really. It's not a secret but not particularly widely known about, either – I think the tabloids ran a story at some point.'

Kirby said nothing and appeared to be deep in thought, distracted even, his eyes fixed on some point she couldn't determine.

'Do you think this is relevant to the woman's death?' Connie asked.

'I thought there might be a reason why the body was left up here rather than anywhere else.' His eyes shifted from whatever they'd been focused on and came to rest on her. 'I'd value your opinion, that's all. You know this place pretty well.'

'It is strange, I agree. Like, there are plenty of other places to leave a body here where they wouldn't be found for months, if not years. Mind you, with the demolition guys coming in, a body would be found sooner or later.'

'Where would *you* hide a body then?' he asked.

164

'*Me?* I hope you don't think I had anything to do with this.'

He smiled. 'No, nothing like that. I'm genuinely curious to know what you think.'

'Well . . .' She began running through the remotest and most inaccessible parts of the site in her mind. 'I suppose the more over-grown areas would be obvious – the small outbuildings by the laun-dry, maybe? There was a groundsman's storage shed somewhere but that got so overgrown it could be anywhere.' She thought for a minute. 'There is one place where no one would find a body.'

'Where?'

'The lake. And if it was weighed down it wouldn't be found until – well, when the lake was drained.' She looked at Kirby, trying to read his thoughts, wondering if this had been some kind of trap.

'Good answer,' he said, eventually. 'Which all rather reinforces the idea that this room is somehow significant.'

'I suppose it might.'

'You said a lot of stuff was left behind here. What about drugs? Not in this room, but elsewhere on the site?'

'You mean like old medical drugs?'

Kirby nodded. 'Have you ever come across any here?'

Connie shook her head. Sometimes there were old supplies left, but she'd definitely never found any drugs here.

'Where would they be if there were drugs here?' asked Kirby.

'God, I don't know. They'd all have been stolen by now.'

Kirby looked thoughtful. 'Did Ed ever mention finding any drugs here?'

'Never. Why are you asking?'

'I just wondered, that's all.'

'It's certainly possible. I've visited abandoned veterinary prac-tices in the past that have still had drugs in them.'

'Interesting,' said Kirby. 'Thanks.'

Connie went over to one of the windows and looked down over the frozen lake. It really did look beautiful today. Then her eyes wandered to the right and to the old water tower, dark and brooding in contrast to the white snow – the place where Sarah had fallen to her death. 'That's where it happened,' she said, quietly. 'The water tower.'

Kirby joined her by the window and followed her gaze. 'I know. I read the report. Have you been up there?'

'Several times. You?'

Kirby shook his head. 'I imagine the views are incredible.'

'At night, the red lights on the cranes at the power station look like a constellation. It's pretty magical.'

'Aren't you frightened of falling, like your sister did?'

'Not really. In any case, that part is boarded-off now.' Connie stared down at the lake and beyond it towards the Thames, brown and sluggish, and an overwhelming sense of loss swept over her – first Sarah and now Ed. 'Apparently Ed had found out who she was with, the day she fell. He was going to tell me on Tuesday.'

'You didn't mention that on Thursday when we spoke,' Kirby said.

'I didn't know then. Our friend Mole, the one I mentioned who was in Poland, told me last night.'

'I see. Well, let's hope that Ed surfaces soon and can still tell you.'

'You don't think it could have anything to do with his disappearance, do you?' Connie asked.

'I've seen the report on your sister's death, and it was an accident. Whatever's going on now is something entirely different.'

'I've tried to imagine what kind of person would just leave her. I guess they didn't want to get caught and took the coward's way out – called the ambulance and scarpered.'

'I dare say they've paid the price over the years, not that it excuses their behaviour in any way. They should have made themselves known,' said Kirby.

They walked back the way they'd come. Downstairs, the ECT machine that Connie had remembered was still there. It was a Siemens Konvulsator and sat on a rusted metal trolley, its four wheels at disjointed angles – mobility something even a good squirt of WD-40 would be unable to fix. The plastic case of the machine was covered in a thick layer of dust and had a deep crack running along its top. A dead fly lay on its back next to the handle.

'Someone's had a Spinal Tap moment,' said Kirby, indicating the machine's two dials, both of which were turned past maximum.

When they got outside the air felt slightly warmer, as though Keats Ward emanated an Arctic chill all of its own, and they started to walk back. When they reached the main gate, a dishevelled-looking man in a woollen hat and overcoat was lumbering down the road towards Battersea. Connie recognised him as Raymond Sweet – Ed had pointed him out once.

'Do you know him?' asked Kirby, as they waited for the guard to unlock the gate.

Connie shook her head. 'I know *of* him. It's Raymond Sweet, isn't it?'

'Yes. Lives in the Old Lodge. Does Ed know him?' Kirby asked, as they began walking towards his car.

'I don't think so, or not very well at any rate. He tried to befriend him once, get some inside intel on the asylum, but it never came to anything. Do you think he has anything to do with the murder?'

They had reached the car, and Kirby took out his keys. They were on what looked like a vintage Citroën fob, the chevron logo unmistakeable.

'Off the record?' said Kirby. 'No. He's—' But he didn't get any further as he was cut off by his mobile, which he pulled out of his pocket. 'Excuse me, I need to take this.' He took a few paces away from the car and turned his back.

'Shit,' Connie heard him say under his breath.

'What's happened?' she asked, as he turned back to the car.

'Sorry, but I've got to go,' he said, abruptly. 'Thanks for your help.'

Connie watched as he climbed into the car and slammed the door. Whatever it was must be serious, and she became aware of a sense of disappointment as the car cruised away leaving an exhaust trail in its wake. She looked at her watch – it was gone twelve, and she'd promised Harry lunch. She began walking and paused at the top of Daylesford Road. In the distance, Raymond Sweet was visible, his ungainly figure strolling towards the river and the Daylesford Road entrance to Blackwater, near the damaged fence where she and Ed had planned to get in on Tuesday night. She checked her watch again; twenty minutes wouldn't hurt, would it? In a split second, Connie made a decision and ran after him – Harry would have to wait.

CHAPTER 26

There had been slim pickings at the bring-and-buy that morning, so to make up for it Raymond had treated himself to a hot sausage roll, which was now keeping his right hand warm as he walked home. He should have bought two, he realised – one for each hand – as it was so bitterly cold. He reached the corner of Daylesford Road and turned down the familiar street towards home, mulling things over in his head. There was so much going on that his brain could hardly keep up, but there was one thing he was now sure of: the Creeper had been in the bone jar. The canisters had definitely been moved, like the things in his house. And then there was his smudged drawing in the old pillbox. It hadn't been an animal, he now realised – it was the Creeper telling him he knew about the bone jar. He was glad now that he'd told the policeman about the Creeper, although whether they believed him or not, he couldn't tell.

He was about halfway down Daylesford Road, and looking forward to his sausage roll, when he heard a shout.

'Wait! Mr Sweet!'

It was a female voice, and he turned to look. A young woman – he'd passed her coming out of Blackwater a few minutes ago with the detective who had the shabby notebook – had just turned the corner and was jogging towards him, waving. 'Mr Sweet, wait! I'd like to talk to you!'

He carried on walking, the entrance gate now within sight. What did she want? He could hear her muffled footsteps getting nearer.

'Raymond! Stop!' she shouted.

He reached the gate and took out his keys. As he undid the padlock, he could see her a few feet away. She slipped on a patch of ice and nearly lost her balance. As she righted herself, he nipped through the gate and began locking the padlock, pulling out the key just as she appeared on the other side.

'Mr Sweet,' she panted, her breath trailing out in long plumes. 'I just want to talk to you, that's all. Please—'

Raymond took a step backwards and looked at her through the wrought-iron gate, the key still in his hand. 'What do you want?'

'Ed Blake, the man who's missing . . .' She was out of breath.

The police had asked about him yesterday. 'What about him?' Raymond replied. The girl had very large eyes.

'I think something might have happened to him,' said the girl.

Raymond nodded, slowly. He wasn't sure what to make of her.

'The night he disappeared – Tuesday – he was coming here.'

He frowned, uncertain how to respond.

'I mean coming *here*, to Blackwater. I should have been too,' she went on, 'but I got held up on the train. It was the anniversary of my sister's death.'

What was she on about, her sister's death? He was about to walk away when something stopped him.

'My sister had an accident at the water tower five years ago. You might remember,' the girl was saying. 'Her name was Sarah Darke?'

Raymond did remember; he'd drawn a sad face on the tower's wall a few days later. He'd been questioned then, too, and now he nodded slowly, wondering exactly what it was she wanted.

The girl continued. 'Me and Ed, we planned to go there on Tuesday. Only, as I said, I was held up, so Ed was going to go there alone, and he's now missing. You didn't see anything, did you, on Tuesday night?'

'No,' he replied, quickly. Raymond wished people would stop asking him about Tuesday.

'I just want to find out what's happened to him.' The girl paused. 'He lived nearby as a kid – his grandfather, Harry, worked here. He's been interviewing people about the place. Maybe he interviewed you?'

Raymond shook his head, feeling a bit put out that he hadn't.

'I'm Connie, by the way.' She stuck a gloved hand through the gate.

He shook her hand tentatively; it wasn't something he did very often.

'You're quite well known,' she said. 'I bet you know more about this place than anyone else does.'

Raymond shrugged. He wondered whether he should tell her about the Creeper – perhaps her friend had seen him too.

'Listen, I don't suppose you'd let me in, would you?' she asked.

He hesitated. He liked her, but even so. 'I can't,' he said. 'Sorry.'

'Okay, we'll take a rain check. Perhaps I could ask you a few questions, interview you?'

He nodded. He would like that very much, although what a rain check was he didn't have the foggiest. 'I've got a film too,' he added.

'Really? What kind of film?'

'Oh, erm, just a film. About Blackwater. My friend Gregory is in it.'

'That's nice. Perhaps we could watch it together, when I interview you – maybe at your house? You could tell me about your friend.'

He liked this girl. She seemed genuinely interested – was she *actually* inviting herself to his house? He really would need some sherry glasses if that ever happened; the thought made him giddy. Then he remembered that he didn't have a DVD player.

'Well, I'd better be going then,' said the girl. 'It's been lovely meeting you, Raymond. I'm glad you've agreed to talk me.'

'Er, yes,' he said, unable to recall agreeing to anything, but he didn't really care and stood nervously. He'd never been good at goodbyes – was he supposed to kiss her? The giddy feeling returned.

'How can I contact you?' she asked. 'Do you have a phone?'

Raymond shook his head. 'You can leave me a note.' He nodded towards the small metal letterbox attached to the fence.

'Cool, thanks. Okay, bye then.' She gave him a small wave and began walking back up Daylesford Road.

Now that she was leaving, Raymond didn't want her to go, and he desperately tried to think of something interesting to say that would make her come back. 'There was someone here that night,' he suddenly blurted out, almost looking behind him to see where the voice had come from. It had the desired effect though, and the girl called Connie came back and grabbed the metal gate with her gloved hand.

'Who?'

'I – I don't know,' stammered Raymond, now feeling under pressure to tell her something useful. 'The Creeper.' There! It was out; he'd said the name out loud!

'The Creeper? Who's that?'

'I don't know.' He hesitated. 'I think it's a ghost.'

'A ghost? Right . . . And what does this ghost do?' She was smiling now, which he liked, but like the policeman yesterday he wasn't sure that she believed him and he began to feel stupid.

'It moves things. In the house. One day I couldn't find my torch, then the next day there it was, on the table. And the face—' He stopped.

'What face?'

'Um, I drew a face and then its mouth got wiped away.' Now he felt really stupid.

She seemed a little taken aback at this. 'Have you told the police?'

'Um, of course. The ghost bit was a joke,' he added, in an attempt to redeem himself. 'But I can't tell you anything else.' He was suddenly afraid that he'd said too much. 'I have to go now.' He turned and began walking back to the Lodge.

'Raymond, wait!' he heard the girl shout. 'Raymond!'

He didn't break his stride until he entered the clearing by the Lodge. Only then did he stop and take stock of what he'd just said to the girl, about the ghost bit being a joke. What if it really was a joke and the Creeper wasn't a ghost after all? Worse, what if it was the murderer? It knew about the bone jar and if it knew about that then . . . Something suddenly clicked into place and a sense of dread ran through him. If the Creeper really was human and had killed Ena, then how much longer he could keep the bone jar under his hat was anyone's guess. Gregory was safe at the lodge, along with Alardice and Barnes, but the rest of the ashes were still down there; he needed to move the remaining canisters pronto. He hurried over to the porch and up the steps. The key slid reassuringly into the lock and he felt the comfort of the Lodge envelop him as he stepped inside. Just as well, because there was another task he had to perform, one that filled him with even more dread than the bone jar being discovered. He felt in his pocket – the sausage roll was still warm and he gave it a gentle squeeze to reassure himself, because the truth was he was scared.

CHAPTER 27

The call Kirby had taken at Blackwater had been the news he was half expecting and half dreading: the body of a young man had been pulled from the Thames, possibly that of Ed Blake. By the time he'd arrived at Westminster Pier, where the Marine Policing Unit had retrieved the body, the snow had been so bad that the body bag was already white. It hadn't taken long for Kirby to establish that the body did, indeed, belong to Blake. A black snake's head poked out from the man's jacket sleeve, its forked tongue brushing the base of his palm – an identifying mark mentioned to Kobrak by the man's grandfather, Harry Joyce.

When Kirby returned to Mount Pleasant the mood was gloomy. Everyone on the investigation had hoped that Edward Blake would come strolling back after a few nights of hot passion, tail between his legs at the trouble he'd caused – his phone stolen, chucked over the fence, picked up by a dextrous fox and placed carefully in Keats Ward next to a dead former nurse. All bollocks, of course, but that's what they'd hoped, willing the fantasy to come true.

'Anyone seen Pete?' asked Hamer, who looked harassed, as he addressed the assembled officers.

'He was going to the hospice to return the visitors' book. The weather's probably nobbled him,' said Kirby, who'd spoken to him on the way to Westminster.

Hamer let out a frustrated sigh and went on. 'We'll have to start without him then. As you all know, we now have a second body. Lew?' He nodded in Kirby's direction.

'We're certain it's that of Edward Blake, the missing urban explorer. The body has a tattoo identical to the one Blake has here.' Kirby indicated his wrist. 'Initial examination shows that he was hit on the head and then strangled and dumped in the river. Probably dead when he hit the water, but we'll know for sure once the pathologist has done his work. The grandfather, Harry Joyce, will have to make a formal ID – I'll go and see him after we finish here. By all accounts they were very close, and it turns out that Mr Joyce used to work at Blackwater, so he might be able to tell us something.'

Hamer looked up sharply. 'Did we know about the grandfather working at Blackwater?'

'Yes,' said Kirby, glancing at Kobrak, who he knew had inter-viewed Harry Joyce about his missing grandson. 'Connie Darke mentioned it to me when I spoke to her earlier today.'

Hamer looked exasperated.

'Mr Joyce was only questioned in relation to his missing grand-son. What he did for a living nearly twenty-odd years ago wasn't touched upon,' said Kirby.

Kobrak threw him a grateful look.

'Okay, so there's a possible link between Blake and Ena Massey,' said Hamer. 'Make sure you ask him about it, Lew.'

Kirby nodded. 'Regardless of that, we now know for certain that there's a third party involved. Blake didn't strangle himself.'

'They could have been in collusion,' said Kobrak. 'Perhaps Blake and the third party fell out and Blake got killed.'

'Or, Blake and Ena were killed by the same person for different reasons,' said Kirby. 'Why would Blake arrange to go to Blackwater with his friend, Connie, on the anniversary of her sister's death, if he planned to kill someone there the same night? It's more likely that he witnessed something.'

'Okay, get over to Blake's flat, see if there's anything of interest,' said Hamer, directing the order at Kobrak. 'Computers, phones, paperwork – anything that could link him to Ena Massey. Newlands are going back over his emails and phone calls, but he might have had several devices. Lew, when you see the grandfather, check if Blake kept anything there – maybe a second computer, or another phone. And what about Sweet? Pete had him in yesterday, didn't he?' Hamer looked around the room, as if to say, *Where the fuck is he?*

'Sweet admitted knowing Ena when he was a patient at Blackwater,' said Kirby, wishing to God that Anderson would suddenly appear. 'He didn't like her, not that he said it in so many words. He said she kept putting him to sleep, whatever that means. Oh, and there's a ghost.'

'A ghost? Give me strength,' said Hamer.

'That's what I thought,' Kirby went on. 'But apparently he saw it on the night of the murder, down near the lake, which is only a stone's throw from Keats Ward.'

'Can we believe anything Sweet tells us? He's hardly a reliable source.'

Kirby shrugged. 'Could be something, could be nothing. My guess is that he did see something but that it's easier for him to deal with the spiritual world than the human one.'

Hamer grunted. 'I want to know *why*,' he said, standing up and moving across to the crime scene photos, where he stared at the images of Blackwater and Ena Massey's beaten body. 'Why *her*. Why *now*. She's the key.' He prodded a photograph. 'And another thing. I'm going to have to give Patrick Calder the green light to start work. I can't hold him off any longer.' Hamer's eyes avoided Kirby's as he spoke. 'I'll make the call first thing on Monday.' He then dismissed the group and disappeared into his office, closing the door behind him.

Hamer was under pressure, Kirby could tell. Poor bastard, running four understaffed murder teams and answering to the commissioner, who had a reputation for ball-breaking. Telling him their only suspect was of the spiritual variety wasn't going to go down very well. Never in a million years, thought Kirby, as he returned to his own desk.

'Thanks, Lew,' said Kobrak, who'd followed him over. 'About Harry—'

Kirby held up his hand to stop him. 'It's fine. Hamer's stressed, that's all. Everyone seems to have a connection to Blackwater round here.' Just then, the door to the office banged open, and he didn't need to turn around to know it was Anderson.

'Oh boy, are you going to be pleased with Uncle Pete,' Anderson said, plonking himself down. 'The old luck of the paw strikes again—'

Before he could get any further, Hamer came out of his office with his coat and scarf on. 'I'll be on the mobile,' he barked without looking at any of them, and headed for the lift.

Anderson raised his eyebrows.

'Not pleased you missed the briefing,' said Kirby. 'Where the hell have you been, anyhow?'

'At the hospice. Drinking tea.'

'Really. How frightfully fucking wonderful. And what did the tea leaves tell you?'

'Ahh, well,' said Anderson, twirling the rabbit's paw dramatically. 'First off, no one had a bad word to say about Ena, no one recognised any of the jewellery we found at her house and none of the names on the letters rang any bells. Then, just as I was leaving, one of the staff members told me that Ena regularly visited an old colleague of hers – an old colleague from Blackwater.'

Kirby leant forward. 'Bingo. Who?'

'Margaret Halliday. She was a nurse at Blackwater at the same time as Ena. Worked alongside her for years, according to this staff member.'

'And she's still alive?' he asked, feeling a tingle of excitement. He was sure Ena's murder had something to do with her past.

'Yep. Nursing home in Epsom . . .' Anderson looked the name up in his notes. 'Littledene Care Home.'

Kirby turned to Kobrak, who'd been standing by listening. 'Get on the phone. See if it's okay to visit Margaret Halliday tonight – tell them it's urgent.'

'Will do,' said Kobrak, scurrying off.

'Did they say anything else about these visits?' Kirby asked Anderson.

'Only that she visited every few weeks, as Margaret Halliday had no one else.'

'How thoughtful. And no one at the hospice mentioned any complaints about Ena?'

'None. An example to us all, apparently,' said Anderson, pulling a pious face.

'Well, she sure as shit pissed *someone* off.'

'And there's something else,' said Anderson, holding up the rabbit's paw like a talisman before rummaging about in a carrier bag he'd brought back with him. 'The pièce de résistance.' With a flourish, he pulled out a framed photograph and handed it to Kirby.

The photograph was colour, taken on the steps of the hospice, and showed Ena Massey being given a small trophy by a tanned-looking man in a suit. Beneath the picture, it said: *Ena Massey – Volunteer of the Year 2014*.

'You are fucking joking,' said Kirby, staring at the image. 'How did Kobrak miss this?' Maybe he'd been too lenient on the young sergeant after all.

'He obviously didn't go into the kitchen. Staff manager offered me a cuppa.' Anderson smiled and stroked the rabbit's paw. 'How could I refuse?'

Kirby looked at the photograph again and studied the man giving Ena her award. There was no mistaking who it was. Patrick Calder.

CHAPTER 28

Kirby arrived at Calder's house having left Anderson with the unenviable task of telling Harry Joyce that his grandson was dead. Calder's secretary had told Kirby that her boss was at home, and when he'd rung to check Mrs Calder had answered the phone.

'Of course he'll see you, Detective. I'll tell him you're coming.'

As Kirby walked up the steps of the large house on Clapham Common Westside, he wondered whether he should have informed Hamer he was going. He'd barely spoken to his boss since their conversation the night before, and after this evening's briefing Hamer had left before he'd had a chance.

Kirby rang the bell and waited, listening to it echo in what sounded like a large hall behind a front door that was at least twice the size of most. After a few minutes it opened, and a rather glamorous-looking woman appeared. She introduced herself as Saskia Calder and invited Kirby in, closing the door just as Patrick Calder emerged from one of the rooms off the hall. She glanced at her husband, and without saying another word disappeared upstairs. Whatever charm Calder had once had, with his velvety voice and perfect teeth, it seemed to have stopped working on Mrs Calder a long time ago.

'What's this about?' he asked, making no move to invite Kirby any further into his house. 'I would offer you a drink, but I have to leave soon for a dinner appointment. You've come to tell me we can begin work, I hope.'

'I'm afraid not,' said Kirby. 'Ena Massey, the woman whose body we found, won a Volunteer of the Year Award four years ago. It seems you presented it to her.' He held out the photograph for Calder to look at. 'St Elizabeth's Hospice.'

'What of it?' said Calder, his eyes barely looking at the framed image.

'She was found murdered on your land, and you told us that you didn't know her. That's *what of it.*'

'I don't – didn't – know her. Maybe I did present her with an award. Honestly? I can't remember.'

'So you have no recollection of meeting her?'

'None. I meet a lot of people, and you'd be surprised at how few are worth remembering.' Calder smiled, and Kirby wondered whether he was included in that category.

'Why did the hospice ask you?'

'As a successful local businessman I'm often called upon to present awards, give speeches, and so forth. It comes with the territory.'

'That's not quite what I meant,' said Kirby. 'I meant why did they ask *you* specifically? They could have asked anyone – and, well, I'm surprised that you had the time.'

Calder regarded him for a few seconds. 'They nursed my grandmother when she was dying. I owe them a debt of gratitude.'

'When was this?' asked Kirby.

'I don't see what my grandmother's death has to do with any of this, but if you must know, it was 1996. And before you ask, no, Ena Massey never had anything to do with the care of my grandmother.' He took a step towards the front door. 'I'm sorry to rush things, but a table at The Ivy isn't something one wants to be late for.'

'We pulled a body out of the Thames earlier,' said Kirby, as they stood by the door. He wasn't letting Calder off the hook just yet. 'Edward Blake. It was his phone that we found at the crime scene. I don't suppose you've thought any more about whether you know him?'

'Of course I haven't. Why would I?'

'You'd forgotten that you knew Ena Massey, and so I wondered whether you might have forgotten knowing Mr Blake too. As you said, you do meet a lot of people.'

'Meeting someone is one thing, knowing them is quite another. I don't recall doing either with Mr Blake. I'm genuinely sorry that I can't be of more help.'

'In that case, I'm sorry to have kept you,' Kirby said, stepping outside and on to the driveway. 'Say goodnight to Mrs Calder for me, won't you?'

Calder said nothing and closed the door with a soft whoosh, as though sealing a vacuum. Kirby noticed it had a handsome Hand of Fatima doorknocker, and wondered how good a job it did of keeping evil out of the Calder household. Something made him look up, and he saw Saskia Calder watching him from an upstairs window. Their eyes met briefly and then she moved away, leaving him to wonder what kind of marriage they had. Not a happy one, by the looks of things.

CHAPTER 29

It took Kirby over an hour to reach Littledene Care Home, where Margaret Halliday lived, and he was just pulling up outside when Anderson called.

'Get anything from Calder?' he asked.

Kirby told him about their brief conversation. 'I can't see what motive he'd have for murdering Ena Massey and leaving the body on his own land. Doesn't make sense.'

'Plus, he's got an alibi.'

'There is that,' said Kirby. 'How'd it go at Harry Joyce's?'

Anderson sighed. 'As you'd imagine. Poor bastard's devastated. Although you'll never guess who was there with him.'

'Who?'

'Connie Darke.'

'I didn't know they knew each other that well,' said Kirby, remembering Connie mention Harry briefly when they were at Blackwater earlier that day.

'They don't, not really. She's been keeping an eye on him since Blake went missing. She showed me a room upstairs where Blake kept some of his things. No computer or anything, just research and junk connected to his exploring. There was quite a lot of stuff on Blackwater, including a few cuttings of Ena. Seems she made the headlines a few times, allegations of misconduct and the like. Never charged with anything.'

'Interesting – let's get them checked out. Could be a long-held grudge, although it doesn't sound very likely. How did Connie seem?' Kirby thought about their conversation earlier and how Blake had been going to tell her what he'd found out about her sister's mysterious companion. He wouldn't be doing that anymore.

'Upset. Kept it in check for the old man though.'

Kirby noticed the time. 'Look, I'd better go, otherwise I'll be talking to Margaret Halliday in bed.'

Anderson chuckled. 'What with Karen McBride in her onesie and a retired nurse in a winceyette, you'll be getting a bad rep.'

'Fuck off,' said Kirby, and hung up.

The care home was a handsome Victorian house set within what looked to be well-tended grounds. The street lights cast an orange glow over the front garden, and even beneath the snow Kirby could tell that the grass was cut, the hedges had been trimmed and the flowerbeds were neat. It certainly didn't look like your average care home, and he wondered what the fees were to stay in a place like this.

He rang the front bell, and after a few minutes was admitted into the hall, where he could hear the clinking of glass and the vague sound of activity coming from somewhere in the house. It felt more like a private club than an old people's home.

'I'm Theresa Bethell,' said the woman who'd answered the door. 'Was it you I spoke to on the phone earlier?'

'No, that was Sergeant Kobrak. I'm DI Kirby.'

'This way.' She led him through the hallway and into an impressive, large room with a roaring fire in one corner. 'Some of the residents are just having a small sherry or cocoa before bed.'

Armchairs were scattered around the room in small groups, about half of them occupied by residents, the rest empty. Of the people there, the average age looked to be around eighty.

'Sorry, I realise this might be a bit late. I was held up,' said Kirby, suddenly feeling guilty.

'That's all right. Margaret doesn't retire until gone nine most nights. She's over there.' Theresa pointed to a woman sitting in the far corner on her own, staring out of the French windows into the garden. Kirby followed her eyes and was surprised to see a large, brightly lit pond at the end of the garden. It was like a miniature version of the lake at Blackwater.

'I'll introduce you,' said Theresa, and Kirby followed her across the room.

'Margaret, this is the detective I told you about earlier, Detective Inspector Kirby. He'd like to ask you a few questions.' She turned to Kirby. 'Would you like anything to drink, Inspector?'

'No, I'm fine, thanks.' He sat down opposite Margaret Halliday and waited as Theresa walked off.

The woman opposite had probably been quite formidable in her day. Even sitting down, Kirby could tell that she was tall. Her shoulders were now stooped, but they were broad and looked as though they had once been strong, like a swimmer's.

'Miss Halliday, I'd like to ask you a few questions about your time at Blackwater Asylum, if you don't mind. I'm investigating the death of Ena Massey, who I believe you knew.'

Margaret Halliday continued to look out of the window, blinking every now and then but staring with such intensity that Kirby wondered if she'd heard what he'd said. 'I'd really like to ask you about—' he began, when she suddenly turned and interrupted.

'It was a long time ago,' she said, looking at him just as she'd watched whatever it was outside that had held her attention.

'Yes, I realise that. I wondered what you could tell me about Ena Massey, as I gather that you worked there together in the 1960s and that she used to come and visit you.'

Margaret frowned, two deep ridges forming between her eyebrows. 'Ena Massey,' she repeated, before slowly shaking her head and looking out of the window again. 'Ena Massey never once visited me. You have been misinformed.'

'She never came to see you here?' He wondered if Margaret Halliday had the beginnings of dementia, although it hadn't been mentioned when the visit was arranged.

'Never. Why would she?'

Her voice was firm, and instinctively he felt that she was telling the truth. 'Can you think of a reason why Ena would tell people that she came here to visit you, when in fact she didn't?'

Margaret shifted her gaze once more to Kirby's face, as though searching for something. 'I haven't seen her in nearly thirty years, but I imagine that she hasn't changed much. To whom did she tell this lie?'

'A hospice where she was doing voluntary work.'

Margaret slowly began to shake her head, a smile forming on her lips, which turned into something more ugly. 'So she hadn't changed then.'

Kirby waited for the retired nurse to continue.

After a few moments, she began to speak. 'To understand Ena, you have to understand that she was a complete fraud. From start to finish. I can only conclude that telling the hospice that she visited an old friend in a care home was to reflect well on herself. There is simply no other explanation.'

Although he'd had his doubts about Ena's character, he hadn't been expecting to hear this. He'd even begun to think his cynicism was clouding his judgement. 'When you say a "fraud", what do you mean, exactly?'

The old nurse smoothed the blanket over her knees, as though choosing her next words carefully. 'There's no point in lying about it now, I suppose,' she said. 'A fraud. Exactly that. Ena pretended to be a good nurse. Pretended to care about her patients. Pretended that she knew what she was doing – she even pretended to be a good mother. She was none of those things.'

'Can you explain a bit more? How did she get away with it? Didn't people see through her?'

Margaret's hands were clasped on her lap, the joints distorted by arthritis. Her right thumb rubbed a ring on her middle finger, and Kirby thought about the rings found in Ena's house, which were now in his pocket. 'It was a different time. There was a private ward, which wasn't subject to the same regulations as the rest of the hospital. Dr Brayne, who was in overall charge, gave Ena full rein.'

'Why? Surely if his reputation was on the line—'

'It was safer to have Ena where he could keep an eye on her. If he let her go, she would have ruined him. He wasn't without fault himself, Ena being a case in point.'

'What do you mean?'

'The girl, Ena's daughter . . .'

'Karen,' interjected Kirby.

Margaret nodded. 'Brayne was the father.'

Dr Alistair Brayne was Karen McBride's father? He wondered what Karen would make of the information if she ever found out.

'A proper little madam,' Margaret Halliday went on, inspecting something in the distance before continuing. 'I felt sorry for her though. Ena paid her almost no attention whatsoever. No wonder she left as soon as she could.'

'Did she know who her father was?'

'No. Ena would tease her about it. It was cruel to watch.'

'Ena *teased* her daughter about who her father was?' He tried to imagine why anyone would do that to a child.

'Oh yes. She'd point at him and say, "That's your father, Karen." And then when Karen asked why her daddy never cuddled her and why they didn't live together, Ena would laugh and say, "Only joking! You didn't really think that was true, did you? You didn't really think that someone like that could ever be your father?"'

Kirby was stunned. 'Didn't anyone say anything to Ena?'

'We wanted to keep our jobs,' said Margaret. 'As I said, it was a different time.'

'Didn't Dr Brayne do anything about it – he must have known Karen was his daughter?'

'Dr Brayne was very charming and charismatic – handsome, even. He was also very bright, very academic. But compassionate?' Margaret shook her head. 'Alas, no. And that extended to his daughter.'

Talk about being unsuitable for a job. Kirby pulled the evidence bag containing the rings out of his pocket. 'Do you recognise these?' he asked, handing it to Margaret.

She took the bag and squinted at the contents. 'They're wedding rings,' she said. 'Never seen them before. Why do you ask?' She passed them back.

'They were found among Ena's possessions. As were these.' He took out the copies he'd had made of the letters. 'They were addressed to patients at Blackwater.' He handed her the correspondence and watched as she looked through them.

When she'd finished, she let them fall on to her lap and was silent for a few minutes.

'I remember a few of these patients,' she eventually said. 'Ruthie, that rings a bell, although . . .'

Kirby waited expectantly.

'Sorry.' She shook her head. 'My memory isn't what it used to be.'

A fox crossed the lawn, stopping momentarily to look at them. They watched as it lazily went on its way.

'We've been speaking to an ex-patient, Raymond Sweet, who now lives in the Old Lodge at Blackwater. Do you remember him?' asked Kirby.

'Raymond.' She smiled. 'I do. A sad soul. I saw in the paper that he'd won the right to stay.'

'Do you think he's capable of murder?'

'Not the Raymond I knew. I think if he had been, Ena would have been dead years ago.'

'What makes you say that?'

'Dr Brayne dealt in sleep,' said the old nurse. 'Deep Sleep Therapy, it was called. He believed that the brain could regenerate itself if it was switched off for a period. Looking back, I think he treated his patients more as experiments than human beings. Some of them were sedated for weeks, including Raymond.' She paused, and then said quietly, 'Ena was in charge of that.'

So that's what Raymond had meant when he told Anderson that Ena kept putting him to sleep. Kirby dreaded to think what the long-term effects were, and wondered whether Raymond's ghost was a figment of his imagination. 'What about the people in the letters, did they undergo Deep Sleep Therapy – did it work?'

Margaret looked down at the letters on her lap and nodded. 'It was a long time ago, but I'm fairly certain that they did. And no, it didn't work.'

'Can you think of a reason why Ena would have kept these letters?'

'None. They weren't hers to keep.' She handed them back as though she no longer wanted anything to do with them.

Kirby folded up the letters and returned them to his pocket. 'You said that Ena was in charge of patient sedation – can you elaborate?'

'Up to ten patients were sedated and kept asleep in what became known as the Narcosis Room. Male and female. I was in charge of the nightingales – those were the nurses who did the real work. I say "real work"; they were the ones who looked after those poor souls, took them to the toilet, bathed them, combed their hair. Ena was incapable of any of that. When staff were short, the smell was awful. Sweat, urine, sometimes worse.'

'Where was this Narcosis Room?' he asked, hoping she'd corroborate what Connie had told him.

'In the private ward, Keats Ward.' Margaret turned to look at Kirby and began reciting a poem. '*Turn the key deftly in the oiled wards, And seal the hushed Casket of my Soul.* "To Sleep", by John Keats.'

'Were there any . . .' He hesitated, aware that this might be difficult for the retired nurse. 'Were there any accidents?'

Margaret fell silent and stared out of the window towards the floodlit pond. Kirby waited patiently, trying to read her face. It was as though her mind were elsewhere. After a few minutes, she slowly began to nod her head and whispered a barely audible '*Oh yes.*'

Kirby swallowed, feeling like he was on the brink of something. 'Did any of them involve any of the patients in the letters?'

A glass of sherry lay untouched on the side table, to which she now pointed.

He picked up the small glass and passed it to her.

'Thank you,' she said. She took the glass in her bony hand – which he now noticed had a slight tremor – and sipped the golden liquid. He found himself wondering what vintage it was.

'There was a girl and a young boy, possibly others,' she began. 'The girl was the daughter of one of Brayne's cronies. It was all handled very discreetly.' She wet her lips again with the sherry and passed the glass back to Kirby, who placed it on the table.

'What happened?' he asked.

'She died during childbirth.'

'At Blackwater?' Kirby was shocked, unaware that the hospital had a maternity ward.

Margaret nodded. 'Pass me those letters again.'

He took out the letters and handed them to her, and watched as she went through them one by one. 'This one,' she said, nodding as she examined its contents. 'I remember now, Sarah Carswell.'

Kirby took the letter, which began *My Darling Sarah* and was signed *Your loving Tom*. It was the only one out of the fifteen that didn't have a corresponding name on the envelope. He had assumed that Ena must have lost the original envelope and stuffed it into one she had spare.

'The envelope we found this one in was addressed to Catherine Edwards,' he said.

'Perhaps they didn't want anyone to know that she was there. As I said, it was all handled very discreetly.'

'You mean covered up?' asked Kirby.

Margaret nodded.

'Who was Tom – her boyfriend?'

'I had very little to do with Sarah, but she did have a young man who came to visit her. Different class to her, so I doubt her family approved. It could have been him.'

'Do you remember his surname?'

Margaret shook her head. 'I didn't even remember his name until you showed me the letter. Poor lad, he was smitten with her.'

'What year was this?'

She thought for a minute. 'It must have been in the mid-sixties. I can't be more specific than that.'

'What happened to the baby?'

'He was sent away, to an orphanage. Ena saw to that.'

Kirby was incredulous. 'Why on earth did the family allow that – what about the father, Tom?'

'Poor man had no say. The daughter was an embarrassment, and I think the family simply wanted shot of the entire situation. At least, the father did.'

Christ, thought Kirby. What sort of family did that? 'Can you remember which orphanage the baby was sent to?'

She began to move the blanket off her legs as though she needed to get up. 'I don't – it was all so long ago.'

'Let me help,' said Kirby, and he took the blanket and folded it over the back of her chair. 'You mentioned a young boy—' Suddenly a commotion broke out, distracting them both, and someone let out a wail followed by breaking glass. Kirby turned around to see an elderly gentleman being led out of the room by two care workers. The man looked distressed and confused. *God save me from ending up in a place like this, as posh as it is with its vintage sherry and floodlit bloody pond.* He saw Theresa making her way over towards them, tapping her watch, indicating it was time for him to leave. 'The boy, Miss Halliday?' he prompted.

'Oh, yes. He was young, about the same age as Raymond, anorexic. He had no family or friends and had come from an orphanage. Raymond took a shine to him. Two lost souls.' She shook her head. 'So sad.'

'What happened to him?'

'I wasn't privy to the details; all I knew was that he died during the Deep Sleep Therapy. Gregory Boothe was his name. Raymond was distraught. He'd recently lost his mother and then that happened.'

'Are you nearly done, Inspector?' said Theresa Bethell, who had now joined them. 'Only it's getting late.'

Kirby would have liked to hear more about Gregory Boothe, but he stood up and turned to Margaret, who was struggling to get out of her chair. 'Here, let me—'

She waved him off and stood unsteadily. 'I'm fine, thank you.'

'Margaret, you know that you should have your frame with you. What have I told you?' Theresa turned to Kirby. 'She's so stubborn,' she added with a smile.

'You fuss too much. Let me be.' Margaret held out a bony hand to Kirby. 'Good night, Detective Kirby.'

Kirby shook her hand and was surprised by how strong her grip was. 'You've been a great help. If I need to ask you anything else, may I call you here?'

'Of course.'

He thanked the old nurse again and gave her his card just in case. He told Theresa that he would make his own way out.

He was waiting for one of the staff to unlock the front door when something suddenly occurred to him. He rushed back towards the room he'd just come from as Margaret and Theresa emerged.

'Sorry, one more thing and I'll promise I'll leave you in peace,' he said, putting on his best smile. 'You mentioned the patients were sedated. Can you remember any of the drugs used?'

'There were so many,' the old nurse said. 'Mainly barbiturates . . .' She trailed off.

'I see,' said Kirby, disappointed. 'Thank you.' He was about to go when Margaret stopped him.

'But there was one,' she said. 'It wouldn't go amiss here sometimes.' She cast a mischievous look at Theresa. 'Long out of use now, of course. Ena swore by it.'

Kirby found himself holding his breath as Margaret recalled the name.

'That's it,' she said. 'Mandrax. Or, as the Americans called it, Quaaludes.'

CHAPTER 30

It was late when Kirby got back to the boat. It felt like an icebox, so he whacked on the heating and made hot chocolate, the thick Italian stuff you could stand a spoon up in, adding a more-than-generous slug of rum. After his visit to Littledene Care Home, he'd spent an hour or two at Mount Pleasant writing up his report and filling Anderson in on what Margaret Halliday had told him. They'd also done a quick search on Sarah Carswell and Gregory Boothe. Boothe's name yielded nothing but they got lucky with Sarah. She'd been the daughter of Duncan and Miranda Carswell, both now deceased, and had a sister, Helen. It had been too late to call the Registry of Births, Marriages and Deaths, so the details would have to wait. However, Duncan Carswell had been a man of some influence and warranted his own Wikipedia entry. And that was where Kirby had found some rather significant information.

Duncan Carswell had sat on the Blackwater Asylum board of governors and had been a keen supporter of Alistair Brayne's work, doing much to facilitate his career. The bit that caught Kirby's eye, however, was where the Carswells had lived – Marsh House.

Kirby plonked himself on the sofa and put his feet up, spooning a mouthful of the thick, rum-infused chocolate into his mouth. The stuffed three-legged fox eyed him as he went over in his mind what Margaret Halliday had told him. First off was that Ena had lied to her colleagues at the hospice about visiting her, which meant that Ena had been deceiving people right up until the day she died. Then there was her relationship with Dr Alistair Brayne. Whether or not he really was the father of Karen 'Onesie' McBride was open to speculation, and given Ena's propensity for lying it could easily have been another one of her fantasies. The death of Sarah Carswell, however, was most definitely not a fantasy. Exactly what Ena's involvement had been in that tragedy he had yet to discover, but if it turned out that Ena had been responsible in some way, then Sarah's boyfriend Tom Ellis, the father of her child – not to mention the child itself – would both have a motive for killing her. Gregory Boothe had apparently had no family or friends, which if true ruled out that connection. And then there was the Mandrax. Surely it couldn't be a coincidence that Ena kept her patients sedated with Quaaludes, only to be permanently silenced by them herself?

Sarah Carswell seemed to Kirby to be the key to all this – or rather, the only key he had. One question, in particular, had been rattling about in his head ever since he left Mount Pleasant, and that concerned Charles Palmer's recently deceased mother, Mrs Linehan – was she a Carswell? The Carswells could have sold up years ago, the house changing ownership every bloody year for the past thirty, for all he knew. He flipped open his laptop and typed *Helen Linehan Carswell* into the search engine, and clicked 'Return'.

A smile tugged at his lips as he read the results, and he gave the fox the thumbs up. Richard Linehan MP had, in 1967, married Helen Carswell, daughter of Duncan and Miranda Carswell of Marsh House, Battersea. So Helen had been Sarah's sister, which in turn made Charles Palmer Sarah's nephew and a cousin to her mystery son. Margaret Halliday hadn't been able to remember the name of the orphanage that he'd been sent to, but perhaps Charles Palmer could.

Kirby scooped out the last drops of chocolate and was thinking about having another rum, straight up this time, when his phone started ringing; it was Isabel.

'Hey,' she said. 'I saw your lights on.'

'Yeah. This Blackwater case, it's . . . complicated. How're you? Been out?'

'Just a few drinks at the studio.' She paused. 'You want me to come over?'

Kirby closed his eyes and did his best not to think about what would happen if she did. 'No – I mean, yes, I'd love you to, but . . . sorry, Isabel, this case . . .'

'It's okay, don't worry. How was your mother – did you manage a visit?'

'Yeah. She was, well, weird.' He'd been so caught up in the case that his visit now seemed like days ago.

'Did you find out what's wrong?'

'No.' He hesitated. 'I'm worried it's dementia.'

'In that case, she needs to see a doctor, Lew. Will she go?'

'I think so, yes.'

'Good. Changing the subject, you'll never guess who I have a meeting with next week,' she said.

'Who?'

'Patrick Calder.'

'How the hell did you manage that?' asked Kirby, impressed.

'I'd like to say it's because of my persuasive personality, although I doubt it. I don't actually know – he just changed his mind. Who cares, he's agreed to meet and that's what matters.'

'Maybe he's found a way he can use the situation for his own ends.'

'You don't like him, do you?'

Kirby laughed. 'No, is it that obvious? But it's good he's agreed to talk to you. I'm pleased.'

After chatting for a while longer they said goodnight, and he thought about calling his father but it was late by now. He'd tried a few times during the day and had the distinct feeling his dad was avoiding him. So, instead, he googled 'Deep Sleep Therapy Blackwater' and was surprised when an article popped up about unexplained patient deaths during treatment. Mostly it referred to institutions in America, but one section mentioned Blackwater in some detail. It seemed that several incidents had taken place there over the years, not just related to DST – unexplained deaths, the suicide of a young nurse, allegations of abuse – none of which, as far as he could make out, had ever been proven. One thing that did strike him was how confident and charismatic Brayne had been. The doctor had evidently been a maverick, but it was only after his death and the passing of time that people had begun to voice their concerns about his unorthodox – not to mention experimental – methods. No wonder he'd taken all his files with him when he retired. Photographs showed him to be somewhere between Charles Dance and Christopher Lee, and Kirby had no problem picturing him walking among his sleeping patients with the coldness of a vampire.

After another hour trawling the internet for information about Alistair Brayne, Kirby eventually crawled into bed. The river was still, the boat barely moving, but he could still detect the feeling of suspension that being on board gave him and that he found so comforting. He thought of Isabel, on her own boat at the end of the pier, and a pang of longing surged through his body, which almost had him up and running along the jetty. Instead, he focused on his next move – tomorrow he'd try to trace Tom, the man Sarah Carswell had run off with and who had fathered her child, as well as trying to trace the child itself. The obvious place to start was with Charles Palmer.

With no family and no medical records, Gregory Boothe was more problematic. And then there was Ena's involvement with Deep Sleep Therapy. It was all but forgotten about in the public domain, but the laying out of the body in Keats Ward suggested someone hadn't forgotten. The question was, who?

CHAPTER 31

Early the next morning, Kirby was at his desk at Mount Pleasant, eating a bacon sandwich 'Anderson style' – mustard, no ketchup – as he waited for Births, Marriages and Deaths to call him back. He'd spoken to them as soon as he'd got in, and they'd promised to call back with information on the Carswell family. He'd also called his father, who still wasn't picking up at home – or on his mobile. Where the hell was he?

Kirby's phone rang and he grabbed it without checking who it was, hoping it might be his dad.

'It's Linda Maltby from Births, Marriages and Deaths. I have the information that you requested.'

'Great. Hang on.' He grabbed a pen. 'Go ahead.'

'Duncan and Miranda Carswell were married in 1932 and had their first daughter, Sarah, which is the one you specifically asked about, in 1942. Their second daughter, Helen, was born five years later, in 1947.'

Kirby scribbled the dates down on a notepad. 'Okay, so no other children, just the two girls?'

'That's right. Sarah died in 1964, the same year that she gave birth to a son, Ian Thomas Carswell. We have no other records for him, just his birth certificate.'

'Does it say where he was born?' asked Kirby.

'Let me see . . . Blackwater Hospital, Battersea. The father wasn't noted.'

'What about cause of death for Sarah, are there any details?'

'None. They weren't always noted back then. You'd have to look at her medical file for that information, which, as I'm sure you know, would be confidential.'

Kirby underlined *cause of death* on his notepad twice. 'What about the other sister, Helen? What do you have on her?'

'Let me see . . . Helen married a Richard Mark Linehan in 1967 and there were no children. Richard died in 1998.'

'Sorry?' Kirby thought he'd misheard her. 'Did you say no children?'

'That's right. And she died last year, December 17th.'

'Does it say where she died?'

'Marsh House, Battersea. Sounds like a care home,' said Linda.

'And there's no other family?'

'Not immediately obvious, no. Duncan and Miranda Carswell were both only children. Helen's husband, Richard Linehan, had a brother, but he died a bachelor in 1995.'

'Okay, thanks. What about Gregory Boothe?'

'Born in 1951 to Alice Boothe, who died a month later, and the boy himself died in 1968. Father listed as unknown.'

'Thanks, Linda – you've been a great help. Can you email me this information?' He gave her his email address and hung up.

Kirby remained still for a long moment staring at all the notes on his pad. Eventually, he got up and walked over to the window. In stark contrast to the day before, today was bright and sunny and the sky a brilliant blue. An aeroplane came into view, leaving an Arctic-white vapour trail in its wake. The post he'd seen on the small table in the hall at Marsh House had been addressed to Mrs H. Linehan, who Palmer had said was his mother. Kirby stood and watched until the vapour trail had disappeared completely, which could have been seconds or minutes, he had no idea. He went back to his desk just as the office door flew open, almost banging off its hinges.

Anderson's strides could eat a room whole, the small floor space of the Mount Pleasant office gobbled up in three easy movements. 'Oh, morning,' said Anderson, flopping down at his desk opposite Kirby's. 'You're in early. That an Anderson Special?' He nodded at the half-eaten sandwich on Kirby's desk. 'I thought you were more of a bircher muesli man – keep you fighting fit for that new girl of yours.' Anderson's eyes caught sight of the notes scribbled on Kirby's pad and he pointed. 'What's that about?'

'BMD called about Sarah Carswell,' said Kirby, glad to be off the bircher muesli subject. Anderson had an irrational hatred of the stuff and had ribbed him mercilessly ever since he carelessly mentioned he quite liked it. 'She had a sister, Helen Linehan.'

'Hang on, Helen Linehan. Remind me . . . Palmer's mother?'

'Yes – and no.'

Anderson frowned. 'The bacon's turned your brain, you're not making sense.'

'Yes as in he told us she was his mother, but no because she didn't have any kids.'

'Maybe Palmer was adopted.'

'Could be.'

'What about Sarah's son, anything on him?'

Kirby nodded. 'Ian Thomas Carswell.' The information had come through from Linda and he skimmed through Duncan and Miranda's paperwork, going straight to Sarah Carswell's death certificate. It was as Linda had said – no cause of death had been noted for Sarah, and Alistair Brayne had signed the certificate. He then looked over Ian Thomas Carswell's birth certificate and smiled. 'If he lives in the UK, he's still alive. There's no death certificate.'

'Lew?' said a voice. It was Hamer's; he'd opened the door to his office just enough to make himself heard. 'A word.'

Anderson and Kirby exchanged looks as Kirby got up. 'Run Ian Carswell through the system, will you?' he said to Anderson on his way over to Hamer's office.

When he walked in, Hamer barely looked up. 'Shut the door, will you?'

Kirby did as he was asked and then sat down. 'What's up?'

'I've just had Patrick Calder on the phone. Again,' said his boss.

'What do you mean, *again*?'

'He called me last night. After your little visit.' Hamer stared at him, as though that was all that needed to be said.

'What did he want?' Kirby didn't remember upsetting him. Unless he'd lost his table at The Ivy.

'He wanted to know why you'd virtually accused him of murdering Ena Massey. And what *I* intended to do about it.'

'What? All I did was challenge him about knowing Ena Massey. And for the record, I didn't accuse him of anything. Virtually or otherwise.'

'You should have told me you were going,' Hamer said quietly.

'Why? He's a legitimate suspect. He's bloody lucky I didn't bring him in.' Kirby was fuming.

Hamer leant forward and tapped the desk with his index finger. 'He has an alibi. He has no motive. I know you don't like him, but please, from now on, leave Patrick Calder to me. He needs handling carefully; he could cause us – *me* – a lot of trouble.' He started shuffling papers on his desk, avoiding Kirby's eyes.

Kirby stood up. 'Is that all?'

Hamer nodded, now seemingly engrossed in a crime stat report. Kirby left without another word, wondering what the fuck was going on.

Back at his desk, he said nothing to Anderson about Hamer's warning. 'Did you find any other link between Calder and Ena Massey?'

Anderson shook his head. 'Nothing. As far as I can see, they met for the first – and only – time at the hospice on the day that he presented her with the award. And staff verified that Calder's grandmother was a patient there long before Ena joined. They had nothing to do with each other. Why?'

'Nothing. Shame, that's all.'

'He was really cut up about his gran dying, apparently. Oh, and Ian Carswell isn't in the system, so he's clean. That's if he's in the UK.'

Kirby thought for a moment. 'Charles Palmer, he's what, early fifties? That fits with Carswell's age.'

Anderson nodded. 'You think it's him?'

'It's certainly possible,' said Kirby. 'And if it is him, that makes him our number-one suspect.'

CHAPTER 32

Raymond's eyes roamed over the crumbling brickwork, ivy clawing its way up over the entrance as though trying to suck it down into the depths of the earth, and shivered. His gaze kept returning to a window on the first floor, arched, with a crack running diagonally from corner to corner. The fragments of memory that had been pushing their way forward since seeing the video at Mrs Muir's on Thursday evening, and subsequently being questioned by the police, were becoming more and more persistent. He thought of Gregory and what had happened to him beyond the arched window, but there was something else, something he'd been party to himself. It wasn't the treatment, he had very little recollection of that . . . This was *different*. Ena's death had unlocked something in his memory, he could feel it – and now he knew it was there, he had to know what it was. Which was why he'd decided, for the first time in decades, to enter Keats Ward.

He climbed the steep bank that led up to the old ward block from the lake and stopped, panting, at the top. Police tape hung across the entrance, jogging some event half buried in his memory. He pushed on, thinking about his friends in the bone jar and especially Gregory. Ducking under the tape he stepped into the dark interior, where he made his way to the staircase and began to climb. He didn't stop to look in the rooms on the ground floor – they were of no interest to him today; it was the room upstairs that drew him.

Now he was inside the building his inner being fought to leave, but he knew he had no choice but to continue up to the room where they'd found Ena's body. To the room where he'd been put to sleep for months and the room in which Gregory Boothe had died.

Reaching the top of the stairs, he paused and looked around. Pink paint flaked off the walls and ceiling; a row of doors leading to small rooms stood half open, their mesh panels brown and rusted. He didn't remember the walls being pink before, but that was hardly surprising as he remembered very little of how he ever got here. On the ceiling the light fittings hung dark and crooked where once they had shone brightly, strobing through his eyelids as he was wheeled semi-conscious beneath them. Ahead of him lay a door, half open, the arched window just visible beyond. He felt his body spasm and almost turned and ran, a hot sweat breaking out as he inched slowly forward, the junk shop of his mind beginning to open up. On the threshold of the room he hesitated, then stepped inside.

The first thing he noticed was a dead pigeon hanging from the light fitting and he quickly looked away. There was something about birds, especially dead ones, that he didn't like. He took a moment to compose himself before taking in the rest of the room. The beds had all been pushed to one side; some still had mattresses, stained and decayed, and the smell of sweat and urine flooded his memory. Sunlight filtered through the grimy windows and he could see that black powder covered the bedframes. Now he looked, it was all over the window and doorframes too. Was it fingerprint powder? He'd seen it on telly and he recoiled, not wanting to leave any trace of his visit.

He let his eyes roam the remaining space, his body still, braced for whatever was to come. But nothing happened. He looked around the room again, this time coming to a halt on the arched window. That, too, was covered in fine black dust. But there was something else. He moved a bit nearer, the angle of the light shifting on its dirty, cracked surface. And then he saw it as clear as day: a smiley face, winking at him, crudely drawn in the dust. At first he simply stared at it, confused. How had one of his faces got here? He hadn't drawn it and no one else had been here since the murder, as far as he knew – apart from the police, and he couldn't imagine them drawing smiley faces. Then it hit him: the Creeper had been up here. His face flushed red hot – it did that when he got angry – because everywhere he turned the Creeper had been there before him. It was like it was in his head. He'd cycled himself up, or whatever the word was, to come back into Keats only to find that a ghost – if indeed it was a ghost, as he was now seriously beginning to doubt – had beaten him to it. There was no chance of him remembering anything now, and in a small gesture of defiance he went up to the window and with the back of his sleeve he wiped the smiley face away.

Feeling slightly mollified he turned to leave, but he had only taken a few steps when he stopped mid-stride. The hot flush of anger he'd just experienced was now being replaced by the cold sweat of shock. On the floor in front of him was a small white feather, and in a split second a memory so strong that he gasped out loud flashed before him. Stumbling towards the door he steadied himself, not caring if he left traces, and closed his eyes for a moment. When he opened them he could almost see the flashgun going off in his head. Again and again the image flashed in front of him, so fast he could barely focus on it, and then snow, lots of it, floating across his vision – except it wasn't snow, it was feathers. Hundreds of them, small white feathers in his eyes and up his nose – one caught in his throat and he couldn't breathe – and he ran out of the room and down the stairs as fast as he could, tumbling out of the building like a madman, the police tape catching on a coat button and stretching until it snapped. He fell on to the snow outside, the sun blinding him as he lay staring up at the blue sky, his face smudged with black, images of Ena suffocating Nurse Abbott imprinted on his mind like a negative.

CHAPTER 33

Connie had barely slept the previous night, and had now been walking for a couple of hours, her face raw with cold, tears for Ed mingling with those brought on by the fierce wind. Her fingers and toes were numb but inside she felt brittle, as though a sharp gust of Arctic wind would break her. How could Ed be dead? How could Blackwater have claimed a second person in her life?

She was on Clapham Common and had reached the tennis courts – empty apart from a lone snowman; beyond lay some flats, a 1930s block called Parkview House. Consciously or otherwise, this was where she had been heading the whole time: to the address scrawled on the Post-it in Ed's room. She'd been upstairs at Harry's when DI Anderson had arrived last night and quickly pocketed the note, not mentioning it to the detective when she'd later shown him Ed's room. In truth, she'd forgotten about it until this morning, when she'd found the scrunched-up bit of paper in her coat pocket and then it suddenly became the most important thing in the world. It really was her last chance to find out who Sarah had been with that day, because Ed wasn't going to tell her, not now – not ever.

She climbed the steps up to the flats' entrance and went in, the warm air inside making her face smart. The address on the Post-it had said *45 Parkview House*, and instead of taking the lift up she decided to walk. She should have been nervous. She'd waited the best part of five years for this moment – to finally confront the person who'd left her sister dead, or dying, at Blackwater. But now it was finally here, she felt ambivalent; it wasn't how she'd envisaged it at all.

Number 45 was halfway along a corridor of doors all painted pale green. It was empty and quiet, the residents either out or the doors well-soundproofed. She stopped outside number 45 and rang the bell. She thought her face must look a mess, red and puffy, and she tried to smooth her hair a bit, in a bid to look slightly less of a mad stranger. Eventually, she heard the door being unlocked and braced herself.

'Yes?' said a croaky voice. 'Who is it?' The door was open as far as the chain would allow, and she could see half a pale face on the other side.

'I'm looking for Tom Ellis? My name's Connie Darke.'

The door closed, and she heard the chain being slid off. When it opened again, a man who had to be at least seventy, if not older, stood in the doorway. His age was hard to determine as illness had ravaged his face. There was no hint of colour – he didn't even have dark rings under his eyes – and his skin was like a flat grey mask. Even his stubble was grey.

'I'm Tom Ellis,' said the man.

She'd had no idea of what to expect, but it hadn't been this. 'I – I'm sorry,' Connie said, momentarily confused. 'I think I've got the wrong person.'

'Well, there's only one Tom Ellis here,' he coughed.

'Oh . . .' She stalled, not knowing what to say. 'Sorry, I was here because a friend of mine, Ed Blake—'

'Ed?' the man asked, suddenly peering behind her as though Ed might appear.

'Um, yes.'

The transformation was miraculous. A smile broke out on his face, the crease lines around his eyes and mouth highlighting the contours of his face, bringing it to life. 'Why didn't you say? Come in.' He stepped aside and Connie found herself walking in without a second thought.

She stood uncomfortably in the small hallway while he fiddled with the door chain. A tattoo, now faded and distorted with liver spots, was visible on his left hand; Connie guessed a heart of some kind. 'Old habits,' he mumbled, double-locking the door.

The hall was painted white, and a few small landscapes were hung on the walls. They weren't bad, either.

'Come through,' he said, and showed her into the sitting room. 'Take a seat.' He switched the television off and lowered himself slowly into a leather chair.

Connie took a seat on the sofa and looked around the room. It was full of framed photographs, mainly family portraits. Tom Ellis coughed again, wincing in pain. Her guess was cancer of some sort.

'So, you're a friend of Ed's then? Is there any news? I saw he was missing.'

'Um, they've found a body. It's Ed's.' Her voice almost cracked saying the words.

'Dear God,' said Tom. 'That's terrible news. He was such a lovely bloke.' He had a strong South London accent, softened with age. 'I appreciate you coming to tell me.'

'Actually, that's not why I'm here,' she said awkwardly.

'Oh?' said Tom, looking puzzled.

Connie wasn't quite sure how to go on. 'I gather Ed came to see you last weekend?'

Tom nodded. 'That's right.'

'About Sarah – my sister?'

'I'm afraid not,' he said, shaking his head.

'You mean he didn't come here about her accident?'

'No, why would he? He was here for another reason altogether.'

Connie was crestfallen; she'd got it all wrong. The stress of Ed going missing and the shock at his body being found had made her jump to conclusions – the wrong ones. She stood up, embarrassed by her mistake. 'I'm so sorry – I thought you were someone else. I don't know what I was thinking . . .' She felt tears running down her face from the disappointment that this wasn't who she thought it was. 'Sorry, what an idiot. I'll leave you be.'

'Here, take this,' said Tom, holding out a tissue with his bony hand. 'And sit down. You can't leave in this state.'

Connie took the tissue gratefully and blew her nose. Christ, she felt like a prize fool. This was going nowhere; not even Mole was going to hear about this balls-up. 'Thanks, but really, I should be going. I'm sorry to have bothered you.'

'Sit down, please.' He gave her such a pleading look, she relented. 'Connie's your name, did you say?'

She nodded.

'Ed mentioned you.'

A small jolt went through her. 'He did?'

'Said you were almost as obsessed as him, about Blackwater.' He smiled. 'Been thinking about him a lot since I heard he went missing. Especially after what I told him on Sunday.'

Suddenly, her interest was aroused. 'What do you mean?'

'Well, that's what I was trying to say. He wasn't here about your Sarah – he told me about that, by the way. Terrible. No, he was here last weekend about my fiancée, Sarah.' He got up with effort from the chair and went over to a dresser, where he picked up a framed photograph. 'This was taken in 1964, just before she was admitted to Blackwater. Four months later and she was dead.' He handed her the picture.

'I don't understand . . .' She stared at the young woman's face, and a sudden irrational fear ran through her.

'He came to interview me. About what happened.'

Connie looked at him. 'What did happen?'

'Ena bloody Massey, that's what happened.' He began coughing again and wiped his mouth with a tissue produced from his pocket. There were flecks of blood on it.

Connie was now desperate to hear what he had to say, and waited patiently for the coughing fit to subside. She couldn't help but wonder how long he had left.

'Sarah was the black sheep,' he finally began. 'Came from a well-to-do family. Nasty bunch, especially her old man. Tyrannical bloody bastard. They expected her to marry some toff and settle down, but she had other ideas, did Sarah. Ran off from the family home and came to Soho looking for some excitement – and to get away from her father. I was working down Covent Garden Market at the time. Had a stall selling flowers and that. I was young and full of myself then.'

'Is that where you met?' asked Connie.

He nodded. 'We fell in love. Just like that. It was right mad.' He smiled, and for a second she saw the young Tom, fit and healthy. The tattoo was now clearer on his left hand. A heart with a scroll across it. And a name.

'How did her family take it?' she asked.

'They didn't know to begin with – she had nothing to do with them apart from her sister. It was only when she fell pregnant and things started to go wrong that they became involved.'

Connie listened as he told his story. They'd fallen head over heels in love and Tom had proposed to her after three months, down on one knee, a bunch of his finest carnations in his hands. Despite their initial happiness, it soon became clear that Sarah suffered from some kind of depression, not that he knew what it was back then, but she was prone to melancholy periods, and when she became pregnant these bouts got worse. In the end, her sister told the family what was going on, and they intervened. They had her admitted to Blackwater.

'What happened?'

'She died. During childbirth.'

'At Blackwater?'

Tom nodded. 'It did happen, childbirth at Blackwater – not that they had a maternity ward there as such. I've since learned that Dr Brayne, who was head honcho back then, and this Massey woman practised what they called Twilight Sleep. That was on top of his Deep Sleep Therapy.'

'What on earth is Twilight Sleep?' Connie had never heard of it.

'Women going into labour were heavily sedated with drugs and that; the theory being that they wouldn't remember nothing.' He coughed again. 'So no memory of the pain – or anything else, if you ask me.'

Despite herself, Connie couldn't help thinking that it sounded like a good idea – a pain-free childbirth? She'd sign up for that if she ever had children. 'So what went wrong?'

'God knows. Brayne told us that she had a severe reaction to the drugs used, but I didn't really believe him.'

'Why not?'

'Just a feeling. Every time I visited, Sarah was more out of it. It was like she was a zombie or something.'

'What did you do?'

'Kicked up a bit of a stink. Said I wanted an autopsy. A second opinion. But it was no good, Brayne was a powerful man – and Sarah's family were and all. No one would listen to me.'

'What about the baby?'

Tom shook his head. 'That was the worst part.' He looked up at Connie with such a pained expression on his face that she could barely hold his gaze. 'I never even saw the little fella. The family took him, and that was that. The only person who showed me any sympathy was a young trainee nurse. Badly affected her, it did. Heard she topped herself a few years after.'

'Jesus,' whispered Connie. 'What happened to the baby?'

'The family looked after him, but I later heard from the sister that he was sent to an orphanage.'

'Why on earth would they do that? He could have come to you.'

'He could have done, but really, a market trader like me, looking after a kid? I barely had rent and beer money, never mind money for a little one. My family were pretty shit too – pardon my French. No, he was probably better off going somewhere else. At least I hope so.' Tom began coughing again and disappeared into the kitchen. Connie could hear pills being shaken from a bottle and the kitchen tap running.

She got up and went over to the dresser for a closer look at the photographs. There were several of Sarah before she became pregnant and, although she was smiling for the camera, there was a haunted look in her eyes. As Connie picked one up, a smaller photo fluttered to the floor. It was another picture of Sarah, but this time her face was devoid of any emotion. An image of Keats Ward flashed through Connie's mind from the day before, followed by Kirby's words. *On a bed, over there . . . with the number nineteen on it.*

'What have you got there?' asked Tom. She hadn't heard him come back into the room and felt as if she'd been caught doing something she shouldn't.

'Oh, um, this fell out.'

Tom looked at the picture. 'Day before she died. I'd forgotten I had it.'

'And you're sure Ena Massey was involved?'

'On my life – or what's left of it. Used to write to Sarah, I did. Never had mobile phones or email in them days. Good old-fashioned letters is what we relied on. Only, Sarah said she never got my letters, not all of them at any rate. When I asked Nurse Massey, she just told me that Sarah's memory must be playing tricks on her. I didn't believe her, but what could I do?'

'Tom, could I borrow this?' asked Connie, tapping the picture. 'It's important, and I'll make sure it's returned, you have my word.'

'Go ahead. Take it.'

Connie made her farewells as fast and politely as she could, and left Parkview House with her heart racing. Yesterday, when Kirby had asked whether a bed with the number 19 on it had meant anything, it hadn't. The photograph in her pocket changed all that. Now she knew exactly what it meant.

CHAPTER 34

Kirby found Charles Palmer leaning on the railings by St Mary's Church in Battersea, staring out over the river. He looked like a man who hadn't slept – a five o'clock shadow crept around his chin, his eyes were bloodshot, and despite his tan his face looked sallow in the cold, bright air. When Kirby had called at Marsh House earlier, Palmer's car had been in the drive but the curtains had been drawn, and after ringing the bell several times and getting no response, he'd called Palmer's mobile. Looking at him now, Kirby's guess was that he hadn't been home, and he wondered whether he'd had a long night at the Vauxhall Tavern – or one of the other gay bars nearby.

'What do you want, Inspector?' Palmer asked, wearily gazing across the water towards the Lots Road Power Station. The church was in a beautiful position, directly on the riverbank.

'Your cousin, Ian Carswell. I was hoping that you might know where I can find him.'

'Sorry, I can't help. I have no idea where he is. Why do you want to know?' he asked, a bit too casually.

'His name cropped up in relation to the Blackwater case.' He studied Palmer's face and noticed lines he could have sworn weren't there a few days ago. 'Is something bothering you, Mr Palmer?'

'No.' He turned and looked at Kirby. 'Was there something else you wanted to ask me?' He pulled out a pair of sunglasses and put them on, as though suddenly aware of how exposed his face was.

'Yes, your mother – Helen Linehan – she adopted you?'

Palmer returned his gaze to the river and clasped his hands together as he leant on the railings and half smiled. 'Yes, she did.'

'Do you mind telling me about that? Only you said that you grew up in Perth, Australia, not here in London.'

'It's complicated . . .'

'So you said, the other day.'

Palmer shoved his hands in his pockets. 'It's not something I like to talk about. My mother and I never really got on. Her husband, Richard, had a brother in Australia, and I spent more time over there than I did here. I suppose I did grow up at Marsh House; it just didn't feel like it.'

'She still left it to you though.'

'There was no one else. I'm under no illusion that it was left to me out of love – more a sense of duty, guilt even.'

Guilt for what? wondered Kirby. 'Going back to your cousin, Ian, can you tell me anything about him? Are there any other family members who might know where he is?'

Palmer turned to look at Kirby, shaking his head. 'Like I said, I can't help. He wasn't part of my life. In any shape or form.'

Something in the way Palmer spoke felt like it was the truth, and yet Kirby sensed he wasn't being entirely honest. He tried to see beyond the polarised lenses and into Palmer's eyes, but all he could see was his own reflection staring back.

'I need to get home,' said Palmer abruptly. 'I have a company coming in the morning to put things into storage, and there's still a lot to pack up. You know where to find me.'

Kirby watched him walk up past the small church and turn left on to Battersea Church Road, eventually disappearing from view.

There was a sadness – palpable and raw – that he hadn't seen before, and it seemed to seep from Palmer's very being. Kirby wondered what it was that he wasn't telling him.

His mobile buzzed in his pocket.

'It's Connie Darke.' She sounded breathless. 'I need to see you.'

'Is everything okay?' he asked.

'Yes, but I need to show you something. Can we meet?'

'Where are you?'

'Near Clapham Common. Battersea end.'

'There's a small café at the top of Battersea Rise near the church. I can be there in fifteen minutes.'

He wondered what it was that was so urgent as he drove through Battersea towards the Common. Had Ed Blake's death prompted her to open up about something? When he arrived at the small café, Connie was already waiting and he could tell that she'd been crying. The place was empty apart from a couple, both engrossed in their mobile phones. Kirby ordered a macchiato and sat down. 'What was it you wanted to show me?'

She slid a black-and-white photograph across the table towards him. 'This.'

He picked it up and studied the image. It showed a young woman in a bed that looked identical to the one they'd found Ena Massey's body on, the number 19 clearly stencilled at its foot. 'Where did you get this?'

'From a man called Tom Ellis. Her name was Sarah Carswell,' said Connie, tapping the photo in Kirby's hand. 'They were engaged to be married.'

'*This* is Sarah Carswell? But—' The barista brought his coffee over and asked if they wanted anything else. 'We're fine, thanks,' said Kirby impatiently, waiting for him to go back to the counter before continuing. 'How do you know Tom Ellis?' He remembered the letter Margaret Halliday had singled out, signed, *With all my love, Tom.*

'I found his name and address at Harry's place – with the name "Sarah" underneath. I thought it was the person Ed had found who'd been with my sister when she had her accident – or at least someone who knew who it was. Only when I got there, it was immediately apparent I was wrong.'

'So it was Sarah Carswell, not your sister?'

Connie nodded and then described her visit to Tom Ellis, Sarah Carswell's former fiancé. 'He's in no fit state to kill anyone, let alone get into Blackwater in sub-zero temperatures,' she said, when she'd finished.

'So he has no idea what happened to the child?'

'None. Only that he was sent to an orphanage, but he doesn't know which one. The Carswells closed ranks, shut him out. The father was a total bastard, apparently. No wonder Sarah left.'

This appeared to fit with what Margaret Halliday had told him, and if it was all true it was a tragic story. It looked as if the one place Sarah Carswell should have been safe turned out to be the most dangerous place she could have gone.

'Can you write down Tom Ellis's address for me?' Kirby pushed a napkin towards her and pulled out a pen. 'I'm sorry about Ed, by the way,' he said, as she wrote.

'Thanks. I've been a bit all over the place to be honest. This' – she indicated Tom's address as she wrote – 'I don't know, it gave me something to do. I guess I'll never know who Sarah was with now.' She pushed the address over to him.

'Thanks.' He glanced at it before slipping it into his pocket. It was five minutes away.

'Do you think that's why Ed was killed?' asked Connie. 'Because of what Tom told him about Ena Massey?'

'It's certainly something we'll look into, but . . .' He paused. 'But I'm not convinced. It could be that Ed was extremely unlucky that night, stumbling into something he knew nothing about.'

'What about the Creeper? Do you think they have anything to do with this?'

'How do you know about that?' asked Kirby.

'Raymond Sweet told me about it. He thinks there's a ghost creeping around Blackwater. As if.'

'You've spoken to Raymond Sweet?'

'I bumped into him yesterday after you left. He mentioned it then.'

'What exactly did he say?'

'Not much. I think he was embarrassed and wished he'd never mentioned it. All he said was that it moved things in his house.'

'It's been in his house?' Sweet hadn't mentioned that to Anderson. Christ, maybe Raymond was more unstable than he'd thought.

'So he says. He mentioned a torch – said one day it was gone, then the next day it was back. Just little things . . .'

'Well, he's either imagined it or someone *has* been in his house. Why anyone would do that, I can't—' He suddenly noticed Connie had gone very still. 'What is it?'

'This is crazy . . .' she said, shaking her head.

'What is?'

'When I came home the other night, the boiler had been switched off. The cat flap was locked but the cat was outside – remember, when you called I was fiddling with it? I thought I was imagining things, losing the plot with all this stuff going on, but . . .'

'What are you saying?'

'If Raymond hadn't said anything, I wouldn't have given it a second thought, but now . . . Now, I think someone's been in the Four Sails.'

CHAPTER 35

Kirby drove Connie home and checked all her doors and windows before leaving. Everything appeared to be in order, and there was no sign of any kind of break-in. The only puzzling thing was the door to the pub cellar; the key was missing. Connie couldn't remember the last time she'd seen it. She never went into the cellar, or very rarely, and the key was always left in the lock. It could have gone missing weeks – or even months – earlier. Kirby suddenly remembered Palmer saying that he'd lost the remote for the gate at Marsh House, and wondered if there was a connection.

Once he'd felt comfortable about leaving her alone, he drove to Tom Ellis's place. But he was too late; Tom Ellis had been found by a neighbour, collapsed in his hall, and been taken to St George's. His condition was serious and there was every chance he wouldn't pull through.

Back at Mount Pleasant, Kirby felt deflated. *Someone* had to know what had happened to Ian Carswell. Palmer had said that he'd spent a lot of time in Australia with his uncle while he was growing up, so Kirby went back over the information from BMD, remembering Linda saying that Richard Linehan's brother had died a bachelor in 1995. According to his death certificate he was living in the UK at the time, which didn't mean to say that he hadn't lived abroad before then. It did strike him as odd that Helen Linehan would adopt a child when, in theory, she could have been a mother to her sister's child.

Why was the baby sent away? Unless Tom Ellis recovered, they might never find out.

He brought up the government's probate research service on his computer and typed in Helen Linehan's details. She had died on 17 December last year and probate had been granted on 3 February. Two weeks ago. He made a note of the probate number and picked up the phone.

'Dianne? It's Lew Kirby. How are you?' A small smile crept over his lips as he spoke.

'My oh my, Lew Kirby. It's been a while,' said a husky voice on the other end of the phone. 'I'm fine. How about you? Still on that damned boat?'

'I am. I'm surprised you remember.'

'I'm hardly likely to forget a three-legged stuffed fox,' she said with a soft laugh. 'And it was quite a night.'

'Yes, it was,' said Kirby, remembering all too clearly. Dianne Halloran worked at the Probate Registry, and he'd met her at a party a year or so ago. She had been sitting in a corner with a bottle of Chablis, reading a book about magic tricks that she'd pulled off the hosts' bookshelf. After helping her finish the Chablis – which had actually been rather good – he'd suggested they went somewhere else. Several pubs later, they'd ended up on his boat.

'What can I do for you?' she asked. He couldn't tell if the comment was loaded or not, as everything Dianne said sounded loaded. She just had one of those voices.

'I need you to trace a probate number for me. I'm after a will.' Probate had only recently been issued on Helen's will, so the information might not yet be available, although technically it was now in the public domain.

'Give me the number,' said Dianne. 'Slowly.'

He concentrated on reading the number, wondering why they'd never become an item.

'You're in luck,' she said, after a minute or so. 'It's just gone online. Shall I send it over?'

'Thanks.' He gave her his email address.

'You want to go for a drink, for old times' sake?' she asked. 'No strings.'

'Thanks, but I'm a bit tied up at the moment – no pun intended.'

'Another time then,' said Dianne. 'When you're not so tied up.'

Her voice seemed to melt down the phone with such seductive intent that he found it quite alarming. 'I'm not sure my girlfriend would approve,' he said.

'Are you saying you don't trust me now?' He could tell she was smiling.

The details of Helen's will landed in his inbox, so he ended the conversation before he agreed to something he might regret. He put the phone down and was about to turn his attention to the Last Will and Testament of Helen Linehan when his mobile rang. It was a number he didn't recognise.

'Detective Kirby?' said a woman's voice. The line crackled.

'Yes, speaking.'

'This is Margaret Halliday.'

Kirby could hear music in the background – Radio 3, at a guess. 'Miss Halliday, how can I help?'

'I've remembered something. Are you ready to take this down?' she asked, briskly.

Kirby grinned to himself. 'Poised for action, Miss Halliday.'

'I remembered the name of the orphanage that Ena sent that poor child to. House of Nazarene.'

'Do you know where it was?' he asked, jotting down the name.

'Mitcham. I'm sure you'll find it listed somewhere, although whether it still exists is another matter.'

'Thank you, Miss Halliday, that's extremely useful. Was there anything else?'

'Well, it might be nothing,' she began. 'But those letters you showed me.'

'Yes?' He waited.

'The one addressed to Ruthie – I knew there was something about it, only I couldn't pinpoint what it was.'

He remembered how she'd picked out the name and had appeared on the brink of remembering something. 'What about it?'

'I could be wrong, but if it's who I think it is, she wasn't a patient – she was a nurse.'

'Why would Ena have a letter addressed to a nurse?' he asked, thinking out loud.

'I have no idea. Unless . . .'

'Unless what?' asked Kirby.

'Well, unless it arrived after she died.'

'You'll have to explain.'

'She killed herself. She'd taken drugs from the dispensary and took an overdose. Allegedly.'

He swallowed, a nasty feeling beginning to bloom in his stomach. 'What do you mean, *allegedly*?'

After a pause, Margaret spoke. 'Ena found her.'

'What exactly are you saying, Miss Halliday?'

'Her family were adamant that she would never have taken her own life. You may draw your own conclusions.'

'Do you remember where she was found, or what she took?'

'I don't, I'm sorry. I hope I've been of some help.'

'You have – and thank you, Miss Halliday. You take care now.'

He ended the call and immediately dialled Kobrak's extension, the feeling growing that they were finally on to something.

223

'Take a look at the letters we found in Ena's bedroom again, will you?' he said when Kobrak picked up. 'In particular, the one addressed to Ruthie. Looks like she was a nurse, not a patient, and that she committed suicide. Find out what you can.'

'I'm on it,' said Kobrak, the excitement in his voice palpable.

A quick Google search revealed that the House of Nazarene orphanage was now a care home – Christ, he'd seen enough of care homes and hospitals in this case to last him a lifetime. He jotted down the address and called the general enquiries number. The girl who answered sounded as though she was at the end of her shift and couldn't care less, but she did say that the home's manager, Dan Christie, would be in at 8.30 a.m. And that, yes, they did hold a few records from 'the past', but she couldn't be sure what. He put the phone down and thought for a few minutes. There wasn't much more he could do tonight, so he decided to go back to the boat and try to get the case straight in his head. There was also the small matter of speaking to his father, who he still hadn't managed to track down.

Before leaving, he opened up Helen Linehan's will, which Dianne had sent over, and skimmed through the legalese until he came to the section marked *Beneficiaries*. He read the section several times just to be sure. Helen Linehan had left Charles Palmer not only Marsh House but also a sizeable amount of money; in fact, she'd left him virtually everything. The only thing she hadn't left him were some drawings of the house, which he noted were bequeathed to RADE, where Connie worked. Not that Palmer would give a damn about a few drawings, because whoever he was – Helen's son or Ian Carswell – he was now a very, *very* wealthy man indeed.

CHAPTER 36

It was Monday morning and the atmosphere on the roads was fractious, everyone thoroughly fed up with the weather and just wishing it would get back to normal – and that included Kirby. He'd finally managed to speak to his father the night before, albeit briefly, which wasn't helping his current mood either. His dad had remained tight-lipped about Livia and their conversation had been strained, exacerbated by bad reception. He couldn't remember the last time he'd had such an awkward conversation with his father, and had actually felt a sense of relief when the signal finally gave up completely and cut them off.

After what seemed like an eternity of red lights, being beeped at and cut up, he pulled up at his destination, the House of Nazarene care home. Like Littledene, it was situated in what had once been a Victorian house, but that's where the similarities ended. It was smaller than Littledene and had been added to over the years – and not sympathetically. The 1960s additions clung to the original building like parasites; leaching whatever character it had once had into a miasma of grey panels and peeling paintwork. Ramps with corporation-yellow handrails led up to double doors with wire-mesh security-glass panels. It looked more like a halfway house than a care home, and Kirby felt his already-low spirits plummet even further as he entered the hallway. If the day carried on like this, he'd be scraping them off the pavement by lunchtime.

'Can I help?' a young woman asked from behind a tattered reception desk. She looked worn out, her navy uniform crumpled and flecked with unimaginable things.

Kirby explained who he was and asked whether Dan Christie was in yet. With a bored look she picked up the phone and spoke to someone – presumably Christie – to tell them 'the fuzz are here', and then buzzed him through another set of double doors into a corridor painted pale blue. By comparison, Blackwater was rather attractive – despite standing empty for nearly twenty-five years. The artificial lighting, scuffed skirting boards and the cold shade of blue all gave Nazarene an intensely depressing atmosphere.

Christie's office was first on the right, and soon after knocking a chirpy voice from within called, 'Come in!'

The contrast was astonishing – although, admittedly, it would have been hard to get much worse. The office was painted – freshly, judging by the smell – in orange and yellow. Potted plants lined the windowsill, which looked out on to a car park. Photographs of ageing film stars adorned the walls, and a small two-seater sofa had been crammed into the room along with an old wooden desk and antique swivel chair. It was quite a sight. As was Dan Christie. He was a small man, in his forties, wearing a checked shirt and knitted tank top. Either he or a family member was an amateur knitter, Kirby guessed, looking at the uneven V-neck. Even his tie was knitted, something Kirby hadn't seen since his school days. Christie wore wire-rimmed glasses whose lenses were so thick that they made his eyes look the size of golf balls. He wouldn't have looked out of place in a Big Top.

'How can I help?' He stood and extended a hand, which Kirby took, half expecting a mild electric shock.

'I'm interested in the records you hold for the House of Nazarene orphanage,' he said, sitting on the small sofa, which despite its size felt like it could swallow him whole. There was probably a whoopee cushion inside. 'I called yesterday and was told that you still have some.'

'Ah, the House of Nazarene orphanage. What period were you thinking of?' Christie sat down on the wooden swivel chair and regarded Kirby with interest. The chair creaked as he leant forward eagerly.

'I'm looking for someone in particular. A baby who came here in 1964, possibly 1965, name of Ian Carswell.'

'I can tell you right now that we won't have his personal records,' said Christie. 'All those would have been sent to the local authority.' He pushed his glasses back up his nose, the lenses so heavy that they kept slipping down. 'Good luck with trying to trace anything there,' he added.

'Do you hold any records at all for that period?' Kirby asked, feeling disappointed already.

'That's what I was coming on to. We do hold a few – they tend to be more general records about the orphanage. Its day-to-day running, finances and so forth.' He smiled. 'Let's see what the old Wheel of Destiny has to say, shall we?' Dan Christie swivelled – if that was the correct terminology for a man in knitwear – to his left, deftly stopping just in time to pull out what looked like an enormous, oversized filing cabinet drawer. Within the drawer was a circular filing system, a bit like an old-fashioned Rolodex – Kirby's mother still had one – only on its side.

'We don't hold a lot of files for that period, but you never know,' he said, spinning the file like it was a roulette wheel, stopping it with his fingers at a tab, which Kirby could see from the sofa said *1965*.

Christie pulled out a file and twisted round to put it on his desk. 'Bloody chair, only goes one way,' he said, continuing his swivel until he was facing Kirby again. He opened the file and began going through its contents.

After a few minutes, Christie looked up. 'What were the child's circumstances?' he asked. 'Do you know where he came from?'

'He was born in Blackwater Asylum in 1964. His mother died during childbirth.'

Christie went back to the file. 'This could be something.' He pulled out a page and began going through the text, running his finger under each line, as though fearful he would miss something. 'Minutes from a meeting held on 5th January 1967,' he mumbled. 'Interesting . . .'

Kirby could feel himself gradually being swallowed by the sofa. The springs had gone, and he kept having to shift his weight forward to sit on the edge of the frame.

'Ah-ha!' said Christie all of a sudden. 'I think this is it!' He rummaged about in the file and pulled out another piece of paper. 'Here we are. The pages were out of order – this was originally stapled together.' He held out the papers to Kirby. 'Third paragraph down.'

He skimmed the text on the first page, but couldn't spot Carswell's name, and so glanced at the following page. He looked up at Christie. 'What is this? It looks like some kind of travel document.'

'That's exactly what it is,' said Christie. 'Take a closer look.'

He went back over the third paragraph and stopped halfway. 'Baby C?'

Christie nodded. 'If you read further, you'll see why.'

A short itinerary was listed, beneath which several declarations had been signed. They briefly outlined the suitability of each child for the journey and had then been signed by a guardian or representative. 'Christ,' he muttered, looking up at Christie. 'Is this what I think it is?'

Christie nodded. 'The list you have in your hands is the final list of child migrants sent from the House of Nazarene to Australia. The last boat sailed on 24th January 1967, and your baby was on it.'

Kirby looked down at the document in his hand and felt a flutter of excitement. Baby C had been sent to Perth. Not only that: his declaration had been signed by Ena Massey.

CHAPTER 37

It had just turned midday when Connie walked up the drive of Marsh House. She'd called Bonaro earlier, to explain what had happened at the Four Sails over the weekend, and he'd said that once she'd collected the drawings bequeathed by Helen Linehan, she would be free to take the rest of the day off. She planned to get the lock changed on the cellar door, and the ones on the front and back doors, just to be sure. Why anyone would break into her house and fiddle with the boiler and cat flap was a mystery, but the idea freaked her out. Perhaps it was meant to.

An expensive-looking Merc was parked at an angle across the drive, as though someone had stopped in a hurry. Circumnavigating the car, Connie approached the front door and was about to knock when it opened, and she found herself face to face with a tall, tanned man in what looked like a very expensive suit, with a clutch of papers under his arm.

'Yes?' he asked. She noticed that his eyes scanned the driveway behind her before coming to focus on her.

'My name's Connie Darke. I work for the architectural archive, RADE, on Queen's Square. I'm here to collect some drawings.'

'What drawings?'

'The owner Mrs Linehan bequeathed them to us in her will – drawings of the house. The executors called us last week, and my boss, Richard Bonaro, arranged for me to collect them.' She watched as the man processed what she'd said. He didn't seem to know what she was talking about. Had there been some mistake?

Suddenly his face changed. 'Drawings of *this* house?'

'That's right. I was told to contact a Charles Palmer. I did call earlier, but it went straight to answerphone. I left a message.' There was something about the man's gaze that was unnerving.

'Oh . . . I'm sorry. It's been a busy morning. There are areas in the house where there's no signal.' He smiled. 'Do come in.' He stepped aside to make way for her, and she went inside.

The hall was dark, all but one of the doors off it shut, some light filtering down the stairs. It was crammed full of packing boxes, and freezing cold.

'The house is being cleared, as you can see.'

'So, are you Mr Palmer?' she asked.

'Sorry, how rude,' he said, extending a hand.

'Pleased to meet you, and my condolences,' said Connie, taking the hand, which felt unnaturally soft. They stood awkwardly in the hallway for a few seconds, Palmer making no move to get the drawings.

'How many drawings are there?' she prompted. 'We're very excited to be acquiring them. We hold the entire James Neville collection – apart from Blackwater. Unfortunately no one knows what happened to those.'

'Actually,' he smiled, 'I have no idea how many there are.'

'Okay, perhaps I could take a look? If there are too many I'll call a cab.'

'Would you like a cup of tea?' Palmer asked, suddenly.

The question was so unexpected that she accepted without thinking. She could do with a cup simply to warm her hands, if nothing else. Palmer led her into a sitting room, which was equally cold, and told her to wait. She went over to the window and looked out across the garden and wondered what it would be like to live in a place like this. Terror would love it, she thought, as a robin landed on a frozen birdbath. The garden was large and ran down to the river, where there was a boathouse – she'd seen it once on a boat trip down the Thames. Lost in thought, she didn't hear Palmer when he came back in the room a few minutes later.

'Your tea,' he said, making her jump.

She took the mug of steaming tea. 'Thanks. You not having one?'

'Oh, no. I finished one before you arrived. Right, this way then,' he said, sounding far jollier than he had on her arrival.

She followed him into the hall and up the stairs, noticing the papers still clutched in his hand.

'I suppose they're in some kind of portfolio?' he asked, as they reached the landing.

'That's what I was told. So you haven't looked at them then?'

'To be honest, stuff like that has been left to the solicitor to sort out. I've had more important things to attend to.' He opened a door to a room on the left. 'Here you are,' he said. 'They'll be in here somewhere.'

Connie looked around the room. It was packed to the rafters with boxes of books, clothes and household ornaments. It looked as though Palmer had swept all the shelves of ornaments and shoved them randomly into any box he came across. It was chaotic, to say the least. She couldn't see a portfolio anywhere.

'And these are definitely drawings of the house, you said?' he asked.

'Yes – plans.' It was odd that he didn't seem to know where they were, especially as it had been prearranged for her to collect them.

'Perhaps they're behind here,' he said, moving to close the door of the room.

She moved back a step and felt a box against her legs, spilling scalding tea over her hand in the process. There was really no room to move up here. 'Ouch,' she muttered, wiping the back of her hand on her jeans.

Palmer seemed not to notice, and had almost pulled the door to the room shut when the doorbell rang. For a moment he seemed unsure what to do, turning to look at her. The room felt claustrophobic with the door pulled to, and she suddenly felt trapped.

'Don't mind me,' she said. 'See who it is.'

'Of course.' He collected himself. 'Let me know if you find anything. You have me intrigued now.' He smiled. 'And don't let the tea get cold.'

Fat chance, it was positively Vesuvian. When he left the room, Connie looked for somewhere to put the mug down. The tea smelt dreadful, worse than the builder's tea Mole drank, and she put it on the mantelpiece. She could hear Palmer hurrying down the stairs as the doorbell rang again, and was relieved to be alone.

She picked her way over to the window and peered out. It overlooked the drive, and a van marked *Opus Crates* was parked in the driveway. They must have come to collect the boxes in the hall. She was glad Palmer was out of the way; there was something about him that gave her the creeps. Turning back to the room, she scanned the jumble of boxes. At least she was only looking for something that might contain large architectural drawings, which narrowed it down considerably, although the journals could be anywhere. Outside, the van's doors slid open.

Not wanting to waste any time, she began rummaging through some of the boxes. It was mainly knick-knacks. There was nothing resembling a roll of papers, or journals – let alone a portfolio. She tried moving boxes to make sure the plans weren't buried beneath, lying flat on the floor, but found nothing. Within a few minutes she realised the search was pointless. Perhaps they weren't in this room after all, Palmer hadn't seemed that sure. She idly began flicking through a box of framed photographs by the window, which were mainly family portraits featuring the same four people – two adults and two young girls, one of whom was several years older than the other. Deciding that she was wasting her time, she was about to leave when something made her stop in her tracks. The girls in the photographs. She went back and looked again. The older girl looked different, resembling the mother but not the father in any shape or form. The younger one had her father's brooding eyes, and they were unmistakably related. Her eyes went back to the older girl. She could only be about ten years old, but something about her made Connie's hair stand on end. It was the melancholy in the child's eyes. The same haunted look that she'd seen recently at Tom Ellis's flat, when she'd looked at the photograph of Sarah Carswell.

'Christ,' she muttered, realisation dawning. It was the same family; they'd never left.

Downstairs, she could hear voices. She quickly replaced the photos and picked her way over the boxes, creeping out on to the landing. Opposite, she could see the bathroom and suddenly remembered the mug of tea. She went back and picked up the mug, sniffing it again. Rank. She poured the offending liquid down the sink and noticed a packet of sleeping tablets lying open on the shelf. Palmer must be a bad sleeper, and she was about to take a nosey peek when something caught her eye in the bathroom mirror.

It was behind the bathroom door, a strange place to leave such a thing, and stranger still not to remember it was there. It was a red leather portfolio with black corners. She quickly undid the ties, the front of the portfolio flopping to the floor with a loud smack. Some of the smaller papers inside slid out, skidding across the tiled bathroom floor; the larger ones secured by inner flaps. She bent down to pick up the smaller pages and realised that they were sketches of the house and garden.

She hastily sifted through them, aware that it had gone quiet downstairs. They really were rough sketches – ideas, more than anything. About to put them back in the portfolio, one caught her eye; it was bolder than the others, more definite. Picking it up she found that, in fact, it was two drawings on fine tracing paper, one laid over the other. She flipped the top sketch up, looking at the one beneath, then flipped the top one down again. It was like an old-fashioned flick book – *now you see it, now you don't*. She did it several times, making sure she wasn't imagining things. It was a tunnel – or rather two tunnels – linking Blackwater and the garden at Marsh House.

Adrenalin pumping, she swiftly rolled the small drawings up and slid them into one of her front pockets. After replacing the portfolio where she'd found it, she silently slipped out on to the landing, grabbing the mug as she went. Someone below was whistling – she guessed the van driver – but there was no conversation. Making her way down the stairs, she saw the man from Opus Crates lifting one of the boxes from the hallway. She nodded to him and waited as he hefted the heavy box out of the front door and into the back of his van. There was no sign of Palmer anywhere. She put the mug down on a small table by the front door, next to a mobile phone, and peered out of the front door. Strange, the Merc was gone.

'Funny bloke, your husband,' said the Opus man. 'He said just to carry on.' He was looking at her more carefully now, as though registering the age gap between her and Palmer and wondering if he'd put his foot in it. 'Okay with you, Mrs Palmer?'

'Oh, yes, sure,' said Connie. 'Just do whatever he told you.'

She walked quickly down the drive before he could ask her any more questions, and turned right on to Battersea Fields Drive, narrowly missing a man who'd just crossed the road. 'Sorry,' she muttered, dodging past. He looked vaguely familiar.

As she walked, she thought about the drawings. What she should do was call Kirby. Or she could do what any urbex worth their salt would do – go and investigate. The tunnels might not even exist. In fact, it would be a minor miracle if they did, as she'd never once heard mention of them. How could something like that stay hidden for so long?

When she reached the junction with Daylesford Road she paused, even pulling out her phone and bringing up Kirby's number. But the thought of discovering a disused secret tunnel was intoxicating, and instead she slipped the phone back into her pocket and turned right towards the river.

Connie had read about asylums that had secret entrances for the wealthy to come and go discreetly, but never something on this scale. It was, simply, too good an opportunity to miss. There was, however, one small problem: she first had to get into Blackwater, and there was only one person who could help her do that.

Raymond Sweet.

CHAPTER 38

'About bloody time,' said Charles Palmer. 'I've been here over an hour, and no one is telling me anything. I thought I was just here to help answer a few questions.' Today he was clean-shaven and didn't look like someone who'd been out all night, but the worry lines were still evident.

'Sorry about the wait. I know that you have things to do this morning,' said Kirby, dropping a file on the table and sitting down opposite. 'Has anyone offered you a drink – tea, coffee? I'm afraid it won't be up to your standards.'

'I'd rather get this done and back to the house.'

'Of course.' Kirby opened the file in front of him and took out a photograph. He placed it in front of Palmer. 'Marsh House.'

Palmer looked at the photograph and then at Kirby, as though it were some kind of trick. 'What about it?'

'It's been in your family for a number of years.'

He hesitated. 'Yes . . .'

'You don't seem sure.'

'Yes, I am sure. Look, what's this about? I thought this was to do with next door?'

'We'll get to that in a moment. First, though, perhaps you could tell me about your childhood,' said Kirby. 'Your adoption.'

'What's that got to do with anything?'

'You told me that Helen Linehan adopted you. But she didn't, did she?'

Palmer stared at him.

'You see, this morning I went to Mitcham. Not the greatest way to spend a Monday morning, driving to Mitcham. But it turned out to be worth it, because I found this.' He took a photocopied sheet out of the folder and handed it to Palmer. 'Take a look.'

Palmer took the sheet, and Kirby watched his eyes as they darted across the text. 'But . . .' he began. 'I don't understand.'

'Towards the end, Baby C . . .'

Kirby watched carefully as Palmer read, his eyes coming to a sudden halt and the colour draining from his face. 'You mean . . . ?' He looked up, confused.

Kirby nodded. 'That's right. I think you're Baby C.'

Palmer looked stunned. 'Where did you get this?' he finally managed to ask.

'The House of Nazarene care home, formerly the House of Nazarene orphanage.' Kirby paused. 'Just to be clear, you *are* Ian Carswell?' Something shifted inside the man in front of him – almost indiscernibly, but it was there.

'I was born Ian Carswell, if that's what you mean. But when I told you yesterday, down by the river, that he was never part of my life, I was telling the truth. Ian Carswell died a long time ago.' Palmer put the sheet down as though it were contaminated.

'Tell me what happened.'

Palmer was quiet for a few moments, and when he spoke, he seemed to choose his words carefully. 'I was orphaned. My mother died during childbirth – I never knew her – and my father was nowhere to be seen. As there was no one to look after me, I was sent to an orphanage, the House of Nazarene. And then . . . then, I was sent away.'

'Go on,' said Kirby.

'I was almost three. All I remember being told was that I was going to a farm.' Palmer's fingers scratched at the surface of the table, as though trying to pick off an invisible piece of dried-on food. 'I loved animals, so it sounded like paradise.' His hand swept the imaginary bits off the table, and he sat back in his chair. 'It wasn't.'

Kirby didn't say anything, just waited for Palmer to continue.

'I was sent to a farm school. Harsh doesn't begin to cover it, not to mention the other stuff. There was no love or attention, and as soon as I was strong enough to work I was sent out on the land. To put it bluntly, I lost my childhood and any sense of hope. *That's* when Ian Carswell died. Out there on that stinking farm.'

'And who do you blame for what happened to you?'

'Blame?' Palmer snorted and shook his head. 'It's not about blame. It was government policy – who can I blame for that?'

'How about Ena Massey?'

'I don't know what you're talking about. I told you, I don't know her.'

Kirby tapped the sheet of paper in front of him. 'Take another look.'

'Why?'

'At the end, the person who signed Baby C's declaration of fitness to travel,' said Kirby.

Palmer slid the sheet nearer with the tip of his finger and glanced at it before pushing it away, sending it fluttering off the table on to the floor. Kirby could hear him breathing – deep, controlled breaths – as he stared at his hands, flat on the table.

'Mr Palmer?' he said after a few moments. 'Did you see the name?'

Palmer looked up slowly. 'I don't need to see the damned name. It's Ena Massey.'

CHAPTER 39

'The Creeper is as real as you and me,' said Connie, as Raymond finally unlocked the gate. 'Ghosts don't kill people, that's why the Creeper has to be a real person. Who else killed Ed and Ena?'

'Yes . . . but if it *is* the Creeper, what do they want with us? Why aren't we dead?' he asked, relocking the gate.

It was a good question – unless, of course, no one had been into either of their homes, and they'd both imagined it all. Goodness knows she'd been distracted enough these past few days, and as for Raymond, who knew how reliable he was? Then something occurred to her: what if the Creeper and the murderer were two different people? The more she thought about it, the more sense it made. She and Raymond had nothing to do with Ena Massey and her dodgy past – not directly, at any rate.

'Those drawings you showed me,' said Raymond, as they began walking into the grounds. 'There's something that's not there.'

'What do you mean, something that's not there?'

He stopped and looked at her as though she were stupid. 'There's something missing. Something that's not on the drawings.'

'Like what?'

'You'll see,' he said, grinning. 'And it's a lot more exciting than the tunnels.'

Connie's head buzzed with excitement as she followed him through the asylum grounds. For such a shambolic figure, Raymond moved with surprising dexterity; once in a while, indicating places for her to avoid. It wasn't until they were down by the lake, Keats Ward looming above them, that Raymond stopped.

'What is it?' she asked, following his sightline. He was looking up at the first-floor window that she and Kirby had looked out of the week before, and for a brief moment she thought she saw someone move behind the glass.

'That's where the real ghosts are,' Raymond whispered, before resuming the walk.

'What do you mean, the *real ghosts*?' Connie asked, hurrying to catch up. Was he alluding to the Narcosis Room that she'd told Kirby about?

Raymond either didn't hear her or ignored her, skirting the lake and leading her into an area so overgrown that Connie could see no way through. There was actually a path, but so vague that if you didn't know it was there, you'd miss it. No snow lay on the ground here – protected as it was by the canopy above – but after a few minutes they emerged into a small area that was marginally less overgrown. Here, some snow had penetrated the twisted branches and the tangle of weeds, frosting the ground with fine flakes like crystals.

'We're here,' said Raymond, pointing. Ahead was some kind of structure covered in moss and algae; ivy clung to its walls and knot-weed sprung from every crevice. It looked like an old pillbox, or bunker. 'Promise me you won't tell Mr Calder I showed you here.'

'Course I won't. We'd both be in trouble then,' she said.

Raymond went in first. It was a small space, no more than ten feet square, and on entering she felt slightly disappointed. She'd been expecting something bigger, maybe Tardis-like, on the inside.

Certainly something more exciting, because this was no more than a glorified shed judging by the old pitchfork propped against the wall. 'This is it, the place not marked on the drawing?' she asked.

'Oh, no,' said Raymond, bending down and removing what looked like a small piece of wood from the floor. 'That's down here.'

She immediately saw that there was a latch for a trapdoor, and watched as Raymond heaved it open to reveal a narrow flight of steps. This was more like it, she thought. An overpowering smell of damp and decay hit her nostrils, smells she was familiar with from years of exploring forgotten places, but there was another layer, something metallic.

Raymond shone his torch into the hole and began making his way down. 'Are you coming?' he asked, when he reached the bottom.

Just for a second, she hesitated. Was she being really stupid? Maybe, but how many opportunities like this came along? Fuck it, she wasn't turning back now, and she went down the steps after him.

'This way,' he said.

They were in a narrow brick tunnel, and as she followed him she tried to work out which way they were walking. Now they were below ground, her sense of direction was distorted. They should be heading towards Marsh House, surely, which was to their right, but the tunnel appeared to veer towards the river. The smell that had hit her when Raymond lifted the hatch was getting stronger and more pungent. It was like the river, only ten times more potent. The brickwork, although in good condition, was riddled with damp, and there were large areas of calcification. It wasn't unlike some of the sewers that she'd explored, except the smell down here wasn't sewage. Connie also had the sensation that they were walking downhill, as if they were being pulled into the earth's very core. It was warmer than above ground, also like the sewers, and she realised she was sweating beneath her layers – she could also feel a headache coming on, as if pressure were building in her head.

After a minute or so, the beam of Raymond's torch hit something ahead – a door. It was made of cast iron with huge studs across the top and bottom, rusted around the edges, lending it a subterranean feel, and looking down she saw that the ground was much damper here than by the steps. The metal door wasn't locked, and Raymond pushed it open easily. Beyond lay a darkness so utterly black it was as though the torch beam were trying to push through treacle. Raymond took a few steps in and disappeared.

Connie's eyes were unable to focus on anything, the darkness was so absolute – not to mention the silence, which was so intense that it was like drums banging on her eardrums. She stifled a brief wave of panic.

'Raymond?' The darkness seemed to suck the words from her throat, and she had the crazy notion that he couldn't hear her, although in truth he couldn't be more than a few feet away.

All of a sudden, pinpricks of light appeared in the darkness like distant stars, and for a brief second she was transported back to a school trip to the London Planetarium. She blinked a few times in case she was imagining it, then heard a loud click before a second set of lights came on, much brighter.

'My God!' she whispered, not quite sure what she was looking at.

'This is it,' said Raymond, reappearing. 'The place that's not on the drawing. I call it the bone jar.'

Connie's first thought was that they had somehow – impossible, she knew – come up into an old greenhouse or palm room, because they were standing under some kind of giant, circular glass dome. Metal ribs, streaked with rust, fanned out from the apex above, arching down to the floor. Puddles of water reflected the lights, and the effect was like some weird sci-fi movie set.

'What is this place?' she asked, taking a few tentative steps into the room, which felt more like a spaceship than a room. 'Where are we?'

'Under the lake.'

'*Under the lake?*'

Raymond nodded towards the edge of the room. 'That's water out there.' His voice fell flat in the strange circular space – it should have echoed but didn't, as though something contained it. The air felt strange too – humid, the atmosphere dank with an overpowering smell of what she now recognised as algae and rust.

'It's incredible,' she said, wandering over to the edge of the room, where she ran a hand over one of the metal ribs. How on earth was something like this built – and more's the point, how come no one knew about it? When she touched the cast-iron work, the metallic smell was almost overpowering and it left a brown mark on her skin. She laid her palm flat on one of the glass panels, and half expected to feel a heartbeat, because that's what it felt like: being in the belly of some large, underwater beast. It was beyond her wildest dreams to have found a place like this, and for the briefest moment she forgot why they were there.

'No one knows about it apart from me,' said Raymond. 'Or that's what I thought.'

Connie turned to look at him. 'You mean the Creeper?'

Raymond nodded. 'He's been down here.'

'What makes you say that?' she asked, wondering if she actually wanted to know the answer. Her throat felt dry and nerves tickled her insides, the reality of why they were here suddenly kicking in.

Raymond walked over to the edge of the strange room, where Connie now noticed a cabinet. It was about half a metre in height and ran the periphery. Raymond slid open one of its doors, but the inside was so dark that she couldn't make out what it was he was showing her, until he switched on his torch and shone its beam inside. It was full of what looked like some kind of canisters, and she went over for a closer look, picking one up. The canister itself appeared to be copper with a label on the front – the paper brittle and cracked – which read *Blackwater Asylum London*. Above, a name had been typed, followed by a number. She was about to ask him what they were when a distant memory began pushing its way back. She'd read of something similar in an old American psychiatric institution, but never in the UK.

'They're unclaimed ashes?'

Raymond nodded. 'I started coming to look after them, only now I'm evacuating them before Mr Calder and that site manager, Mr Catapult, get here.'

'Mr Catapult?'

Raymond tapped his head as though trying to dislodge the name. 'Mr Kaplinsky,' he said, after a few seconds. 'But I call him Catapult. Anyway, I keep them in order – see?' He gestured towards the canisters, which Connie could now see were more or less in alphabetical order. 'But when I came here the other day, Gregory Boothe – he was my best friend – was next to Alardice. That's not where I left them.'

Her first thought was that Raymond had imagined it. Why on earth would anyone want to move them? Then she thought about the strange goings-on in Raymond's house and her own place – the missing cellar key, the locked cat flap, the switched-off boiler – and changed her mind. It was almost as if someone were making their presence known in the subtlest of ways, and she shivered at the thought.

'How do they get in and out?' she asked. 'Where's the other tunnel, the one that leads off the asylum?'

Raymond moved to the opposite side of the room, and suddenly another light came on over a door that she hadn't noticed, identical to the one they'd entered through. 'Here,' he said.

She put the canister back in the cabinet and went over for a closer look. 'Is it locked?'

'It used to be,' said Raymond, glancing at her. 'But it isn't anymore.' He made no move to open the door and instead took a step back. For a moment they both stared at the door, saying nothing.

She had to take a look; it was why she was here, after all. Tentatively she took hold of the handle. She expected it to be stiff with age, so was surprised when it moved easily, as if recently oiled. More blackness greeted her as she let the door swing open, and for all she knew, she could have been looking into a black hole, or a small cell, it was so dark.

'There's a light switch,' said Raymond, sticking his arm out to the side of the door. A series of bulkhead lights flickered on. They were placed at regular intervals along a narrow, elliptical tunnel. Unlike the tunnel they'd come in through, this one was metal, streaked with years of rust.

She looked at Raymond. 'Have you been down there?'

He shook his head. 'It's always been locked.'

'But you know where it goes?'

He nodded, silently.

Her heart was thumping in her chest, part fear, part thrill; this was by far the most incredible place she'd ever been to on an explore. The truly extraordinary part was that no one knew about it. Blackwater had been the Holy Grail for urban explorers for years, and yet she'd never heard a whisper of a room under the lake.

'What are you going to do?' asked Raymond, beginning to look worried.

'I'm going to see where it leads,' she replied, staring down the elliptical tunnel in front of her. 'And then we call the police.'

CHAPTER 40

'You lied to us about not knowing who Ena Massey was, which makes me wonder what else you've lied about. I think you need to tell me what's going on here, Mr Palmer,' said Kirby. Palmer took a few sips of the water Kirby had just fetched for him, and seemed to be weighing up his options. After a minute or so, he appeared to make a decision.

'My aunt, Helen Linehan, she told me about Ena Massey,' Palmer began.

'Go on,' said Kirby.

'Helen contacted me last spring, after a diagnosis of cancer. She'd been given less than a year to live and decided to try to put right some of the wrongs done in the past.' He shook his head. 'As if it were that easy. At first it seemed like a miracle, hearing from my mother's sister after all these years. Then, the more I found out, the more it became apparent what a twisted, dysfunctional family they'd been.' He took another sip of water. 'My mother, Sarah, was older than her sister and left home as soon as she could – she and their father, Duncan, fought like mad. Anyhow, Sarah fell pregnant with me and quickly became ill – depressed – and that's when Duncan Carswell stepped in. He took over and had her admitted to Blackwater. Helen never knew exactly what happened, but Sarah died in childbirth, *having me*. Can you imagine?' He stopped and drank the rest of the water in one go. 'I mean, Christ, you'd think the family would be broken, would do anything to help that poor child. *Me.*' He tapped his chest. 'But no, Duncan Carswell saw to it that I was removed. Like I'd never happened. Helen and her mother, Miranda, were forbidden to talk about it to anyone, ever. And they didn't. *They didn't* – can you believe it? That was the hold Duncan Carswell had over them. He was an evil, manipulative man, and his wife and daughter were too spineless to stand up to him.' He spat the words out in disgust.

'Why was he so keen to see you gone?' Kirby was grappling with Duncan Carswell's motivation. 'He sounds like the kind of man who might have been pleased to have a son. An heir.'

'He might have been, but there was one small problem – Duncan wasn't Sarah's father.'

'Miranda had an affair?' Kirby asked. That would be enough to send a misogynist like Duncan off at the deep end.

Palmer nodded. 'It's why Duncan Carswell and Sarah never got on, and why she left home as soon as she could. Removing me was his way of punishing Miranda. He made sure that she not only lost her daughter, but also a grandchild.'

What was it that Connie had said to him? *The father was a total bastard, apparently. No wonder Sarah left.* She hadn't been wrong. 'Do you know who Miranda had the affair with?'

Palmer shook his head. 'My aunt didn't know – or rather, she never said if she did.'

'So where does Ena Massey fit into all of this?' Duncan Carswell had no doubt been an ogre, but this was all over fifty years ago.

'I didn't kill her, you have to believe me,' Palmer pleaded. 'When you told me it was Ena who had been killed, I – I panicked. My aunt told me about her last year, said a nurse at Blackwater took care of everything for Duncan, arranged for me to be sent to an orphanage, and when that wasn't enough for him, got me shipped off to Australia.'

'What about your mother's death? Was Ena involved with that – did Helen say?'

'She . . . she . . .' Palmer put his head in his hands. 'She said, "I wouldn't be surprised if Ena got rid of her for Duncan's sake."'

They sat in silence for a moment, Kirby trying to imagine what kind of person Duncan Carswell must have been in order to sanction the death of his illegitimate daughter – and then remove the grandchild as punishment for his wife for having an affair. If Palmer had killed Ena, Kirby would quite understand why.

'Why would Ena do something like that for Duncan Carswell? She must have had a good reason,' Kirby finally asked.

'Duncan was very close to the doctor who ran Blackwater.'

'Dr Brayne?'

Palmer nodded. 'Apparently Brayne would have done anything for him – Duncan funded his research. And, in turn, Ena would have done anything for Brayne.'

Like have his child. Kirby took out the photograph of Sarah Carswell and slid it across the table towards Palmer, who picked it up.

'Where did you get this?' said Palmer, so quietly he was barely audible.

'Never mind that for the moment,' said Kirby, not wanting to get on to the subject of Tom Ellis, who was dying in hospital. 'That *is* your mother, Sarah Carswell, isn't it?'

Palmer nodded. 'Yes.'

'Have you seen this photograph before?'

Palmer shook his head. 'No.'

'Are you sure? Or perhaps one like it, in the same bed?'

'No,' said Palmer, emphatically. He laid the photograph back on the table and slid it back towards Kirby. 'I've never seen it before. Why?'

'Ena Massey's body was found on a similar bed, marked with the number nineteen.' He watched Palmer carefully and saw no flicker of recognition on his face. Instead, he saw something else – Palmer was making a connection. To what, he didn't seem sure, but something was dawning on him.

'What about Edward Blake? Did you know him too? He was the missing man we were looking for.'

'*Were?*' asked Palmer, looking up.

'We pulled his body out of the Thames on Saturday.'

'Christ,' said Palmer, putting his head in his hands again. 'What the fuck is going on? You have to believe me when I say that I had nothing to do with this – any of this.'

Kirby felt his phone vibrate in his pocket and ignored it. 'Tuesday night – the night of Ena's murder – you told me you were at the Vauxhall Tavern, and the barman Vihaan James confirmed it. However, I went back to the Vauxhall Tavern. It seems Vihaan went on his break at 10.30 p.m. and doesn't remember seeing you again until just before midnight.'

'I . . . I . . .' Palmer looked confused. 'I went to get something to eat. Then I went back. It's the truth.'

'Can anyone verify that? Let me be blunt: so far, you are our only suspect, who not only had motive but also opportunity. You could easily have slipped back to Blackwater, disposed of Ena Massey and then returned to the Vauxhall Tavern for closing time. It would have been tight – and I can't figure out the details – but it would have been possible.'

Palmer had broken out in a sweat, and Kirby could see panic written on his face. 'No! That's a ludicrous suggestion.'

His phone vibrated again and he pulled it out of his pocket to see what was so urgent. It was Connie. The previous missed call had also been her, as well as a text: *call me. i know how killer got in.* 'Would you excuse me for a moment?'

'Where are you going?' Palmer pushed his chair back, as if to stand. 'You can't just leave me—'

'Two minutes,' said Kirby, leaving the room and calling Connie's number.

She picked up instantly, and before he had a chance to say anything she began talking excitedly. 'I know how the killer got in and out of Blackwater. There's a tunnel from the asylum, which leads into the grounds of Marsh House. It comes up in the old folly – I'm there now.'

Kirby swore to himself. That must have been how Palmer got the body into the grounds and how he then made his escape unseen. Christ, he was a good liar.

'And what's more,' Connie went on, 'there's this room under the lake. It's incredible.'

What the hell was she on about now? 'What do you mean, *a room under the lake?*' he asked.

'Exactly that. Raymond goes there sometimes but says that someone else has been down there too. He's with me now – well, he's waiting for me.'

He heard footsteps in the corridor and looked up to see Kobrak hurrying towards him. 'Hang on a moment, will you?' he said to Connie.

'Sir, you've got to see this,' said Kobrak, waving a piece of paper in his hand.

'What is it?'

Kobrak came to a halt in front of him, out of breath. 'The letter, sir. The one to Ruthie. The one Margaret Halliday said wasn't a patient?'

'Yes?'

'Margaret was right. Ruthie Abbott was a nurse. She killed herself in 1966 – at least that was the official account. Seems her mother believed otherwise, thought Ena and Dr Brayne were involved.'

Hadn't Tom Ellis mentioned a trainee nurse to Connie?

'And look at this,' said Kobrak. 'It was amongst Edward Blake's stuff that we brought back from Harry Joyce's place.'

He looked at the piece of paper Kobrak had handed him. It was a photocopy of a newspaper cutting, showing a blurred image of a young child being led out of a cemetery by an older woman. He read the caption below and felt something inside himself shift. *Ruthie Abbot's mother, Stella Calder, with grandson Patrick, after the funeral.*

'Holy shit,' he muttered.

'And guess where her body was found?'

He looked at the young sergeant. 'Don't tell me: Keats Ward.'

'Not only that – bed number nineteen.'

Kobrak was just about to say something else when the door to the interview room flew open, and Palmer came out. 'You said two minutes and it's been—' He stopped mid-sentence and looked at the two policemen. 'What's happened? Wh—'

Kirby held up his hand to silence Palmer, as he spoke with urgency into his phone. 'Connie, you still there?'

'Yes, what the hell's going on?' she asked.

Kirby could feel his heart racing in his chest. 'Listen, do exactly as I say. Go back to the Old Lodge with Raymond and wait for me there. Do not mention this to *anyone*, understand?'

'Does this mean that Charles Palmer killed Ed?'

He looked at Palmer standing opposite him. 'It's not him you need to worry about. Now, get back to the Old Lodge immediately.' He hung up before she could ask any more questions, and spoke to Palmer. 'All that we've been talking about – the orphanage, Australia, Ena Massey – have you mentioned this to anyone else?'

'No . . . why?'

'Are you sure?' he pressed. 'It's important.'

'Well . . .' Palmer hesitated. The look Kirby had seen earlier returned. He knew something. 'There was one person but . . .' He shook his head. 'But he can't possibly have anything to do with this.'

Kirby handed him the news clipping Kobrak had found.

Palmer studied the photograph and began slowly shaking his head. 'No, it can't be. I don't believe it.'

'Who did you tell?'

Palmer looked up, the truth dawning on him as he spoke the name. 'I told Patrick Calder.'

CHAPTER 41

Connie stared at her phone after Kirby hung up, as though the call might magically spring back to life. There was something he hadn't told her – she'd heard it in his tone of voice when he said it wasn't Palmer she should be worried about. The tunnel came up on his land, so if it wasn't him, then who? After taking a last look at the snowy garden of Marsh House through the locked gate of the old folly, she quickly made her way down the spiral staircase that led to the tunnel entrance and back to the lake room, where Raymond was waiting.

'Raymond?' she called, halfway along the tunnel. 'We need to leave . . .' Except Raymond wasn't there. Bollocks, now really wasn't the time to play silly buggers. 'Raymond, where are you?'

Cautiously, she made her way to the doorway of the lake room and stood on the threshold, looking around. There was no sign of him anywhere. *Shit*, where was he? Since her conversation with Kirby, she'd started to feel jumpy, and getting back to the Old Lodge was now a priority. Suddenly she became aware of something moving in the shadows. 'Raymond, what are you doing over there?'

'Well, if it ain't Miss Hoity-Toity,' said a man's voice.

The voice was vaguely familiar, although Connie couldn't quite place it – but one thing was certain, it definitely didn't belong to Raymond. 'Who is that?' she asked, searching the room for a weapon of some kind, should she need it.

'You don't half have bad taste in men,' said the voice. 'First you're looking for that old codger Harry Joyce, then I find you hanging out down here with a fucking loony. You can do better than that, know what I'm saying?' The man stepped out of the shadows, and Connie could now clearly see his face. She recognised the puffer jacket first, then the hat, which he now pulled off. It was Skinny from the Welcome Inn. The man she'd narrowly missed walking into as she left Marsh House. *Fuck.*

'What are you doing here?' she asked, trying not to sound as scared as she felt. How the hell had he got into the grounds? 'Where's Raymond?'

'He's gone. Don't you worry about him.' Skinny smirked.

Connie remembered the voice, the bad breath, the pinprick eyes full of mean lust, and felt sick. Something about him had changed though – his voice had a confidence to it which hadn't been there before. He almost sounded like a different person. Then another thought entered her head: where was the fat one? He wasn't down here but that didn't mean he wasn't up top, keeping watch or dealing with Raymond.

While all this was going through her mind, she scanned the subterranean room for something to put between them. She moved towards an old hospital bed, its frame rusted, a clipboard still attached. Skinny was quick, though, and darted in front of it, knocking the clipboard, which swung from a chain clipped to the frame. Connie moved the other way, wondering whether she could make a run for the tunnel, which led back up to Blackwater – unlikely, but there wasn't much choice.

'The police are on their way,' she said. 'Neither of us wants to get caught down here, so I suggest we get out while we can.' She tried to sound assertive and began walking towards the exit, but he grabbed hold of her wrist. He was surprisingly strong for a wiry man.

'So the coppers are coming, are they?' He smiled. 'Better not waste any more time then, eh?'

'Let go of me,' she said, trying to pull free.

'Now, why would I want to do that?' He pulled her close, and she could feel his breath on her face. 'Aren't I good enough for you? You never did give me an answer.'

'Fuck you.'

'Dirty talk now, is it?' He gave a lascivious lick of his tongue and smiled. 'My favourite.'

She was struggling to break free of his grip when his other hand grabbed her arm and she felt herself being pushed backwards.

'Let me go, you fuckhead!'

'That's more like it,' he said, pushing her back until she felt her legs come into contact with something – a table or a cabinet. 'Fighting talk.' She struggled to keep upright, his body weight pushing into her.

'Stop it!' she screamed. 'Let me *fucking* go!'

Suddenly, his hands released her arms and went up to her head, holding it vice-like as he moved to kiss her. Bracing herself on whatever she was leaning against, she brought her right knee up as hard as she could, straight into his crotch. His hands automatically let go, and she kicked out again. He staggered back, pain and confusion on his face, and hesitated – but only for a second. Suddenly he was on her again, quick as a snake.

Connie felt the wind being knocked out of her as she fell backwards and hit the cold, damp floor. Skinny was on top of her now, pinning her down. She struggled, kicking out with her legs, shouting for him to stop, but he was strong, his hands crushing her shoulders, as he leant his weight on her.

'Get off me!' she shouted. 'You fucking maniac, get off!' She tried kneeing him in the balls again, but he knelt across her legs so she couldn't move. Her coat had ridden up with all the struggling and was bunched up round her chest, rendering her even more incapacitated. She felt him fumbling with her belt when suddenly she heard a voice.

'Stop!'

Connie felt Skinny being hauled off her and saw him stumble backwards and trip over.

'What the fuck . . .' Skinny began, surprise written all over his weaselly face. 'What the fuck did—' But before he could get any further, the other man kicked him in the chest with his foot and he fell backwards, stunned. Connie watched in horror as the figure then violently kicked Skinny in the stomach, again and again, making him curl like a hedgehog.

She pushed herself back against the wall and hugged her knees to her chest, watching as the stranger laid into him. The man kicked again, this time making contact with Skinny's head, and Connie was sure she heard teeth break. Blood was now pouring from Skinny's mouth, and he raised a feeble hand in front of his face to ward off the next kick. 'I'm sorry—'

Connie couldn't stand it any longer. 'Stop it!' she shouted. The bloke might have been a sleazeball, but she didn't want to see him beaten to a bloody pulp before her eyes.

The stranger froze, foot drawn back to strike, Skinny on the floor, panting and bloodied, eyes wide with fear. His attacker relaxed, drew himself up and looked down at him and spat. 'You're pathetic. Get out of here.'

Skinny staggered to his feet, clutching his stomach with one hand, the other wiping the blood from his mouth as he spat out what looked like a tooth. 'Why do you always spoil my fun?'

'Shut up!' yelled the stranger, moving towards him. Connie was sure he was going to lash out again, but the threat was enough.

'Okay, I'm going,' Skinny said, and he lurched towards the Blackwater exit. 'You've broken my fucking teeth,' he muttered as he stumbled into the tunnel. 'Mad cunt.'

Connie watched Skinny's shadowy figure disappear, the occasional swear word bouncing off the tunnel walls, until all she could hear was the thunderous sound of her own beating heart.

CHAPTER 42

Patrick Calder had befriended Helen Linehan. He'd had to – he desperately wanted to buy Marsh House. She'd been on the brink of selling when she announced that she'd changed her mind. By way of explanation, she had confided in Calder that she had found her long-lost nephew and that she was finally going to make some small amends for the wrong that had been inflicted upon him by her family – by leaving him Marsh House. Until that point, it might never have crossed Calder's mind to kill Ena; or at least, not seriously. With Sarah Carswell's long-lost son on the scene, however, Calder suddenly had a fall guy, or possibly an accomplice.

Not only that, but the two men had begun an affair, the feelings seemingly genuine on Palmer's side, but whether Calder was simply using him remained to be seen. Or that's how Kirby was seeing things, as he gunned it towards Blackwater.

Anderson was on his way to Marsh House with Palmer, to pick up the only key to the folly. No one knew where Calder was – his secretary had no idea, there was nothing in his diary, and his wife, who was at home preparing supper, hadn't heard from him since the morning. The site manager, Kaplinsky, had met Calder earlier that day at the asylum, but had no idea of his whereabouts now. He could be anywhere. Kirby had tried calling Connie's number several times, but it had gone straight to voicemail. He just had to hope that Patrick Calder was anywhere but the asylum.

He came to a halt at some traffic lights, and while he waited for them to change he thought about the conversation he'd just had with Hamer. Kirby had expected his boss to be pleased – this was a major breakthrough – but instead he'd been circumspect. There was something Hamer wasn't telling him, and Kirby was sure it was connected to Calder.

The lights changed and he took off, swerving to avoid a fox as it ran into the road and narrowly avoided becoming a new roadkill project for Anderson.

His phone rang and Kobrak's animated voice came down the speakerphone.

'Calder lied,' Kobrak began. 'Sort of.'

'What do you mean, *sort of*?'

'He did go to Edinburgh on Tuesday morning, the 6.45 a.m. from Gatwick, and he did return from Edinburgh on the 6.05 a.m. flight on Friday morning.'

'Yeah, we checked the flights,' said Kirby.

'But we didn't check the charter helicopters. Calder flew back to London on Tuesday afternoon, private charter into Battersea, and then flew back up on Wednesday morning.'

Kirby cursed, banging the steering wheel. 'How the fuck did we miss that?'

'Because we weren't looking,' said Kobrak, unhelpfully.

Kobrak was right. Calder hadn't really been a key suspect, and Hamer hadn't wanted to make things any more difficult with him than they already were. Patrick Calder had been under their nose from the word 'go'; he had access – and now, it appeared, he had a motive. Kirby hung up and, taking a corner too fast, skidded on the icy road, narrowly missing a Mini parked on a double yellow. 'Fuck,' he muttered under his breath as he regained control of the

Corsa. He turned into Battersea Fields Drive and came to a sliding halt outside the main gates to the asylum.

He jumped out of the car and pushed the buzzer. No reply. He buzzed again. Where the fuck was the security guard? He tried the number he had for the Portakabin and was about to hang up when the guard appeared.

'Sorry,' the man said, his breath streaming out of his mouth. He'd clearly jogged to the gate and was out of puff. 'I thought I saw something on the Daylesford Road camera. I went back to check, but it must've been Mr Sweet coming home. He's the only one who uses that entrance so it must've been him. I was a bit on edge after you called.'

Alarm bells went off in Kirby's head; Raymond was with Connie.

'Have you got the key?' he asked impatiently.

'Here,' said the guard, handing it to him. 'Sorry—'

'If you see anyone else coming or going, including Mr Calder, call the station immediately,' Kirby said, getting into the car. He did a U-turn on Battersea Fields Drive and then hung a right down Daylesford Road towards the river. Someone else had entered the grounds, and he hoped it wasn't Calder. He banged the steering wheel again in frustration.

As he neared the river, mist funnelled up the road, becoming thicker as he approached the water; it was like the John Carpenter movie, *The Fog*. Suddenly, the phone box on the left loomed into view, its receiver hanging uselessly from its cord, swaying gently like the dead pigeon in Keats Ward. Kirby slowed down and pulled up outside Raymond's entrance and got out. The familiar smell of the Thames prickled the inside of his nose – it was particularly strong, its pungency amplified by the damp and the cold. As if on cue, the one street light that was there flickered and finally gave up, shrouding the road in dim shadow. He struggled with the padlock on the gate; it was so cold that it might as well have been carved from ice. Eventually it opened, and within seconds he'd slipped into the gloomy, eerily silent grounds of Blackwater and begun making his way towards the Old Lodge.

CHAPTER 43

Raymond had run back to the Old Lodge as fast as he could, veering off course, tripping and at one point finding himself about to hurtle on to the frozen lake. He paused for breath only once, at the mortuary, sure then that he wasn't being followed, and ran the final distance at full pelt. He was now back, the door locked, all the lights on. He stood in the kitchen, panting, his breath misting the small space like a cheap magic-show effect. He began to shiver, the sweat he'd built up running now turning to cold, icy rivulets that ran down his back and sides. Looking down at his coat, he realised that he was covered in caked snow from where he'd fallen. He took off the coat and shook it, but the room was so cold that the frozen snow only clung to the fabric like some scaly second skin. He draped it over the back of a chair and lit the paraffin heater. His hands were shaking so badly that it took him three goes to light the match. Once it was lit, he sat down as near as he dared without setting himself on fire.

An unopened packet of Jaffa Cakes sat on the table, a treat forgotten after Connie's arrival – or, as Mrs Muir would have said, after his day had gone tits up. He reached for the packet and ripped it open, popping the first biscuit in whole. He barely chewed it, squashing the cake part with his tongue before swallowing the disc of rubber-like orange jelly. Before he knew it, he'd done the same with the next, and the next, and the next – until there was only one left.

He pushed the packet aside and sank his head into his hands. He felt terrible. He'd left Connie alone in the lake room with Lloyd, and he knew what Lloyd did to ladies. Why hadn't he stood up to him? Lloyd could make his life hell, he knew – him and Calder between them. Raymond loathed them both; his victory in court over Calder had, in truth, been bittersweet. He had every right to stay at the Lodge, the court had said so, but that didn't mean Calder would make his life easy. Especially when he had pricks like Lloyd to do his dirty work.

Raymond suddenly realised his face was wet and that he'd been crying. He rubbed away the tears with his hands and popped the last Jaffa into his mouth, this time managing to chew, and thought about Connie. He had to go back, he had to help her. She'd promised to watch his film with him, and she'd never do that if he didn't go back and help her. He liked her, as well, and she looked at him when she spoke – not many people did that, let alone someone as pretty as her.

He needed to pull himself together and began looking around the room for anything that might be useful as a weapon – not that he had any real notion of what he'd do with a weapon, only that it would make him feel safer if he was carrying one. He remembered something Mrs Muir had once said, while they were watching an action movie. *The element of surprise, Raymond, that's what's needed.* He turned the phrase over in his mind as he looked around the Lodge. He didn't like knives, knew they could be dangerous, so he quickly ruled out the one chopping knife that he had.

Eventually, his eyes came to rest on the kitchen shelf above the kettle, where he kept his teabags and sugar – and the urn. He got up, and after crossing himself he took down the urn containing his mother's ashes. His mother had died in a house fire, so Raymond was under no illusions and knew that what he actually held in his hands was more likely to be the remains of the two-up, two-down that they had lived in on Pike's Road. Maybe even a bit of their cat and the budgie.

He carefully prised open the lid of the urn containing Cynthia Mae Sweet's ashes and set it down on the table. He slid his hand inside and slipped his fingers between the bag of ashes and the cold metal wall of its surroundings. Suddenly, his fingers felt something small, round and smooth, and with care he pulled it out; it was as good as new. He remembered the day his mother had bought it. She'd been so pleased. He turned it round in his fingers, pulled the old wine cork off the end and tested its end on his thumb. *Ouch*, it was still sharp. It was perfect.

Replacing the cork, he quickly put the lid back on the urn and returned it to the shelf. He turned off the paraffin heater and put his coat back on, slipping his mother's hatpin into his outer pocket, a real sense of urgency racing through his veins. He'd recently been rescuing the dead from the dark confines of the bone jar, but today he was going to save someone living. *The element of surprise*, he whispered to himself as he left the Lodge.

He was going to save Connie Darke.

CHAPTER 44

Now that they were alone, Connie took a proper look at the man who had pulled Skinny off her, and to her surprise recognised him as Charles Palmer.

'Are you all right?' he asked.

'Um, yes, I think so. Thanks for what you did just now. That could have ended, um, badly.' Her heart rate was slowing back to normal, but she could still feel her hands shaking. She must be in some kind of shock. 'That man, who was he?'

'I've no idea,' said Palmer, brusquely. 'Right, shall we get you out of here, back to the house where you can warm up?'

'Yes, thanks, that would be good, although—' She wondered about Raymond, he'd be worried. She hoped that Skinny hadn't harmed him in any way.

'Although?' asked Palmer. 'Surely you don't want to go back the other way? Fine by me if you do.' He shrugged.

Palmer had obviously been home and changed, as he was out of the stuffy suit and in jeans and a sweatshirt. Even so, he still looked like someone who had private healthcare – Bonaro fitted into that category too. *Christ, Bonaro!* She'd just remembered. He'd be wondering where she was, or at least why she hadn't called.

'Nothing,' she said. 'I just need to make a call when we get outside.'

'Excellent.' Palmer gestured towards the tunnel leading to Marsh House. 'After you.'

'By the way, what were you doing down here?' she asked, as they walked along the rusted subterranean tunnel.

'I was fetching something from the boathouse and thought I heard something.'

She wondered how that was possible but was just relieved that he had – she didn't want to think about what might have happened if he hadn't. Her hand gripped the comforting shape of her phone, icy-cold to the touch, in her pocket. She'd call Kirby as soon as she was above ground and tell him where she was. She was concerned about Raymond, hoping that Skinny had just frightened him off and nothing more serious.

They were nearing the end of the tunnel, and she could see the spiral staircase ahead. As she climbed the stairs, she thought about Palmer again. What had he been doing in the boathouse at this time? And, now she thought about it, how could he possibly have heard her screams from the garden? She listened to his feet on the metal staircase behind her, and an unexpected wave of new fear swept over her. And there was something else – what was it Skinny had said, after he'd been pulled off her? *Why do you always spoil my fun?* Despite the cold, she felt herself break out in a sweat – *they knew each other*.

Don't be daft, she told herself. *Why would a wealthy man like Palmer know a sleazeball like Skinny?* And, in any case, hadn't Kirby said he wasn't the one to worry about?

Reaching the top of the spiral stairs, she briefly considered whether she could swing round and push him back down and make a run for it, but the gate to the folly was padlocked – she could see it clearly as she stepped up into the small brick building.

'Here, let me,' said Palmer, coming up the steps and joining her in the cramped space. The same sense of claustrophobia that she'd felt earlier in the house with him, in the upstairs room, returned. He took a key out of his pocket and unlocked the padlock. 'You never know these days. Danger can come from the most unexpected of places,' he said, smiling as he held the gate open. She stepped through and was aware of him right behind her.

'This way,' he said, gently steering her by the elbow to their left.

'Aren't you going to lock up?'

'It can wait,' he said curtly.

She had no idea of the time, but since she'd spoken to Kirby from the folly it had not only got much darker, but also freezing fog was coming off the river, blurring the already-white garden into a series of opaque shapes that seemed to shift before her eyes. Her sense of direction felt distorted, as though emerging from the subterranean tunnels had skewed her senses, although she instinctively felt as though they were walking towards the river and not the house.

'Where are we going?' she asked. There was a sharp tang in the air and sudden cold patches, like when you swim in the sea and move from warm to cold water. She shivered and pulled the zip of her parka up as far as it would go.

'To the house, of course,' he replied casually, over his shoulder. 'Where else?'

CHAPTER 45

Once inside the asylum's grounds, Kirby found himself in almost complete darkness. He thought he knew where the path through the trees was – it had been trampled enough by SOCOs after all – and yet he found himself disorientated and lost. The mist seemed even worse within the grounds, clinging to the foliage and following him like a lost ghost. Using the torch on his phone, he made his way through the undergrowth, but before long he realised that he'd gone round in a loop, when he saw the same broken tree stump twice. He was about to try calling Connie again when he detected a faint glow ahead and made a beeline for it.

Every light was on at the Old Lodge, and Kirby breathed a sigh of relief as he stepped into the clearing – Raymond and Connie were here and safe. Just as he was about to knock on the front door it burst open, and Raymond appeared. He had something brown smeared down one cheek and it looked as though he'd been crying.

'What's going on?' Kirby asked, alarmed. 'Where's Connie?'

'She – she's with Lloyd in the room under the lake. I should never have left her . . .' Raymond spluttered, trying to push past.

Kirby caught him by the arm. 'Who's Lloyd, Raymond?'

'I didn't mean to leave her,' he said, blinking and wiping his nose on the back of his hand. 'Honestly. Only, Lloyd came and said if I didn't go he'd come and burn my house down and take my mother and that he'd tell everyone what I've been doing and—' He was talking so fast that Kirby could barely follow.

'Raymond, slow down.' He noticed Raymond's coat was covered in chunks of ice, as though he'd fallen in the snow. 'Tell me exactly what happened.'

Raymond took a deep breath and squeezed his eyes shut in concentration, and then began talking. 'She wanted to see the bone jar—'

'Bone jar?' Kirby cut in.

'It's the room under the lake,' said Raymond. 'It's where the Creeper gets in.'

'Shit. Why didn't you tell us?'

'I took her, and when we got there she wanted to see where the other tunnel went. I said I'd stay and keep watch – only, when she was gone, Lloyd showed up and told me I had to go—' He stopped suddenly, and opened his eyes. 'Have I got chocolate on my face?'

'Who's Lloyd, Raymond? What's his surname?' Kirby was desperately racking his brains trying to remember anyone called Lloyd who'd been interviewed in the case.

'Templeton. He does things for Mr Calder.'

'What kind of things?'

'Anything.' He sniffed.

Kirby wondered why someone like Calder would use someone like Lloyd; assuming Raymond was telling the truth.

'We need to go. Now,' said Raymond.

'Have you seen Calder tonight, anywhere?'

'No . . .' stammered Raymond. 'Will I be in trouble with him?'

Kirby shook his head. 'You'll be fine. Now, show me this lake room.' He pulled out his phone and punched the autodial for Kobrak, as Raymond led him away from the Old Lodge and into the darkness of the asylum grounds.

'How did Lloyd get into Blackwater?' asked Kirby, as he waited for the call to connect to Kobrak.

'He must have a key,' said Raymond.

'*Fuck*,' muttered Kirby. Kobrak came on the line, and as briefly as he could, Kirby explained the situation while trying to keep up with Raymond. 'Looks like we have a suspect on the premises, a Lloyd Templeton. He has a key to the Daylesford Road entrance – get someone over there now. And tell Pete.' Then he hung up and concentrated on not breaking a leg or losing an eyeball.

Despite the darkness and the mist, Raymond moved through the grounds with an impressive ease. Kirby tried not to think about what might be happening to Connie as they tramped through the snow and round the lake, eventually coming out near Keats Ward.

'Over here,' said Raymond, pointing ahead to an area so overgrown it looked impenetrable.

Suddenly, out of the gloom, a figure appeared. 'Lloyd,' gasped Raymond.

'What the fuck you doing here, Raymond? Didn't I tell you—' Lloyd saw Kirby and stopped. '*Fucking filth.*'

Before Kirby had a chance to say anything, Lloyd darted past both of them and ran towards the lake.

'Wait here,' he said to Raymond as he went after him, crashing through the undergrowth like a blind elephant. After a minute or so, he realised it was pointless; branches and trees blocked his every move, and at one point he nearly ran straight into what was left of a wall, isolated and adrift in a morass of snow-covered vegetation. He stopped to catch his breath. Lloyd was gone, and the sound of his footfall slowly dissipated until silence engulfed Kirby. He had to leave Lloyd to whoever was at the gate on Daylesford Road – and he hoped to God that someone was. His priority now was Connie, and he ran back to where he'd left Raymond only to find him gone.

'Raymond!' he shouted, frantically looking around. Where the fuck was he? 'Raymond!'

He suddenly heard a noise ahead, from where Lloyd had appeared, and took off. *Goddamn you, Raymond,* thought Kirby, as branches scratched his face and tore at his trousers. The torch on his phone at least enabled him to make out a vague path through the jungle-like undergrowth, but he was no match for someone who knew where they were going. He eventually came to a small clearing and stopped. He held his breath in order to hear properly, his own breathing making so much noise that it masked anything else; but there was nothing, only silence. As he shone his torch around, he realised that there was some kind of structure ahead, covered in vine and knotweed and all but invisible.

He made his way over to the small building and aimed his phone's beam inside. A hatch in the floor lay wide open, exposing a narrow flight of steps – it had to be the way into the tunnels Connie had mentioned, and where, presumably, Raymond had just gone. He quickly texted Anderson and Kobrak a rough location of where he was – then, shining his light down the steps, he began his descent into what he knew must be the lake room. He just hoped that he wasn't too late.

CHAPTER 46

Connie was following Palmer towards what he said was the house, but she wasn't so sure. Since they'd emerged into the garden his demeanour had changed, and she felt as if an invisible leash tied them together. Running away in this fog would be problematic; she could barely see a few feet in front of her. He had saved her, she kept reasoning, so maybe she was being paranoid. Why would he have saved her if he had something more sinister in mind?

Palmer walked faster now, and she was having a difficult time keeping up; his steps had a purpose beyond her well-being – they were almost arrogant.

'I'm sorry, but can we stop for a minute?' Connie's energy levels were low, and she felt chilled to the marrow. 'I need to make a call.'

Palmer slowed down but kept moving. 'Surely you want to get to the house as soon as possible, then we can put an end to this traumatic event.'

'Well, yes, but—' At that precise moment her phone pinged in her pocket, indicating a text, and then began ringing. The signal must have kicked in, backlogged messages finally coming through. She pulled the phone out of her pocket and saw that it was Kirby calling. Before she realised what was happening, Palmer had wheeled round and snatched the phone from her hands.

'What do you think you're doing?' she asked, confused.

'You won't need that,' he said, slipping the phone into the inside pocket of his coat and grabbing her arm. 'This way.' He began pulling her towards a bank of trees, which appeared out of the thick fog ahead. 'The quicker we are, the sooner we can put an end to all this.'

'An end to all what?' she said, struggling to free herself from his grasp. 'What the hell are you—'

'Just do as you're told,' he said, yanking her arm painfully and continuing to drag her through the snow.

'Let go of me!' she yelled.

'Save it. You're going to need all the lung capacity you've got.'

Desperately trying to free her arm from his grip, Connie kept tripping and stumbling; Palmer dragged her along regardless. Snow was going down the tops of her boots, and her jeans ripped on something as she desperately tried to remain upright; all the while, her brain was fighting to make sense of what was happening.

As he hauled her along, she became vaguely aware of a building ahead, and the air becoming noticeably colder. They must be nearing the river, and she realised the building had to be the old boathouse. A sudden vision of Ed being thrown into the river came into her mind, and she felt panic starting to rise in her stomach.

'No,' she shouted. 'Please.'

The boathouse emerged out of the fog, and next to it the weeping willow, which in summer was a curtain of bright green but was now a snow-covered shroud, its white branches hanging like tendrils towards the dark water below. Maybe if she screamed loudly enough, a passing boat would hear her. Then she realised what a ridiculous idea it was; no one would hear her from here. She wondered whether Kirby was at the Lodge yet and would realise something was wrong. Her only hope was that Raymond had simply been scared off by Skinny, rather than anything more serious, and that he could tell Kirby where she was.

They'd reached the old boathouse by now, Palmer's grip beginning to cut off the blood flow in her arm. With one final burst of energy she lashed out, managing to scratch him on the face, while desperately trying to free herself from his grip. It was no use – he was too strong – and soon he had pushed her face first against the side of the boathouse, her arm twisted up behind her. An agonising pain shot through her shoulder, and she was sure he was about to break her arm.

He leant his body weight against her so that she couldn't move, pinning her to the side of the wooden building, his breath hot on her neck. 'There's no point in trying to run,' he hissed. 'We're way beyond that now.'

Keeping his weight on her, he unlocked the door to the small building, the padlock making a dull thud as it fell to the ground, and pushed her inside. She landed awkwardly on the floor, against something metal and sharp, and lay there dazed. The arm that had been twisted behind her back felt limp and numb, and she tried to get some feeling back into it. The door slammed, bouncing on its hinges, the latch not catching, and for a moment they were in total darkness. The only sound was coming from below, and it took a few seconds for Connie to realise what it was: the river, gently lapping against the underneath of the boathouse, like an animal licking a wound. She struggled into an upright position, and with her good arm began feeling about the floor for anything that she could use in self-defence. Her hand had just found something cold and metallic when the light came on. It was blinding, and for a few moments she couldn't see anything. Within seconds Palmer had grabbed her parka and was dragging her along the floor towards the far end of the boathouse.

'Let me go!' she yelled as her hands desperately tried to grasp on to something; splinters pierced the tender flesh under her nails as she scrabbled at the wooden floor. The end wall had a large set of double doors in it, which opened out on to the river. She'd seen them, that day on the boat trip, flung open as though expecting a boat at any moment; tonight, they were padlocked shut with a heavy chain. Perhaps that would be her chance – when Palmer was unlocking them, as he'd need two hands for that. She stopped resisting in order to preserve her strength, and hoped the feeling in her arm would return when she needed it.

However, Palmer didn't make for the doors, instead stopping a few feet away. He released his grip on her so unexpectedly that she crumpled to the ground. 'Wh-what are you going to do?' she asked, her teeth chattering with the cold. No wonder she couldn't feel her arm; her fingers were now blue.

'Shut up,' he said. 'You're not going anywhere.' He placed his foot on her arm and slowly began to put his weight on it. '*Yet.*'

She tried to claw at his legs with her other hand, managing to partially roll over and grab his shin. If she could just bite him hard enough he might release his foot, but she didn't get the chance. He kicked her away with his other foot, and she remembered what he'd done to Skinny in the lake room, as the cold, gritty leather sole of his shoe made contact with her cheek. She tasted blood in her mouth and lay gasping, looking up at the ceiling, where a faded kayak hung suspended from the rafters. When she looked back, Palmer was heaving open a trapdoor in the floor of the boathouse, which she hadn't noticed until now. With a grunt of effort, he lifted one side of the pair of doors. The sound of the river beneath was now much louder, its tang stronger. With one side open, the other door flipped up easily, and Connie could make out the inky blackness below.

Rolling on to her front, she tried to crawl back towards the entrance, but Palmer grabbed her by the hood of her parka and yanked her back. 'Oh no you don't,' he said, dumping her dangerously near the edge of the hatch, where she lay on her back cradling her arm, which was now throbbing violently.

'Up,' he said, nudging her in the ribs with his toe.

'I can't,' she said.

'No such word. Surely your mother taught you that.' His foot nudged her again, this time harder, and she felt the edge of the hatch on her back.

With effort, she managed to roll away from the open hatch and haul herself on to all fours – or rather, all threes, as her left arm was now virtually useless; she even wondered whether it might be broken. After a great deal of concentration, she eventually managed to push herself off the floor and into a standing position. Once upright, her head swam and she felt herself sway. Instinctively, she reached out to steady herself, only there was nothing there – Palmer had stepped back, just out of reach, and she teetered. The snow had numbed her legs, and when she looked down she was surprised to see blood on her jeans. She must have cut herself while being dragged along, her leg too numb to feel anything.

'What happens n-now?' she asked, attempting to focus on the boathouse wall behind Palmer. There was some old gardening equipment, a lawnmower and a kayak paddle, but there was no way she could get past him to reach any of it.

'You're going for a swim. That's what's going to happen,' he said, pointing towards the hatch and the black water below. 'You stumbled in the dark, the hatch had been left open, and you fell. A tragic accident.' He smiled. 'Just like your friend Blake.'

'You m-mean this is where—' Before she could finish the sentence, she felt the bile rise in her throat and, turning, she vomited into the Thames. When the retching finally subsided, she wiped her mouth with her sleeve and straightened up.

Palmer was watching her with mild disgust on his face.

'But why?' she managed to say, her throat sore from the retching.

'Wrong place, wrong time.' Palmer shrugged. 'He saw me. Shame, he was a good-looking boy. But like I said, it was an accident.'

'You lying bastard,' she whispered.

CHAPTER 47

When the policeman took off after Lloyd, Raymond saw his chance and legged it. He careened through the undergrowth like a wild boar after carrion, and threw himself into the old pillbox at full pelt, stopping a moment away from tumbling head first down the steps. As it was, he took them two at a time and misjudged, missing one and falling the last few. Landing with a painful bump on his right hip – he was sixty-seven, after all – he felt in his pocket, his fingers finding the cork. Thank goodness it was still in place. He'd look a right idiot if he managed to impale himself.

He stood up and fumbled around in his other pocket for his torch, his hip aching from the fall. Where was it? There was no light in this tunnel, and either the door to the lake room was closed, or someone had turned the lights off. He checked all his pockets but there was no torch; he must have dropped it when he fell earlier, or left it at home. He had been down here before with no torch – it wasn't as though he could get lost, as the tunnel only led to one place – but that was before the Creeper had started poking about. The darkness now scared him.

Feeling his way along the tunnel wall, he made his way as quickly as he dared. The sensation of walking in total blackness was unnerving, so he focused on the task in hand. He hadn't been able to save Gregory all those years ago, or Nurse Abbott – but maybe, just maybe, he could save Connie. His heart pounded uncomfortably in his chest; he'd had an adverse reaction to a tuna sandwich once, which had produced a similar reaction, and he now regretted eating the packet of Jaffa Cakes. He silently burped, the bitter tang of the orange jelly making him grimace.

As he slowly felt his way along the tunnel, he became aware of the darkness ahead changing quality, and he knew the door to the lake room was open, the blackness ahead even deeper than that in the tunnel. At the door, he hesitated, listening for any sign of life, but all he could hear was deafening silence.

'Connie?' he whispered, groping about for the light switch.

When the lights came on, it took him a few seconds for his eyes to adjust, but he soon realised that there was no one there. The door leading to the folly tunnel was open, and a feeling of dread blossomed in the pit of his stomach. Was he too late? He noticed a table had been pushed against the wall, and he could see marks on the floor. He moved closer and saw a few drops of blood and something else, paler. He bent down for a better look and recoiled. It was a tooth – or at least part of one. He couldn't imagine Connie knocking anyone's teeth out, and an alarming thought crossed his mind: the Creeper. He looked at the open door that led to the folly and knew there was only one thing he could do, Creeper or no Creeper. He flicked the tunnel lights on and began making his way along the elliptical passage. The overhead lights gently buzzed as he walked, slowly at first and then faster and faster until he was running, his steps bouncing off the metal walls. He didn't want to be in there a moment longer than was necessary.

Fresh, cold air hit his lungs as he emerged into the folly, the gate mercifully unlocked. He stood on the threshold, panting, his breath pouring out into the garden in long plumes, heart thundering. His hip was now throbbing painfully, and he looked wildly about for Connie, cursing himself for losing the torch. Suddenly he noticed fresh tracks in the snow. A freezing fog was coming in off the river, but somewhere to his left he could make out a vague glow through the thick, white haze. He slipped his hand into his pocket, carefully removing the cork from the pearl-tipped hatpin, and began following the tracks in the snow. After a few feet, the tracks changed into drag marks, and at that point he knew he had no time to lose. He quickened his pace, his fingers tight round the hatpin, his thumb resting on the pearl that sat on its top.

As he went, he thought back to Lloyd as he'd come running out of the undergrowth. Lloyd hadn't looked like a man who'd done something bad that he'd enjoyed; more like a man who'd been denied his prize. And as far as Raymond knew, there was only one person who could do that.

As he ran, the truth began trickling into his brain, like chocolate sauce running down one of Mrs Muir's steamed puddings, a sense of finality looming. There was only one person who could stop Lloyd doing something he wanted to do, and that person was Lloyd's father.

CHAPTER 48

The Thames was a dangerous river, full of eddies and undertows that could pull you down within seconds, not to mention the cold and the obstacles you'd encounter along the way, such as boats, piers and bridges. If she survived going into the water, which was extremely unlikely, it would be down to luck and nothing more. She peered into the blackness, and the drop and the moving water increased the feeling of dizziness that washed over her. Dragging her eyes away from the water, she tried to focus on Palmer. She had to keep him talking – she was too weak to fight him, as he was a fit, strong man. It was her only option.

'I want to know what this is a-about,' she said. 'It has to be about Ena. T-tell me what happened.'

Palmer grinned. 'You *really* want to know?'

'Y-yes,' she stammered. 'You owe me that, at least.'

He thought for a moment. 'Okay, I'll give you the short version.' He folded his arms and stared at her. 'That bitch, Ena Massey, killed my mam. There you have it.'

'Y-you're Tom Ellis's son?' Connie gasped, searching Palmer's face for any trace of similarity between father and son and finding none. 'You do know he's dying?'

'Dying? No, I didn't. Well, maybe that's something he'll be good at. He certainly didn't stand up for his fiancé, let alone his son.'

'What are you t-talking about?' She nicked the end of her tongue and tasted blood. Her entire body was becoming numb; she needed to move and get the circulation going. A sudden vision of Sir Ranulph Fiennes slicing his own fingertips off with a micro-blade flickered across her mind. Fuck, how *was* she going to get out of this?

Palmer suddenly started laughing, his breath clouding around him. '*Nid* Charles Palmer *ydwyf*.'

'What?' What was it, Welsh?

'*Nid* Charles Palmer *ydwyf*,' he repeated. 'You don't get it, do you? You *really* don't get what's going on.' Amused, he moved closer, and when he spoke his breath felt deliciously warm on her face. '*I'm not Charles Palmer*,' he whispered.

She opened her mouth to speak, but nothing came out. It was too late anyway, Palmer's hand gently rested on her chest, and with one, sharp push she was falling.

It was as though the world had entered into slow motion: she felt her balance going; the sensation of falling backwards; her heels on the edge of the ledge; her right foot stepping backwards into the void; the anticipation of the coldness that would soon engulf her entire being as the water entered her lungs. She wanted it to be over. *Just let it happen.* Then, all of a sudden, she caught a flash of movement over Palmer's shoulder. A shape came through the door and lunged at him from behind, just as she felt her right foot hitting something solid. Her left foot followed instinctively, and she crashed backwards expecting the Thames' icy grip to drag her under at any moment. But it never came; instead, she found herself hitting a hard surface, one leg painfully twisting up underneath her thigh, and the other desperately trying to grip the wooden floor as it pushed her body away from the edge of the hatch.

By some miracle, Connie had managed to step over the corner of the hatch, landing on the other side. It took her a few moments to realise that she wasn't in the water, that she wasn't about to die from hypothermia or a wheel spoke through her brain. She was alive, and more importantly, on dry land. Lifting her head slowly, she saw a figure wrestling with Palmer on the opposite side of the hatch. Through her blurred vision, she gradually recognised the coat, the scarf.

'Raymond!' she shouted, struggling to sit upright, the pain in her leg making her gasp as she tried to get up. With horror, she watched as Raymond and Palmer rolled perilously near to the edge of the drop opposite.

'Raymond!' she shouted again, dragging herself over to the hatch doors. With difficulty, she managed to flip one of them shut just as the pair rolled on to what would have been, a second ago, thin air. They were now half on, half off, the door – Raymond straddling Palmer, who was wildly punching at him. She was edging herself towards the two men, to position herself behind Raymond so that she could try to drag him back, when she heard a yell and saw Raymond lift his right arm and bring it down hard on Palmer's neck. Palmer let out a strangled yowl, his hands reaching for his neck, and in that split second Raymond rolled off him.

Palmer's hands clutched at his throat, blood trickling from between his fingers, something sticking out of his neck. Raymond backed away, a mixture of blood and shock on his face, unable to take his eyes off Palmer. Palmer tried to get up, but he misjudged, a look of surprise on his face as he realised his mistake.

Connie and Raymond watched as he plunged into the water with a loud splash. Neither of them spoke for a few seconds – the water lapping at the underside of the boathouse and their breathing the only sounds.

'He k-killed Ed and Ena,' said Connie. 'P-Palmer did.'

'No,' said Raymond, shaking his head. 'Palmer didn't. That was Mr Calder.'

She looked at him in confusion and then back to the water. 'W-what are y-you talking—' But before she could finish the sentence, a hand shot out of the murky water. Connie hadn't spotted them before, but recessed below the hatch was a set of wooden steps leading into the water, which Calder was now desperately trying to cling on to.

'Fuck!' she screamed as his head emerged from the water like a monster from the deep, his other hand grasping the next rung on the ladder. Something protruded from his neck.

Raymond got to his feet, and they both watched, transfixed, as Calder hauled himself up until his hands were on the edge of the hatch; it was like watching a zombie rise from its grave. The current was strong, and Connie could tell that he was having a hard time holding on. Calder looked at them both in turn.

'Help me,' he rasped.

'Why?' asked Raymond, matter-of-factly.

Connie was now shaking uncontrollably and instinctively took a step back, unable to take her eyes off the man she'd thought was Charles Palmer.

Calder tried to smile. His lips were turning blue, his grip on the edge of the hatch weakening. Blood was oozing out of his neck, running down his shirt.

Connie glanced at Raymond, but his eyes were fixed on Calder.

'You killed her friend,' said Raymond.

A boat went by outside, sending waves over Calder, and he spluttered, struggling to hang on. 'He was on my property. And like I said.' He gulped. 'Wrong place, wrong time.' He spat out a mouthful of river water and, summoning all his strength, once again tried to haul himself up out of the water.

'No,' said Raymond quietly, before lifting his foot and bringing it down with a sickening thud on Calder's remaining hand. 'You're wrong. It's *my* property.'

CHAPTER 49

Connie and Raymond were standing by the open hatch when Kirby burst into the boathouse, Connie trembling violently. He'd seen the tracks in the snow, and then the light from the boathouse glowing through the greyness, when he emerged from the folly.

'What happened?' he asked. 'Are you hurt?' His mind was still reeling from the lake room, wondering if he'd imagined it. It was like something from another planet, strange and otherworldly, but he hadn't had time to stop and take it in properly. He'd seen the second tunnel and knew it had to be the way into the grounds of Marsh House, so had wasted no time.

'C-Calder tried to kill m-me,' Connie stammered.

'He was *here*?' Kirby asked, staring at the gaping hatch.

'He fell,' said Raymond, glancing at Connie as he spoke.

Kirby looked into the water and felt like he was staring into the mouth of a beast that had just eaten, and he half expected a belch. All the Armani suits in the world wouldn't save Calder now.

'If R-Raymond hadn't come when he d-did . . .' Connie's voice trailed off.

Kirby pulled out his phone and punched in the number for the Marine Policing Unit. 'When did he go in?' he asked them, waiting to be connected. It couldn't have been that long ago; he'd only been ten minutes behind Raymond.

'J-just now,' said Connie. 'A m-m-minute?' She looked at Raymond, who simply nodded.

Mart Stevenson picked up the phone on the third ring, and Kirby explained to him what had happened. 'We're on our way,' Mart replied. 'He's not going to stand a chance in this weather,' he said solemnly, before hanging up.

Kirby heard a noise outside, and Anderson suddenly appeared at the door, breathless, Charles Palmer behind him.

'What's going on?' Anderson asked, looking around. The small building suddenly felt crowded.

'Calder's in the river,' said Kirby. 'MPU are on their way.'

'Shit,' said Anderson.

Palmer had edged around Anderson and stood staring at the open hatch, realisation dawning. 'Oh my God . . .'

'What happened?' Kirby asked, looking at Connie and Raymond.

'He f-found me in the l-lake room,' Connie stuttered. 'There was a man down there, after I spoke to you on the phone. He attacked me. C-Calder pulled him off.' She looked into the water. 'I thought I was s-safe. B-but he brought me here and t-tried to kill me. I th-thought he w-was Palmer.'

Palmer said nothing, in shock, taking it all in.

'He said Ena k-killed his mother,' she went on. 'What did he mean?'

'The trainee nurse that Tom Ellis mentioned to you, the one who killed herself? That was Calder's mother. Her name was Ruthie Abbott,' said Kirby.

'But—' began Connie.

'Calder was convinced that Ena killed her,' said Kirby. 'Something which, sadly, we'll never know for sure.' No one said anything for a few moments, the water's rhythm now gentle as though nothing had happened.

It was Raymond who broke the silence. 'I saw Ena do it.'

They all turned to look at him.

'In Keats Ward, I saw Ena put a pillow over Nurse Abbott's face. There were feathers everywhere and—' He stopped, looking embarrassed that he was the centre of attention.

As Raymond was speaking, Kirby felt the strangest sensation come over him, and for a brief moment thought he might faint. He quickly pulled himself together, thankful that all eyes had been on Raymond.

'And you never said anything, all these years?' Connie asked.

Raymond shook his head. 'Ena made me promise. She put me to sleep to help me forget. But then I went up there, a few days ago, to where you found her body.' He looked at Kirby and Anderson. 'And that's when I remembered. I didn't want to, but I had to know. Will I be in trouble?'

'No, Raymond, you'll be fine,' said Kirby, catching Anderson's eye. 'Take them back to the house, will you?'

'Sure,' said Anderson, looking like he'd just woken from a bizarre dream. 'Come on, Miss Darke, let's get you warm and call an ambulance. You too, Raymond.'

Kirby watched them go, leaving him alone with Palmer. He couldn't help but wonder whether Raymond had been telling the truth when he said that Calder had fallen. He'd seen the look on Connie's face.

'This is just insane,' said Palmer, running a shaking hand through his hair. 'Will Patrick survive?' The open hatch transfixed him.

'Not with the currents and the temperature, no.'

'Christ,' said Palmer, hugging himself. 'I can't believe it.'

'Did you tell him about Ruthie Abbott?' asked Kirby.

'I had no idea . . . he never said anything to me, about her being his mother. This is all my fault.'

'How did you find out about Ruthie?' Kirby was having difficulty trying to piece it together in his mind.

'My aunt mentioned her. She told me there were two people there when my mother died – Ena, and a trainee nurse called Ruthie Abbott. She never mentioned a son.'

'And you told Calder this?'

Palmer nodded. 'It was why I was here, why I'd been left the house – why I was selling to him. He was sympathetic. I had no reason not to trust him and . . .' He shook his head. 'He had a key,' he said, quietly. 'Patrick did. To Marsh House. I gave it to him. Then one day, I came home unexpectedly and found him at the house. It seemed a little odd, but I forgot about it.'

If Calder had keys to the house, he could have let himself in on the night of the murder and taken Ena's body into Blackwater via the tunnel. It didn't explain how he'd got her there in the first place though. 'Why didn't you say anything?'

Palmer shrugged. 'Why would I? I . . . we were sleeping with each other, for Christ's sake!' He was doing his best to hold back tears.

'Does his wife know?' asked Kirby, remembering the frosty atmosphere at the house in Clapham.

Palmer nodded. 'I got the feeling there was no love lost on either side but that it suited them both to be seen to be married.'

'You mean married to someone of the opposite sex.'

'There's still a lot of prejudice out there. Especially in Patrick's world.' Palmer looked at him. 'I don't expect you to understand.'

Kirby could hear the familiar sound of the Targa's engine approaching outside – the boat the MPU used.

'He was going to buy the house from me, help me sort my life out. He . . .' Palmer shook his head. 'I can't believe he killed those people. Did he, really?'

'It does appear that way,' said Kirby. Based on Connie's attempted murder, Calder was certainly capable of it, but there was also Lloyd's involvement to take into account, if he was involved at all. He could see Palmer visibly flagging and decided the best thing was to get him back to the house and continue the conversation later. 'Come on, let's get out of the cold.' He led him away from the hatch and out of the boathouse.

The freezing fog was even thicker now, creeping up the garden towards the house. The folly gate hung open in the murk, like a prop from a Hammer Horror film. 'Why did you need the key?' Palmer asked, staring at the small structure.

'There's a tunnel, which leads next door to Blackwater.'

Palmer looked completely bewildered.

'You didn't know?'

Palmer shook his head and fell silent again as they made their way through the snowy garden, and Kirby wondered whether he was telling the truth. He and Calder could easily have been in it together, two men drawn together by events of over five decades ago – events which had shaped both their lives profoundly – both seeking retribution. But Kirby didn't think so. Palmer appeared visibly shaken by the evening's events, so he either knew nothing about the murders or he was a very good actor. He also wondered where Ed Blake fitted into all this. He'd known about Tom Ellis and Palmer's mother, so had he also known about Ruthie Abbott? And then there was Ellis, who lay dying in hospital and who was more than likely Palmer's biological father. Kirby wasn't quite sure where to begin with that – Palmer seemed fragile and now wasn't the time, although time was one thing Tom Ellis didn't have.

All the lights were blazing on the ground floor of Marsh House as they approached across the lawn: Anderson, Connie and Raymond's footprints were clear in the snow, heading to the French doors. Inside, someone had lit a fire, and Connie sat huddled next to it as the warmth took hold, a mug of tea in her hands. The shaking had almost stopped, although the occasional shudder still ran through her.

'Where's Raymond?' Kirby asked her.

'With Detective Anderson. Looking for biscuits.'

'Are you okay?'

She nodded. 'I cut my leg and my shoulder hurts, but I'll live.'

Palmer had slumped into a chair at the table at the far end of the room, his head in his hands.

'Lloyd, the man in the lake room,' said Kirby, lowering his voice. 'Did he—'

'No,' she cut in. 'Calder, he – he stopped it happening. I'd seen him before, the man who attacked me, at the Welcome Inn. He threatened me then too, but I left before it got out of hand.'

'Were there any witnesses?' asked Kirby. It would help when it came to charging him.

'He was with a mate, big bloke. I don't know his name.'

'We'll find him.'

'I just can't get my head around Calder,' said Connie, staring into her mug of tea. 'I mean, he killed Ed – was going to kill me – and yet he stopped that animal attacking me.'

'Try not to think about it too much. You're safe now and that's what matters.' He left her staring into the fire and went to the kitchen, where he found Raymond pulling on some nitrile gloves. 'What are you doing?'

'Mr Sweet is hungry,' said Anderson, rolling his eyes. 'Said I'd help him find some biscuits, only I don't want his prints everywhere.'

'What about the ambulance?' Kirby asked.

'On its way.'

Raymond was now frantically opening cupboard doors and then closing them.

'Go and sit next door, Mr Sweet. We'll fix you up with something just as soon as we can. Go and keep Miss Darke company.'

Raymond reluctantly did as he was told, still wearing the gloves.

Anderson let out a long breath. 'He keeps asking if Calder was this Creeper character. I can't see why Calder would break into the Old Lodge, or the Four Sails for that matter, can you? Perhaps he and Connie did imagine it after all.'

'It could be Lloyd, who attacked Connie.'

Anderson shook his head. 'Raymond is adamant it's not him. Fuck knows.'

'Who else could it be? Calder never did anything unless there was something in it for him. Unless, of course, he had a gold-plated set of skeleton keys and a Gucci balaclava and just got a kick out of it.'

'Nothing would surprise me,' said Anderson. 'People get a kick out of the weirdest shit. Look, I'll wait for the cavalry if you want to get over to Calder's place. How much do you think his wife knows?'

'My guess, very little.' Kirby's eyes darted to the doorway and he lowered his voice. 'Calder was sleeping with Palmer, and according to him the marriage was a sham.'

'Shit. We'd better call the boss,' said Anderson, pulling out his phone.

'No, wait,' said Kirby. 'I'll call him on my way to Calder's place.'

Anderson gave him a questioning look.

'Can I take your car?' He wanted to change the subject before Anderson insisted on calling Hamer. 'Mine's on Daylesford Road.'

Anderson tossed him the rabbit's paw keyring. 'You okay, Lew? Only I saw you just now, in the boathouse.'

The pair locked eyes for a few seconds, Kirby's brain buzzing like electrical interference, before he managed a smile. 'Yeah, I'm fine. Need to eat something, that's all. I'd better get going.'

Anderson seemed happy with the excuse, mumbling something about bircher muesli not being proper food, then he suddenly began grinning. 'Hey, at least one thing's pretty certain.'

'What's that?' asked Kirby.

'I doubt Mrs Calder will be wearing a onesie with a gravity-defying zip. Or fondling a bottle opener.'

'No,' said Kirby, with more than a tinge of disappointment. 'I very much doubt that she will.'

CHAPTER 50

The following morning, Kirby stood in what everyone was now referring to as the bone jar – Raymond's name having stuck. Kirby was alone, the first there after only a couple of hours' sleep, and still awestruck by the room's very existence let alone its construction. He stood with the lights off for a moment, letting what fragments of natural light there were penetrate the thick film of algae, which coated the glass panels that made up the domed roof. The thick layer of ice and snow covering the lake blocked out most of the light, but there were mottled patches on the glass where the tone altered. He didn't know if there were fish in the lake – Kirby knew nothing about fish and their habitat – and he wondered whether Leroy Simmons knew. Did carp eat algae? He stuck out his hand and flicked on the lights.

Police floodlights, which had been set up the night before, revealed the domed structure in all its bizarre glory. Sixteen cast-iron ribs – Kirby had counted them only a few hours ago in a caffeine-fuelled moment – fanned out from the central circle at the apex of the dome, arching downward to the ground like a giant spider. Two tunnels ran off the room, on opposite sides, connecting the subterranean bone jar with Marsh House and Blackwater Asylum respectively. *In space, no one can hear you scream*, the tagline to the first *Alien* film, hadn't left Kirby's mind since he'd first set foot in the place. No one would hear you down here, either.

As he gazed around the bizarre space, he thought back to the previous night and his visit to Patrick Calder's home. Saskia Calder had taken the news of her husband's almost-certain death with equanimity. The real shock had come when Kirby explained the circumstances. Apart from his dalliances with men, of which there had been several over the years, it became clear that she knew nothing of what her murderous husband had been up to. She'd been happy to let Kirby look around the room Calder had used as an office when at home, and it was there, in a desk drawer, that Kirby had found the letters and the photograph.

The letters were from Patrick Calder's mother, Ruthie Abbott, to her mother – Calder's grandmother, Stella Calder – and they made grim reading. In the same drawer, shoved right to the back, he'd also found the pay-as-you-go mobile that Calder had used to contact Ena, although her phone was still missing. Then, as he'd been about to leave, he'd asked Saskia Calder if the name Lloyd Templeton meant anything. Raymond had told them that Lloyd was Calder's son, something Kirby found almost impossible to believe, but it turned out to be true: Lloyd Templeton *was* Patrick Calder's son, the product of a fling Calder had had early on in his career. That Saskia Calder found Lloyd as distasteful as Kirby did was only too evident.

He wasn't sure how long he'd been standing there, but gradually a stream of forensics officers, SOCOs and police photographers trickled back in around him, starting work in hushed tones. Kirby began walking around the circular space, parts of which were cordoned off, his protective suit making its familiar rustle as he went. On one area of the floor, they'd found fresh blood and part of a human tooth, which they believed belonged to Lloyd Templeton, who now sat in Wandsworth nick with a lisp and broken nose, not to mention a few choice bruises. There was also a medical cabinet where they'd found drugs dating back to the 1950s, including Mandrax and other barbiturates. Kirby was about to open the cabinet that housed the unclaimed ashes that Raymond had been looking after when he heard his name being called; it was Hamer, who he hadn't noticed come in. With everything that had gone on, Kirby hadn't yet had the chance to speak to his boss one-to-one.

'An extraordinary place,' said Hamer, coming over. 'How come no one knew about it?'

Kirby shrugged. 'Things get forgotten over the years – even extraordinary things. Out of sight, out of mind.'

'Indeed.'

They fell silent for a moment, Kirby sensing a tension between them.

'Has Calder's body shown up yet?' asked Hamer.

'Marine Police are still searching. There's no chance he survived going into the water unconscious.'

'I see. Maybe it's . . .' He hesitated. 'Maybe this place is cursed. How long's it been empty, twenty-three years?'

Kirby nodded. 'Something like that.'

'Sometimes there's a reason why buildings stay empty after their primary function has ended. At least, that's what my wife tells me. How's Connie Darke doing?'

'Torn ligament in her shoulder, minor cut on her leg and a few bruises. She was lucky Raymond turned up when he did, otherwise we'd be trawling the Thames for her body, not Calder's.'

'And Palmer?'

Kirby had been up half the night with him, trying to piece together what had happened on the night he was born and what had subsequently happened to Ruthie Abbott. The letters found at Calder's house had helped, and Kirby was now convinced that Palmer had had no involvement in Ena Massey and Ed Blake's murders – and so far, the lack of DNA evidence in either Keats Ward or the bone jar supported this. 'It's been difficult for him,' said Kirby. 'He knew his mother died in suspicious circumstances, possibly at the hand of Ena Massey, but he had no idea about Ruthie Abbott's death or Ena's involvement in that.'

'Do you believe him?' asked Hamer.

Kirby nodded. 'Yes. He was happy to cosy up to Patrick Calder – Calder was going to buy the house from him, for a very tidy sum, I might add – and had no reason to suspect what he was up to.'

Hamer raised his eyebrows at this. 'Calder wasn't going to redevelop the house as well, was he?'

'It's listed, but they were going to sign the papers yesterday morning. Only we hauled in Palmer before Calder arrived. That must have been when Connie showed up. She said Calder was clutching papers when he showed her in.'

'Palmer must have had suspicions, surely? Especially if they were . . .' His boss left the sentence hanging.

'When I first visited him, we didn't know Ena's identity. The second time I went, I really don't think he made the connection. Plus we have absolutely no physical evidence that he ever set foot in Blackwater, at least not as an adult.' Kirby tried to picture the newborn Charles Palmer being whisked to another part of Blackwater by Ruthie Abbott, while Ena Massey killed his mother. 'I feel sorry for him. He's had enough shit in his life, and just when something good happens, like finally finding out the truth and inheriting the house, he meets Calder and falls in love.' He paused. 'Calder would have happily watched him go down for everything.'

Hamer was staring at something on the other side of the bone jar. 'Do you think Patrick was in love with him?'

'Who knows, he might have been.' Kirby watched his boss from the corner of his eye and could have sworn he saw the smallest twitch of his mouth. Then it was gone.

'Does Palmer know about his father yet?'

Kirby nodded. He'd broken the news to him during their conversation last night. 'He's probably at the hospital right now. Kobrak was taking him.'

'What a way to meet your father,' Hamer sighed. 'I had a look at the letters Ruthie Abbott wrote to her mother.' He shook his head. 'No wonder Calder wanted revenge.'

The letters had painted a picture of a scared young woman. She'd found herself in an impossible situation and had eventually made the brave decision to leave Blackwater and speak out. Unfortunately, it was too late, because she had made one fatal mistake: she'd kept a diary.

'It's a shame we don't have the diary,' said Kirby. 'It wasn't among Ena's things, and we didn't find it at Calder's place.'

'Ena must have destroyed it. Wouldn't you?'

'I suppose so. We have Raymond Sweet's account of Ruthie's murder though.'

'Can we believe him?' asked Hamer.

'He has nothing to gain by dragging it all up now – quite the contrary, he's been trying to forget it for the last fifty years.'

The two men stood without speaking for a few minutes. Eventually, Hamer looked at his watch. 'You heading back to Mount Pleasant?'

Kirby shook his head. 'I have the delightful prospect of telling Karen McBride what's happened.'

'Oh dear,' was all Hamer could muster in response. Karen McBride's onesies and porcelain dog collection – not to mention the poodle lighter and minibar – were now legendary at Mount Pleasant. Anderson had made sure of that.

'There is one other thing,' said Kirby, lowering his voice. He took an envelope from his pocket and handed it to Hamer. 'I found this in Calder's desk. It was the only one, and you might want to look at it when you're alone.'

Kirby left Hamer holding the envelope, his expression unreadable, and walked back along the tunnel to the pillbox, where he removed the plastic bootees and protective suit. It was a beautiful morning, the sun bright in the sky, and for the first time in months he felt its warmth. As he walked, he could hear the sound of dripping, the sun slowly beginning to melt the snow – even the odd bird chirruped. When he reached the lake, Kirby stopped for a moment and looked out across its smooth, white surface, then turned to gaze up at Keats Ward, where Raymond had witnessed Ena Massey murdering Ruthie Abbott over fifty years ago and where, according to Raymond, his friend Gregory Boothe had also died. He thought about the photograph he'd found in Calder's desk and Hamer's wife, Andrea, who he liked very much, and whom he doubted knew anything about her husband's extracurricular activities with the property developer. He hoped it would stay that way.

On the way back to the admin block and the bastard Corsa, Kirby's phone beeped: it was Anderson.

'You'll never guess what Forensics turned up at the house: Mandrax, in a mug in the hallway. Looks like Connie was right to tip that tea down the sink. She'd have been out cold if she'd drunk it. And if the Opus Crates guy hadn't shown up, who knows what might have happened.'

Kirby heard another call trying to get through and saw that it was Livia. 'Look, I've got to go, Pete. See you back at MP.' He cut the call from Anderson and took the incoming one from Livia. 'Mum, everything okay?'

'Fine.' She hesitated. 'Lew, I need to talk to you. I've got something to tell you.'

Finally, he thought, rummaging about in his pockets for the car keys. 'Okay . . .'

'Can you come over?' she asked.

He found the keys and pulled them out of his pocket. 'What, now? I can't, we're in the process of—'

'This evening then. Please? It's important.' Her tone was insistent.

'Okay, I'll do my best. I'll call you later.' With everything that had gone on in the past twenty-four hours, Kirby had managed not to think about what might be wrong with his mother too deeply, but now the dread re-emerged, sharp and piercing. He really would try to get over there later, no matter how many reports he had to write up for Hamer.

He was just about to get into the car when his phone went off again.

'Sir?' It was Kobrak.

'What is it?'

'Thought you'd want to know – Harry Joyce has just been brought into St George's. Looks like a stroke.'

CHAPTER 51

The conversation that Kirby had had with the nurse looking after Harry Joyce had been less than optimistic, and as he waited outside the door to Karen McBride's house, he wondered how long the old man would last. Anderson had offered to give Karen the news, his curiosity about the onesie and minibar momentarily taking over, but Kirby felt that it should come from him. He also wasn't sure Anderson would survive an assault from The McBride; even the luck of the paw might struggle against that. After a minute or two, the front door opened, and Karen appeared.

'Bleedin' hell,' she said, giving Kirby the once-over. 'You've seen better days. Better come in, I suppose.'

At least she wasn't in a onesie, Kirby thought, stepping over the threshold. He caught sight of himself in a mirror and saw she was right: he did look tired, not to mention the angry scratches on his face from the night before. He rubbed a hand over his chin and realised that he'd forgotten to shave.

'Hope she was worth it,' said Karen, leading him into the dreaded sitting room, where, thankfully, the ambient temperature was lower than it had been on his previous visit. 'Take a pew,' she said.

'Thanks.' He took a seat as near to the window as possible. 'I have some news about your mother,' he began.

'You want a drink? Look like you could do with one,' said Karen, who was already at the helm of the hull-shaped bar, tapping the bulldog bottle opener on the palm of her left hand. 'Cold beer?'

Before Kirby could begin to articulate a refusal, an ice-cold bottle of Heineken was in his hand. 'Thanks,' he said, moving what looked like a porcelain Shih Tzu out of the way so that he could put it down; it wasn't even midday. 'About your mother – we're fairly certain of what happened.'

'Well, we know who *didn't* do it, don't we?' she said, snorting. 'I hear you got his mate in custody though. Nasty shit, that Lloyd.'

'Yes, we do have Lloyd Templeton in custody, that's true. But he didn't kill your mother. Do you know Lloyd's father?'

'Do I fuck,' she replied, taking a long slug of WKD, which was orange today. 'What about him – crashed his Ferrari, has he?' Karen emerged from behind the hull and began a hunt worthy of Forensics for her cigarettes. Today she was sporting a pair of wet-look leggings and a jumper featuring an appliquéd dog on the front.

'Not exactly, no.' Kirby gave Karen a brief account of what they believed to have happened to Ena, beginning with Calder luring her to Marsh House on the pretence that Helen Linehan had left her something in her will, to her eventual death. He left out some salient details, although he doubted that even a stomach full of disco biscuits and a battered head would faze Karen.

'Well, I'm a bleeding Dutchman,' she said when he'd finished, the cigarette hunt now elevated to high-priority. 'So Patrick Calder killed my mum?'

'We believe so, yes, and also a man called Edward Blake.' He took a swig of beer. It was the only way to deal with the outfit. Kirby loved dogs, but this was an affront to his senses.

'Did that shit Lloyd know about any of this?' Karen eventually found her cigarettes exactly where Kirby had guessed they'd be

– down the back of the sofa – along with the poodle lighter, and lit up, blowing smoke out of both nostrils.

'He's not saying much. He's facing a sexual assault charge.'

'What?' Karen exploded, almost literally, as smoke poured from every facial orifice. 'I knew they got up to no good, them two, but I never thought they'd do something like that. I'll fucking kill my Douglas, I will.' She drained the WKD bottle in one go, somehow managing to fill that with smoke too.

Karen could have her own circus act, and Kirby almost expected smoke to appear from the appliquéd dog's mouth and ears. He got up and opened the window without asking. 'There's no evidence that Douglas was involved, Karen. Lloyd was alone when it happened. He'd threatened the victim before – Douglas was there on that occasion – but nothing physical took place then. Douglas needs to be more careful with who he hangs out with.'

'Too fucking right he should. Inherited my mum's genes, by the sound of it. Little sod. Told you that she was an evil cow, didn't I?'

'I'm afraid it's a little more serious than that,' said Kirby, sitting down again. 'Do the names Sarah Carswell or Ruthie Abbott ring any bells? Sarah was a patient at Blackwater, and Ruthie was a nurse. Ruthie was also Patrick Calder's mother.'

Karen tapped the empty WKD bottle on her teeth as she thought about this for a moment. 'It was forty fucking years ago,' she said, eventually. 'But Ruthie, she's the one that topped herself, right?'

'That's what was thought at the time, yes.'

'I can hear a ruddy great "but" coming along,' said Karen.

Kirby braced himself – for what, he wasn't entirely sure. 'We have a witness who says he saw your mother kill Ruthie. And we are also led to believe that she killed Sarah Carswell.'

For the first time, Karen seemed stuck for words – although not for long. 'Well, fuck me,' she said, stubbing out her cigarette. 'A murderer in the family – who'd have thought?'

Christ, did nothing faze her? 'Patrick Calder had his mother's letters, ones that she'd written home after Sarah Carswell's death in Ena's care. She was convinced that your mother killed her, but that's something we'll never be able to prove. She also kept a diary, which unfortunately we don't have.'

Karen looked thoughtful for a moment, if such a thing were possible. 'Hang on a sec,' she said, getting up. 'Won't be a mo.'

Kirby watched her leave the room and heard her tread on the stairs. Somewhere in his head he prayed it wasn't a costume change. After a few minutes, he heard her come back down, and to his relief he saw that she was still in the same clothes.

'You might want to have a butcher's at this,' she said, holding out a book of some sort.

It was an A5 leather-bound book with *Diary* embossed in gold on the front. He opened it and looked up at Karen. 'Where did you get this?'

'When I walked out in 1978 I didn't take much – we didn't have much. I took my clothes, but I was determined to take something of hers too, something that would piss the old cow off. I thought that was hers.' She nodded at the diary in his hand. 'Only, when I looked at it a few months later, I seen that it wasn't.'

'But you still kept it?'

'Only 'cos it was in a box full of my own shit,' said Karen, firing up another cigarette with the poodle lighter. 'Moved house with me more times that I've been hitched – and that's saying something.'

Kirby didn't even notice the acrid cigarette smoke as he flicked through the diary in his hands. 'Can I take this?'

'Be my guest. You want another beer? I could put some music on, bit of Rod—'

'No, thank you,' said Kirby, quickly standing up. 'I have to be going.'

Karen showed him out and leant on the doorframe, watching as he headed to the car. 'Whoever she was, she ain't worth it,' she called after him. 'You need a *real* woman, Mr Kirby. You know where to find me.'

He heard her laughing as the front door slammed shut. So much for dropping the bombshell her mother was a murderer; water off a duck's back to Karen.

Inside the car, he put the key in the ignition and stared at the diary; it wouldn't hold all the answers, and it wouldn't prove anything, but it would certainly shine a light on the recent tragedy, as well as the ones more than fifty years ago.

He opened its first page and read the name at the front, written in blue ink, the handwriting small and neat: *Ruthie Abbott*.

CHAPTER 52

After being checked over at the hospital, Connie had been driven home, arriving back at the Four Sails in the early hours of the morning. Mole had been waiting for her, a fire lit in the grate and her bed made up with clean bedclothes. He'd also fed Terror, who had all but ignored her when she walked in, his allegiance now firmly with Mole, his new provider of food. When she woke up the next morning, the reality of what had happened at Blackwater was undiminished, and if anything, more vivid. In her dreams she'd constantly experienced the sensation of falling, which had woken her at least a half a dozen times, and then when she was awake she kept reliving the moment when Calder had tried to push her into the Thames. As awful as they were, for the most part they overrode those of Lloyd's wiry body pushing himself on to her. There was another recurring image, too, one that she hadn't mentioned to anyone, not even Mole, and that was of Calder's face as Raymond stamped on his hand.

'How're you feeling?' asked Mole, who'd slept on the banquette in the bar, apparently, with Terror.

'I could do with another painkiller for my shoulder. I can barely move it.' She sat down at the bar as Mole placed a cup of coffee in front of her.

'I'll get them for you,' he said, and disappeared into the bathroom.

Terror jumped on to the bar and sat gazing at her curiously, as though she'd changed in some way. She tickled him under his chin and was pleased when he purred and stood up to bunt her hand. 'You're still my big, bad boy, aren't you?'

'I do try,' said Mole, appearing from the bathroom. 'Oh, you were talking to the cat.'

'Don't make me laugh, it hurts.'

'Here you go.' Mole placed a glass of water and the painkillers next to her coffee.

'I remembered something last night.' She paused to swallow a tablet. 'When I left Marsh House yesterday with the drawings, I almost bumped into a bloke crossing the street. It was that bastard from the pub, Lloyd. I knew he looked familiar.'

'Hope I never run into that fucker,' said Mole. 'He'll get more than a broken tooth if I do.'

'He must've followed me to Raymond's. God, I was stupid.' She hadn't really thought about why Calder had turned up at the bone jar, as Raymond called it, when he did. At the time, she'd just been relieved that he had. 'He's got to be the Creeper, don't you think? Lloyd, I mean?'

'Ask your detective. Talking of which, what time do you have to go and make your statement?'

'Twelve. Then I thought I'd go and see Harry, tell him . . .' She didn't quite know what she'd tell him. That she'd looked Ed's killer in the eye and watched him fall to his death, and that she'd done nothing to help him? She felt deeply conflicted: on the one hand she was glad Calder was gone, that she'd never have to see his face again; on the other, he'd never have to face up to what he'd done. A small part of her felt that they'd given him the easy way out, but there was no going back now. Bloody hell, she still hadn't called Bonaro! God knows what reception she'd get from him after not turning up at work yesterday with the drawings from Helen Linehan.

'Look, call your boss, get it out of the way,' said Mole, as if reading her thoughts. 'He'll be cool once you've explained, I'm sure.'

'Yeah, you're right.' She picked up the phone and took it into the bedroom, closing the door behind her, and dialled Bonaro's number. When he answered, she took a deep breath. 'Richard, I'm sorry about yesterday, I can explain . . .' She carefully took him through the events of the last few days and felt satisfied that he was suitably horrified. If anything, he was simply angry that she hadn't called to let him know she was all right.

'Everything okay?' asked Mole when she went back to the bar.

'Yeah, I'm forgiven, but his trip's been brought forward. He's going in two weeks.' How was she going to deal with all that in the next two weeks? Bonaro had arranged a meeting with the trustees of RADE in Wimbledon for later that week, which couldn't be rescheduled, and had also suggested they spend a few afternoons going through the finances and any other things that she needed to know before he went. It was the last thing she felt like doing.

'It might help, you know,' said Mole. 'Keep your mind off things.'

'You mean like the funeral.'

'Well, yeah. Come here,' said Mole, wrapping his arms around her. 'We'll give the old bugger a good send-off, I promise.' He gave her a gentle hug, and it felt good. 'Hey, you seen the time? It's almost eleven.'

'Christ, I'd better get ready,' she said, slipping off the barstool. 'I'm going to have a quick shower.'

'Let me know if you need any help with anything. You know, with the shoulder and that.' Mole winked.

'Thanks, but I think I can manage.' She headed to the bathroom and stood for ten minutes under the hot water in a trance, letting it run down her face, warming her shoulders, as the painkillers

307

kicked in. A sharp knock on the door brought her back to reality, and it opened a crack, Mole's arm appearing with her ringing phone in his hand, an old Nokia she'd found in a drawer. He really was on his best behaviour.

'Answer it, will you?' she called, turning off the water and wrapping a towel round her. She wiped the mirror with the back of her hand, and through the steam could make out the bruising on her face. Her leg throbbed from the hot shower – where she'd cut it as Calder dragged her along – yet despite the heat of the small room, she shivered, goosebumps covering her arms.

She opened the bathroom door, releasing a cloud of steam into the pub. As soon as she saw Mole's face, she knew something was wrong.

'What is it?' she asked.

'It's Harry. He's had a stroke. He's been taken to hospital.'

'Fuck,' she mumbled. 'Who was it on the phone?'

'Your good-looking copper bloke.'

'Who said he was good-looking?' She could feel herself beginning to blush. 'Certainly wasn't me.'

'You didn't need to. Not that I care, of course.' He smiled.

'No, course not. Me neither. Feel like I don't care about very much at the moment.'

'Oh, Cons, come here.' Mole went over and put his arms round her. 'And I do care, really. Just keeping you on your toes, that's all.'

'Yeah, well, that makes two of us.' She kissed him on the cheek and started towards the bedroom, pausing by the door. 'I might need some help. Getting dressed. You know, with the shoulder and that.'

'What, really?'

'Yes, really.'

'Well, this is a first,' said Mole, walking towards her. 'Being asked to help a girl *into* her clothes.'

CHAPTER 53

Ruthie Abbott would have made a bloody good nurse had she not encountered Ena Massey. Many of the attributes that led Kirby to this conclusion – attention to detail, meticulous notes and a strong moral sense of duty – had probably also helped seal her fate. Had she been less meticulous, less attentive and less concerned, Ruthie Abbott might have lived to see her son grow up. Unfortunately, the diary was like an unexploded bomb that Ena Massey had made sure never went off. It wasn't just factual evidence. Ruthie had carefully documented her observations on Ena's working methods and on Deep Sleep Therapy and her instinct that it was intrinsically wrong: worse than wrong, inherently dangerous. No wonder Ena had taken the diary and kept it safe. Why she hadn't missed it when Karen took it in 1978 was a mystery. Unless, by then, Ena had simply moved on and forgotten about the entire thing – it wouldn't have surprised Kirby if she had.

He locked the diary in his desk and headed out to the car, where he texted Livia to say he was on his way. Now he knew that Ena Massey had deliberately killed Ruthie Abbott, he had no reason to think that she hadn't done the same to Sarah Carswell but with an overdose of barbiturates. Whether or not Ena knew she'd been seen killing Ruthie by Raymond, Kirby didn't know. It seemed unlikely, given that she'd made no attempt to kill him; then again, perhaps she hadn't needed to. Who would have believed someone like Raymond? It would have been his word against hers.

Kirby pondered all this as he drove to Ealing, desperately trying to push aside thoughts of what Livia might tell him when he arrived. Of everything that had happened – Calder seducing Charles Palmer, luring Ena to Blackwater via the old folly, murdering Ed Blake because he'd been in the wrong place at the wrong time – the one thing that still bugged him was the Creeper. He'd thought it was Calder's errant son, Lloyd, but this was looking increasingly unlikely, as his alibis for the specific occasions for which Raymond and Connie could pinpoint either an intrusion or a sighting were watertight.

Kirby swung into his mother's drive and switched off the engine, sitting for a moment. What possible reason could Patrick Calder have had for snooping around Raymond and Connie's houses? It made no sense; he hadn't even known Connie until he met her at Marsh House – or, at least, as far as they knew.

He got out of the car and locked up, unable to put off his conversation with Livia any longer. He'd been desperate to know what was wrong with her, and yet now he was about to find out, he suddenly didn't want to.

He rang the bell, and as he waited for her to answer his phoned pinged. It was a text from Anderson: *Harry Joyce popped his clogs.* It was hardly a surprise, but nevertheless it felt as though Ena had claimed another victim.

He heard his mother unlocking the door and put his phone away.

'Lew, darling, come in,' said Livia, quickly ushering him in.

He had to repeat the same ritual as on the weekend – taking his shoes off and leaving them by the door, Livia watching from a distance – only instead of being led into the kitchen, his mother steered him into the living room, where she offered him a drink and asked him to sit down.

'What's this about, Mum?' he asked, thinking she looked nervous.

His mother sat stiffly on the edge of the sofa, a wine glass clasped in her hands. 'There's no easy way to say this, so I'm just going to say it,' she said, looking him straight in the eye. 'Your nonna, it was me – I killed her.'

Kirby sat stunned, trying to comprehend what his mother had just said to him, a brief memory of seeing her hunched over his grandmother's – his nonna's – bed just before she died, flickered across his memory. Before he could summon up any form of response, Livia continued.

'She was dying, Lew – a terrible, terrible death. I couldn't let her go like that, I just couldn't. You saw me that day, I know you did. You just didn't know what you'd seen. And now . . .' She paused. 'Now it's my turn.'

'What do you mean? I don't understand . . . Nonna died in her sleep. The doctor said so.' He searched his mother's face for some kind of affirmation that this had been the case, and could see none.

'It's not true. She didn't die in her sleep,' said Livia. 'And it's not true because it would have been impossible.'

What was she talking about – how could dying in your sleep be impossible? It occurred to Kirby that she was losing her mind, that whatever was wrong with her was affecting her mental capacity. That she'd lost her grip on reality. 'Mum, you don't know what you're saying.' He heard the lack of conviction in his own voice, the image of his mother standing in the doorway of his grandmother's bedroom and her words – *It's over, she's finally asleep* – refusing to fade. 'What do you mean, *now it's my turn*?'

'It means I'm dying, Lew, of the same disease. A disease that means you can't sleep. There's no cure, and – oh God, this is the most difficult thing I've ever had to say . . .'

311

'More difficult than telling me you killed your own mother? That would be pretty hard to top,' said Kirby, immediately regretting it.

Livia looked at him with such pain in her eyes that he suddenly realised that she wasn't going mad at all. This was the truth, and what she was about to say was going to be ten times worse. Then it hit him. 'No, Mum, please don't tell me—'

Livia nodded slowly, her words barely audible. 'It's genetic, so there's a fifty-fifty chance that you have it too. *I'm so sorry*,' she whispered, as the tears rolled down her face.

CHAPTER 54

Kirby slipped into the church just as the service was about to begin. It was packed, so he sat at the back, glad not to be noticed. It had been just under a week since Livia had given him the news, although in truth it had felt like a lifetime. Words from their conversation refused to stop floating around in his head: dying, fatal, incurable, insomnia, hereditary. None of it joined up – just random words looking for somewhere to go. He still hadn't spoken to Isabel about it; he didn't know where to begin and had stayed at work late every night. When he got back to the boat in the early hours of the morning, he couldn't sleep – hardly surprising, given what he'd been told.

The congregation began to rise, and he caught sight of Connie by the aisle near the front; her trademark black clothes now pathetically appropriate. His eyes wandered up the aisle and settled on the two coffins that sat side by side at the front of the church, Harry Joyce's and Edward Blake's, a simple white wreath on each. Soon he'd be doing this again, only then it would be his mother. He bit his lip to focus on the present, and thought about Livia and the secret she'd carried with her for all those years. He wondered whether she'd ever spoken of it on the rare occasions that she went to confession. Kirby wasn't religious, despite the Catholicism on his mother's side of the family, and had never been to confession in his life. He couldn't imagine confessing his sins to a priest and he wondered if that was how his mother had justified her silence over the years.

The congregation grew quiet as the vicar greeted the church from her lectern and indicated that they should sit. Kirby lowered himself on to the pew and closed his eyes as she spoke. Her voice drifted in and out of his consciousness, and he caught the odd word, but it was like trying to catch snowflakes: they were there for a second, then gone. A pause came in the service, followed by a new voice. Kirby opened his eyes and saw a tall, good-looking man in his early thirties standing before the crowd. He'd been seated next to Connie, and Kirby wondered whether they were an item. The man spoke fondly and eloquently about Blake, about his passion for exploring and his near-obsession for recording things; so much so that Kirby was transported from his own dark thoughts just for a few minutes. The man ended his eulogy by saying that no coffin, and no amount of earth, would ever contain the spirit that had been his friend, and that if anyone could find a way out, it would be Ed Blake, the best drainer in the business.

Kirby slipped out as someone got up to speak about Harry, and stood in the graveyard. He didn't want to hear any more. Harry Joyce – not to mention Tom Ellis – had died a heartbroken, lonely old man, and it was something Kirby didn't want to dwell on. Was that how he would die? He hoped not, although if he inherited the disease that his mother had – this Fatal Familial Insomnia, or FFI as she called it – that might be preferable. Looking out over the graveyard, he spotted Raymond Sweet on a bench and made his way over.

'Mind if I sit down?' Kirby asked.

Raymond shook his head.

They sat in silence for a few minutes.

'This is where I come for the bring-and-buy,' said Raymond. 'There should have been one today but . . .' He trailed off.

'How have you managed all these years, alone in that place?' asked Kirby.

'I'm not alone,' he replied. 'I have my mother. And the ashes. What will happen to them?'

'At the moment they're being kept at the funeral director's. Unless any of the families can be traced, which is unlikely, they'll probably stay there for a while. They're safe, though. You needn't worry.'

Raymond took out a packet of mini Jaffa Cakes from his coat pocket. 'Would you like one? I got them specially.' He offered the packet to Kirby, who took one.

Kirby must have been a child when he last ate a Jaffa Cake, and the taste took him straight back to his parents' garden in the summer: the greenhouse full of tomatoes and the odd cannabis plant; his father chasing him with the garden hose when it got too hot; and his mother's homemade lemonade. Happy times, before they split up. Now he knew why: Livia had made his father promise never to tell Kirby that she'd euthanised her own mother, releasing her from the living hell of incurable insomnia. Not only that, but that she, too, had inherited the same disease, and that one day it would also claim her and possibly their son. The secret had been too much for Kirby's father to bear, and he'd left.

'I'm sorry about your mother and Gregory Boothe,' he said. 'You must miss them.'

'Every day. Nurse Abbott was the only one who understood how I felt.'

And paid the price for it, thought Kirby. 'Are you happy, Raymond?'

He smiled. 'I'll never have to see Mr Calder again, and the redevelopment is on hold. Another Jaffa Cake?'

Kirby shook his head. 'No thanks.' People began filing out of the church, and he saw Connie emerge with the man who'd given Blake's eulogy, his arm around her shoulders.

'Will there be a buffet?' asked Raymond.

'A buffet? I don't know,' said Kirby, standing up.

'Only, Mrs Muir said there's usually a buffet after a funeral. We didn't have one when my mother died though.'

'Thanks for the Jaffa Cake, Raymond. You take care now.' Kirby left him on the bench and made his way down towards the crowd.

Connie was standing with a group of people who he guessed were from the urbex community, and they fell silent as he approached.

'Connie.' Kirby nodded. 'How have you been?'

'Oh, you know, okay.' She managed a smile. 'You?'

'Yeah, fine. That was a great eulogy, by the way,' he said to the man next to her. 'They're not easy.'

'This is Mole,' said Connie, introducing them. 'Kirby's the detective I told you about. The one I kept annoying.'

'Got the bad guy in the end though, didn't she?' said Mole.

Kirby couldn't tell if he was joking or having a go, so he ignored it. He didn't have the energy to argue.

'I'm just going to talk to Dan,' said Mole, wandering off to join the rest of the crew, who'd drifted away while they'd been talking.

'He doesn't approve of you fraternising with coppers then,' said Kirby.

'Mole's all right. He was just a bit annoyed, that's all. Said I was doing your job for you.'

'How's the shoulder?' he asked. 'Getting better?'

'Slowly. Swimming's helping.'

'Good. Raymond's here,' he said, turning to point over at the bench, but it was empty. He must have gone in search of the buffet.

316

'Will you find his body? Calder's?' asked Connie. 'I'll sleep much better knowing he's really dead.'

He shrugged. 'Perhaps.'

'I can't believe he was the Creeper, I mean—' But she was cut off by Mole, who came jogging back over.

'Hey, Cons, you need to hear this,' said Mole, pointing excitedly. 'That bloke over there, Jimmy Rae. He was the one Ed met. You know, the one he told me about, as I was getting on the plane to Poland, the one who knew who your sister was with when she had the accident.'

'Oh my God,' said Connie.

'He's been living in Germany for the past five years, didn't even know Sarah had died. Came back for a family wedding and bumped into Ed on his first day here. C'mon, I'll introduce you. You need to hear what he's got to say.'

Connie looked at Kirby. 'Do you mind if—'

'It's fine, you go.' He watched as they went over and joined a man in his mid-thirties wearing a dark suit and a black coat. Judging from their body language, Mole already knew the man. He introduced Connie, and the three of them began talking animatedly. Kirby genuinely hoped that Connie would find out what had happened to her sister that fateful day five years ago. It wouldn't bring her back, but it would bring some kind of closure.

After waiting for a few minutes, he decided to slip away. Connie was absorbed in whatever it was that Jimmy Rae had to tell her, and the truth was that he just wanted to leave, to escape the smell of death that hovers over every funeral.

He had just reached the gates of the cemetery, the Citroën parked a few feet away, when he heard Connie calling his name.

'Kirby! Wait!' She was jogging after him, holding her arm awkwardly, still clearly in pain when she ran. 'Hang on.'

He stopped at the gates and waited for her to catch him up. 'Sorry, I realised I need to be somewhere,' he said, by way of explaining his sudden departure. 'Did you get what you wanted?'

'Yes,' Connie said, catching her breath. 'He knew the bloke my sister was with. Said he was a bit strange – nothing serious, just a bit odd.'

'Did he have a name?' asked Kirby.

'Yes.' She nodded. 'His name was Kaplinsky, Brian Kaplinsky.'

CHAPTER 55

Raymond left the churchyard after sharing his Jaffa Cakes with the detective and walked home. With no buffet, there wasn't much point in hanging around. He'd kept quiet about Gregory's ashes, as well as Alardice's and Barnes's, and so far no one seemed to have noticed that they were missing. He would have liked to speak to Connie, but she had been surrounded by people and he didn't want to intrude.

He strolled down Daylesford Road, enjoying the fact that he no longer had to wear his scarf turban-style. Although still cold, it was considerably milder, and he could almost imagine sleeping without thermals and pyjamas. He let himself into the grounds and was walking through the small copse of trees to the lodge, when he saw a figure coming towards him. It was Calder's site manager, Catapult or whatever his damn name was.

'Raymond,' said Catapult.

'Mr, erm . . .'

'Kaplinsky.'

'Oh, erm, yes, Mr Kaplinsky.'

'I've just been having a last look round the site. You know, making sure everything is in order.' He looked at Raymond, as if it were somehow down to him. 'There's one piece of machinery that needs removing from the site, then that's it, Patricey Developments are out of your hair.'

'Oh, right. That's good then. I mean, that's, erm, useful to know. Thank you.' Raymond tried to edge past the man, but despite the fact they were outside, the trees seemed to hem them in.

'Going back to the Lodge?' Kaplinsky asked, not moving.

'Yes,' said Raymond. 'I've just been to a funeral and . . .' He couldn't think how to end the sentence. 'There wasn't a buffet.'

'No. Well.' Kaplinsky stuck out his hand. 'Goodbye, Raymond. I'll miss you in my own way.'

Raymond went to take his hand, then withdrew. 'Bye, Mr Kaplinsky,' he said, and pushed past him. He'd never liked him and now he didn't even have to pretend to. As he hurried back to the Lodge he was still aware of Kaplinsky standing behind him, and could feel the man's eyes boring into his back.

'Oh, and Raymond?' he heard Kaplinsky shout. 'Say goodbye to your mother for me, won't you?'

Raymond stopped in his tracks. *What did he say?* He must have misheard him. He turned slowly. 'Pardon?'

But Kaplinsky was gone.

Raymond peered through the trees, wondering how someone could just disappear like that. Then a nasty feeling began creeping through his stomach, accompanied by a slow but very stark realisation. He turned and ran back to the Old Lodge as fast as he could, hurling himself up the steps and fumbling with the lock, until he burst into the living room and ran over to the kitchen. He noticed his mug on the draining board – a present from Mrs Muir with *I Heart Benidorm* on it – exactly where he'd left it earlier. Then he looked up at the shelf where he kept the tea caddy and almost screamed. Next to it, where the urn containing his mother's ashes should have been, was an empty space.

Unable to move, Raymond blinked a few times, swallowing the panic that was rising up and threatening to tip him over into somewhere he didn't want to go. Eventually, he tore his eyes away from the empty space and down to the kitchen table. And there she was. '*Mother*,' he whispered to himself, grabbing the urn. He checked inside, just to be sure, then clutched it to his chest and wept for joy.

AUTHOR'S NOTE

Blackwater Asylum and its patients are entirely fictional, however certain elements are based on real places and events. During the 1960s and '70s, Ward 5 of the Royal Waterloo Hospital did house a 'Sleep Room' where Deep Sleep Therapy was practised. In Australia, a royal commission was held into the treatment after it led to the deaths of twenty-seven people at the private Chelmsford Hospital in a suburb of Sydney. The 'bone jar' itself is based on a real building at Witley Park in Surrey.